TORMENT

COURTNEY KONSTANTIN

DEDICATION

To the mister in my life. For always being so happy for me as I follow my dreams. Even when my nose is pressed against a computer screen half the time.

PROLOGUE

Two months since the end of the known world. It had been two months since commercial planes sounded in the sky as they criss-crossed the wide blue expanse. Two months since cellphones were connected to every person's ear. Two months since the news reports went dark, no longer reporting on the rupture in normal life. Two months since that first bite. And two months since the dead no longer stayed dead.

Thick clouds obscured the sun above the Montana mountains. Below the gray, moving transportation was rare. Cars sat, crashed and abandoned along every major roadway. The black shells of some told the story of fire and destruction. Among the empty husks of the modern world the dead reigned. Truly dead bodies littered the pavement, birds and other animals finding their feasts in the rotting flesh.

A crow perched on the head of a dead body leaning against a car. The bird bent and pecked until it was able to pull the intact eyeball from the skull. Another bird landed nearby, and its scream was one of annoyance and jealousy over the crow's find. The black bird didn't take notice of the insult and instead it flew off quickly to enjoy its meal in peace.

Deep in the nearby forest a compound sat behind high walls. Here a family, bonded not only by blood but by the need of survival, resided. Alex, Rafe, and Max Duncan, with their family and friends, had created a working day-to-day life in the safety of their father's compound, their childhood home. Every day, they work at finding a semblance of normal in the new decaying world they are a part of.

The laughter of children often rang through the house, having dinner together as a group in the evenings where everyone gathers to talk about their days and the tasks to come. It's easy to fall into a sense of normal when they stay behind their stone walls and barbed wire. The animals are fed, and the gardens are harvested. Food is plentiful for the group and no one has to suffer hunger.

However, that is not the case everywhere. Each day the destruction of the human race intensifies. Those that are left behind, that are able to survive and avoid the plague, find themselves suffering and lost. There are those that war against each other, not knowing how else to make it on their own. The fall from humanity had taken less time than anyone would have imagined. With no answers from the government, or cure in sight, humans slowly fall into ruin and society deteriorates further and further.

The Duncans work hard to keep those close to them safe. But for Alex Duncan, turning her back on those that are in need is something that goes against the grain in her heart. As a team the Duncan siblings make choices and run the compound together with no one getting the entire say. Alex being the oldest is the unspoken leader, but she chooses to not to take that role without her siblings' insight. Leadership was never something Alex wanted. However, it was what her father trained her for.

Mitch Duncan would have thrived in the turbulent plagued world. His preparations and paranoia built a place that comfortably kept his family safe, years after he passed. His lessons are in every fiber of his children, creating people that brought knowledge on how to live now. They were strong and experienced in the ways of life without the modern technologies most relied on before the plague started. As the power grid failed, their solar power gave them the opportunities to have lights and movie nights. As the water system became polluted, they relied on well water and rain filtrations systems to keep their household well watered.

The walls continued to keep the sick out. Yet, it didn't stop the living. The Duncans didn't have enemies, minus one. The government faction responsible for the start of the plague, for creating something so vile it seemed incurable. They didn't know as much as they wished about them. The little they had surmised was a combination of firsthand experience during the time Max was tortured, from Rafe working at a government facility, and a third unlikely ally. From this knowledge the Duncans knew it was only a matter of time before the faction made a run at their home again.

Alex didn't like the silence. She waited every night for another attack, but it seemed things were quiet. As she imagined the walking dead wandering the woods, she knew that quiet was a false sense of compliance she couldn't take a chance on. Billie and Henry, her young children, relied on her wit and intelligence to keep them safe. Believing the government had just decided to give up would be foolish and Alex reminded herself of it daily. Her nightly routine always included a round of checks with the weapons they had stashed in the case of emergency. She would unload, check, and load all the weapons before she could chance going to sleep.

Montana was slowly allowing spring to enter its mountains. A chill still hung tightly to the air, as if to remind them that winter would eventually return. With spring, tasks around the compound changed. Pigs would be bred, and some would be slaughtered. Gardens would be tended to, ensuring the largest production possible. Canning and preserving of fruits and vegetables would go into high gear, replacing the stores they had tapped into the last two months.

Alex could feel the change in the air. Something spoke to her over the crisp breeze, calling to her, warning her. Something more was coming, and they needed to be ready.

CHAPTER ONE

The smell. That smell was something burned into Alex Duncan's senses and imprinted on her brain. The smell of decomposing flesh, similar to roadkill that had sat too long in the sun. The scent lingered on the air around those infected with the deadly plague. After two months Alex thought she would build a tolerance to the nauseating smell, but it was the same every time. She found herself fighting the desire to vomit on the spot.

"I hate this part," a grumble sounded behind her.

Alex turned to look at Easton Reynolds, the teenage boy she had saved at the beginning of the plague after his mother had fallen to an infected. He and his sister, Candace, had joined with Alex, Billie, and Henry on their trek to Montana and safety. She looked upon the boy with fondness.

His eyes shown with water above the bandana he had tied around his nose and mouth. They had started carrying them and Vicks in their packs, just in case. That just in case came around more often than Alex wished.

During a routine check of the woods around the perimeter wall, Alex and Easton stumbled on a small horde of infected. Easton had trained and had become a skilled fighter when it came to the dead. Alex didn't question the idea of going into battle with the boy at her back. She watched his, as he watched hers. They were a well-oiled machine. The small horde was a small surprise, but not one they were unprepared for.

Easton was armed with the wooden bat he always fought with. Alex had taught him to never leave it behind, as threats could be anywhere at any time. She carried the machete that once belonged to a man that threatened her family's survival. She'd allowed the man and his companions to leave alive, but she kept the machete, finding it to be an adequate weapon in the quiet battle against the infected. As a backup precaution, she always had her 9mm strapped to one hip and a bowie knife sheathed on the other.

Alex stepped forward first to engage the nearest infected. With a wide arc, she brought the machete down on the head of the short female infected; the soft flesh and bone no longer held the structure of a living being. Her blade sliced into the brain, ending the life of the walking dead immediately. As Alex moved forward, she chopped at legs and arms as infected attempted to rush to grab her. This practice was a typical dance for her and Easton. She would chop down the infected, creating easy targets for Easton's bat. The rhythmic sound of the wood crushing skulls met Alex's ears and without looking she knew Easton was following close behind.

The pair fought through the horde, allowing bodies to fall where they finally died. Until, breathing heavily, they were the last things to stand among the trees. Alex looked to Easton, who nodded to her. He knew without a word that she was asking if he was whole. Each time they fought together; Alex was forced to fight down the terror she felt putting the boy at risk. Over time, she had begun to feel like a mother to Easton and Candace. She couldn't fathom losing either of them, just as she couldn't imagine losing her younger children, Billie and Henry.

As they were right outside of the walls, the infected bodies had to be cleaned up. This task was not a favorite of any at the compound. However, as they were often faced with infected in the trees, they couldn't leave the bodies to just rot. Together Easton and Alex pulled the bodies into a rough pile in a nearby clearing. Using the rags of clothing still on the bodies, they started a small fire and waited while the bodies smoldered to ash and bone.

Alex stared into the flames, her mind wandering over the tasks of her day, week, month. The list never seemed to diminish, only growing in size as the days went by. The pressure felt like a lead weight on her shoulders. The occupants of the compound, including her siblings, looked to her for guidance. Alex was even-tempered and thoughtful in her actions. Where her sister, Max, was wild and erratic at times, Alex was the complete opposite with her planning and clear view on how the future should look. Rafe was more like Alex, but he avoided the responsibility of leadership like the plague itself.

That left Alex to lead the group. Everyone was extremely willing to help in any way Alex found fit. Over the first few weeks, Alex had sketched out a rough list of all the duties needed to keep the compound viable and running smoothly. Each duty was then grouped by similar skills necessary. Once she had that organized, she decided on who would rotate through each group weekly. Everyone was given the chance to do different things, as well as learn new skills they were interested in learning.

Rafe was teaching people about the animals. As he had been alone on the compound since their father had died, he was the one most acquainted with the workings. Rafe was also talented with the technical tasks. He alone had created and set up the surveillance system they had around the compound. That system had helped them during the attacks of the military, as well as notifying them when the sick were too close to the gates.

Even with all the security, Alex felt routine walks around the wall were necessary. She didn't believe the government was gone.

The government who was responsible for the outbreak of the plague and were also on the hunt for Alex's siblings. Rafe, because he and his girlfriend, Charlie, knew more about the origins of the plague than anyone else. And Max, because her escape was nothing but a humiliation to the Major after he'd tortured her for information. The images of her sister being tortured still haunted Alex. Even now, thinking of it, her stomach began to feel queasy again.

"Alex?" Easton asked, his voice muffled by his bandana.

"Hmmm?" She replied absently.

"Where did you go?"

"Nowhere, I'm right here," she said, laughing a little to lighten the mood.

"You get that same look when you're worried or stressed," Easton replied.

"I think that's just the way things are now. Worrying and being stressed," Alex replied.

She stepped forward and started kicking dirt over the outer-most flames. The last thing she needed on her hands was a forest fire. Easton followed her cue and moved to the other side of the bonfire to repeat the dirt kicking. They were silent as they moved around, checking their work. The crackle of the walkie talkie on Alex's belt caused her to jump.

"Alex, come in," Max's voice came from the small speaker. Alex quickly pulled the radio and replied to her sister.

"Saw the smoke outside the wall. Everything ok?" Max asked.

"Ran across a small horde. Only about ten. Easton and I handled things," Alex answered.

"No problems?"

"Nope. It was quick. We'll continue our check around the walls before coming back in," Alex replied.

"Need any backup?" Max asked, her voice hopeful. Alex had to smile at the walkie talkie.

"No, Max, you need to finish your chores."

"Alex...I'm not meant to garden," Max said with a groan.

"You know how to garden. It's your turn. You're meant to garden this week," Alex said, laughter in her voice.

"I hope you run into a bear. Over and out," Max said, causing Alex and Easton to laugh.

Mitch Duncan would have felt he failed if one of his children didn't know how to grow their own food. Countless chores and lessons throughout their childhood were about gardening and the wild plants that were edible. Much to Max's annoyance, Alex was well aware of her abilities with plants, so she was required to do a gardening rotation just as Alex and Rafe were. Max groaned about it, but she was very talented in the garden, it just wasn't enough action for her. She wanted to constantly be moving and fighting, this new world being perfect for her.

Alex had enough of the fighting by day one. That was also the day she became a widow, after she had to put down her infected husband, Blake. Her heart had finally come to terms with what she had been forced to do. She knew that Blake would want nothing more than for their children to be safe. So, Alex made the impossible choice to end him and run with their kids. When they arrived at the Montana compound, the weight of the loss still clung tightly to Alex. Though she knew that she did the right thing, she still missed her husband.

The companionship she had found with the people at the compound had helped some. She had her children, healthy and happy. Easton and Candace fit like puzzle pieces into their family and Alex had come to adore them as her own. She even found a friendship with Marcus, the man they found on their way to Montana. While his antics still seemed to grate on her nerves, he was useful and was able to make the kids or Alex laugh at any time. She had appreciated the way he paid attention to the kids, letting them help with his projects while helping to keep them safe and provided for.

However, at night, Alex still found herself thinking of Blake.

She often wondered if he watched her from above and if he approved of the decisions she'd made. When she found herself in those musings, she would laugh to herself. Without asking the question, Alex knew Blake would trust her instincts when it came to the new life they were having to build. Alex had the ability to create a haven for their family, something not everyone had the knowledge to do.

As Alex and Easton moved around the perimeter of the walls, Alex stopped to check on the snares Rafe had set. They had been lucky to have plenty of pigs on the farm to feed the population of the compound. Rafe had been smart about the breeding and if they continued his practices, they would have pork year around. But, pork could get old, so they continued to hunt outside their walls when necessary. Alex could make a delicious stew out of a rabbit where no one actually knew they were eating rabbit at the moment. She smiled widely when she found a rabbit in the first snare. She unwound the tight cord from its neck and set the snare again.

"Rabbit stew again?" Easton asked.

"You like my rabbit stew," Alex replied with a smile.

"I did. Until I saw it was rabbit you put into it."

"This isn't the time to be picky about our food," Alex admonished.

Easton didn't reply. Alex knew he understood her point. Over the two months since they'd arrived at the compound, she had worked hard to instill survival instincts into Easton. He was a smart, strong boy, he'd more than proved it when he and Candace were separated from the family for a week. Alex had been wrecked when she thought she had caused the deaths of the teens. When they arrived on the compound after being missing, Alex swore to herself that she would make sure they could always survive without her. Easton was an attentive student, wanting to absorb all the information she had to give him. Candace was slightly more wary of the dirty aspects of survival.

She didn't care for the blood and gore that came with the infected.

With the check done, Alex and Easton arrived back to the large metal rolling gate that allowed access into the compound. Alex had three rabbits hooked to her belt. Checking the snares took a bit longer on their check, but it was worth it when they had foods to add to their stores. Thinking about cleaning rabbits, Alex entered the code for the gate. Easton slid through first, waiting by the keypad to enter the code again on the inside. As soon as Alex stepped through, he pushed the numbers and the gate immediately began to roll closed.

"Why don't you take the weapons and get them cleaned up? Store them in the shed with the rest," Alex said. Without a word, Easton nodded and started to jog up the front hill.

Alex took her time, letting herself soak in the silence of the moment. She didn't get to enjoy the quiet very often. Being the mother to two young children, she was mostly used to that. But now it wasn't sibling rivalries she needed to handle, it was adult questions about chores and schedules. Alex knew as soon as Max realized she was back her sister would come to complain about garden duty again. And there were other issues. Rafe needed more supplies for the garden, to start the spring planting he wanted to do. Charlie had a long list of medical supplies she was hoping to get. Cliff was still closed off and Alex always took a special interest in getting him to converse and be part of the group.

All of this was daily. Leadership was what Mitch Duncan had told her would be needed when the world fell apart. She didn't dispute his point. However, she never wanted the job solely on herself. There was no leadership from the government, local or federal. Part of Alex had hoped someone would come through with the strength to get things on track. But after Max had showed up, beaten from torture at the hands of the government, Alex began to have her doubts. Later, they added the information that Rafe and Charlie had from the beginning of the plague, and Alex knew they were on their own. She looked back toward the zombie burn pile, small wisps of smoke still rose. No one was coming to help them.

So, she did what was needed. With that in mind, she trudged up the hill to the barn. She avoided running into Max, because she just knew that would be the biggest issue of the day. When she entered the cool interior of the barn, she paused, allowing her eyes to adjust and to determine if she was alone. Her ears immediately picked up on glass and metal clicking. She walked toward a stall that was now separated from the rest of the barn by thick plastic, sealing the room off from the outside. Alex stood outside watching the blonde woman inside, who seemed to be sorting through samples.

"Morning, Charlie," Alex said.

Charlie's green eyes flew up, surprised by Alex's quiet approach. Alex had worked on being as accepting and welcoming as she could be to the woman it seemed Rafe had finally set his eyes on. Rafe had endured years of teasing from his sisters, never letting them in on his romantic life. Since the start of the plague, Rafe and Charlie had been bonded. Rafe confided in Alex that he hadn't been lying when he told his sisters he didn't have girlfriends. He didn't, until Charlie. Now he was in love with the pretty blonde doctor, who was on a crusade to cure the plague.

"Morning, Alex. You scared me," she laughed.

"Sorry. Was just trying to hide from Max for a while, figured I'd skin the rabbits in here," she said as she held up her haul.

To her credit, Charlie's grimace only tightened her eyes. But Alex saw it and it only caused Alex to smile wider. Charlie had been exposed to survival in a thrown into the fire sort of way. When the lab she worked in mistakenly created the plague, that now turned the bitten into the infected dead, Charlie was forced into being on the run with Rafe. The government that was behind the experiments wanted Charlie for her knowledge. Though after being questioned by Alex, and then grilled mercilessly by Max, it was clear Charlie didn't know how the plague was created. That didn't stop her from being determined to cure it.

"Max is in rare form today. I think she's getting stir crazy," Charlie replied, clearly ignoring the rabbit subject.

"We all are. But going out often isn't safe. Not only because the number of infected that seem to grow every time we're out, but also, we don't know what 'The Suit' or Callahan are up to," Alex replied.

Charlie's face was a mask of anger and fear when Alex mentioned the government members that were attacking the Duncan family. 'The Suit' was the nameless man that ran the facility that Charlie and Rafe both worked at; Charlie as a doctor and Rafe in security. After the outbreak, an attack on the compound forced Rafe and Charlie to flee into the mountains. They lived in a cave for close to a month, not wanting to bring the government down on the Duncan family. Little did Rafe realize, the Duncan family had already been added to the list of wanted. In another state, Max had been captured by Major Callahan, who seemed to work for 'The Suit'. When she arrived at the compound, she had been bruised and broken. All because she wouldn't give up the location of her siblings.

With the family together now, they had compared their information and were able to create an understanding of what was happening to them. There was no way for them to believe that 'The Suit' and Callahan weren't working together. Their goal was the same. And the Duncan family immediately was on their radar once the plague arrived. Both seemed determined to cure the illness. They wanted Charlie for that. Neither realized, nor cared, that Charlie hadn't created anything that could even slow the pathogen down.

Now, two months later and they hadn't become complacent. Daily checks were scheduled to make sure they weren't under surveillance. They rotated on nightly shifts to ensure someone was always awake in the chance of an attack. To anyone outside of the Duncan family, it may have seemed extreme. Yes, they had a security system that would alarm the moment someone broke over the wall. And yes, over the past month Rafe, Marcus, Griffin, and Cliff had added barbed wire to the top of the walls. But, the Duncans had been raised to never feel safe, to never believe it was over and to never trust the government.

"I still believe we should go after them," Charlie said, breaking into Alex's inner musings.

"Part of me agrees with you. The other part doesn't feel like we have enough information to go on the offensive yet," Alex replied.

"I know you're right. Things feel different now. With Rafe and Aiden...." Charlie said, trailing off at the name of the little boy she and Rafe had rescued.

"I understand where you're coming from, Charlie. I consider everyone on this compound family. We are here to protect each other. It makes it so much more difficult when you have something so precious to lose."

"That's exactly it, Alex. I've never had anything precious like that in my life. Now that I do...."

"You'll do anything to keep it," Alex finished.

"Yes."

"So will I. Don't worry, Charlie. We are in this together."

Alex left Charlie to complete whatever she was working on. Alex had to admire the work Rafe had put into creating her little lab. Part of the stall was for her tests and specimens. The other half she had started working to create a triage center. Charlie most recently did lab work, but before that she was a doctor. That was invaluable to the compound members now. She had quickly stitched up Marcus when he'd slipped off the ladder during the barbed wire installation. It was an event he didn't like to speak about, but the healing gash on his forehead told it for him. Charlie had also helped with antibiotics when Aiden seemed to come down with an ear infection. She realized how her knowledge could be of use and Rafe went out a number of times to retrieve whatever he could from local clinics, pharmacies, and hospitals.

A section of their large barn was used for slaughtering of animals with all the proper instruments hanging from the wall of the room. Before, Rafe hadn't worried about making a mess that he would need to clean up later, now he did all the dirty work inside, so the kids weren't completely scarred from seeing the animals they loved being killed. Alex knew Billie would be traumatized to see her mother gutting and skinning rabbits. No need to let her daughter know she had eaten Peter Cottontail more than once.

Alex went about the work of cleaning the rabbit. The task allowed her to easily relax and leave her worries to their own accord for a while. Catching, cleaning, and preparing animals was just one of the lessons Mitch Duncan had taught Alex during her childhood. She thought of her father now, wondering if he would approve of how she was running the compound. She had a feeling her dad would have some comments and corrections. However, he raised Alex with the skills to handle leadership on her own. She needed to make her own choices. So far, she felt she was doing ok.

Once she had the rabbits cleaned, she cut off the useable meat, so no one saw where it came from. Most of the adults were able to see beyond the source of the food, realizing eating was what was important. But they had four little kids that wouldn't understand. Equipped with a bowl of meat, Alex stepped back into the sun. She immediately saw Billie and Henry outside the fence, watching the cows. Henry saw Alex, and he came running for her. She held the bowl above his head to avoid spilling. Her young son threw his arms around her legs and looked up at her. His dark eyes smiled at her, though he tried to look very serious.

"Mommy, tell Billie we aren't gonna eat the cows," Henry said.

In his five-year-old mind the idea of eating the animals he watched every day was a nightmare.

Billie, her blonde hair shining in the sunlight, came running to continue her argument with her brother. Two years older, Billie believed she was the boss of her brother. Alex appreciated when she wanted to protect him and show him the right ways to behave. But more often than not, she was full of mischief. Watching her now, Alex was sure that it was one of those moments.

"Of course, we're going to eat them, Henry. Why else would we keep them here?" Billie stated.

"What did you drink with breakfast this morning, Billie?" Alex asked, deciding it was time for a lesson.

"Milk."

"Where does milk come from?"

"Cows," Billie answered with a smile, happy she knew the fact.

"Correct. That is why we have the cows. We are not going to eat the cows. Not anytime soon at least. We have other food. Don't worry, honey," Alex said, using her free hand to run her fingers through Henry's hair. She took the moment to note that it was getting a little long and wondered if she should just let it go, or trim it up.

"See, told you," Henry said, shooting his sister a look.

"Did you two finish your morning chores?" Alex asked.

The kids were young at seven and five, but they were old enough to help with the smaller tasks around the compound.

"I fed the chickens," Billie replied.

"I helped Auntie Max in the garden," Henry said. Alex winced slightly.

"How did that go, buddy?" Alex asked.

"She's not happy with you today, Mommy," Henry replied, his face extremely serious.

"That's all right. Auntie doesn't like having chores. But just like you two, everyone has to help, right?"

Billie and Henry both nodded. Then Billie decided they were going to go find their cousin Jack and little Aiden to play hide and seek. The compound was large with a good number of buildings on it, including the main house, a bunkhouse, barn, greenhouse, root cellar, and several large storage containers. The kids found great joy in playing large games of hide and seek, as the places to hide seemed to be endless. Alex gave her normal warnings of being safe and keeping an eye on the younger Aiden, before Billie and Henry went running off, screaming for Jack.

Inside the house, Alex found Margaret in the kitchen. She was cleaning the fresh vegetables that were picked that morning. She turned when Alex came into the mudroom, kicking off her boots to not track mud through the house. Though spring had officially started, Montana still had its moisture and would probably still have spring showers for a month or so. Alex brought the meat into the kitchen and Margaret smiled at her.

"Successful outside today?" She asked.

The woman had been a lifesaver for Alex. When they first met, and the feisty older woman had pointed a shotgun at Alex's face, Alex couldn't have predicted how much she would lean on the woman. Her gray hair was getting longer, not the same spiky wildness it was when she'd joined Alex in survival. But looking at her, you could never mistake her for a regular grandmother. She was maternal but also spunky and funny. When Alex first told her the whole story of Blake and the struggles they had faced in the beginning of the plague, Margaret was the first person to tell Alex it wasn't her fault. Until that moment, Alex hadn't known how much she needed to hear that.

"It was. I reset the snares. I think spring is bringing the animals closer. I wonder too if the infected scare them? Either way, they tend to run into our snares. I was thinking stew for dinner."

"Perfect. We just pulled potatoes today. That will go perfectly."

Alex didn't say anything else, just covered the bowl with plastic wrap and popped it into the refrigerator until it could be cooked. She evaluated the rest of the fridge, taking in the half empty bottle of milk, the small bit of butter, the vegetables and fruits, the leftover pasta from dinner the night before. They were doing all right when it came to food. But Alex would always want to scavenge more. That thought created an itch in Alex's mind that she wanted to reach out and scratch.

"Alex?" Margaret's voice came from behind her. "What's going on?"

"Nothing. Why?"

"Honey, I know it's only been a few months. But I feel like we've been through some stuff, which has given me some insight into you. I can tell you're troubled," Margaret said.

She leaned her hip against the counter and laser focused her gaze on Alex. Her look caused Alex to sigh and roll her head to stretch some of the tension from her muscles. How did she tell her that she was tired of the responsibility? Alex wasn't like Max; she didn't want action. But she needed a break from the constant leadership of the compound.

"I'm just tired. It's been a long few months."

"It has. Why don't you get some rest?"

"I don't think it's a physical tired. My mind just feels foggy and overwhelmed. And it's every day."

"Ok. What can I do to help?" Margaret asked immediately.

"I think I need to go on a run, head back into town. See what else we could scavenge and bring back," Alex said quickly.

"You've been keeping everyone inside unless absolutely necessary. Why now?"

"Because I need a break. I need to get a break away from the constant management of everyone. I need a break away from Max fighting with me about daily assignments. I want to breathe, away from being some sort of leader here. I'm just not sure I am built for this...." Alex finally finished, trailing off as she looked at her feet.

"Alex Duncan," Margaret's strict tone made Alex look up quickly. "There is no one else better suited for the leadership of this group. Your father ensured that you would be ready for this. And you are doing a fantastic job. I understand you are under a lot of stress. So, if you need to get outside of these walls and change things up, you do that. But I will not hear you doubt yourself again, understand?"

"Uh, ok?" Alex replied timidly. She had never felt so put in her place as an adult ever.

Margaret nodded her head once and turned back to the vegetables. Alex stood and stared at the back of her head for a moment. The words had deep meaning, and she worked to absorb the impact of what the older woman was saying. Despite the stress and uncertainty Alex was feeling, she wasn't seen as a total failure. The thought did help her breathe a little easier. She moved to stand next to Margaret for a second before giving her a quick side hug.

"Thank you," Alex whispered.

CHAPTER TWO

"I don't understand, why can't I go out and handle the scavenging? Why do I have to stay and finish a rotation in the garden?" Max demanded.

Alex forced herself to not roll her eyes. They were sitting around the dinner table. All the adults sat together, with the kids at a small folding table on their own. Rabbit stew steamed in a large pot in the middle of the table. A salad of arugula, tomatoes, and green onions sat in a bowl nearby. Margaret did wonderful things in the kitchen and Alex appreciated her touch in making meals more filling. The topic of a scavenging run had come up after everyone had eaten their dinners and Max wasn't all too happy with the choices Alex was making.

"Because you are on a garden rotation. And just like everyone else, you have to finish the rotation," Alex said, patience lacing her voice.

"Well, our fearless leader shouldn't be barging out in the dead world while we all sit behind these walls," Max shot back.

"I didn't ask for any titles, Max. If you'd like to take over, be my guest," Alex said. Her patience was waning and from the looks around the table, people knew it.

Max flopped back in her chair, saying nothing in response. No one was under the impression that Max wanted to be in charge. Alex knew her sister well enough to know she wanted the least responsibility possible but also not have any requirements. Max wasn't lazy or suffering from a lack of dedication. She just didn't like the finer details that came with survival after the end of civilization. Alex knew her sister wanted action to keep herself distracted from other things. Such as dealing with talking about her torture at the hands of Callahan.

Thinking of that, Alex swung her gaze to Private Smith. As with most meetings and meals, he stared at the tabletop with no opinion in the matters discussed. The man who could barely grow peach fuzz on his face had participated in the beating of Max. If Max hadn't stepped in when they found Rafe, and Smith by extension, Alex or Max's boyfriend, Griffin, would have killed him outright. But Max saw him for what he was, a boy barely into bootcamp before Callahan yanked him out and put him into compromising situations under the guise of following orders. Though the man still slept in a cell that had been created in the barn for him, they had recently allowed him to join their meals. He had been a wealth of information about Callahan once he realized they weren't going to kill him. Now he was assigned chores just like the rest of their group.

"Everyone needs to make a list of items they need. Practical items, please. I will take the lists with me and work on retrieving everything requested. While I'm gone, Rafe will be in charge of chores and managing the compound," Alex continued, moving on from Max's temper tantrum.

"Who's going with you?" Margaret asked.

Alex hadn't thought about who would accompany her. As she looked around, she could see reactions from each person. Many she could read easily. Easton wanted to accompany her; the teenage boy had taken the task of watching her back very seriously. Griffin looked to Max because he wasn't leaving her side unless necessary. Rafe had his arm around Charlie and just nodded his head at Alex, reassuring her that he would handle things while she was gone. That only left a few people that were able fighters. Margaret would always be willing, but Alex wouldn't put her at risk in that way. Issac, another survivor that had joined them from town, was too old for the heavy hand to hand combat with the infected. He would disagree with that, but Alex just wouldn't let him know her thoughts.

That left a few able-bodied people to go. Marcus was staring at her when Alex turned her gaze to him. He waggled his eyebrows at her, causing her to snort.

"Well, I guess I'll take Marcus. I would be doing you all a favor to get him out of your hair for a few days," Alex said.

Despite the lingering grumbling from Max, dinner quickly ended and everyone went about spending their free time as they wanted. Alex pulled Rafe aside to discuss the upcoming few days of scheduling and needs. He kissed Charlie's hand before sending her off to give Aiden a bath before bedtime. Alex had a notebook she had been using for basic scheduling and a running to-do list for items that were a high priority.

"Alex, I know how to run a schedule," Rafe said as he sat down with her.

"I know. I just have this worked out in advance, to ensure everyone has their fair share. Especially our whiny sister," Alex replied.

"You can't let her get to you. You know she's dealing with some things," he said.

"Aren't we all, Rafe? I just think hoping for some understanding and peace with my own sister isn't a lot to ask."

"You're testy, Alex. That's not like you. What's up?" Rafe asked. His blue eyes searched hers. It felt as if they bore into her and Alex knew she couldn't lie to her brother.

"I'm just feeling weighed down. This is a lot to handle every day. I know you all are doing the work with me, but I feel like there is more expected of me. And I've been thinking a lot about Dad."

"What about him? His unrealistic expectations or his absurd lessons on which bugs to eat in the wild?" Rafe replied. Alex knew he was partially joking, but his comment also hit home for her.

"I think it's the expectations. I have them for myself, because of what he taught me to do. I feel like everyone is going to expect the same from me, as if he's standing right next to me."

"Alex, that's silly. No one here is like Dad. No one is stringent and unyielding. No one here believes you are more than human and are going to behave as one. Dad left us with impractical beliefs. Not only of the world around us, but of ourselves. You need to let that all go," he said.

Alex sighed and scrubbed her hands over her face. She knew Rafe was right. But something about living up to her father's expectations had always haunted her. Even before the plague, she had prepped and stored foods to provide for her family. But a lot of Mitch's lessons were lost in city life. There were times over the years where Mitch would call and lecture her. Alex would always reassure her father that everything was in order. She often lied about things, knowing Mitch would never visit her family in Las Vegas. He would never see that she didn't have barrels of water saved or a large greenhouse providing fresh produce.

"I know you're right. I'm hoping this run will give me some time to clear my thoughts," she replied.

"With Marcus? You know he still has a thing for you, right?"

"We've had a discussion about that. I think we've found our happy medium. He's been a good friend."

The conversation had her rewinding and thinking about when she had a come to terms talk with Marcus. Shortly after they met, he had shown obvious interest in her. But he was never inappropriate or overly obvious around Billie and Henry. Alex as a woman could tell when a man was showing interest in more than a friendship. She ignored it at first, hoping it would fizzle and go away.

But eventually she had to have the conversation with him. It went surprisingly well, Marcus already knowing she was still mourning the loss of her husband. They agreed to be friends. And since then, Marcus had been nothing but a supportive friend to her and her children.

"I hope he heard you loud and clear. He still does anything for you. Which I could appreciate if you were interested in that from him."

"It's not his fault. I'm not in the best place right now," Alex said softly.

"I know, sis. Losing Blake, doing what you had to do, I'm not sure any of us could stomach that."

"And of course, you get it now, since you have Charlie," Alex said, pushing at her brother's shoulder, lightening the mood.

"Don't be like Max. I'm not talking about it," Rafe said with a grin.

"You'll have to talk about it, eventually. We're all under this roof together now. You can't hide anything."

After a few more minutes of ribbing each other, they got down to business of creating a scavenging list. Charlie was looking for additional items for her lab. Alex wasn't sure how she was going to locate the things she described, but she would just bring everything back if that was the only solution. They needed additional clothes for Aiden, as they hadn't grabbed enough when they found him in his home. Slowly they had been collecting sturdy outdoor clothing, better boots and summer clothes for the boy. Alex also planned on keeping anything Henry grew out of for Aiden to wear shortly after. Rafe also produced a list of seeds he'd like to have. While he was harvesting seeds as a continuation plan for the produce, seed packets would be a wonderful backup.

"And, Alex," Rafe said as he was walking out of the dining room. Alex turned to look at him.

"Work it out with Max before you leave. She will be hell to

deal with when you're gone if you don't," he finished, flashing a grin before walking out.

Alex stared at the wall for a long while. He wasn't wrong about Max. The siblings all respected each other. But Max was the biggest rebel when it came to any sort of hierarchy. Putting Rafe in charge would have rubbed Max wrong, even when she herself knew she didn't want the responsibility. Max wanted to run free and do as she wished. But her safety was now a concern for everyone as she was part of a group. Whether she liked it or not.

Making her decision, Alex stood from the table and went in search of her sister. She had a good idea that she would be wandering outside, instead of being cooped up indoors for any reason. The cool fresh air washed over Alex as she walked into the darkness. She stood very still at first, listening. Partially to find Max but also to listen for danger, even though it was unlikely that danger was nearby without the alarms being triggered. However, it was a habit to be extremely aware of her surroundings. When she heard the sound of wood being chopped or possibly abused, Alex knew which direction to go.

Circling around the back of the house, Alex found Griffin leaning against the wall. His eyes were glued to Max, who at the moment was hefting an ax over her head. Alex stopped to watch, thinking that talking to Max when she had a weapon in hand was dangerous. The ax came whistling down and embedded into the log of wood Max was working to split.

"She been doing this since dinner?" Alex asked Griffin.

"Yup."

"How pissed is she?"

"Anyone's guess. She's not telling me the problem either," Griffin sighed, the sound heavy with meaning.

"What's going on, Griff?" Alex asked.

"She's shutting me out. The last week or so she's been distant. I know she's been fighting with you over chores and wanting to do something else. But it's not only that. I'm pretty sure it's rooted in something more," he explained.

"You've tried to talk to her about it?"

"Of course. She tells me I'm being obsessive and then becomes typical Max, avoiding the issues."

Alex looked back at her little sister. Her physical wounds had faded to scars. Her broken fingers were close to healed up. Her ribs still felt slightly bruised, but Charlie was pretty sure they weren't broken and just needed time to heal. Chopping wood wasn't something that would give her the chance to heal, but no one had the guts to tell Max that. She finally set the ax down and stacked the pieces of wood she had chopped. She looked over and finally noticed Alex with Griffin. Only because she knew her sister did Alex see the slight widening of her eyes, the only hint of surprise.

"We need to chat, Max," Alex called out.

"Why? You've already dictated your decisions," Max snapped back.

"Can we have a conversation without the attitude? You can be pissy all you want, but you know that I don't make choices in this compound that aren't for the safety and health of everyone within our walls. You don't have to agree all the time, but you can't be mad at me every day," Alex said.

"I don't agree with that. You are going out on a supply run, with no one else getting a choice."

Finally, Alex felt she had had enough. She strode forward and grabbed the ax from where it was stuck in the log at Max's feet. She turned and returned it to the small overhang they used to keep the wood dry throughout the winter. They were slowly refilling the piles of logs they would need for the next winter. With the weather warming slowly, they no longer needed large fires to warm the larger rooms of the house. Alex figured getting the ax away from Max would work in her advantage.

"You don't have to agree. You just need to be agreeable to the people around you. You need to stop shutting out the ones that love you. I need to go on this run. I need to breathe. I need to get away from constantly managing and leading. And I need a break from the fights with you," Alex said.

She gulped a deep breath after she said the last sentence. She hadn't particularly meant to say it to Max that way, but she needed her sister to know how hard it was on her to be at odds every day.

"We don't fight," Max said, her voice becoming unsure.

"Yes, we do. You want to fight about every chore. You get mad when I won't let you go off half-cocked into town when it's not necessary. You question every single thing I do to try to keep this compound running," Alex replied. Max didn't respond, just looked at her feet. Alex stepped closer and put her hand on her shoulder.

"Max, you have been through things. And you aren't dealing with them well. Your body may be healing, but in your mind, there are things you are struggling with. No, don't argue," Alex said as Max started to look at her and shake her head. "We all see it. We all want to help. But you are too busy pushing against us to actually get that help."

"I feel like I'm drowning here," Max said, so quiet that there was no way Griffin could hear her.

"You aren't alone. You are loved. That man over there," Alex said, gesturing to Griffin who hadn't left his post against the wall, "Wants nothing more than to be there for you. To hold you and help you through this. Why aren't you letting him?"

"I don't need anyone's help," Max said defiantly.

"Keep telling yourself that until you self-destruct. I need you to back up Rafe while I'm gone. And please just stay on the compound and help with the chores without complaint. Can you do that for me?"

"I'll behave...Mom," Max said with a grin.

"I somehow doubt that, but ok. Why don't you and Griffin

turn in for the night? Maybe tell him what's on your mind a little? It couldn't hurt anything," Alex said.

She knew she was pushing the issue, but she didn't want Max to suffer alone. Griffin also had a hard time with the pain they shared. Max gave Alex a side hug and walked to Griffin. Without a word he slung an arm around Max's shoulders, and she slid one around his back. Alex found herself sending a silent prayer to whoever was listening that her sister would find a way through her demons. They were no longer in the age of therapists. They were on their own to work through their troubles.

The couple turned the corner of the house before Alex turned to the Bronco she and Marcus would be taking the next day. She lowered the tailgate and climbed into the back to check the normal bug out bags that were kept in the truck. At any time if they needed a quick escape all the compound vehicles were equipped with enough supplies for the occupants to survive for a week. Cases of water were stacked on one side and Alex mentally noted to take all but one out for their trip.

As she worked, Marcus came up to the Bronco. He began to take out the water cases Alex had moved to the end of the tailgate. He brought the additional food that Margaret had packed for them and Alex moved it into the back seat for easy access. Then the man stood and watched Alex evaluate the packs.

"What's up?" Alex asked.

"You sure about this trip?"

Alex stopped what she was doing to look over at Marcus. She shined the flashlight she carried into his face, so she could better see his expression. She had learned that what Marcus said wasn't always what he was meaning. A lot of the time he led with jokes, when it was a serious situation. He never seemed to know when the right time was to not be a joker. This time, his face seemed to be completely serious.

"Of course, I am. If you aren't, you don't have to go," she replied.

"And you'd just go alone, wouldn't you?" He said.

"No. I'd take Cliff or Easton."

"I'm hurt. I'm just replaceable, huh?" Now his face softened into a sarcastic look.

"Yes, yes you are Marcus. Now are you going to help me get ready, or are you just going to annoy me? We are leaving first thing in the morning."

Together the two quietly loaded the extra supplies into the Bronco. They pulled out the weapons from the shed they would want. Alex chose her 9mm, machete, shotgun, and a Bowie knife to put on her hip. Marcus also chose a 9mm after Alex insisted he have a gun. He typically only used knives, but he had shown Alex he was competent with a handgun as well. There was no guarantee of what they would face when they went into town.

With the guns and extra ammo loaded, Alex shut the doors on the Bronco and slid the keys into her pocket. Excitement shivered through her veins. She was ready to walk away from the compound for a little while. To feel free of decisions and responsibility for other people. She loved her family and had come to care greatly about the other survivors that lived with them, but the pressure of leading them, keeping them safe and provided for, was a weight she was having a hard time carrying.

"We're all here to help you, ya know," Marcus said.

They were standing in the dark, the moon only a sliver in the sky. Marcus was a good friend and Alex knew there were times he got her better than others did. And instead of adding more stress, he often used humor and cockiness to lighten her mood. She knew he thought she took things too seriously. But there was nothing more serious than survival when the dead walked and tried to eat your family.

"Everyone does help. I've never said otherwise," she replied.

"But you take all the responsibility on yourself. No one wants you to do that. And that's why you are so ready to run away from here."

"Stop trying to analyze me, Marcus," she scoffed.

"I don't need to analyze. It's clearly written on your face every day. New lines seem to deepen every day and before you yell at me, I'm not just talking about wrinkles. You frown more. You don't play with the kids as often. You avoid long conversations," he said, ticking off all the things that Alex knew she was doing wrong. But thought no one noticed.

"I have a lot on my plate," she replied.

"I know that. We all know that. But you need to stop being so hard on yourself. Things are getting done. We are all safe right now. You need to relax."

"Sure. Relax. During the apocalypse," she quipped.

"You know what I mean. Hopefully this trip will do the job for you."

With that, he walked away, disappearing into the darkness toward the bunkhouse where he slept. Alex watched for a moment as a lantern flared to life inside the building and she could hear quiet murmuring between Marcus and Cliff, who also slept in the bunkhouse. The bunkhouse was really a converted log shed that her father had insulated, with bunk beds throughout. It gave the compound an additional twelve beds for those that joined them.

Alex made her way back into the main house, thinking about getting her kids to bed as well. Easton stopped her short inside the mudroom.

"What's up, East?"

"Can I come with you tomorrow?" Easton asked.

Alex was anticipating his question. Anytime he was left behind he felt abandoned and useless. Alex always marveled at the emotional disaster of a sixteen-year-old boy. Easton tried hard to be a grownup, but in his heart, he was still sensitive and looking for approval. Alex understood he needed her reassurance and understanding, and she worked hard on that.

"Not this trip. I need as many hands on deck here to keep

things running. You are in rotation with chores and it's best if you stay with that."

"I could be helpful," Easton continued.

"This isn't about you being helpful, East. You know I trust you to watch my back and help me when it's necessary. But this time, the smaller the group that goes, the better. We need to slide in and out quietly to not draw any sort of attention."

"I guess. Candace has a small list," Easton said, handing a slip of paper to Alex.

A smile spread across Alex's face when she saw what the young girl wanted. No, the items weren't all practical as Alex had requested. But entertainment and comfort were things they could still provide. The nail polish, teenage romance DVDs and sports bras were all things Alex would do her best to find and bring back for the girl.

"I know it's not the stuff we really need...." Easton said, trailing off.

"No, this is great. This list reminds me that we still are living lives here, that aren't just chores and survival," Alex looked back to Easton and smiled.

By the time Alex made it to her bedroom, a half hour had passed. She had lists from almost everyone in the compound. Some requests were outlandish, and she wasn't quite sure how she would bring back the items they wanted. But she smiled and said the same to each, that she would try. That wasn't a lie. She wanted to provide for each of the people behind their walls. They were becoming a unit, and she cared about them all. She took all the lists and folded them carefully into the pack she would take with her in the morning.

Stepping into the bedroom she shared with Billie and Henry, Alex found the kids cuddled up in her bed. Billie held a book and was reading aloud to her brother. Alex stood in the doorway for a moment and listened as Billie explained how volcanos worked. When she started to dive into death and destruction Alex smothered a laugh. Listening to a seven-year-old talk about how lava burns everyone alive and the ash filled their lungs until they choked was entertaining. Alex realized they were reading a book about Pompeii and she wondered where it had come from.

"People weren't frozen, Billie. Lava is hot!" Henry argued.

"Their bodies were burned immediately, so they were frozen in place," Billie explained.

"What are you two reading?" Alex said, stepping up to the bed.

"I'm teaching Henry about Pompeii. It's a city that was lost to a volcano," Billie said in her best teacher imitation.

"Teaching him?" Alex asked.

"Well, we don't have school anymore. I don't want Henry to not be smart because he won't go to school," Billie explained.

"That's a great idea. But can you even read the book?"

"Some of the words. I figured it out from the pictures," the little girl turned the book and pointed to the illustrations of lava chasing people.

"Well it's time to end the lesson tonight. Time to get ready for bed."

As Alex changed the kids' clothes, and they cuddled in bed for a while, her mind whirled thinking about education. Not only her kids and her niece needed their studies, but Easton and Candace were still only middle school and high school aged. And Aiden would soon need to learn to read and write. Mentally she added a school to her list for places to scavenge. They needed to get some general study books for the kids. Then they would start adding school times to the chore rotation. Training the mind was just as important as training the body for survival. Maybe they wouldn't be using algebra anytime soon, but someday the world may mend itself and she didn't want them extremely behind.

Henry was curled up with his head on her chest. Billie was on her other side, cuddling with her arm tightly. The kids didn't understand why Alex had to go on a scavenging run. But after some conversations and some promises to bring home special items for them, the two of them finally fell asleep. Though they both had cots in the room, often the kids just slept with Alex in her queen-sized bed. Tonight, Alex was too exhausted to even suggest they sleep in their own beds. The sweet smell of Henry's hair lulled Alex to sleep

Her dreams were erratic and bloody. Infected dead were hiding in every dark corner of her brain. Part of her subconscious knew she was dreaming and that part of her hoped the dreams weren't a sign of things to come.

CHAPTER THREE

Alex poured over the maps they had started to maintain since they all came together at the compound. Each place that was searched was marked. Some were marked in black, meaning there was no reason to go back. Either all the supplies were gone, none were ever there, or it was too overrun with the infected to risk it. There was a lot of black on the map of the nearest town, Kalispell. However, there were still places Alex wanted to check before they headed to another town.

There were locations they had circled in green. These were places like small stores that maybe no one had scavenged from yet. The Duncan group only took what could be trucked at one time, without taking a lot of time in the open. They hadn't been to the school yet, as it had been a military outpost in the beginning of the outbreak. It was overrun and now it was a shell of its former structure. With the idea of education in her mind, Alex assumed no one would be concerned about the learning materials. She hoped a lot of it was left around the rooms. The last time she drove by the area, she noted that all the doors had been left ajar. Going in would be a risk. She had confidence in her ability to handle things and thought it would be a good first stop.

Marcus came into the dining room where Alex was going over maps. He yawned loudly before taking a drink of the coffee he held. His face screwed up at the taste and he looked into the cup as if something had died.

"Did Max make the coffee this morning?" He asked.

Alex answered without looking up, "That's my assumption since it tastes like sewer sludge full of dead rats."

"Great visual," Marcus disappeared into the kitchen again. When he came back, he had a bottled water in his hand instead.

"What's the plan?" He asked.

Alex turned the map toward him. She had circled the places they were going in blue. They started out with the school, then a small pharmacy owned by a local family that they hadn't seen since the plague started. After that Alex wanted to attempt to go to Wal-Mart. She knew it was a risk and possibly a waste of time. But it was the one place that had the most clothing and toiletries to fulfill some of the lists they had. Lastly, she has plotted a route to Whitefish, a nearby resort town. There was no knowing how many tourists were there when everything fell apart. Alex thought some of the smaller shops would be intact and useful. She also wanted to venture further away from their little area. They wouldn't know what was happening in the other states if they didn't find others to talk to.

"Seems you're planning on being gone a while. These locations will take a few days at least," Marcus commented.

"Well, eventually we were going to need to head further out."

Marcus nodded. He handed Alex a list she hadn't seen yet. She looked at the scrawling letters and knew it was from Cliff. The man kept his distance from everyone but the children. After he lost his wife and child to the infected, Max literally slapped him out of his despair and brought him to Montana with her. Once there, Alex had welcomed him with open arms. They had talked a number of times, but the man was shuttered. It was clear he didn't want serious connections that could be lost again.

However, when it came to the children, he was different. Max had told a few stories of how Cliff had protected her daughter, Jack. Alex could only guess what he saw as a failure with his own flesh and blood, fueled his need to see all the children safe. On the compound the only time he smiled was when he played with the kids. They all immediately trusted him, and Alex always took that as a sign of a good heart.

His list consisted of a few toiletries, but the rest were all things he wanted for the kids. Games, cards, stuffed animals. Alex sighed and closed her eyes for a moment. A stab of pain went through her heart when she thought of his loss and how he battled it. Alex had her own loss, but she couldn't compare it to having a child ripped from your arms by the infected.

"It's sad," Marcus said when Alex didn't comment.

"It is. But we'll get him the things he wants."

Alex packed the lists and maps into her bag. She double checked her fire starters, food, compass, extra ammo, and first aid kit. She knew everything was there. But she always double checked. She pulled on her thick hiking pants and hiking boots. She made sure to pack her motorcycle gloves, a thick leather that would protect her hands when they had to fight the infected. She rubbed her fingers over the soft leather thinking about her husband, Blake. When the picture of his face floated into her mind, her heart seemed to break a little less each time. But that fissure would always be there.

"Mommy!" Henry exclaimed as he ran into the room. He flung his arms around Alex, burying his face into her side.

"Hey, buddy, what's wrong?"

She stooped so she was eye level with her little boy. His eyes were hers, brown and inquisitive. She knew he saw everything around him. When he leaned back to look at her, his eyes shimmered with tears.

"Do you really have to go? What about the sick people?" He asked.

"I need to make sure we have all the things we need to be comfortable here. I can handle the sick people, remember?"

Alex hugged him close to her again and his little arms twisted around her neck. He squeezed tightly for a moment before releasing her. She kissed his forehead just as Billie entered the room as well. As usual, her daughter had a brave face. Alex felt her heart twist just a little again. When Billie looked at her, she saw Blake's eyes so clearly. A part of her was so thankful for the pieces of him that would forever be with her. She would always do what was necessary to keep their children safe.

Outside of the house Max and Griffin waited by the Bronco. Griffin handed a brown paper bag to Alex as she met them.

"Breakfast and lunch for today from Margaret. She's in the garden, avoiding a goodbye I think," Griffin said.

"Why is everyone acting like this is something different from what we've been doing out here? This is no different from other scavenging runs," Alex said, her exasperation showing.

"Because it's you. The solid, dependable Duncan is leaving us all to fend for ourselves," Max said. Alex could tell she was barely keeping the roll of her eyes to herself.

"Well I guess that means you need to learn to be the dependable one, Max," Alex replied.

Max snorted in Alex's ear as she hugged her. "Doubtful," Max said.

Climbing into the Bronco Alex didn't hesitate to start the engine. She was starting to feel panicked as the goodbyes continued. All she wanted was to breathe and get away from the moment. Marcus climbed into the truck next to her and the slam of his door was all the signal she needed that it was time to go. She refused to look into the rearview mirror as they pulled down to the gate. She could feel eyes on them. Her children were probably at the top of the hill waving. Alex couldn't stomach anymore guilt from doing what she needed, so she kept her eyes forward.

When they got to the gate, it opened automatically, proving

that someone was watching them on the monitors. Alex carefully pulled the Bronco out as soon as there was enough space. Once through, the gate began to move again immediately. They sat, waiting for it to completely close. Marcus watched out his side of the truck, ensuring no infected somehow stumbled into the opening. As soon as the clang of the metal sounded the completion, Alex took a deep breath. She released it in a rush as a large weight seemed to feel lighter on her shoulders.

They spoke very little as she drove toward town. Alex knew that was unlike Marcus, to keep his mouth shut for any length of time. She was thankful for it now. Without someone asking, she would have gone on this run alone. That thought was ludicrous because Alex had forbidden anyone to go on runs alone. Nothing was safe anymore and everyone needed someone to watch their back. But she was in such a hurry to get away, she didn't even want to wait for arrangements to be made. She needed the silence for her brain to unwind. Stealing a glance over to Marcus, she knew that he realized what she needed.

"You're a good friend, Marcus," Alex said, breaking the thick silence. His eyes swung to her for a moment before looking back out his window.

"Well you don't always make it easy."

"I know."

"Wow, no argument from you?" Marcus asked, his snarky attitude revving up.

"Nope. I know I've been difficult. But I'm glad it's you out here with me. It's easier because I don't have to worry about you getting eaten," Alex joked.

"You're such a good friend too," Marcus said with a smirk.

"I try...wait...what's that?" Alex said, her joke lost as she trailed off.

"That wasn't there before was it?"

Alex shook her head. She slowed the Bronco to a crawl as they approached the large gray tour bus. The windows were blacked out, making it impossible to see what was happening inside. From their distance, they could see the door stood open. But the bus itself was parked across the road, blocking almost the entire path. They could slide the Bronco around, but Alex felt apprehension crawl up her spine. As they got closer, she could see the distinct drying red smears against the side of the bus.

"Where do you think it came from?" Marcus asked.

"The question I'd like answered is where are the people that were on it?" Alex said.

Marcus nodded as he leaned forward in his seat. Alex stopped the Bronco ten yards from the bus, trying to make a plan of how to go around the bus. With the way it was stopped, she couldn't see what was on the other side. The idea of an ambush or a hidden horde made her feel jumpy. Another part of her brain wondered what was on the bus still or if there was anyone still alive. *Wouldn't they come out at the sound of a vehicle,* her inner devil's advocate said. She had to agree with that opinion as well. But some part of Alex always stopped her from ever walking away from possible survivors.

"We should check the bus," she said.

"For what? More blood? Because there's plenty right there," Marcus replied.

"What if there are supplies in there?"

"What if there are dead in there?"

"We could play a lot of what ifs here. But this bus came from somewhere and it's too close to the house. I don't like it sitting there like that."

"You want to move it?" Marcus asked, raising his eyebrows at her.

"If we can find the keys. Maybe they left so fast they are still inside," Alex replied.

"You don't make anything easy, Duncan," he said. But he

started double checking his weapons as he spoke. Alex knew she had won the point.

She took her keys and pushed them low in her front pocket. In case this was some sort of ambush, she wanted it to be hard for anyone to get her keys. Marcus had an extra key; in case she was killed, and he couldn't get the keys off her body. Making extra keys for the vehicles had been something Alex wanted done quickly. When she explained why, she knew it was a gruesome thought, but she didn't want anyone left stranded should the worst happen.

Alex clicked off the safety on her 9mm when she jumped out of the Bronco. She had it in a two-handed grip, pointed slightly down, prepared for any attack that may come. She didn't have to look to know Marcus was behind her, with a similar stance. Both of them swept the area for any movement. When they saw none, Alex had an idea. She motioned for Marcus to stop and watch. Placing her 9mm back into its holster, she quickly dropped to her front, in a push up position. From that vantage point, she could see under the bus to determine if there was anything hiding on the other side. She jumped up a moment later and shook her head at Marcus. There were no feet or legs from what she could see.

Leading toward the bus, Alex held her gun again. When they got to the open door, Alex did what they always did before entering anything, she tapped on the glass with the butt of her gun. The sound echoed into the bus, exactly what she had hoped for. A groan sounded from inside and they both stepped to the side of the door, waiting for the infected to come. After a few moments, the groaning and hissing continued, but nothing appeared. Alex decided to investigate. She pointed toward the door and again motioned for Marcus to stand watch. He shook his head at her vigorously. Alex had to roll her eyes. She knew he wouldn't follow her instructions while they were out.

Deciding to just ignore whatever he was going to do, she stepped onto the bottom step. Leaning down slightly, she could see down the middle aisle of the bus. There was no driver in the seat and no blood there. She immediately noticed that the keys were in the ignition and in her mind she cheered. The middle aisle seemed clear near the front, so she took two more steps. In the middle of the landing of the entrance, Alex panned through the bus with her gun. It didn't take long to find the infected that had heard them.

Alex couldn't help but stand with her head cocked as she looked at the infected. It was a woman, wearing only a bra and ripped shorts. There was only one bite on her that Alex could see, directly on her forearm. The same arm that was pinned above her, where her wrist was cuffed to the metal pole that ran down the entire bus. Alex was sure the pole was usually used as a handhold when you walked in the bus while it moved. But this woman had been handcuffed to it at some point. Alex wondered if someone had tried to restrain her, knowing she would turn.

"What in the world?" Marcus hissed from behind her.

"Maybe someone couldn't kill her after she was bitten and turned?" Alex suggested.

"Can't leave her like that," Marcus said sadly.

"Nope."

Alex put her gun away and pulled her bowie knife. There was no need for the loud gunshot when the infected was restrained. The bus had other riders at some point and Alex didn't want to draw their attention, dead or alive. She walked carefully down the middle aisle, checking the seats as she went. However, she made it to the infected woman without finding any other threats. The woman's free hand swiped toward Alex, her low guttural growls and moans intensifying as she thought her meal was within her grasp. Alex easily pushed her arm to the side and slammed the blade into her temple. Immediately the infected body went limp, hanging from the wrist that was handcuffed.

Standing next to the hanging body, Alex started to notice other things. The first was small slices that were made in her skin

near her breasts and down her bare arms. Nothing deep enough
to bleed profusely. And with the way there was no scabbing, Alex
guessed the cuts were made after she turned. The infected was
also missing three fingers from one hand and two from the other.
Alex lifted the one hand that was free and swinging from the dead
body. The removal of her fingers had to be after she died and rose
again, because there was no clotting and no signs of significant
bleeding. Instead, black thickness now covered the areas.

"I don't get it," Alex said as Marcus joined her near the back
of the bus.

"What happened to her fingers? Infected bite them off?"

"I don't think so. I think someone tortured the woman, after
she became infected. Notice the lack of blood from these chest
wounds?"

"What kinda sick crap is this?" Marcus hissed as he looked
closer at what Alex had noticed.

He then extended his finger, pointing at the infected's bare
thighs. Alex cursed quietly. Somehow in all the filth Alex hadn't
seen the circular burns that covered the skin that was visible.
Some were the size of cigarettes. Some were larger, as if something had been heated up just to burn the infected.

"I don't know what happened here and I'm not sure I want to
know. Let's move this bus and get out of here. This is giving me
the creeps. More than any infected has."

Marcus agreed, and the two began to check the bus for
supplies. They scored with three boxes of Cup of Noodles soups.
Each box looked to be from some sort of warehouse, holding
twenty soups each. They weren't ideal with the nutritional value,
but they were easy. They also grabbed a bat and a crowbar that
were abandoned when the bus was left. Alex easily started up the
bus, to find it had a half tank. She mentally noted that lack of gas
wasn't the reason the bus was left. She moved the bus to the side
of the road, leaving a mostly clear road again.

Sitting back in the Bronco, they sat in silence again. Alex

didn't drive, her hands tapping the wheel as she tried to go over everything they had found.

"That was weird right?" Alex asked.

"Weird doesn't really cover it."

"If she was tied up, but they abandoned the bus anyway, there must have been more infected on there. The blood on the door and side of the bus seem to tell that story," Alex said. She didn't really expect any response from Marcus. She was talking to herself, rolling the situation around in her mind.

"Unless the blood was from a previous attack. Still, doesn't explain where the driver is. We know at least there was a driver. We can't guess about the rest," Marcus reasoned.

He was right, Alex knew. The mutilation to the infected didn't sit well with her. She realized that the fall of civilized society would open doors to the most demented. Having them so close to her home made her skin crawl. If they hadn't been on watch when they left the compound, Alex would feel the need to turn around and check again. But nothing had been moving near the wall when they left. If anyone approached the compound, they would be picked up by the cameras and sensors. Alex calmed her panic by remembering their security system was second to none and Rafe had created it himself. Moments like this were the only times she really missed cellphones. She mentally noted that they needed to search again for long range radios to communicate with the compound when there were problems.

"Let's get out of here. I think I'm going to have nightmares about this one," Alex mumbled.

"Just going to add it to my ever-revolving terrors," Marcus replied.

The rest of the drive into town was quiet. At times in the distance they could see the stumbling forms of the infected. When they passed any closely, the infected heads would swing toward the moving vehicle. Their bodies, strange moving, with limbs flopping with little care for control, would stumble toward the Bronco. They wouldn't get close and they would lose interest as soon as the Bronco turned a corner and they could no longer hear it. Early into the plague Alex realized the infected were drawn by sound and sight. When they didn't have a clear visual of something that made them think of food they easily gave up.

They pulled up to the school Alex had circled on their map. It was an elementary and middle school combination, a large gym seeming to be the center point of the campus. The exterior had once been surrounded by temporary chain link fencing, hastily erected by the government officials taking over the school. Now that fencing laid haphazardly in places, some completely pushed over. Most of the doors stood open from where they sat. Alex looked around at the blood stains and destroyed tents. A small tremor of fear entered her mind, but she fought it down. She knew they could handle anything they faced in this place.

Marcus looked more incredulous. He looked at the building then to Alex. He shook his head before looking back to the school.

"This is really necessary?" He asked.

"The kids need education. Just because the world is no longer civilized, doesn't mean we shouldn't try. Plus, we don't know what type of supplies could still be in there."

"Maybe we should start at the portables over there," Marcus suggested, pointing in the direction of temporary buildings set up on the field next to the school.

Alex studied them for a moment. The words and logo for FEMA were on the side. She assumed they were either offices or storage. Storage would be what they were looking for and FEMA would have brought supplies, if they had the chance before everything fell apart. The white outer walls of the mobile units were now stained with dark smears, an ominous sign of what they were likely going to face inside. While she watched, two infected shambled from between the buildings. They had little destination until the rumble of the Bronco caught their attention. Alex sighed, shutting the truck off.

"Pulling any closer could be risky. I'll leave it here for now. We can move it if we find anything," she said.

Marcus was already double-checking weapons before Alex had spoken. With the engine off the quiet was piercing. No other engine sounds, no planes, no helicopters, no other life making itself known. This was the world they lived in. The click of safeties and rounds being loaded echoed in the truck as they prepared to step out. The sound of weapons was more commonplace than hearing someone calling to a friend in town. Gunfire, explosions, and fire were normal occurrences as the living fought through every day.

Today was no different. Alex had no doubt that they would have their hands full after they left the Bronco. However, the risk was necessary when it came to the survival of their group. The quality of life was important to Alex. That quality didn't include having to see infected dead every day or struggling to eat. So, she handled those things as often as she could.

"Ready?" Alex asked, looking to Marcus.

He said nothing, but his hand was on the door handle the next moment. Together they popped open the doors. They locked both before slamming them shut. The loud noises riled the infected, their howls and hisses rising in level. Alex looked around them, having an eerie feeling that these two infected were calling more to the feast. But when she glanced to the sides nothing moved but the two infected walking toward them.

One of the infected was a small woman in a lab coat which was splattered with blood and mud. The ripped flaps of it hung from the infected's shoulders. Her head hung at a strange angle and as she got closer Alex could tell why. The side of her neck was completely missing, all skin and tendons ripped away. Without the muscles to keep her head upright it lulled to the side. That didn't stop her from snapping her jaws and stumbling toward her prey.

The doctor's partner was in worse shape if that was possible. Alex had to swallow hard to keep bile from rising to her throat as she watched the lanky man head toward them. His stomach was an empty cavity, skin, muscle and organs completely gone. Something had feasted on him for a good period of time before he rose as a walking dead. Alex imagined the only thing keeping him upright were the bright white ribs and spine she could see even from a distance.

The sickness didn't give her pause. She immediately began to stride forward, always more willing to meet her enemy than wait for them to reach her. Marcus knew her habits and didn't protest when she walked directly toward the danger. He was close on her heels, Alex didn't even have to look to know he was ready. They had gone on other runs together and had fought side by side a number of times since the beginning. It was second nature already.

Alex met the infected doctor first. The woman's snapping intensified, and an inhuman growl left her throat. She tried to lunge for Alex, but Alex was ready to pivot and move. As she turned away from the infected, the dead woman couldn't quickly react, and Alex easily plunged her Bowie knife into the back of its head. She swung toward the second dead, but Marcus was already pulling his blade from under its chin where he had pierced its brain. Marcus leaned down and wiped the blade on the infected's remaining clothing before looking to Alex, nodding his head.

They didn't speak or use guns. The additional noise could attract anything else within hearing distance. Alex was sure that if they didn't come to the howling of the two infected they put down, there weren't any more dead nearby. But her mind didn't allow her to let go of even slim possibilities. Staying silent was their best option. Alex slid her own cleaned blade back into its sheath that rested on her hip. Though she knew her 9mm was ready, she quickly rechecked it before she left it unclipped on her opposite hip.

Together the pair stalked toward the FEMA portables. Alex slid to the side as they approached a window, while noticing the door wasn't open like the rest of the school. She couldn't tell from the outside if it was reinforced. Finding anyone inside wouldn't be a large surprise. But to ensure they didn't get shot by a survivor trying to defend their hideout, Alex wanted to check inside carefully. She walked on the balls of her feet along the wall, until she was right at the corner. Marcus shadowed her, following her lead as they went.

At the window, Alex lifted onto her toes for a moment and peeked into the dim interior of the portable building. The light from the windows didn't shine very far, and she was only able to see vague shapes in the shadows. None of which looked like a human, alive or dead. She stayed still as possible while balancing on her toes to make sure nothing moved. Tapping on the glass a few times with her finger confirmed her suspicions that the building was empty.

Alex looked over her shoulder at Marcus, who was watching their backs as she checked the portable. When his eyes met hers, she nodded her head toward the door once and they started moving again. At the stairs into the portable Alex slowed, stepping onto the aluminum steps carefully. There was some creaking from the stairs, but it was minimal as they climbed. At the door, Alex pulled her 9mm as a precaution. Again, possibilities were always her worst enemy. Marcus shadowed her movements, also making sure his gun was in his hand.

The doorknob turned easily, surprising Alex. She not only expected it to be locked, but she had expected other people to be there. This was easily one of the best places to scavenge, knowing the government would have come with supplies. Alex pulled the door open slowly, her 9mm leading into the darkness. The light from the opening door gave her more of an idea what was in the room. The stacks of boxes filled the back of the portable. Alex and Marcus stepped inside and Marcus allowed the door the click shut quietly behind them.

Marcus pulled a small flashlight from his pocket and the beam of light cut through some of the darker shadows, illuminating labels on the boxes.

"Jackpot," he breathed.

CHAPTER FOUR

Alex whistled low in agreement to Marcus's reaction. It was indeed a jackpot. A part of her brain niggled, making her question why the items hadn't been taken by any survivors yet. But the rest of her wanted to rejoice in finding such a large supply of substantial foods meant for survival. Boxes of MRE's lined one wall. Another wall seemed to have boxes of canned tuna, chicken, fruits, and vegetables. In the center were boxes that were labeled with powered foods such as potatoes and flour.

"We can't even fit this all into the Bronco," Marcus said.

"No. Maybe we should grab another vehicle while we're here?" Alex wondered aloud.

"And drive two to Whitefish?"

"Thinking we could load this stuff up, hide the vehicle to pick up on our way home," Alex explained.

Marcus agreed with a nod of his head. He stepped into the room further, popping open the first box he came to. They were taped up and he confirmed that the box he opened was full of supplies. While he was searching, Alex turned to the small desk that was in the building as well. The papers on the desk were logs of supplies, delivery schedules, and orders from leadership. Those communications caught Alex's attention the most.

Grabbing a stack of papers, Alex stepped to the dirty window where she could get the most light. The beginning of the communications were typical coordination, set up, and guidelines. She found it odd that they were all printed out because there was no visual computer in the portable but they looked like memos. Once the Wi-Fi fell, they may not have had any way to connect and receive their orders without someone bringing the papers to them.

The communications continued to become more panicked and erratic with the suggestions and orders. Alex looked at the dates and times and realized the memos weren't days apart like she originally assumed. They all seemed to happen over a 48-hour period of time. The panic of the communications reminded Alex of the major breakdown of services when she was fleeing her home in Las Vegas. It was clear the government hadn't been prepared for the illness. Now, having more information about where the pathogen came from, Alex found the panic even more telling. Charlie was sure the laboratory she worked at was a secret site, maybe even a black site that the top levels of government didn't know of. The smaller groups within the government weren't given any information to protect themselves or to escape in time.

"They weren't planning on giving the supplies to anyone. These were specifically for the military that were stationed here," Alex said.

"Why wouldn't FEMA try to help the public?" Marcus asked, his voice slightly muffled by the boxes he was behind.

"No way of knowing. My guess is the military was supposed to help the public. FEMA was here to support them."

Though her hypothesis rang true, Alex still felt as if the entire rescue situation was disorganized and chaotic. She flipped through a few more of the memos where the number of dead was

noted in pen. The number wasn't as high as Alex would have
thought, but if all they cared about was the military, it may have
only been their numbers. On the final sheet of paper Alex
scanned it like she had done before, realizing this memo was
different. It was orders to abandon camp. The last line made Alex
pause and stare.

"Son of a bitch," she said, her voice louder than she had
intended.

Marcus popped his head around a stack of boxes and when he
saw her face, he rushed over to join her. He looked over her
shoulder and they both just stared. The name at the bottom of
the memo, the one sending the orders, was Major Callahan. Alex
saw red when she saw the name. She could hear her heartbeat in
her ears, the vision of Max, beaten and broken when she finally
got the compound came to her mind. Without thinking, Alex
crumpled the memo, gripping her fist as if she could smash it into
Callahan's face.

"He was calling the troops back to him. His place is called
Camp U.S.?" Marcus asked as he read the memo quickly.

"Makes it sound like the only one, doesn't it?" Alex replied.

"That can't be true?" He replied, raising his eyebrows at Alex.

"I'm not sure of anything," she replied.

She stepped away from the window to toss the crumpled
memos back on the desk. There was no information there worth
taking home. Alex knew she needed to get her mind set straight.
Thinking about Callahan's reach wasn't going to help them find a
vehicle and load it up with the supplies they wanted to take. Plot-
ting to kill a man she had never met was a distraction she didn't
need when they were out in the open. Her mind had a hard time
breaking away from that train of thought. Alex shook her head
roughly, as if to shake Callahan directly out of her mind. When
she finally looked up again, she found Marcus watching her.

"It makes sense that you're pissed."

"I'm not pissed," she replied.

"Sure you are. After seeing Max when she made it home, there's no way you wouldn't be mad at the man that did that to her," Marcus said.

"Right now isn't the time to be mad."

"Uh, the dead aren't staying dead. Oh, and they want to eat us. There are also some crazy government guys after us. When would be a better time to be mad?"

"Being a smart ass doesn't change things," Alex shot back.

"Always good at the avoidance," Marcus said with a laugh.

"Not avoidance. I just can't face that right this moment. We have other things to concentrate on. Like finding a vehicle to put this stuff in."

Marcus, realizing he was fighting a losing battle, dropped the conversation and looked out the windows. Alex joined him, checking for any infected that may have wandered in. Nothing was moving, for now. Alex noticed a FEMA pickup that was parked next to a nearby portable. She pointed it out to Marcus, who agreed that they could fit plenty of the supplies in there. They also planned on taking a few additional things with them, just in case they found any survivors that needed help.

Running together, they left the supply building and headed for the building the truck was parked next to. Alex checked the truck for keys. As she suspected, they weren't in the vehicle. Quickly they went up the metal stairs to the door of the building. This one had a small window on the door. Marcus hesitated, checking the inside. Before he could say anything to Alex, a bang against the door made him jump back slightly.

"Looks like just one," he said, as he tried to look around the infected.

"Open the door and jump back," Alex instructed. She backed down the stairs to await the infected.

Marcus turned the doorknob and allowed the door to open a crack, before he jumped down the stairs. They both waited as the infected banged against the door again. It stumbled out of the building as it found the door to be open. The shirt on the man had a FEMA logo on the chest pocket. Alex looked closely as he stumbled down the stairs, almost falling face first as he tried to get to the living at the bottom. She saw that the man had one circular bite to his hand, some of the flesh was missing. A black mark was left where blood and muscle should have been. Alex guessed that after the man was bitten, he ran into the building hoping to protect himself. Instead he probably got sick, died, and rose as an infected dead. Without the coordination to open the door, he was stuck inside until someone ended his torment.

Alex had no problem being the person that handled that. As the FEMA worker reached the ground, he immediately focused on Alex and began to hiss and growl. He began to lumber toward Alex, but before she could lunge and end him, Marcus stepped up from the side. The infected fell at Alex's feet, Marcus's knife sliding from its skull. He bent immediately to clean the blade.

"I had that," Alex grumbled.

"Of course, you did. I was just handling your light work."

When they stepped into the building, they both began to cough. Alex fought hard to control her gagging as the rancid smell of decaying meat filled her nostrils and mouth. Immediately she pulled her bandana from her back pocket and tied it around her face. The portable building was completely enclosed, allowing the smell of the infected to permeate the walls. Alex didn't know how long the man had been dead in the closed portable, but it was long enough to make it smell worse than anything Alex had encountered so far.

They agreed to search quickly for the keys. Before coming back to the building, Alex had checked the pockets of the infected and found them empty. She had high hopes the keys were inside somewhere and tried not to imagine them in the pocket of some infected wandering miles away. As they looked, Alex took in the condition of the room. In the corner there was a makeshift bed with coats and wool blankets thrown on the ground. By the amount of blood in that area she assumed the man died there while trying to hide from the infected that swarmed the safety zone. There were empty food wrappers as well. Judging by that, Alex guessed the man was only alive a day before succumbing to the illness.

The sound of shaking keys pulled Alex's gaze to Marcus. He held up two sets. Both had fobs on them, so Alex motioned for him to try them. She cheered quietly when the car lights blinked when Marcus hit the unlock button. Before leaving the office, Alex wandered around. She didn't find any additional information that may give them any idea of what Callahan had control over. She avoided touching any of the walls, as they were all covered with blood and black gore. In her mind she could see the infected man bouncing off of the walls as he tried to find a weak spot to escape from. The sound of any nearby vehicles or people would have riled him into a frenzy in the small building.

They made one more check of the area before starting up the truck and backing it up to the supply building. Alex stood watch, keeping an eye out for any threats, while Marcus started loading the truck with boxes. She knew the process would go faster with two sets of hands, but she didn't have time for one of them to get hurt. She smiled ruefully at her thoughts, realizing her concern was really about the inconvenience of getting hurt, not the possibility of real trouble. Marcus came out of the building just in time to see the strange smile on her face.

"Something funny?" He asked, looking around for the joke.

"Nope. Just thinking to myself."

"I feel like I should be worried that you're smiling like that when thinking to yourself. Have you officially cracked?"

Alex turned to look at him as he hefted another box into the truck. In thirty minutes, he had almost two layers of boxes loaded. They wouldn't be able to fill many more. Marcus was a hard worker and Alex appreciated that trait about him. She never had to worry that he wouldn't get his work done in a day. As he loaded boxes and Alex just stood watch, he never complained or asked for a break. He knew the process of getting things done and getting back into the safety of their vehicle.

"Not completely cracked, but maybe a small scratch is starting," Alex said, only partially joking.

Marcus seemed to realize it was closer to truth than she was letting on. He didn't continue with the joke, but nodded his head and walked back into the building. A shuffling sound from behind the storage building caught Alex's attention. Seconds later she pulled her gun and had it up in a two-handed grip. She slowly circled around the truck, keeping it as a protective shield between her and the building for the moment. She could see the door where Marcus would come unaware of a possible danger. Using the gun, she tapped on the truck. She was answered by a hissing growl that could have come from the throat of a four-legged predator, but Alex knew better.

She didn't turn when she heard Marcus on the metal stairs. He immediately realized the threat, and he pushed the last box into the truck quickly before pulling his own weapons. Alex nodded toward the back of the building, just as a dark form stumbled around the side. *Only one,* thought Alex. *Nothing more challenging or dangerous?* Her own callous thoughts shook her, realizing she wasn't as concerned about her life as she should be. She allowed Billie's and Henry's faces to flash in her mind. Then Easton and Candace. What would those children do without her?

While the inner war waged in Alex, Marcus stepped forward to end the dead life of the infected. Alex assumed it was another FEMA worker, wearing a similar color to the man they found in the office building. It was hard to see any sort of logo on his shirt, as it was completely covered in dried blood. This infected had feasted often after waking as a zombie. The idea made Alex sad. How many had this infected been able to kill before he came across Marcus and Alex? The numbers could be huge, and Alex had to stop thinking about it. There was nothing they could do to save everyone that was still alive. They could only end those they came across as they survived every day.

With the truck packed, Alex ran back to the Bronco. Marcus followed her to the school parking lot. Alex insisted on entering the school to look for the education materials she wanted to collect for the compound. The dark doorways seemed ominous, but Alex just told herself it was because there were no windows in the inner corridors. Though that was probably true, it didn't account for the dead that could be inside as well.

"They left fast," Marcus commented as the two stood in front of the wide-open front office door.

"Everything fell apart too fast. They weren't ready," Alex replied.

"All set?" He asked, nodding toward the dark entrance.

"As ready as you can be in the apocalypse," she replied.

Leading the way, Alex held her 9mm up with one hand and a flashlight under it with the other. She had learned the technique from her father, though it wasn't practiced often. He was very clear about moving your hands together as one, so your flashlight beam was pointing at whatever you wanted to shoot. Her light cut through the dingy darkness of the school hallway. It was the destroyed chaos that Alex had pictured in her mind.

The school office had clearly been taken over by the military. Papers and school handbooks were strewn across the ground. One desk held a satellite phone and a heavy-duty laptop case that was on its side. When Alex turned the laptop, she wasn't surprised to see the screen smashed. The satellite phone was completely dead, but she added it to her pack to give to Rafe. Her brother was a wiz with technology, and she thought he might be able to do something with the device. She'd noticed the blood splattered across the front desk of the office. An attack happened here, leaving Alex to wonder how many people had made it out and how many were dead wandering the halls they were about to walk down.

After the front office was cleared, they used an inner door to enter the hallways. Just inside they stood quietly, listening for movement. The smell was between dusty and roadkill. The infected had been inside and not long ago. But the question was if they were still there. Far off somewhere in the school a banging could be heard. Alex decided to go the opposite way of where she thought that sound was originating from.

The first door they found that was unlocked led to a kindergarten classroom. They quickly cleared the room and let the door shut behind them. In the relative safety of the room, Alex put away her gun and went straight to the corner that held small bookshelves. She quickly sorted through books that would be good for Henry and packed them in her bag. She then went to the teacher's messy desk. It was easy to tell that no one had used the room for anything after the school was taken over. The desk was still covered with lesson plans and homework pages. Alex grabbed a stack of writing practice sheets and coloring pages and packed those away as well.

Marcus busied himself with gathering the stacking blocks and crayons from around the room. Alex found him putting a few bags of crayons, markers, and pencils in his bag. They could only carry so much, so they had to be selective in what they took. Thinking also of creating the little school time on the compound, Alex took the electric pencil sharpener that sat near the door of the room. She looked back around, wishing she could take the colorful posters from the walls that had cute sayings. Or the bean bag chairs that sat all over the room for kids to lounge in. *Another time,* she thought to herself.

Done with the kindergarten room, Alex pulled her gun again. They opened the door a crack to listen while they held their breath. No sounds came from the hallway and Alex carefully opened the door fully. She pointed her flashlight down both sides of the hallway. It was empty, just as they had left it. They took a left-hand turn to go deeper down the hallway, away from the office they'd entered through. After two more locked doors they opened another door.

This room was in disarray. After confirming the room was empty, they quickly entered and shut the door behind them. This room had sleeping bags along the walls and tables set for meals and toiletries in the center. Alex came to a quick conclusion that this was used as shelter, but the lack of the blood meant these people had evacuated before the slaughter began. Ignoring the shelter items, Alex went to the teacher's desk where textbooks were stacked. She flipped through the mathematics book. She knew that Billie had learned her basics of addition and subtraction, but she was only in the second grade. This book seemed slightly more advanced, but Alex guessed that was the point of school. She took one book each of math, science, and social studies. She found a small stack of library books behind the teacher's desk. It was easy to decide which Billie would enjoy reading. Max's daughter, Jack, was a year older than Billie, so Alex hoped these books applied to her somehow as well.

"I think I have all I can carry," Alex said in a whisper.

"We can always come back another time. Or unload and head right back in today," Marcus replied.

"I need to go to the other side," she said.

"For Candace and Easton? I don't think we'll be alone there."

Alex nodded her head, contemplating. In her mind she envisioned building a library for the kids. This was just the start. She wanted to get into the middle school side, the side she was sure the banging was coming from. That would be where she could find things for Candace and Easton. She knew they had all of their basic learning done, but education had been so important to her at their age. She wanted to make sure she provided what they needed to survive now, but also later when—or if—the world repaired itself.

Deciding that they still had plenty of hours in the day, the pair made their way back to the office and out of the school. They went straight to the Bronco and emptied their bags of all the education materials. Alex noticed Marcus was more focused on the fun items such as math games, blocks, construction paper, scissors, and popsicle sticks. She had to smother a laugh thinking about the difference in their priorities. She carefully stacked the books that she had brought, making room for more.

When they turned back to the school, Alex handed Marcus a bottle of water. They studied the school in silence as they sipped the cool liquid. The sun was high in the sky, Alex assumed it was getting close to lunch time. She guessed if they made one more run into the school they would break for lunch after. Marcus agreed with the plan and they headed back toward the office. Though they cleared the area before, they still moved carefully, checking dark corners and making sure doors were secured as they passed.

Alex took a deep breath before turning the direction for the middle school side of the building. She hoped she understood the layout from the map inside the office. They would have to pass through the large gym and on the other side was where the middle school classrooms would be. As they walked down the hallway, the banging sound became more prominent. The sound felt like they were walking toward the serial killer in a horror movie. Alex had hated those movies, always despising how the heroine would escape death even after running upstairs instead of out the open backdoor.

They arrived at a door with a large sign above it that said "Gym". Alex stood and stared at the door. It shook under the assault of banging that was coming from the other side. *Of course,* her mind ironically thought, *Why wouldn't the killing infected be locked in the very building we need to cross through?* She huffed a breath, trying to make a plan in her mind.

"Sounds like only one," Marcus whispered close to her ear.

She didn't think it mattered if the infected heard them. Clearly it had been banging against the door for a while, with nothing to take its attention away from the last place it heard the living. If there was only one, it would be easy for them to handle. However, she worried about what else was in the gym that wasn't banging against the door.

"Do we take the chance?" Alex said quietly, almost to herself.

"We came this far. Might as well see what's going on. If it's too much, we slam the door shut again."

He made it sound so easy. Nothing was easy in the apocalypse, but they didn't have much choice other than turn around and leave. If there was only one, that would be a waste in Alex's mind. She nodded to him and stepped back. He raised an eyebrow, but didn't argue. Alex knew he expected to be the one that stood in danger's path and that was exactly why she wanted to do it. She knew she could handle whatever came through the door just as well, if not better than Marcus. They quickly agreed to a plan, and they stepped to their necessary spots.

Marcus put his hand on the handle of the door. They could see it was the type that just needed to be turned down to open. Once he opened it, he would swing it toward himself, making him blind for a moment. Alex was to handle the infected that came out and then prepare for any additional attacks. If there was anything she could see, she was to yell for Marcus to close the door. Alex rolled her shoulders, preparing for a fight. She held her gun, not wanting to take a chance at hand to hand with an unseen foe. She nodded to Marcus, and he turned the knob.

Immediately, Alex was glad she didn't think to use her knife. The infected that stumbled out was large, very large. In a quick inventory Alex wouldn't put him much shorter than 6'4" and maybe 250 pounds. She raised her aim. It took a moment for the disoriented infected to see her, but when he did, his black eyes widened, and he raised his hands toward her. With no hesitation, Alex pulled the trigger, punching a black hole into the forehead of the infected giant. Brain matter splashed against the open door and Alex decided to let Marcus know that behind the door was the best location.

The large infected fell and Alex realized that their plan was flawed and in the worst way. She swung her flashlight up to look into the dark gym and she gasped at the number of bodies that moved. The chorus of growling and hissing rose together, and Alex knew they had made a mistake. Alex stepped back, calling Marcus's name, though she knew he couldn't close the door; the giant infected had fallen directly in the way. And he was too large to move quickly.

Marcus popped his head around the door when he realized it wouldn't close. One look at Alex's ashen face and he knew there was a problem. The first of the infected started to fight through the door as Marcus stepped to Alex's side. Alex shot the infected that came close to the open doorway, causing it to topple, only to be replaced by five more. They knew immediately they couldn't fight the number that was in the gym and they turned and ran. Alex tried to hold her flashlight as still as possible, giving them a clear view of where to run. In her mind she prayed none of the infected were the faster ones, because she didn't want to look back and find them bounding after them.

They didn't stop sprinting until they ran into the sunlight of the day. They both gasped for breath. The adrenaline was pumping through them and the fear was enough to take the breath from their lungs. Suddenly Marcus ran back toward the school.

"Marcus! No!" Alex screamed. She didn't know why he would run back toward the danger, but she wanted him to stop.

Quickly Marcus yanked on the two big doors that led to the office. Slamming them shut, he stepped back just as the infected began to run into the doors. It dawned on Alex what he had done. He had trapped them inside again. Alex looked toward the opposite side of the school and saw other doors open. She began to sprint that direction and Marcus's footsteps could be heard behind her. She slid to a stop just as she grabbed one door and slammed it. Marcus repeated the action with the other. They stepped back away from the school. Alex held out her hands as if she expected the whole building to implode at any point.

"We can't be sure all the doors are closed," Marcus gasped.

"No. But we did what we could," Alex replied.

"Do we just leave them?"

"We don't have enough ammo to waste on killing them all. We'll have to come up with a plan at home and maybe we can find a way to end them. Better than someone else being killed by the mob," Alex said.

Marcus nodded as he watched the building warily. The banging noise was now on the outermost side of the building, instead of on the inside when they'd first arrived. Alex guessed that might be a good thing. People would be immediately warned that it wasn't safe to go inside the school. Finally feeling she could turn her back she walked quickly back to the Bronco. She waited for Marcus to settle in the pickup and she pulled away from the school and the nightmares that plagued its hallways.

CHAPTER FIVE

Fingers drumming on a desk and the tightening around his eyes were the only sign of irritation. 'The Suit' took off his glasses and rubbed his eyes roughly. A headache was brewing, and he knew it was entirely the Duncans to blame. Dealing with the rebellious group was proving to be harder than he had ever expected. Occasionally he imagined removing Callahan from his position so he could get someone that would be able to actually follow orders.

Thinking of the Major only made 'The Suit' more displeased. He lifted the satellite phone that he kept in his office. No one else was allowed to use the phone which was well known by all of his staff. Not that regular phones were working, anyway. Only the government links with the satellite phones were working now. Society was without any sort of power grid or form of communication.

"Yes," Callahan's curt voice came across the line.

"The Duncans have once again showed up on camera, Callahan. And they seem to be completely alive. What is the problem?"

"We are doing our due diligence this time, sir. Last round of checks we have found they have added barbed wire to their defenses. We've done some other sweeps to gather information," Callahan explained.

"These don't sound like solutions, Callahan. I just watched one of the Duncan women take off with enough FEMA supplies to keep a family alive for over a year. They are making sure they are well prepared for the long game. This needs to stop," 'The Suit' replied.

The sigh that came from Callahan's side of the conversation infuriated 'The Suit'.

"Callahan, if you can't get this job done, I will find someone that can handle it. You are *not* the last military leader on this planet," 'The Suit' all but growled into the phone.

"Understood, sir. We are going about this the smart way," Callahan replied.

'The Suit' couldn't listen to the man any longer. He hit the end button on his phone, barely resisting the urge to throw the device through the window that he faced. Instead, his put it down and paced his office. He didn't care about barbed wire or research. He wanted results and he didn't care how they got handled. In his own mind he could admit where his strengths were and how they didn't revolve around military action. He had people for that. But what he did know is what needed to happen to control a situation. And getting rid of the Duncans was just one step in ensuring the country fell in line under his control.

If there is any country left, he thought to himself. He looked down at the lab that he now had under his command. He could admit to himself that the pathogen that was released was more than he had anticipated. Granted, it wasn't released in a way he wanted or could control ahead of time. However, it was an opportunity to enact a plan that he had been working on for well over two years. When he made the commitment to open the black site that tested unknown pathogens, he was doing it for very specific reasons. One was biological warfare. It was coming and the US was not prepared for it. And two was to have a chemical in his pocket that could bring the country to its knees when he deemed it necessary. It all happened faster than he had wanted.

Turning away from the doctors he found to be useless, 'The Suit' was nothing if not one to take advantage of a situation when he could. His plan had been to be in Washington DC at the time of whatever outbreak he started. He had wanted to be close to the President and the sitting members of the government. He wanted to watch them all die and be the last person standing. He would have spared anyone that agreed to fall under his rule. But the President and his cabinet had to go first. Now, he was stuck in a bunker near the California Coast, with scarce information coming from DC. He had silently rejoiced when he heard the news of the First Lady being bit, turning and killing her husband while they slept in the underground bunker they had been evacuated to.

Washington went downhill from there. No one had realized how fast the illness would sweep through every person in its path. The First Lady had done 'The Suit' a favor, by hiding her bite and then her illness, until she died and went on a rampage. The last secret service agent in the bunker was believed to have committed suicide to escape the horrors of the attacks. No one was entering or exiting the bunker now. While the gruesome scene played out underground, the White House quickly fell to the illness. 'The Suit's' contact had long gone dark and 'The Suit' assumed the man had fallen to the same fate as the rest of the workers in one of the most secure buildings in the country.

'The Suit' would only admit to himself that he felt the situation slipping from his control. Part of his plan had hinged on a cure being developed. His incompetent scientists insisted the infection was something they couldn't even begin to understand. Even after he executed one of them for not having any results, there was still nothing forthcoming. They were afraid of him, just the way he enjoyed it. However, that fear wasn't creating results.

Without a cure, he didn't see an easy path to rebuilding the country and controlling how they moved forward.

The headache took that moment to roar back into life in the front of his head. He went into the adjoining bathroom, rooting around the medicine cabinet until he found pain relievers. He downed a few of them with a glass of water. Looking up into the mirror, he stared at his pale reflection. The man had never had much color, but the pallor of his skin now was even a paler shade of white, if possible. 'The Suit' wasn't sure how long he could live underground without ever seeing the sun. When he entered his office again, he turned back to the monitors.

It was sheer luck that the US satellites that circled the Earth were still useful. With his connection to them he was able to keep some monitoring live around the country. He could see the vague color of the sun in nearby San Francisco. He knew there were survivors in the large city. He had seen groups come and go from some of the larger high rises. At times when he stared out over the water, he would note the number of boats he saw wandering in the bay. There were survivors now. But how many would be left as this infection continued to rage through the population?

CHAPTER SIX

"How did they all even get in there?" Marcus asked.

They had just finished hiding the pickup truck with its heavy load of supplies off the highway. Using the camouflage of wrecked vehicles and tree limbs, the truck was barely visible from the road. Sitting in the Bronco, they finally opened up the bag that Margaret had sent for them. There were sandwiches, thick with cooked pork, arugula, mayonnaise, and mustard. She also had packed small bags of potato chips, granola bars, and her homemade brownies. Marcus, being the child at heart that he was, ate his brownie first.

They had debated about the school and what they had seen since they pulled off the road to hide the truck. Alex was lost in her own thoughts, trying to put the situation into order. The danger kept them from staying to do an infected headcount, but Alex estimated no less than 100 bodies in the gym when she had swung her flashlight through. In the moments she stood there in shock she noticed things that looked like cots, iv poles, and a lot of broken glass. Now that they were in the Bronco, sitting in silence, they both were throwing out their ideas of how the school had fallen.

"I think the gym was set up as a triage or quarantine, maybe?" Alex replied.

"That plays. But why were all the doors shut? They weren't locked. Seems someone would have left something open."

Alex shrugged as she chewed her bite of sandwich. If she had been in charge, the doors would never have been open except for doctors to come and go, or for the infected to be brought in. She tried to think cruelly, the way she knew Callahan functioned. The man knew how deadly the pathogen was. He would have known those bitten, but not dead, would turn.

"I think they set them up that way on purpose. They knew those people weren't going to make it from the start. Putting them in a shut room ensured they stayed in. My guess is when they evacuated, no one even went to the gym, because those people were already considered a lost cause," Alex said, bringing her random thoughts to light.

"They didn't even try to execute them, like they had done in other places," he replied.

"No. Probably thought it was too much of a waste of ammo. They were leaving the area anyway, what did it matter to Callahan?"

"Because he doesn't care about people dying. Just taking control," Marcus mused.

"Exactly."

The idea of just giving up on people made Alex feel sick. As the population was wiped out by a plague, the first priority had to be to save everyone they could. Someday the idea would be to repopulate. 'The Suit' and Callahan had a different plan entirely. And while they came after the Duncans, there was no cure for them to hide or create. Charlie had been working hard on it every day, but she was starting to become discouraged. Knowing that, Alex continued with the belief that the survival of the human race was up to them. She would never look at anyone as a lost cause.

After they finished their lunches, Marcus worked to pack away the reusable Tupperware that Margaret had sent. Alex checked the map and looked at their plan. Though it was only one in the afternoon, she wanted to only check one more place before setting camp for the night. She'd pinpointed a small pharmacy that they had gone through a few times before. They had only taken what they needed at the time. Now Charlie wanted to stock up more of the basic pharmaceuticals. Having a doctor on the compound was a huge benefit to survival. She had already started files on the residents of the compound. Alex was grateful when they sat down to talk about Billie and her problem with strep throat. It gave Alex comfort to have a doctor capable of treating the illnesses the children could come down with.

Marcus climbed back into the Bronco after double checking the hidden truck. Driving away from their hiding place, Alex moved the Bronco forward slowly. They both checked their surroundings carefully, making sure no one living was watching them. Alex wanted to help other people, but she didn't discount that people could be at their worst when in survival mode. They would share their supplies, but they wouldn't stand for being stolen from. Some respect and basic human decency needed to reign at times.

Confident that their hiding place was secure, Alex finally picked up speed and headed back into town. The pharmacy they were heading for wasn't far into town, sitting in a small strip mall off in a residential area. When they pulled up to it, they waited in the running vehicle. It was the safest way of knowing if any dead were around versus stepping out and being ambushed. When nothing seemed to be moving, Alex shut off the engine, and they both listened as the silence flowed over them.

"I'm not sure when I'll get used to that," Marcus commented, making Alex jump slightly.

"What?"

"The silence of the world now. Before the plague, can you remember the last time it was silent around you?"

Alex thought back into her life. She remembered many silent nights spent in the forest at her father's bidding. Mitch Duncan thought camping in the elements was one of the first steps in being ready for survival. It took the fall of the world for Alex to finally agree with him. However, when she thought about that silence, she realized even then, there were far-off sounds of commercial aircraft or the random helicopter tour happening in the mountains. There was always something.

"No, I can't remember anything like this silence. Thick enough to cut with a knife," Alex replied.

Marcus nodded his reply. They fell back into the quiet, being very aware of their surroundings. Alex opened her door, as the signal to Marcus they were ready to go. She had her gun out as always, though the walk to the pharmacy glass door was only ten feet. When she reached it, she was pleased to see everything still intact. No one had forcibly broken into the pharmacy yet, giving them the chance to clear out the medications and supplies they needed. She stooped and used the card she brought to pop the lock. Any alarms that were on the doors were long gone and only a small bell sounded as they walked through the open door.

Inside, Marcus locked the door immediately. Though they could be fairly certain there were no infected in the pharmacy, they still did a row by row clear of the store. Only then did they split up and start collecting the items on their lists. Alex went straight to the back, where the pharmaceutical medications were kept. She opened the small door that led the way behind the pharmacist counter. She avoided looking down to the floor, as she remembered well the bloody stains that were left after they had to handle the dead pharmacy tech. Alex's heart had hurt when she had to stab the young girl in the head weeks prior. The body had been taken out the back of the store to prevent her from rotting and creating putrid air inside.

Alex sorted through medications. She found a locked area and knew she needed everything inside. She took out her knife and started to pry at the lock. But the sound of keys had her looking up. Marcus held a set of keys that were connected to an elastic wrist coil.

"I grabbed them when we handled the tech the last time we were here," he said.

"Failed to mention that," Alex muttered, but she stepped back and let him start trying keys.

He found the one that worked, and they dumped all the pain medications that were under lock and key into Alex's bag. They also packed up all the antibiotics, decongestants, and allergy relief. After a longer search, Alex eventually found the blood pressure medication that Issac said he needed. She also grabbed the similar types that Charlie said could be used as back up. As long as they could continue getting people their normal medications, Alex wanted to provide them. Alex stepped back looking around the pharmacy area and felt she had taken everything they could need at the moment.

While Alex was busy with the meds, Marcus had been tasked with first aid and medical equipment. The pharmacy was light on equipment, but had two aisles of over-the-counter medications and first aid supplies. His bag was overflowing when Alex met him. She noted the empty shelving as she walked by, approving of him grabbing everything. Once they were done with the pharmacy, it would be marked off their map as cleared.

With a list in hand, Alex walked over to the feminine hygiene products. Most of the females on the compound needed one thing or another. She easily found the brands and products everyone needed and soon her bag wasn't closing either. The last things she wanted to grab weren't so much for survival but for entertainment. The pharmacy had a small DVD display, mostly low budget, never in the theatre movies. But survivors couldn't be picky. Alex grabbed a few that looked like romances and one that looked like teenage angst. Then she grabbed everything that was animated. She also walked down the makeup and nail aisles. She grabbed nail polish and an assortment of makeup for any of the women that wanted it. She knew Billie enjoyed having her nails painted at every possible opportunity.

Checking the door, Marcus found the coast to still be clear. Alex was starting to feel that their luck was too good and knew it wouldn't stay that way. She turned to look back into the pharmacy and all her eyes saw were more things they needed to take.

"One more run?" She said to Marcus.

"Sure. Let's load our packs into the Bronco and grab some spare bags."

An hour later they were loading up the third round of boxes and bags they had packed from the pharmacy. Alex finally felt comfortable enough to mark off the pharmacy. It wasn't that they couldn't come back to it, but she liked to have a clear picture of what they could scavenge from what location. They cleaned out the junk food, drinks, over-the-counter medications, and kids' toys. The haul almost filled up the back of the Bronco and Alex had to think about where they were going to sleep that night as well as where they would put any additional things they got.

"Our lists are doing pretty well now," Marcus said once they were back in the Bronco.

"Yeah. I really want to find the seeds and gardening tools Rafe wants. Also, we need to get some clothes for Aiden and maybe the other kids as well. Maybe we'll only go to Wal-Mart tomorrow," Alex replied.

"Thought you wanted to check out Whitefish?"

"I do. But look at the truck. There's barely room for us to sleep, let alone fit anything else."

"Could just be a reconnaissance mission," he said.

"True. Let's just see how tomorrow goes and we can decide."

By five o'clock they had pulled the Bronco into a section of trees, working to hide themselves from any passing eyes. While the sun was still up, they built a small fire by the truck and boiled left-over rabbit soup to share. With their backs to the

Bronco, they sat and ate in silence. They kept their eyes trained on the small parking lot that was a few feet away. In the far distance they could see movement, but if they were infected, they weren't close enough to see Alex and Marcus in the tree line. Quiet moments like this were what Alex didn't get too often being holed up on the compound. Anytime she tried to sit and just be calm someone was tracking her down for help, questions, or requests. She sighed and leaned back to get comfortable.

"Penny for your thoughts?" Marcus asked.

"Worth more than that," Alex responded, causing Marcus to grunt out a laugh.

Though she knew he waited for her to answer, Alex didn't speak. She stared at the sky that was slowly darkening as the sun sank lower. She could hear her heartbeat, the call of far off birds, and the occasional gunshot. Without reacting her mind knew the shots were so far off there was nothing for them to do. The absence of life was becoming normal and Alex thought she should feel bothered by that. But the quiet was so enjoyable, she couldn't summon any other emotions.

When darkness truly fell, they kicked dirt over their fire, ensuring no light would draw attention. They worked together to move the supplies around the inside of the Bronco, stacking boxes to cover a lot of the windows. They left strategic areas where they could look out if they were to hear anything. There was only enough room for their bed rolls and sleeping bags once they were done. Alex laid on the top of her sleeping bag, her boots and weapons removed. She would sleep with her boots right by her feet, but her weapons were always right by her hands for quick access. With a small penlight she read a book while she waited for sleep to come.

"So, what is it, Alex?" Marcus's voice cutting into the pleasant silence.

Without asking, Alex knew what he was trying to get at.

"You aren't going to let this go?" She asked. His silence was all the answer she got.

"I'm just tired, ok? I never get the chance to hear myself think, let alone read a book," she said, waving the book around in between them.

"So, you decided to take a run so you could start that new romance novel you've had your eye on," Marcus replied sarcastically.

"Me taking a run shouldn't be such a big deal. I'm not more important than anyone else at home. I need to do my fair share too."

She was defensive, and she knew Marcus would play on that. But he made it sound like she was being flighty about a salvage run which couldn't be further from the truth. No one, except her siblings, were more serious about the outside world than Alex. Though she was always busy keeping the compound running, making sure no one bickered, and everyone was fed, her mind was always outside the walls. She was always wondering where all the living people were? Were they surviving? Did they need help? Her thoughts were always full of questions that couldn't be answered from inside the walls.

"It's not about importance. It's about where you're needed," he said.

"And I'm just needed to stay home and handle all the tasks there?" Alex demanded.

"You're the strongest leader among us. It's your strength."

"Maybe I don't want it!" Alex finally exclaimed. Then she sighed and looked over at Marcus in the dark Bronco. With the slight light from the flashlight she held she could see he was watching her.

"I never wanted to be in charge. Everyone just assumed. I thought when we got to the compound things would be easier. Instead, I feel like being behind those walls is harder for me than fighting through the dead to get there in the first place. Everyone looks to me to make decisions. If I make the wrong ones, it could cost people their lives. Do you have any idea what kind of pressure that is on me?"

Alex knew the words were flowing out of her like a torrent. She couldn't stop it. All the stress, fear, and admittedly anger that had welled up in her for two months was bursting to come out somewhere. Marcus was the easiest target at the time. But Alex knew it wasn't his fault. It truly wasn't anyone's fault. She just felt that no one understood how she felt and why. Also, a large part of her felt guilt for even remotely being unhappy with their situation They were safe. What did she have to complain about?

"I have a general idea. But I'm not in your position, so no I can't completely understand," he replied. His tone was casual, but Alex knew he was listening intently to every word she said.

"That's exactly it. No one can really understand. And someone like Max doesn't even care to understand, as long as it's not her having to answer questions and set schedules. I lay awake most nights worried about the crops, if I made the right decisions with the animals. I think about if we are attacked, is the plan that I am responsible for, going to work to protect us," she continued.

"We worked together on that plan. It's not only on you," Marcus reminded her.

"I know. But I take the lead if the plan has to happen. What if I turn right and I should have gone left? What if our people die because of stupid choices I make?"

"Are you prone to stupid decisions?" He asked.

"I...well...I don't think so," she replied quietly, the wind coming out of her sails slightly.

"Did your father teach you how to run the compound?"

"I told you that he taught us all," she said.

"Right. So, he knew you could do this without him, right?" Marcus continued.

"I guess. But we never really had to," Alex replied, thinking about how her father had always been on the compound. He may have sent them into the forest alone, to camp and learn, but he never left them alone on the compound to fend for themselves in a complete survival situation.

"But he knew you could, or he wouldn't have taken all the time to make sure you had the lessons you did. You are the oldest, Alex. And from what I know, you're the most responsible."

"Rafe is..." she started.

"Rafe isn't irresponsible. He's just very in his own head. It's not a fault, it's just not the quality of a leader. You have the qualities of a leader. You care about others. So much so that you've driven yourself to this point with stress and concern over the results of the choices you may have to make," Marcus said.

Alex wanted to mouth off, tell him to not psychoanalyze her. She found herself wondering if he was a therapist in the times before the plague. Marcus had proven to have a number of talents such as doing hair, construction, and being a very accurate shot with a handgun. It wouldn't surprise her if he had been some sort of counselor or therapist at some point and now those talents were spilling over.

"Everyone trusts you to make those choices, Alex. No one expects perfection. The choices you make will be the best that can be made with the information you have at hand," he finally finished.

She didn't really know what to say to that. She huffed out a breath and looked at the ceiling of the Bronco. It was that trust she wasn't sure she deserved. She had picked up people and brought them to safety. During that she lost one person, Margaret's friend. The older woman never blamed Alex for the choices she made that led to the man's ultimate death. Alex knew she grieved for him often, as they had been close friends for years. It was difficult for Alex to not blame herself, even after Margaret let her off the hook telling her it wasn't her fault.

They fell into silence after that. Alex guessed Marcus was done, because he turned to his side and his breathing deepened.

She wished she could fall asleep so easily. In her mind she checked off the items they had already gotten from their lists. Then she thought about the remaining items, wondering if they could just make one more stop and grab the rest. She was still running through those ideas when sleep slid into her mind and pulled her down into the dark.

Morning came before Alex was ready. When Marcus began to stir next to her, she was almost immediately awake. However, once she remembered where she was, she settled back down and closed her eyes. That one moment between sleeping and waking was the time Alex would forget where she was and what she was doing. It happened often at the compound as well, especially when she was plagued with nightmares. Behind the darkness of her eyelids, she concentrated on her breathing as she mentally prepared herself for the day to come.

The sun shone through the small sections of windows they left open. After a quick breakfast of homemade muffins, they rolled up their sleeping bags and rolls. They made quick work of moving the boxes around the back again so Alex could see as she drove the Bronco. There wasn't any traffic to worry about, but she didn't need any infected sneaking up on them because she couldn't see out of the windows. Their place in the trees seemed to be safe since no infected stumbled upon them during the night or as they prepared to leave.

Alex sat in the driver's seat, reviewing the map again for the locations they wanted to stop. She had already drawn a clear route from their forest clearing to their final goal. Marcus sat next to her, checking and rechecking their weapons. They had additional firepower in the Bronco should they need more than their 9mm handguns. Alex knew she would take her shotgun into the large store, the extra power making her feel safer. She realized that it was a false sense of security, but she would take it.

A loud engine caused them both to look up from their thoughts. A black van screamed across the parking lot they sat near. The turn it took was so fast, Alex thought it was possible the whole vehicle would go over. The driver seemed to suddenly get control of the vehicle and it straightened to exit the parking lot again. Suddenly the brakes were slammed, and the van came to a halt. Alex leaned forward, putting a monocular to her eye. She kept the one-piece telescope in the Bronco for times just like this, when they needed to see what was happening, without needing to get closer.

"Is the van rocking?" Marcus asked, squinting against the morning sun, but not having any sort of help to see closer.

"Yes. Odd," Alex replied.

She studied the dark vehicle. There were no back windows to see into, only the backdoor holding a small window that was covered in brown paper. The entire vehicle seemed to be shifting back and forth on its wheels. Alex sat back, wondering what the trouble was and if they should find out.

"No," Marcus said suddenly. When she just looked at him, he continued, "This isn't our problem. And I don't know why, but it gives me a bad feeling. We are staying away from that van."

The discussion was cut off as the van revved its engine again and took off. It quickly rounded a corner, cutting off Alex and Marcus' visual of the vehicle. Alex couldn't shake the feeling that something wasn't right in that van. But Marcus was right. She couldn't involve herself in every issue they came across. They had the compound and their own people to worry about. She would never turn anyone away, but she also couldn't bring any more trouble down on them.

Ten minutes later, Alex pulled the Bronco into the parking lot of Wal-Mart. They had been to the big store a number of times for supplies they couldn't easily get at smaller places. The glass doors on both entrances were smashed, allowing anyone and anything to wander in and out. The inside was dark, no matter the time of day. There were high sky lights that sometimes let in dim illumination, but it wasn't enough to chase away all the shadows. The shadows were the biggest threat, as there was no knowing what they hid.

Though she knew Marcus had already completed the task, Alex checked her 9mm and shotgun for ammo and turned off the safeties. Marcus didn't comment on the lack of trust, because he knew that wasn't really it. Alex was used to doing these things on her own. The only people she worked cohesively with were her siblings. The act of surviving together and managing situations was engrained in them. Each of them had a role from the time they were little. And now that the world had truly fallen to its knees, those roles seemed to be permanent.

"Ready?" Alex asked, as she popped open the door.

Marcus didn't answer, just popped open his own door. He carried his own 9mm on his hip and a bat that he had hammered nails through. Alex had thought it was a foolish weapon at first. She changed her mind after the first time she saw him fight with it. The nails were long enough to pierce the skull, but weren't going to become stuck if he kept a good hold on the wood. She felt confident that he could watch her back as they went into danger.

At the broken door of the store, Alex stopped. She bent and grabbed a larger shard of glass. Tossing it into the depth of the store, the sound of the glass pinging against tile echoed slightly. In a haunting answer, a deep growl emanated from the dark. Slinging the shotgun over her shoulder, Alex pulled her Bowie knife instead. She couldn't be positive, but she thought there was only one infected nearby.

Soon a grotesque face could be seen in the light from the doorway. Involuntarily, Alex stepped back, not in fear, but revulsion. The once man, was completely nude. She couldn't imagine how he ended up as an infected, out in the world, without a stitch of clothing on. When she looked over to Marcus, she could see his face screwed up in a pained expression. Bite marks marred the majority of the man's exposed flesh. The muscles from his right calf were completely torn away, nothing but a flap of skin hung from the back of his knee. The lack of support caused him to drag the foot behind him. Alex was lost in her mind wondering how that was even possible, when Marcus stepped forward and swung his nailed bat.

Marcus stood above the body for a moment, as if he couldn't look away. Alex stepped to him and touched his shoulder. She could feel his shudder as it went through his body. She tried to keep her eyes up, but they wandered down the dead infected of their own accord. The man was covered in black crusted wounds, some clearly bites. Others were ragged tears of skin and muscle, where the infected had taken the time to feast on him. If he hadn't been nude, Alex wasn't sure she would be able to tell anything about him, his body was so destroyed.

"At least they missed one part," Marcus mumbled.

Alex almost missed it, but when she realized what he said, she had to choke back a gagging laugh. Part of her found the humor that a man was going to be more concerned about the manhood of the infected, than the gaping wound showing the white bones of his ribcage. The more rational part of her couldn't move beyond the horror of his body and she realized she needed to get away from it.

"Let's go. I can't look at it anymore," Alex whispered.

Despite their delay outside of the doors, it didn't seem like any additional infected were wandering the store. They made plenty of noise as they crunched across the broken glass in their heavy-duty boots. Alex was at the ready with her knife and a small flashlight as soon as they moved deeper into the dark abyss of the store. She swung the light back and forth, checking for movement. Without thinking, she moved toward the clothing she knew they wanted to pick up. She had a mental map of the store, not wanting to wander to find what she needed.

At the boy's section, she stopped and signaled to Marcus to watch. Using a duffel she had carried in, she began to grab whatever T-shirts in Henry and Aiden's sizes she could find. She moved to pants, concentrating on the heavier jeans that were still in stock despite the plague starting as Spring came around. She made quick work of what they needed, and she whistled low to Marcus to signal she was done.

They repeated their process of searching and bagging in the girl's, men's, and women's sections. They headed to the garden section last, as it was the furthest from the outer doors. There was an outside area to the garden section, that was separated by a sliding glass door. The door no longer worked with no power and Alex had no problem with that. In the garden section they had counted five infected wandering at one point. She didn't know how they had gotten out there, but every time they checked the same five were still wandering aimlessly.

With Alex's duffel full and a second they had taken from the luggage section, the pair set out for the door of the Wal-Mart. As they neared the open doors, screaming reverberated into the store. Alex froze in her tracks and looked at Marcus. He was already looking at her, for a decision she realized. She wasn't interested in losing everything they had just collected. But if someone was in trouble, she couldn't just leave them alone.

Making a quick decision in her mind, Alex began to run toward the door. She was hindered by the duffel but she just tightened her hold and kept running. The Bronco was only a few feet from the door. When they slid to a stop at the back, Alex quickly fished out the keys and opened the tailgate door to throw their bags inside. The screaming was coming from the side of the Wal-Mart now. After she locked the truck again, Alex took off for the noise, Marcus easily on her heels.

They came around the corner of the store and Alex immediately tripped to a stop, before she ran headfirst into a horde of infected.

CHAPTER SEVEN

"Alex, back to the Bronco," Marcus hissed from behind her.

Despite being quiet, not even hearing themselves over the groaning and growls from the infected, they were quickly noticed by some of the outlying infected of the group. Alex knew they needed to make a quick choice. If the horde surrounded the Bronco, they wouldn't be able to escape the mass. There was easily over a hundred dead bodies chasing whoever was screaming. That person sounded like they were in the alley behind the store now and Alex couldn't understand what their escape plan was.

"We'll get the truck, head to the other side of the building and grab whoever is being chased there," Alex said, as she began to backpedal.

Marcus took one step to the side and slammed his bat into an infected that was getting too close. Alex decided it was too late to worry about noise. As soon as she started the truck, the infected would hear that as well. She pulled the shotgun from her back and aimed for the heads of the nearest infected. She easily dropped three that had taken an interest in them. The loud echo of the gun had a lot of the infected changing their target and Alex knew it was time to run.

They easily outran the nearest infected, but as they got to the Bronco, Marcus turned with his 9mm in his hand. Alex only had a moment to glance back to see an infected running toward them. *Ok, what the hell?* She thought to herself. This wasn't her first time seeing running infected, but it had been quite a while. Enough time had passed since her time in the dark forest near the Montana border that she had started to think she had imagined the faster dead. Now Marcus was having a tough time with head-shots as they moved much quicker. That trouble didn't stop him from ending their dead lives, but it took a few more rounds.

As these thoughts ran through her mind, she shoved the key into the lock on the driver's side door. 302RD was the pathogen that Charlie was studying, that she believed released the plague they were now dealing with. It was clear to Alex at that moment that something was changing and she wasn't sure they were equipped to deal with it. Knowing your enemy was part of the battle. They were already dealing with the unknowns of the government and when they may strike again. Right in front of her was proof that the enemy they did know was evolving, they just didn't understand why.

"Drive around the side of the building!" Marcus yelled over the gun fire.

"Get in the truck!" Alex yelled back as she climbed in.

"I'm going to run, see if I can draw them away. You go grab the survivors!"

Without giving her a chance to tell him his plan was ludicrous, he sprinted away. Alex slammed the truck door shut just as quickly, set on chasing him down if need be. But as she sat in the quiet vehicle she watched as a good number of the infected ran after him. She hated his plan and was going to tell him she was tired of his going off on his own all the time, but first she wasn't going to waste the small window he had given her. She couldn't do anything about his actions now. As she started up the truck, she hoped that he didn't die before she had the chance to kill him herself.

The sound of the truck was enough to pull the attention of the passing infected and the noise Marcus was making was further away. She quickly stomped on the gas and sped toward the other end of the shopping structure. The tires squealed as she went around the corner. Just as she was pulling up to the small alley in the back, two men burst out running full tilt toward her. She slammed on the brakes; glad she hadn't accidentally run them down. They skidded to a stop and stared at her through the windshield. She rolled her window down quickly.

"Get in! Quickly!" She yelled.

The two men didn't hesitate. They ran for the passenger seat of the Bronco and jumped into the front and back seats easily. Once they were in, Alex had to make a decision on how to find Marcus. He hadn't exactly given her directions of where he would be. That was the problem with Marcus's half-baked plans, they were never completely thought out. She concluded the easiest way to find him, was to follow the part of the horde that had broke off, heading his way. She just hoped she didn't find them feasting on his remains.

"Thank you for stopping," the man in the passenger seat said.

"Sure," Alex replied.

She glanced over and for the first time took in the image of the man sitting next to her. He was filthy, covered not only in blood and black gore but dirt and possibly other unknown substances. He eyed her in a way that didn't make her feel completely comfortable, but she tried to not jump to conclusions. She glanced into the rearview mirror, pretending to be checking as she drove. The man in the back seat was in just as bad shape, if not worse with his shirt ripped away from the collar and bruises covering his exposed skin.

"Are you bitten?" Alex asked, working to keep her voice calm.

"Nope. Just been fighting to survive like everyone else," the man in the back replied, sounding offended.

"Where are you going?" The man in the passenger seat asked.

"I need to find my friend. He drew away the dead so I could get to you guys."

Alex didn't miss the look between the men, feeling the hair on the back of her neck stand up. Something wasn't right with these men. She immediately knew she needed to find Marcus so together they could get rid of the men that they had just worked hard to save. She circled around the horde, drawing their attention as she passed. Luckily there didn't seem to be any more fast infected, so she easily drove away from the dead as they turned toward the truck. She could see where the line of infected seemed to lead, and she turned the truck that way.

"Stop the truck," a cold voice came from the back seat.

Alex looked up into the mirror and saw the man staring at her and sitting forward in the seat. He wasn't wearing a seatbelt and Alex immediately began thinking about plans of how to get him out of the truck, by any means necessary. A flash of metal caught her attention and when she looked back again to focus, she felt the barrel of a gun as it pressed against the back of her head.

"Bitch, I said stop the truck," the man said again.

She complied, realizing too late what her mistake had been. Without backup, she never should've allowed two strangers into the truck. She slowed the truck to a stop and made sure to keep her hands on the steering wheel.

"Take whatever you want. There's plenty," she said quietly.

Though she knew she had made the erroneous decision to let the men into the truck, cold rage brewed inside her at the insult of being held at gunpoint. Typically, Alex didn't wish harm on people, a fact that had changed over the months since the plague started. Now in her mind she was wondering why she hadn't allowed the infected to rip apart the men.

"We don't want just your supplies. You're going to drive us

where we want. Follow Jackson's directions," the man from the backseat said.

"Jackson?"

"That's me," the man in the front seat replied, sounding uncomfortable with the situation. Despite that, he did nothing to try to help Alex. Instead, he reached across her to remove her knife from its sheath and then her gun. He threw both into the back seat, far from Alex's reach. Mentally she cursed, wondering what else was within the truck that she could use as a weapon without moving far.

Jackson instructed her to turn the opposite direction of the infected horde, away from Marcus. She didn't immediately comply, her mind still trying to figure out a way to dispose of the men. The man in the back pushed the gun against her skull harder.

"We have no problem killing you and just taking the supplies."

Alex decided to give herself more time to plan, and she turned the truck the way Jackson pointed. He had her winding down small roads in town and through alleyways. All the while the man with the gun didn't speak and his gun didn't move. Alex tried to sit as still as possible except her arms as she drove, afraid the man could have a nervous trigger finger. She evaluated them both more as they drove. The filth she had noted before told her they hadn't lived well since the plague started. Their actions seemed to be out of desperation. She thought that was something she could work with.

"Look, I get it. These are hard times. You two have obviously struggled. I can drop you wherever you want. You can take anything you want from the truck, all of it if that's what you want to do," Alex said.

"Slow down and turn here," Jackson replied. Both men ignored Alex's attempt to negotiate.

Alex followed the instructions, but as soon as she made the turn, she realized they had led her down a dead-end street. She let the truck roll to the end, but when they ran out of road she stopped.

"Turn the truck off," the man with the gun said.

"You guys can just get out. I won't follow you," she replied, without moving to turn off the engine.

She had been looking at Jackson and slowly trying to turn to see the man in the back, when there was a tap at her window. The noise caused her to jump. When she swung her gaze back, she saw they were no longer alone. Though they were stopped at a dead end, beyond the barrier in the road, there was an open space behind buildings. Alex assumed the men that now stepped up to stand around the Bronco must have come from there. The one tapping on her window was doing so with a gun that he now pointed at her face.

"Turn the truck off," the man said loudly to be heard through the window.

With a turn of her wrist, she shut off the vehicle and put both hands back on the wheel. She had no weapons on her, except her own body. While she knew that she was a formidable opponent, she knew she couldn't take the five men outside the truck on her own. And she had a feeling that they would shoot her if she became too difficult. She didn't want to put herself in that position. Her mind raced and images of her children flashed across her thoughts. Billie and Henry, then Easton and Candace. Part of her was thankful they were safe on the compound with people that would love and care for them. The other part of her was furious these men thought to threaten her and take her away from them.

Alex was still not sure what the entire plan was of the men, but the one outside her window indicated to the lock on the door. She hit the button that unlocked her side. The door was opened immediately, and the man reached in to pull her out. Jackson hit the button on her seatbelt quickly, making it easy for the outside man to yank Alex to her feet. She stood, staring at the man, giving no indication of weakness or fear. Though she did feel fear deep in her stomach. These men looked a lot like Jackson and the second man in her truck. Dirty, suffering from malnutrition, twitchy.

"Bo, get out of there," the man said loudly. Alex noted the second name, keeping track of who was who.

"Take the truck. I'll walk away," Alex said.

"You were taking supplies from The Noble Lord," Bo said as he climbed over the driver's side seat.

"I'm sorry, the who?" Alex asked, completely perplexed.

"The Noble Lord and he's taken control of this area," the man standing in front of her with the gun said.

"And you are?" Alex asked.

"Lewis, not that it matters."

"Ok, Lewis, well I'm not sure who this Noble Lord person is, but as far as I do know we still live in the United States of America, and we don't have Noble Lords here."

Nervous laughter seemed to come from all the men. She looked around at them. What she had previously figured was twitchy from being hungry or thirsty, she now figured was some kind of ill effect of drug withdrawal. Lewis was close enough for her to see his eyes, his pupils were slightly dilated despite the fact the sun was high in the sky. The fear in her gut rose a few levels, because she realized trying to be rational with a group of addicts was going to be harder than she hoped.

"Have you seen anyone from the government in the last few months, lady?"

"Doesn't mean they aren't there," Alex said.

"Well, while they're hiding in whatever mountains they have, the Noble Lord has been taking care of people around here," Lewis said.

"I've been here this whole time and I've never heard of this person," Alex replied.

"Doesn't matter. You were taking his supplies, so now we're taking you to him," Lewis said.

Alex didn't like the sound of that. She immediately moved her body into a more relaxed fighting stance. And she waited. She knew one of them would make the first move. They didn't know what or who they were messing with by trying to take her. And she had no problem breaking some of them when they tried. Her shift seemed to have gone unnoticed, and she guessed it was because they were all more concerned with other things, such as her body and drugs. She hadn't missed some of the more lustful looks she had garnered. It was the end of the world, that didn't surprise her. However, she was more concerned about what they would do about this interest.

The nod from Lewis was the only warning Alex had that something was happening. She glanced over her shoulder to see Bo, who had put his gun away somewhere, start to move toward her. With no hesitation, Alex spun and hit in him in the face with a fast jab, striking him on his nose. She knew it probably wouldn't break the bones, but it would make his eyes water enough for her to continue her attack. Bo cried out and went to grab his face. But before his arms could come up, Alex kicked him squarely in the groin and the man crashed to the ground. She pulled her foot back and kicked him again, this time in the stomach, causing all the wind to whoosh from his mouth. He no longer made any noises, and he struggled to get any air into his lungs.

As she prepared for the next strike, she was grabbed from behind and Lewis started barking orders.

"Get me something to tie her up with! Where's the hood?"

Alex was disgusted by the smell of the man and his hands on her. Fury rose to extinguish some of the fear. All of her self-defense instincts came to the surface, giving her fuel. Without warning, Alex snapped her head back and connected with Lewis' face, hearing the satisfying crunch of bone as she connected. Pain in her own head was minimal and easy for her to handle. As soon as he instinctively let go of one of her arms, Alex made her next move. Turning quickly, she rotated her wrist and grabbed his arm with the hand he held. She yanked him closer to her as she pivoted and swung her free elbow to connected with his temple. The strike was direct and with power and he collapsed immediately.

A loud shot sounded, and Alex ducked, thinking she was being shot at. She was just about to turn and run for the Bronco when she realized the shot came from Bo. Blood dripped from his nose and he bent slightly at the waist holding his groin with one hand. The gun was back in his hand and no longer pointed at the sky, it was pointed directly at her face.

"If you think for a moment I care about killing you, you are wrong," he croaked out.

"Then do it!" Alex said.

"While I would enjoy it, The Noble Lord wouldn't like me getting rid of such a specimen. We'll let him decide what to do with you," Bo said with a sneer at her.

"So, this guy has control over you? You're that weak?" Alex said. She was goading him, hoping he would strike out at her and she could find a way to grab his gun. But he just sneered at her, letting her know he was aware of her plan.

As she stood there staring at Bo, her world went dark as a black hood was pulled over her head. Her arms were roughly pulled behind her, by more than one man this time. The metal clinking of handcuffs met her ears as she felt them encircle her wrists. She began to fight, her protection response going into overdrive as she knew the handcuffs would prevent her from escaping. But she was roughly moved around and pushed against what she assumed was the side of the Bronco. One held her head, pushing her cheek into the unmovable object. Her thumb was grabbed by another and the way he pulled made her squeak in pain. Loud laughter answered that, and Alex knew with a nauseous feeling that these men enjoyed hurting people.

"Move her to the van. Load all this stuff in there too. The Noble Lord is going to want what she was trying to steal."

"It's not stealing. It's surviving," Alex said, though it was muffled by the hood and pressure on her face.

She was suddenly released, and she stumbled a bit. The hands on her arms increased pressure keeping her on her feet. She tried to get her bearings, but the hood effectively cut her off from seeing anything. Even with the sun high in the sky, shining brightly, she couldn't even make out shapes.

"Get Lewis up. We need to go. That horde will show up again," Bo said.

The moan that came from the ground told Alex that Lewis was coming around. The fact that he had dropped out cold gave her pure satisfaction. The dark part of her wished she had done more. The men all spoke quietly to each other, Alex only catching snippets. She heard another engine, and she assumed it was the van Bo spoke of. Thinking of this van, Alex remembered the vehicle she and Marcus had seen earlier in the morning. It had been driving erratically, possibly like a driver under the influence of something. And if these men were out taking people, there was no knowing who or what else was in the van.

"That bitch!" Lewis suddenly screamed.

"Ah, is Lewis awake? Good morning there, little buddy," Alex said.

She was being patronizing, hoping someone would come at her so she could find a tool for escaping. She was abruptly released and thrown into the side of the truck. Grunts and the sound of shuffling feet met her ears. Using her handcuffed hands, she led herself to the end of the Bronco. She pictured the alley in her mind and knew where they had stopped there was a wall about five feet from the right side of the truck. When she was sure she was at the right back corner, she began to walk that way. The men were distracting themselves and no one seemed to realize she was moving.

When she met the wall, she almost cried out thinking she ran into someone else. But when she turned and ran her fingers along it, she felt stucco from a building wall. As she walked, she bent at the waist, trying to see if she could get the hood off without stopping. She could hear the fighting behind her, Lewis angrily wanting to kill Alex and the rest of the men trying to calm him. She knew it was only a slim chance that she was going to escape and the idea of getting away made her move faster than was safe.

There was no way for her to see the man that had headed her off and waited for to get near. His leg across her path caused her to fall forward. Without her hands to help her fall, Alex tried to twist so she hit her shoulder instead of her face. She couldn't stop the cry that came from her throat at the extreme impact she felt shaking through her bones. Pain screamed through her shoulder and the side of her head that had bounced off the asphalt. She didn't quite get her breath back before the man standing above her kicked her sharply in the stomach.

Alex curled in on herself, her arms preventing her from protecting her body. She gasped, trying to get air through the hood. She felt like she was choking and was near passing out. Everything was dark but she could still tell she was seeing black spots in her vision. *You cannot pass out. Breathe!* Alex screamed at herself. She wanted to be awake for whatever was coming. The idea of being unconscious around her attempted abductors made her feel even more fear.

A hand roughly grabbed her by her belt, halfway hauling her to her feet. Additional hands grabbed at her shoulders and legs until she was being carried. She began to kick and squirm, refusing to make the kidnapping easy. Then she began to scream. Nothing at first, just sound. Then panic started to settle, and Marcus's name tore from her throat. Her body was jostled, the men fighting against her attempt to escape.

"If she doesn't shut up, we're going to be surrounded soon," one man called over her screaming.

"Woman, stop your damn yelling or I will drop you in the middle of a horde myself," Bo hissed at her, his hot breath breaking through her hood. She turned away from the smell of him, too close to her for comfort.

She didn't want to be quiet. She didn't want to make it easy for them. But she knew in the back of her mind that Bo wasn't wrong. The more noise she made, the more likely the horde would find them. They were too far away for Marcus to hear her screaming. Alex had a sinking feeling that she was on her own. Without weapons and being tied up, she wasn't sure how she was going to get out of this one. *Calm, be calm*, Alex thought to herself. She thought of the lessons her father had taught her. Panicking was never going to help anything.

The sound of a sliding door came to Alex's ears. She was roughly tossed onto the floor of what she assumed was the van. Her already injured shoulder radiated pain, her headed pounded and Alex had to grit her teeth against a scream that wanted to escape. She was thankful that she didn't seem to have a concussion. Though, she was sure if Charlie had been around, she would have ordered Alex to bed. Alex could feel warmth on her shoulder. She tried to shift so she wasn't laying on the wound, which she was sure was a pretty picture of asphalt rash. A quiet crying made Alex freeze in her movements. She lifted her head trying to listen.

"Hello?" Alex said. There was no answer, except the hiccuping sounds of someone trying to stifle sobs.

"Hello?" She said more forcibly this time.

"Shh! They'll hear you," came the soft reply.

"What do they do if you talk?" Alex asked.

"Nothing you want to know about," the voice replied.

Alex could tell she was a young woman, her voice soft and pretty. She tried to push her hood up, using her uninjured shoulder. But she couldn't get a good enough angle. She wanted to see the inside of the van, she wanted to see who she was sitting with, and she wanted to see what the men were doing. As she thought about that, she felt the vehicle shift and the sound of things being moved. Alex could guess that they were loading all the supplies she and Marcus had in the Bronco. Clearly, they believed she was stealing from this Noble Lord they referred to. Her legs were roughly shoved to the side, and she felt her knees collide with something soft. The quiet sound of air whooshing between lips could be heard and Alex tried to pull herself to a sitting position.

"Sorry," Alex whispered.

"Not your fault," the woman replied.

"I'm Alex."

"Doesn't matter."

"Of course, names matter. It's a part of who we are. Humans aren't that lost," Alex said softly.

She pushed herself backwards with her feet. Finally, her back met with the metal wall of the van. She could feel the woman sitting next to her, their shoulders touching now. Alex bumped her softly, trying to encourage her to talk.

"Leona, my name is or was Leona," the woman finally said.

"Was?"

"The Noble Lord names his pets as he chooses."

"Pets?"

A shiver ran down Alex's spine, thinking of what Leona meant by pet. It didn't take much imagination to think of what this Noble Lord wanted from his pets.

"Yes. The ones he likes. He renames us. He calls me Bambi."

Alex didn't reply, and she withheld the laugh that bubbled up at the name. The given name sounded right out of a porn movie that she would be willing to bet the Noble Lord enjoyed. Leona sounded resigned to her fate, and it struck Alex as sad. The woman sounded broken and weary.

Her head snapped up when the sliding door slammed shut. The smell of dirty bodies filled the inside of the vehicle and Alex knew she and Leona were not alone. The engine started and Alex braced herself for movement. Using her feet, she moved around to feel what was around them. She was encouraged to find that they were surrounded by boxes.

"Leona, do you have a hood on?"

"No."

"Good. I have an idea."

CHAPTER EIGHT

The screaming seemed so close, but Marcus couldn't find it. Sweat rolled down his face and neck. He felt like he had been running for an hour, trying to outrun the dead and kill the ones that got too close. His arms were killing him, starting to feel numb from the constant contact with the infected. His legs were rubber, threatening to give out at any minute. But he wouldn't stop.

When Alex didn't come around the front of the horde for him, he had known something was strange. When he saw the Bronco driving away in the far distance, he knew things had taken a horrible turn. He and Alex had had their disagreements about things. This horde and how they handled it was one of them. Marcus had expected her to come for him after she had looked after the survivors they were helping. He had anticipated the lecture and possible yelling that would come from Alex. He was prepared for her to tell him he made stupid decisions and she was done with it.

Instead, the last hour had been him running in the direction he'd seen the Bronco last. However, once he got to where he thought it had been, there was no indication of which way she had gone. His heart pounded in his ears as he had stood as still as possible trying to hear any engine. When he thought he heard something, he would run in that direction then he would stop and listen again. He even tried to follow the infected, thinking a group of them may have been lured by the passing of the vehicle. When he realized they were just randomly wandering together, he had been angry and a little scared. He put down the small group before taking a break in a small doorway that was hidden in shadow.

He drank deeply from his canteen. That was when the screaming started. He almost dropped his water it was so sudden. The sound had echoed between buildings. He knew it was Alex. He was sure when almost immediately she began to scream his name. He had stood very still trying to let his ears do the searching, but the screams didn't last. The noise did more than call to Marcus, it also brought the dead out. As Marcus ran in the direction he believed the screams to be coming from, he was faced with infected coming out of buildings, alleys, and from yards of the neighboring houses. His aggravation with the infected was more than it ever was, as they stood between him and Alex.

When Alex first rescued him off the top of a truck, her and Easton swinging in to kill off the infected that had cornered him, he had instantly been attracted to her. She was beautiful, even though she didn't see herself that way. However, after he got to know her a little more and learned of her recently dead husband, Marcus knew there would never be anything between them. Alex still grieved and punished herself for her husband's death. And Marcus knew he was too much of a wildcard for her to find interest in. He didn't believe in changing himself to suit anyone, even Alex. Since they came to the compound, he made sure he was useful with the skills he had. He was kind with the kids, because it was impossible not to love them. He and Alex built a friendship. Something he depended on every day in the dead world.

Now, he had lost her. His recklessness had left her alone with someone they didn't know. He tried to think of the yelling they had heard near Wal-Mart. He believed he heard a man scream, but there was other higher pitched screams, so he couldn't be sure. Alex could handle herself in any situation, he'd seen it many times. If someone had overpowered her, well he didn't want to think of what that could mean. His legs moved faster as he skidded into another road, with too many options of ways to go. There was no way for him to know now where Alex was. A growl from behind him had him whirling. A small woman stalked toward him. Her scalp had been partially ripped from her skull, hair and flesh flopped around as she moved. Marcus didn't think twice before swinging his bat at her head.

He gulped in air as panic and exhaustion tried to take over. Hearing Alex scream had sent him over the edge from worry into fear. She never screamed. She only yelled when fighting with her sister. Rarely, he had heard her yell in the middle of fighting the dead. But those screams were for help, and they were for him. She needed him to find her and he had no direction to go on. For all he knew he was going the opposite direction of where the trouble was. He ran his free hand over his close-cropped hair. He could hear Alex in his mind, admonishing him for not having a plan.

The sound of an engine starting caught his attention, and without a thought he went running in that direction. In the dead world, the sound of a vehicle was far and few between. He knew it had to be Alex, or whoever had Alex. As he rounded the corner of a shopping complex, a black van flew past him on the road. He froze, realizing it was the same van they had seen driving crazy earlier. It seemed to be doing better now, but it was on its way somewhere fast. Marcus ran into the middle of the street to watch the direction it seemed to go. Too soon it was out of sight with no indication of its destination.

Marcus ran toward the alley the van had come from. He stopped short at what he found. The Bronco sat, the door open, the tailgate down. The supplies were gone, only trash remained on the ground and in the truck. He went to the driver's seat and saw the keys were still in the ignition. Without a thought, Marcus ran to close all the doors and jumped into the truck. He turned the key, shoved it into reverse and tried to follow the direction of the van. When he looked down, he realized there was blood on the center console and in the passenger seat. His heart thudded rapidly thinking the worst.

He drove for what seemed like an hour, up and down the main streets, circling the outside of town the best he could. There was no sign of the van. Finally, as he noticed how much gas he was burning, he let the truck roll to a stop. He leaned his forehead against the steering wheel and closed his eyes. He felt tears stinging, and he was moments away from losing it. *Think about what Alex would do,* he said to himself. This made him sit up and look around. He knew Alex was good with plans. But when those plans didn't work out, she found a way to work with what she had. So, what did he have? He had the truck. He had his weapons, though all of their ammo was gone. He didn't have any food, as his go pack had been in the truck as well and it was gone.

What he did have was the town. Those from the compound hadn't met many survivors in town, but they knew they were around. Places they had scouted would be empty upon return, or they would see vehicles in the distance. Their rule had always been to not approach unless someone came to them or they needed help. *Bunch of good that has done*, Marcus thought to himself sarcastically. In town he could find people. Maybe someone saw what happened or knew where the van was from. He could find food easily, even if he went back to the truck they had hidden on the side of the forested road. What he couldn't do was go back to the compound with nothing. He didn't know if Max would let him live if he had lost her sister and given up on the search.

With an idea in mind, he started to drive slowly toward the residential area nearby. As he drove, he looked at each house, watching for a twitch of curtains or a face staring back at him. A small child ran from one house to another and Marcus stomped on the brakes. The child wasn't infected, Marcus realized. He sat in front of the house the child had run into and waited. Deciding that taking the chance was worth it, he parked the Bronco at the curb and stepped out. He left his 9mm in its holster but left his bat in the truck. He wasn't there to intimidate anyone, he just had questions. His hands were out at his sides, palms out to show he wasn't trying to hide anything as he walked slowly toward the door.

"Stop right there," a man's voice boomed. Marcus froze, afraid to look around for the source of the voice.

"What do you want? We don't have anything to spare," the man continued.

"I don't want supplies. I just have some questions," Marcus called back.

"Do you have anything to trade for answers?"

Marcus thought. He had nothing in the Bronco but one case of water that was left behind for some reason. He wasn't willing to part with his weapons because those were the only things that would keep him alive away from the compound.

"Case of water is all I have left."

A man with a hunting rifle came from the far side of the house. A window above him opened, and another man leaned out, flashing a large handgun. Marcus left his hands where they were, realizing he was outnumbered and in a precarious position. When the man spoke again, Marcus realized it was the man from the window doing the talking.

"What's the questions?"

"Have you seen a black van around here?"

The men exchanged a look. They rattled off a quick conversation in Spanish, leaving Marcus wishing he had paid better attention in Spanish class.

"What do you know of the black van?" The man on the ground asked.

"Nothing. That's why I'm here to ask," Marcus replied.

"You've seen the van?" The man from the window said.

"I think the people in it took my friend. I saw it driving away," Marcus said.

A clicking noise from the front door caught Marcus's attention. It was open now, and a woman stood in the doorway. She motioned to Marcus to come inside. He looked at the men holding him at gunpoint in time to see them share an exasperated look. Then the man in the window looked back to Marcus and nodded to him, giving the approval for Marcus to enter the house. Keeping his hands visible, Marcus walked toward the door where the woman stood aside to allow him entry.

The interior was dimly lit, no sun shining through the bottom windows. After a look around, Marcus realized all the bottom windows were boarded up. A decent job by his standards and a smart choice since they seemed to be living in the house. The door clicked closed, and the lock was turned as soon as he was clear of it. Then a thick wooden beam was placed into a slot of metal that had been attached to the walls on either side of the door. This family was clearly concerned about an attack. Marcus wanted to mention that the infected couldn't unlock doors, but he was beginning to believe they had more to fear than the dead.

A young woman approached Marcus. Her face was open and welcoming, with a smile as she spoke.

"I'm Vera. I'm sorry about my brother and uncle, they are very protective."

"My name is Marcus. And it's ok. I don't blame them. But you have nothing to fear from me," he said.

"We know. My mother wouldn't have opened the door if we were worried," Vera said with a light laugh.

When she turned to look at her mother, Marcus noticed a puckered scar on the side of her face. In the small time he saw it, he believed it hadn't happened long ago, but it appeared to be healing well. Her mother was the older woman that had opened the door, much to the disapproval of the men trying to question Marcus. When the two men joined them on the first floor, names were given around, because Vera's mother, whose name was Claudia, wouldn't have rude behavior in the house. Mateo was Vera's brother, the one that held the rifle on him on the ground. The uncle's name was Albert. He was a burly man, one that Marcus wouldn't trifle with plague or no plague. And the last inhabitant who was now playing upstairs was Alonso Jr, fondly called AJ. The boy was named after their father, Alonso, who had died in the early days of the plague. The men had little to say, but both had a few biting words for Claudia. Though Marcus didn't understand the language, he looked away as the argument happened.

"It's ok," Vera said, as she stepped to Marcus's side. "My brother and uncle watch out for us and the house. Especially after what happened to Sylvia."

Her face was sad at that, but before Marcus could ask who Sylvia was, Claudia called him to join her in the kitchen. He had expected everyone to follow, but when he entered a swinging door shut behind him and no one else entered. Claudia busied herself with instant coffee, using candlelight to see her hands. Marcus offered to help, feeling that though society had fallen apart, inside this house manners still ruled. Claudia smiled a sweet smile at him and declined his offer, asking him to sit. He did, but he couldn't stop fidgeting at her nice, white cloth-covered table.

"Cream or sugar?" Claudia asked.

"Black is fine, ma'am," Marcus replied.

"Oh please, just call me Claudia. There's no need for formality here."

The older woman sat next to him. She was wearing what Marcus assumed would be called a house dress. It was colorful with flowers covering every inch. She wore house slippers, which struck Marcus as quite funny. There was no way she could safely leave the house in those if she had to. Marcus wondered if she ever did leave, or if she just stayed safely tucked away in their house. He imagined that as long as they were silent and careful when they came and went, the infected wouldn't show interest in their home. The kitchen seemed well stocked, with additional supplies stacked in corners, organized and carefully put out of the way. Some of it looked like canned goods the Duncans had hoped to grab from a nearby warehouse. When they went to retrieve the cans, most were gone. It was then they were glad to realize they weren't alone in town with all the dead.

"Sylvia, is my oldest daughter. She's a few years older than Vera. She has been missing for two weeks," Claudia said. Her sudden change of subject caught Marcus off guard and he had to put his coffee down again. He didn't want to risk spilling a drop on the pristine white covering.

"Missing? How do you know she's not, well...you know," Marcus hedged. He wasn't sure how to just say she was probably dead.

"Because she was taken by the black van. They took Vera too. But Vera came back."

"With the injury to her face?" Marcus asked. Claudia didn't say anything, just nodded her head with a far off look in her eyes.

"Who drives the van, Claudia?"

"The men that work for the Noble Lord. A man that has tried to take control of the supplies we have here in town. He wants to rule, as if we have that type of leadership in the United States," Claudia said.

"The Noble Lord? There is actually someone out there that calls himself that? So how has he tried to take control? Why do people follow him?"

"The rumor is, from what my brother and son have heard in town, he was a high-level drug dealer before the fall. Once things went to the dead, he still had a good size supply of drugs. Those were the men that followed him first. Then with their help, he started gathering supplies and keeping them locked up. To get a share of supplies, you have to contribute to his cause in some way," Claudia explained.

Marcus sat back in his chair for a moment. He knew he shouldn't feel surprised, but he did. Drugs should be the last concern of the living population, they had plenty to deal with otherwise. However, he realized that addiction was a strong thing. And the fear and panic of people could push them over the edge when looking for a way to escape. If the man then controlled food and water that those people needed, they would probably do anything as long as they were still fed.

"Why would he take your daughters? Why did his men take my friend?" Marcus asked.

"She's a woman, yes?" Marcus nodded his head and Claudia continued. "It's the Dead Brothel. He uses the women they kidnap to work at the brothel." Her voice was quiet and sad.

Marcus stood up in anger and shock, almost toppling his chair in the process. He began to pace the kitchen. A brothel? Now? How had they not heard about such a thing already? Marcus admitted those at the compound had been careful to not cross people unless completely necessary. Behind their walls, they were safe from the threats of someone such as this Noble Lord. Marcus scoffed in his mind, hating to even refer to him that way. Self-proclaimed ruler was what he was trying to be. And his men just took a Duncan. They had now bit off more than they could chew.

"How did Vera escape?" Marcus asked, turning back to look at Claudia. Her eyes were red rimmed, as she fought the tears. Marcus felt sympathy well in him and he calmed himself to sit back next to her.

"She fought with them in the van. Sylvia tried to calm her, believing they would be let go if they just played along. But Vera didn't believe that. She fought and her face was badly cut. The men decided she wasn't worth taking to the Noble Lord, so they threw her from the van on the side of the road."

"Dear god. How did she make it home?" Marcus asked.

"Mateo and Albert were following the van as best they could. They knew the general direction it had gone and were lucky to be on the same road. They found Vera, holding her shirt to her face, stumbling down the road. I was able to sew her up. I'm no doctor but I can do a small stitch," Claudia said.

"Which way did the van go then? What road was it? I need to find it."

"It's a fortress. You won't get your friend out of there, not alive at least," Claudia replied.

"I won't be alone," Marcus said. He thought about how angry Rafe and Max were going to be when he got home without Alex. When he told them this story, Max's head would explode, if that was a physical possibility.

"I thought so. You're from behind the walls, aren't you?" Claudia asked. Her question caught Marcus off guard, and he felt like he knew much less about this woman than she knew of him.

"What walls?" He replied, hedging and keeping his cards close.

"The ones in the middle of the forest. There is a house behind the walls. You live there."

"I'm not sure...." Marcus started, but Claudia cut him off.

"I only know this because Mateo and Albert have searched the area almost daily since the fall. They avoid the dead as much as possible. They saw your vehicle once, and they carefully followed into the forest. They didn't go near the walls though, after they saw the barbed wire and cameras."

Marcus was impressed. It wasn't easy to sneak up on a Duncan. The rest of them though, didn't have the same skills. He thought back to the times he and Cliff traveled out on their own. *Was it one of those times?* Claudia had mentioned the barbed wire, which was a newer addition to the walls. They hadn't found them long ago. And Marcus knew there hadn't been any sightings on the cameras. The alarms had only gone off when the infected were nearby. There was always someone on watch, waiting for the government to attack once again.

"It's very secure. I'm surprised they didn't come close enough to trip the alarms," Marcus finally said, admitting to the truth.

"They used their scopes I believe, but you'd have to ask them. We decided that since you didn't bother us, we wouldn't bother you," Claudia said, shrugging her shoulders.

The woman then stood and went to get more coffee for them. When she handed a warmed mug back to Marcus, he wrapped his fingers around it. His body had gone ice cold hearing all the information Claudia had about the van and the Noble Lord. He knew he had really messed up this time, following his own plans, instead of taking time to decide on something better with Alex. They could have both gotten into the Bronco and taken off. They may have found the survivors before the horde got to them, but it was unlikely with the fast ones he had been trying to kill. Deep down he knew that if the men overpowered Alex, Marcus being with her wouldn't have changed the outcome.

"What are you going to do?" Claudia asked. She had sat back down with her own cup of coffee and a photo.

"I'm going to go home. Get backup and get Alex back," he said.

"If you see my Sylvia, if she's alive, could you bring her back?" Claudia asked, as she slid the photo across to him.

Marcus took the small picture. The smiling face looked very much like Vera, but older. In this image she looked to be laughing at something, her head tossed back, and long black hair flowed behind her. Marcus hated to picture this woman alone, no one protecting her in this brothel. He knew the Duncans well, Alex the most, and he knew Alex wouldn't leave a woman behind to suffer at the hands of the Noble Lord if she could help it. He slid the photo into the front pocket of his button-up shirt. It sat directly over his heart and he realized the symbolism as he made his promise to Claudia.

"I promise, if we can, we will bring her home to you."

Claudia insisted on feeding him a late lunch. They sat around the large kitchen table, everyone eating quietly. Marcus kept his eyes on his plate, feeling the oppressive glares from the men at the table. They didn't appreciate the matriarch overruling them on the situation, but she didn't kick Marcus out immediately. To his right, AJ sat eating cheerily. He had a plastic dinosaur on the table and between bites he rattled off all the facts he knew of that type of animal. Marcus was enthralled, thinking about how much the boy was like Billie Duncan. Claudia's eyes shined when she looked at the boy and she ruffled his hair.

"He was a surprise this one. My Alonso and I were quite done having children. As you can see, there's quite the years in between," Claudia laughed lightly and it was impossible to not smile in response.

"There are children at our home as well. Once this is done, we should let them all meet. I know they would enjoy a new friend," Marcus replied. A scoff answered him from across the table.

"Mateo, I won't have your bad manners at my table," Claudia said, her tone seemingly to be soft and cutting at the same time.

"Mama, you are really trusting this man? Secretive and lives behind stone walls. What do you know of him?" Mateo said. Marcus knew the questions had been brewing in him since he had arrived.

"Mateo..." Claudia started and Marcus could see she was about to set in on her son. He cleared his throat to get her attention. She turned her gaze to him.

"If I may?" Marcus said, waiting for her agreement. He wanted to use every bit of manners he knew where Claudia was involved.

"Yes, we do live behind walls. But those have been there a long time. I guess you didn't know Mitch Duncan, the man who built that home. The Duncans have been a part of this area since their births. That is their home. There is nothing secret there. Only family working to keep each other safe," Marcus said.

"Your family?" Vera asked.

"They are now. Alex, the woman that I'm going after, saved my life. I need to take what you've told me back home to get her brother and sister. Together, I know we can rescue her."

"You don't know what you're dealing with. The Noble Lord isn't one to be messed with. We tried, and we almost lost both of my sisters," Mateo said.

"We may not know him, but you do. And you don't know the Duncans. Not much stops them from getting what they want."

CHAPTER NINE

"There's no use fighting. I tried. They caught me again. Just move on," Leona said quietly.

Alex wasn't sure why the woman wouldn't at least try. Did she really feel like throwing away her life and giving up was an option? In Alex's world, that would never be an option. Allowing men to take her and attempt to force her into whatever they had in mind, was not how Alex had been built. She would continue to fight until one side died. And she knew she would rather die than be a pet to the Noble Lord.

"I won't give up. And you shouldn't either. Once we're free, if you want to stay here you do that. But I'm getting out of here."

The handcuffs were going to be the biggest issue. Alex wasn't carrying anything to pick a lock or an extra key. Her father would have been furious. His obsession with distrust for the government had always gone over Alex's head. She didn't believe those that were entrusted to protect you needed to be feared. She knew differently now, having been faced with Callahan and his men. If she had followed Mitch Duncan's instructions, she would have a handcuff key hidden in her sock or bra. Being put into handcuffs wasn't her first worry when she'd left the compound the day before.

Alex shifted, so her hands were under her thighs. She could hear Leona gasp quietly as Alex breathed slowly and began to contort her body to get the handcuffs down the back of her legs and around her boots. Once she pulled her cuffed hands into her lap she breathed deeply, panting slightly at the exertion. Staying in shape had always been a goal of hers and she was now thankful for the many yoga classes she had taken to keep her body limber and stretched.

With her hands in the front, the first thing Alex did was pat down her pockets. She was pretty sure when the men searched her, they had taken everything, but she needed to be sure. She also realized she still had the survival bracelet on her wrist. She didn't know why they didn't take it, but she assumed they didn't know there was a bottle opener, whistle, flint, and compass hidden on the inside. She ran choices through her mind and right then she didn't believe the bracelet was going to help her get away from the van.

"What are you going to do?" Leona asked.

"Depends, are you going to help?"

"What would I have to do?"

"Create a distraction. Pretend to be sick, get up and go over there like you're going to throw up on them. When they're worried about you, I will get to the door. First though," Alex said as she pulled off her hood.

She blinked in the sudden light of the van. It was dim inside with no windows except the windshield letting in light. The hood had been so black that Alex's eyes needed a moment to adjust. As she figured, the boxes of supplies were built up in a slight semi-circle around the women. The men didn't care if the boxes fell onto the women, as long as they were out of their way. None of the men could see Alex directly, which she was thankful for. She didn't need any of them knowing that her hands were in front of her, at least not yet. She turned to look at Leona. The woman was once beautiful, Alex knew, but now her face was now swollen and covered in bruises. Her vibrant red hair, which looked too bright to be real, was hanging in tangles around her shoulders. Alex could only see some of her eyes in the dim light, but she could tell they were very blue.

The last thing Alex noticed was round burn marks on her arms. She looked closer and her mind flashed back to the bus and the infected tied up inside. Was that infected once a woman kept by these men? That thought played out in Alex's mind and she felt a sickness in her gut. She wondered if the woman was bitten before or after she was tied up. Her mind whirled with anger and disgust for the men sitting in the van. Her fingers twitched thinking of how she wished she had a weapon, something to hurt them all, the way they had clearly hurt these women.

"How long have you been held by the Noble Lord?" Alex asked.

"Too long. I'm not sure anymore. I don't have a way to count the days."

Alex felt more anger, red and pounding in her mind. She couldn't fathom what the woman had been subjected to. But Alex was done with it.

"Ready, Leona?"

Leona looked around, her eyes darting to the men. Alex couldn't read her expression due to the swelling in her face, but she was sure Leona was nervous.

"It'll be all right. Go for the driver's area. Make him slow down. So, when the door is open, we can jump."

"We?"

"Do you want to stay here? I wasn't kidding when I said I was going to get us out of here. Us. You and I."

"Ok," the word was barely audible to Alex. But she finally knew she had Leona's buy in.

Strangely, Leona's hands were free. She gripped them in front her the entire time they sat. Alex assumed the men no longer worried about her, she was broken and fragile. Well, if Alex had her way, they had another thing coming. As planned, Leona got to her feet in a low crouch, so she could move through the van. The boxes blocked off the men in the back and she was able to go directly to the area where the driver and passenger seats were. When she was close enough, she began to feign gagging and Alex could hear her choking out the words "sick, hurl, stop."

The driver, panicked he was about to get covered in vomit, swerved the van, slamming on the brakes, causing Leona to almost lose her balance. Instead of toppling over, she reached through the middle of the seats and grabbed the driver's arm. That got his attention further, and he cried out for the men in the back to help. As yelling and movement began, Alex got to her feet as well. Leona was backing away as the men threatened her and came closer, so Alex went the other way around the box wall. She found the door unsecured and couldn't believe her luck. That was until a face came back around the boxes.

"What do we have here?" Bo sneered at Alex.

"You missed my stop, I'll be getting off here," Alex said, as she yanked open the sliding door.

The driver had slowed measurably, believing Leona needed to be handled. The other woman had crawled to Alex's side. Bo began to move toward Alex and a split-second decision needed to be made. Alex knew she could get away, she could and would fight until her last breath. She knew these men wouldn't get what they wanted from her. But Leona wouldn't fight, she had no more strength to stop them. Alex couldn't leave her. And she couldn't let the men take her either.

"Jump, Leona. Roll when you hit the ground!" Alex cried before she threw herself at Bo.

Bo was ready for her attack and he tried to pivot as she impacted. The interior of the van was cramped with the people and supplies that were loaded up. Alex smashed her shoulder into

Bo's stomach, and he grunted as the air left his body. She wanted to slam him down, but there was no space for leverage to do so. Instead, she drove him back as far as she could. She was quickly grabbed from behind and yanked off Bo, who was gasping to get air back in his lungs. Alex spit on him. She couldn't stop herself. The disgust she felt for the men was a disease that was eating her alive.

"We lost the other one," the man holding Alex said. The sliding door slammed shut and Alex looked around. Leona was gone.

"Damn it. I'm tired of dealing with that woman. This is the third time she's taken off. Let the dead have her," Lewis said from the passenger seat.

Alex noted that he didn't try to join the fray this time. She had to wonder if it was because he liked his balls where they were, and he knew that he couldn't take Alex on his own. Instead he left his lackeys to deal with her. She fought back, yanking her arms away from who held them and made to start toward Lewis. He gave her one dirty look then nodded to another man. Her arms were then yanked above her head just as the black hood was secured once again over her head. She was drug by the handcuffs into the back of the van. The sound of chains met her ears, and she was then left to hang by some sort of contraption. Her knees didn't meet the bottom of the van, so she was forced to crouch awkwardly on her feet as the van shifted under her.

As Alex hung there, with nothing else to do, her mind began to work. She was thankful Leona was out, but how long would the woman survive on her own in the wild with infected everywhere? Alex hoped the woman showed more fight with the dead than she did with the Noble Lord and his men. Alex wondered if she had ensured the woman's death by helping her escape. The Noble Lord and his men were clearly cruel, but was death a better fate than being a prisoner? Alex decided that Leona made that decision on her own by jumping. She took the chance of the dead instead of staying with the cruel leader.

Putting Leona from her mind, Alex began to categorize what she had learned that day. When she met the men, they had accused her of stealing from the Noble Lord. Alex couldn't figure out how they hadn't run into the men before. The Duncan compound was close to self-sustaining. They didn't need to go out often for scavenging runs. They did it more to keep tabs of what was happening in the town and what other survivors were doing. They had tended to avoid those that chose to avoid them. Alex wanted to trust other living people, but they had all experienced negative situations with other survivors. She realized now they had missed something brewing for some time.

The Noble Lord believed he had taken claim to the supplies of the area. Something Alex and her family would never stand for. The belief the Duncans and their friends had was everyone had the right to survive. To do that people needed to work together and share the supplies that were left. Alex had a grand dream that someday trade would be possible. That survivors would band together to keep the human race from going extinct. She knew that her home could be cultivated to provide more fresh produce and meat to those in need. However, she needed to trust the people they would do business with. This Noble Lord was not someone they would open their doors to.

Alex also noted on her list of observations that the Noble Lord's men seemed to be in some sort of withdrawal or under the effects of some sort of drug. From the conversation she had heard, they hoped to gain some sort of supplies from the Noble Lord by turning her over to him. They didn't take the supplies she and Marcus had collected and run with them. Instead, they loaded them up to return to the Noble Lord. Alex could guess that they believed it would gain them additional favor with the man that held some sort of power over them.

Power. That was the last thing. What was it that the Noble

Lord had that had created this vacuum of power? Alex knew one answer was drugs. These men needed more than regular supplies to survive. But what was it about one man that kept other men from overthrowing him? Alex knew she wouldn't get that answer until she met the Noble Lord, something she knew she wouldn't be able to avoid. In her experience no one man held enough leverage to control the actions of so many. Not without an army, laws and a whole government to support him.

Her thighs had started to ache, pain reaching up to her hips as she tried to carefully keep herself balanced. She gave up trying to count turns or figure out the direction they might be going. She knew they had driven away from Kalispell. That was bad enough. She knew Marcus would know something was wrong when she didn't come for him. But how would he track her in the van moving away from their area? Alex found herself cursing Marcus again for going off on his own without a plan. Yet again. But even her inner cursing was halfhearted. Getting captured wasn't Marcus's fault. They couldn't have known what was to come.

Alex snapped to attention when she realized that the van was slowing. The men spoke quietly to each other and Alex could only pick up snippets of what they were saying. She knew they weren't at their destination yet when she heard the words "horde" and "camp" in their discussions. The sounds at the back of the van made Alex jump forward. She knew those noises, the banging and groans of the infected. They knew there was a meal inside the metal vehicle. The van began to move again, but much slower. Alex could feel the rattle as they pushed through the infected that must have been on all sides of the van.

After only a short time of fighting through the horde of infected, the van sped up again, and the men quieted. Alex readjusted her legs, trying to release the tightness in her muscles. She couldn't seem to find a position that didn't ache. As she concentrated on her posture, she was roughly gripped from the side, her body pulled against the metal cuffs at her wrists. She couldn't stop the cry that came from her lips, partially in surprise and partially in pain.

"You think this is bad? Just wait. The Noble Lord will blame you for losing his pet," the harsh growl was near her ear. Alex immediately recognized Lewis.

"Had to wait for me to be tied up again to confront me, Lewis?" Alex taunted.

"I'm not afraid of you. You're nothing. You were easy to lure. Easy to capture. And you'll be easy to hand over to The Noble Lord."

"Untie me and we'll see how easy it is," Alex said, her voice low and threatening.

Instead of answering, Lewis roughly grabbed her breast, squeezing until tears prickled Alex's eyes. His hand began to wander lower. Alex, feeling panic and disgust, tried to judge where Lewis' face was and swung her head in his direction as hard as her bound body would allow. She knew she connected with his cheekbone as pain splintered from the impact. Though she couldn't see, she heard Lewis crash into the boxes that were directly in front of her.

"Touch me again and you'll suffer much worse," Alex yelled.

"You'll learn your damn place," Lewis said as he scrambled back toward Alex.

"I know my place. But you clearly haven't figured out yours. Do you enjoy being my punching bag, Lewis? You make it too easy," Alex said.

Alex could sense Lewis getting close to her and she knew his face was by her ear when his voice hissed out.

"The Noble Lord will enjoy breaking you," he said.

She couldn't see the blow as Lewis' fist collided with her abdomen. She didn't get a chance to avoid or tighten her muscles to help with the pain. The air rushed from her lungs in a loud gasp. Alex couldn't focus as her legs collapsed from under her as the pain radiated from her stomach. She scrambled to find her footing again as all of her weight fell onto her shoulders and wrists secured above her head. Her lungs felt like fire and she coughed and wheezed, fighting for air. All the while Lewis sat nearby, cackling his enjoyment at her pain.

Alex had little idea how much time passed. She had worked on stretching her legs, but found it was near impossible in the position she was stuck in. She tried to track time by counting in her head, but she had lost count of the number of minutes. The van had stopped once, letting men off to relieve themselves. She was yanked from her spot and taken behind a tree. The hood didn't leave her head, but she was told it was her only chance to empty her bladder. Humiliated, but unable to change her bodily functions, she crouched against the tree and did her business.

When she was outside of the van, she could tell that the sun was much lower in the sky. Even with the hood on, she was able to tell when it was brighter, and she knew the sun didn't directly shine on her. She thought of Marcus and the panic he was probably going through. She wondered if he had made it back to the compound yet, or if he was still looking for her? She didn't want to imagine her siblings' reaction to her kidnapping. Max would blame Marcus and Rafe would be a peacekeeper. Alex hoped Max didn't try to kick Marcus up one side and down the other for allowing Alex to be taken. She wouldn't believe it wasn't his fault.

After she was shoved back into the van, they drove a short distance before stopping again. The vehicle passed over rougher terrain, telling Alex they were leaving the road. The men talked about making camp and referred to a cabin they had used before. Alex wasn't sure what direction they went, so she couldn't even guess where the cabin was located. The van came to a sudden halt, and the men began to exit. There was momentary arguing as it was decided who would guard Alex in the van. Using the vehicle as a prison cell was their idea of a good set up. Alex was just glad she would be alone and not inside the cabin at the mercy of her kidnappers.

Alex shifted on the hard van floor. They had removed her handcuffs and hood after they decided she couldn't determine where they were. Once they left her alone, she searched the boxes in the van. She remembered one of them had blankets in them. Using one as a pillow, Alex tried to get comfortable. The blanket was rough against her cheek, but she knew it was better than the cold metal of the van floor. Her first instinct was to escape. However, when she tried to investigate what was happening outside of the van, she quickly realized they had set up camp directly around the vehicle, while one man stood watch.

Her body was exhausted. Though, her mind couldn't seem to shut off as horrible ideas and images continued to flip behind her eyelids. She laid there, breathing deep, hoping to calm herself enough to get some sleep. Alex knew if she didn't rest, she would be no match for the Noble Lord. From the talk she had heard between the men, they would arrive at his compound the next morning. Alex needed to be rested, alert, and prepared to handle whatever was thrown at her when they arrived wherever they were headed. And she needed to be on the lookout for an escape. With ideas of escaping or kicking Lewis's ass one more time in her head, exhaustion finally took control and Alex fell into a dreamless sleep.

Alex didn't sleep deeply, so as soon as a van door was opened her eyes popped open. One of the men she couldn't name began to crab walk to her position, but when she sat up suddenly, he fell backwards. Fear crossed his features and Alex just stared at him, waiting for him to decide on his next move.

"It's morning," the man stuttered out.

"Ok."

"Uh, I'm supposed to take you to pee," the man said. He then pulled a gun awkwardly from his waistband, as if he hadn't handled it often.

Alex climbed out of the truck ahead of the man, who now pointed the gun at her back. She didn't make any sudden moves;

afraid his finger would tighten on the trigger accidentally. He gave instructions on where to walk and then told her to stop behind a large tree. He stood watching her while Alex just stared back.

"Privacy?" Alex finally asked.

"Can't have you running off," the man replied.

"You get off on watching women pee?" Alex said.

"What? No! I...I...I'm doing my job," the man finally explained.

"Well if I make you so nervous, maybe you should just let me go," Alex suggested in her nicest voice. She even pasted a smile on her face, though she could feel it would fail at putting the man at ease.

"Lewis is taking you to the Noble Lord. You will get us supplies. I can't let you go," the man replied.

Alex tilted her head as she studied him. His voice was almost apologetic. She had to guess it was just about the drugs for this one. He didn't enjoy hurting people. The weak needed someone to protect them, and this man would fall right in line with anyone that would show him the way. Alex turned her back on him and unbuttoned her pants. She used the tree to partially hide as she relieved herself. In the quiet, she wondered if she could use the man's weakness to her benefit.

"What's your name?" Alex asked, standing up and fastening her pants before turning around.

"Thomas," the man replied with no hesitation.

"Thomas. I'm Alex. What're you doing with a gang like this?"

"Gang? We're no gang. We're just trying to survive," Thomas argued.

"You kidnap people. You take supplies. You claim to protect the Noble Lord's area. If that's not a gang, I'm not sure what is," Alex said. She pretended to stretch, hoping to keep Thomas in the trees a little longer.

"We...we...do what we're told," Thomas said, his voice small.

"And the Noble Lord is the one giving the orders?"

Thomas didn't speak, just nodded his head vigorously. He then looked over both of his shoulders, as if to make sure no one was listening.

"And he has the drugs you need?" Alex said. She was done pulling punches. She needed to figure out if Thomas was the weak link she was looking for.

Thomas just stared at her; his eyes wide at her statement. Alex wanted to sigh, wondering how none of them thought she could tell there were some real signs of withdrawal in the group. She guessed none of them knew what they looked like anymore. Surviving from day to day with the supplies they wanted to have was all that mattered to them. As Alex stared at Thomas, she saw his face change. A sneer came to his lips and Alex realized she may have said the wrong thing.

"You have a problem with drugs, bitch? That's none of your business. Now shut your mouth and get back to the van," Thomas said, his voice taking on a stronger tone. His hand seemed to tighten on the gun, and he raised his aim at Alex again. She held up her hands in a surrender motions, palms out to not threaten the trigger-happy man.

"I didn't say I had any issues, Thomas. Calm down with the gun a bit, why don't you?" Alex said.

"You need to shut your mouth. All you're good for is being one of the Noble Lord's whores. That's what Lewis says. So, you need to shut your dirty mouth and get to the van."

Alex decided she couldn't push Thomas any further. She replayed their conversation in her mind as she trudged back to the vehicle. As soon as she'd mentioned the drugs, Thomas turned nasty on her. He seemed to immediately assume she was judging him. Internally she may have been, but her question was an innocent digging into who he was. She wanted to determine if he was hooked on whatever poison the Noble Lord was peddling. The more information she had, the easier to get inside the man's head.

Back at the van, most of their camp was cleared, and the men were loading what supplies they had taken out back into the vehicle. When Alex arrived, she was roughly handcuffed and shoved in as if she was just another supply. There wasn't much chatter in the group now. Alex felt tension fill the van, and she guessed it was because they would arrive to see the Noble Lord soon. These men seemed to obey and serve him not only out of necessity, but out of fear.

The atmosphere was somber as the van came into a small town. It would be something described as a one-horse town in the days when there were people living in it. Now it was a skeleton of itself. Alex could only see a small view through the windshield. She saw burned cars and what used to be homes. Bodies littered the road; some were unrecognizable as the tires of vehicles ran them over time and time again. The van bumped over them and Alex felt sick. A part of her wondered if those were infected that had been killed, or people who may have stood in the way of the Noble Lord.

The van wound its way into what Alex assumed was the downtown of the little nowhere town. The van pulled into a makeshift parking spot that had been sprayed onto the street. Alex was yanked from the van as the men exited. Looming in front of them was a large, older white building. The sign from before the apocalypse labeled it a civic center. Old posters advertising for plays known on Broadway and local concerts hung in tatters along one outside wall. Now, a large sign hung from the large windows that seemed to be on a second floor. The sign was made from sheets sewn together. It flapped silently in the breeze. The words smeared across it could only be dried blood. A shiver passed through Alex as she read, "The land of the Noble Lord. Welcome to the Dead Brothel."

CHAPTER TEN

"What do you mean, you lost her?" Max's voice was loud and shrill. Marcus had enough guilt to grimace as Max yelled at him.

"Max, the children," Margaret said quietly.

When Marcus arrived at the compound, in the truck he and Alex had hidden, he immediately requested a family meeting. Those meetings were usually called by Alex and reserved for reviewing duties and plans. Today was a different situation. Rafe and Max had met Marcus at the gate. Both were armed, as he drove up in an unknown vehicle. Once they saw his face, both relaxed, but Marcus didn't want to explain anything while Max had a weapon nearby. Requesting the family meeting was the only way he could guarantee the fiery woman didn't kill him.

"The children are going to know something is going on when their mother doesn't come home," Max hissed through gritted teeth.

"I'm going to go get her," Marcus interrupted.

"Go get her? So, you know where she is? Who has her?" Rafe said, shooting questions in rapid-fire.

"I met this family. I spoke with them yesterday. They know who took Alex. The uncle and son of the woman that took me in are going to help us get her back. They also have a family member that is missing," Marcus explained.

Claudia Vega had insisted he stay the night as dusk started to break during their conversations. Albert and Mateo gave all the details they knew about the men that took the women from town. They described a ruthless leader who used women in his brothel to his whim. Marcus was afraid to give the Duncan siblings those details, afraid Max would fly completely off the handle. Going in half-cocked wasn't going to rescue Alex. After putting together everything the Vega men had shared, Marcus knew they would need a plan. And as many fighting adults as they could take.

"These people that took Alex, what do they want?" Margaret asked.

"They work for a man, he calls himself Noble Lord," Marcus started.

He explained how Alex and he got separated. When he mentioned how he took off to draw the attention of the horde, Max's eyes narrowed as she began to shake her head. Marcus knew without her saying it that he had put Alex in danger with that move. He couldn't have known at the time that the men were kidnappers. As Marcus finished his description of the Noble Lord and how he believed he owned all the supplies in town, everyone sat silent.

"That doesn't explain why they would take Alex," Rafe finally said.

Marcus cleared his throat. His mind raced thinking of ways to avoid the inevitable truth. But whether they found out now from him, or later from the Vegas, or when they found Alex, they would know she was being sold for her body.

"There's a place that the Noble Lord runs. The kidnapped women are taken there. And used. It's a brothel," Marcus said in a rush.

The silence was thick, shattered only by Max jumping up so

fast her chair flipped backward to the ground. She rounded the table at Marcus, who stood up and tried to back away. He was cornered and Max's eyes were ablaze with fury. Max's blow was expected, but it still stung like hell. Marcus knew he would have a red palm print where her hand made contact with his face. She was gearing up to hit him again, with a closed fist this time, when Griffin came up behind her and picked her up off her feet in a bear hug.

"That's enough of that," Griffin said to her.

He carried her back to her seat and physically sat her in it. She made one attempt to move again but Griffin had his hand on her leg, pinning her to her spot. When she looked at him, the fierceness in his face deflated her need for vengeance just slightly. Instead, Max turned to the table and slammed her palm down with a sharp crack.

"You let our sister be taken by men that will sell her body?"

It was Rafe's cold voice that asked the question. Marcus tore his eyes from Max, where he had been preparing to avoid another attack. Rafe's face was red and dark. Charlie sat next to him, one hand gripping Rafe's hand so tightly both of their knuckles were white. Her other hand covered her mouth, and she had gone completely pale. The absolute opposite of her chosen love. Rafe's fury was a surprise, as Marcus had never seen him angry before. The man was always even and calm, nothing ruffled his feathers. Now, there was a damaging storm right under the surface, waiting to explode.

Marcus heard a growl and his dropped his eyes to the white and silver dog sitting at Rafe's feet. Storm clearly knew his master was angry and in turn that meant the dog wanted to bite something. Marcus had seen the dog take a number of instructions from Rafe when in the middle of a fight. And those instructions weren't always vocal. The dog seemed to always know what needed to happen. And at that moment he was sure Marcus was the enemy.

Marcus swallowed audibly and looked back up at Rafe. The normally calm man stared at him for a moment. Marcus worried that Rafe was going to snap and sic his dog on him. Instead, Charlie clicked her tongue at Storm and the dog moved to sit next to her. He rested his muzzle on her leg and she buried her free hand into his thick coat. Though it seemed the dog was controlled, his mismatched eyes never left Marcus.

"I didn't know who they were," Marcus said quietly. He sat down dejectedly at the table again.

"Of course, you didn't," Margaret said, defending Marcus as only the den mother of the group could. Hell, Marcus blamed himself just as the Duncans did. He didn't deserve Margaret's help.

"Do you have a real plan, Marcus?" The older woman asked.

"Part of one. But it will take as many of us that can be spared. According to the Vegas, there are numerous men that work for the Noble Lord and frequent this...this place..." Marcus finished lamely.

"Everyone will go except Margaret and Issac who will stay for the kids. We'll leave Easton for additional protection," Rafe said immediately.

"Wait, no!" Easton started to exclaim. Though he was only sixteen years old, he held many responsibilities of an adult. He always had a seat at family meetings.

"Boy, I will not argue with you on this. Alex would never forgive me for allowing you anywhere near this. Plus, Margaret may need help," Rafe said. His tone left no room for argument or compromise.

The boy flopped back in his chair, as only a teenager could. Marcus could sympathize with him. Alex was a surrogate mother to Easton. They had grown very close over the last few months, bonding over loss and her lessons to him in survival. Having her in danger would make Easton crazy with fear and worry. Marcus felt the same deep in his gut.

"I'd rather take Easton and leave Marcus here," Max practically shouted. That got Marcus's attention.

"What? That's ridiculous, Max. I'm as good a shot as most of you. And I want to get Alex back just as badly," he said.

"Really? Or do you not care because all she is to you is the woman that wouldn't give you the time of day? I've seen the way you look at her," Max countered.

Marcus could feel his face flame. It was the truth. He did originally have a strong attraction to Alex. And maybe those feelings were still there in some ways, but she was very clear that she was still mourning her dead husband. Marcus had never crossed that line once it was drawn. After that, they became good friends. They shared a bond over the children, which Marcus enjoyed being with. They made him laugh, reminding him that life was more than zombies and surviving. It was about living too. Alex's children, Max's daughter, Aiden, the teens, were all the proof that the human race would survive beyond them. He and Alex saw eye to eye on that.

"Max," Margaret started, her tone warning.

"What? It's true isn't it?" Max argued.

"It is true," Marcus replied. He took a deep breath, calming the butterflies in his stomach. "Yes, you are right. I've always been attracted to Alex."

A snort sounded and Marcus turned to look at Easton. He rolled his eyes. The boy had always known how Marcus felt and initially hated him for it.

"Ok, so everyone knew," Marcus said.

"I didn't," Cliff said with a quiet voice.

"Thanks, Cliff. That attraction doesn't matter. I have never made any advances on Alex. She is still mourning Blake. I know that. We are friends, good friends. And I care about her as much as anyone," he finished.

"Of course, you do. Max is just speaking out of anger and

that's not going to solve any problems right now. We are all upset that Alex has been taken. And we need to work together to get her back safely. The smart thing to do is take every able-bodied adult that isn't protecting this compound and the kids," Margaret said.

"So, this family you met is going to join us?" Rafe asked.

"Yes. I told them we would pick them up in town. They'll give us the directions we need to get to the brothel where we're assuming Alex is."

After a long silence and small talk, everyone agreed they would prepare and be ready to leave at first light. Rafe stormed outside with Charlie close on his heels. Max sat, stoic at the table as if she wasn't sure which direction to go first. After a whispered conversation with Griffin, the two of them stood and went toward their bedroom. After a few minutes, Marcus was left alone at the table. He felt like the entire world was sitting on his shoulders. His stomach churned, and he realized he was going to throw up. Jumping up he ran for the door, making it just to the corner of the house before his stomach emptied itself. The burn of the bile in his throat felt like a punishment he deserved. He could feel tears prick his eyes when he thought about what could be happening to Alex.

"This isn't your fault," Margaret's voice came from behind him. She stepped up and held a cloth out to him. Marcus took it and wiped his mouth and damp face.

"Yes, it is. I made the wrong decision again. She's always telling me to wait and work together. I thought it was the right choice, to lead off the horde so she could save the living."

"There was no way to know the living were kidnappers. It sounds like the whole thing was staged. They probably led the horde right to you and then made it seem like they were in danger."

Marcus hadn't thought of it that way before, but it made sense when Margaret said it. How else would they have so easily trapped Marcus and Alex in their plan?

"Thank you, Margaret. I doubt Max and Rafe share your feelings. But I appreciate it," Marcus said.

"They'll come around. Right now everything is colored by fear and anger for what could be happening to Alex," Margaret said, her voice breaking at the end. She cleared her throat and blinked her eyes quickly.

"She means a lot to all of us," he said softly, laying his hand on the woman's shoulder.

"Yes, she does. She brought me here. Gave me a place in the family. I couldn't be more thankful for that."

"We'll get her back. I know it. If anyone can survive being kidnapped, it would be Alex. She's too strong to allow trash to break her," Marcus said with more conviction than he felt inside. It was what he needed to believe, because without that, he wouldn't know how to fight.

After his stomach finally returned to normal, Marcus went back to the truck he had brought into the compound. It had been left at the bottom of the hill where Rafe and Max had found him arriving without Alex. They didn't give him the chance to park the truck near the house before all of them stormed up the hill to have the family meeting. He carefully brought the truck up near the storage units that were next to the barn. Here in the quiet, with no one around, he unloaded the boxes of meals and blankets they had scavenged from the FEMA site. He left one box in the truck, thinking it would be good to have on their mission to rescue Alex.

Marcus sat on the tailgate and made a mental list of what needed to be done. The sun was crossing halfway in the sky, starting toward late afternoon. There was still so much to do. Make sure there were enough supplies for Margaret to feed everyone while they were gone. Ensure Easton had weapons loaded and within reach in case of intruders. He wondered what they would tell the children about all the adults leaving. Jack, Max's daughter, was old enough to realize something had to be wrong. Marcus decided he would leave it to Max to tell the kids what she wanted. He didn't want to frighten them unnecessarily. Even when the situation felt dire.

He went back to the bunkhouse where he, Cliff, and Issac slept. It was really a building meant to be an oversized shed. But Mitch Duncan had insulated it, added additional windows, and a bathroom. Then he lined both walls with bunks. With the men claiming beds, they still had six beds available. Standing in the middle of the large room, Marcus wondered, not for the first time, what Mitch thought would happen to the world that a building with this many beds was needed. He guessed it was what Alex talked about from time to time. Opening the door to those in need and allowing the compound to grow. After what happened the day before, Marcus didn't want to trust anyone.

As that thought crossed his mind, he was also reminded of the kindness of Claudia Vega. They didn't have to open their door to him. Her son and brother would have liked to shoot him, rather than feed him. However, the woman stepped in and provided shelter to him for the night. Now, the men were going to help the Duncans get Alex back and hopefully find their missing family member as well. There was kindness in that family, and it lit a small flame in Marcus. He knew how Alex felt, about not turning her back on everyone. Once he got her back, he would first shake her senseless and then they would discuss a better way of determining who was friend or foe.

Marcus was loading his 9mm when the door to the bunkhouse opened. Max entered and Marcus was on alert immediately. He took his 9mm and the loaded shotgun, trying to hide them behind him on the bunk. He didn't want Max having access to anything that could harm him. She noticed the movement, and a smirk came to her face.

"Ya know, if I wanted to kill you, I wouldn't need a weapon to do it," she said.

"So noted," Marcus replied.

"I figured I'd find you hiding out in here."

"I'm not hiding. I was loading my weapons. I have food loaded in the truck I brought back as well, ready to go..." Marcus said, defending himself. Max cut him off.

"Ok, wrong choice of words. I didn't mean hiding. Look, Griffin told me I had to come out here. Told me I should apologize."

"And you're just making him think you did what he wanted?" Marcus asked.

"I guess. I am sorry I slapped you. I shouldn't have done that. But I'm angry, so angry, that you let my sister get kidnapped," Max said. Her voice was less full of venom, more of sadness.

"If it helps, I'm angry too. And scared. But we'll get her back."

"What makes you so sure?" Max asked.

"Because, she's Alex. She can survive anything," Marcus said.

"I hope you're right," Max said, then she looked at her boots, discomfort clear on her face.

"What is it, Max?"

"I'm sorry for calling you out about your feelings. That was really messed up of me."

Marcus had to admit he was surprised by her sudden apology. He figured that she enjoyed putting him on the spot in that way.

"Thanks. I figured everyone knew anyway," he said.

"Well, it wasn't right to put you on blast. I'm sure it's not easy being in your shoes."

"What shoes are those?" He asked, genuinely curious about where she was going with this.

"Wanting to be with someone that doesn't want to be with you," Max said.

"Well, cut right to the heart there, Max."

"Sorry. I'm just saying, it must be hard to be around her all the time."

"It's not. I came to terms with things pretty early on. It's not like I can just turn my feelings off. Alex is an amazing woman. She has become my best friend in the apocalypse. And I'll do anything I have to, to get her back safely," he said.

Max nodded her head and left without another word. Marcus sat on his bunk awhile longer, just looking at the closed door. The youngest Duncan always burned hot at first, but she came down from it on her own schedule. He admired how strong she was and couldn't blame her for any of her actions. However, being on the right ground with Max made him feel more confident in their mission. He continued with his loading of the magazines for his 9mm. He checked and double-checked everything was close by to strap on first thing in the morning. Once he was satisfied, he went in the search of dinner.

He was greeted with delicious smells as soon as he entered the main house. Margaret and Candace were together in the kitchen, stirring and chopping. He found Billie, Henry, and Jack sitting in the family room with a cartoon movie playing. Marcus was pretty sure he had seen this one at least five times, but he sat down next to Henry, anyway. It didn't take long for the little boy to grab his arm and hug it to him. It was the way he cuddled while watching movies and Marcus wouldn't pry his arm out even if zombies were trying to eat his face. The warmth and trust he felt through Henry's cuddles made him feel more human than anything could in the world they were living in now.

Marcus wondered if Henry would cuddle him the same if he knew his mother was taken, because of something Marcus had done. He tried not to think about losing the trust of the children, who had become dear to his heart. They played and laughed. They had serious conversations about the way life was now. Billie on occasion had gotten a hold of his hair, brushing, combing, and trying to attach bows to the short hair. Usually she became bored because he didn't have enough hair to do all the styles she wanted. More than once they had fallen asleep together on the couch, after long days of chores.

Dinner was more somber than they were used to. The children chattered happily at their own table, oblivious to the discomfort at the adult table. Marcus had been starving before the food was served, but now it tasted like sawdust on his tongue. He knew that had nothing to do with Margaret's cooking. He stared down at the bowl of fresh tomato soup, homemade bread, and pork chop sitting in front of him. During his inner monologue he told himself he needed the fuel. And wasting food during the apocalypse was something Alex would seriously lecture.

"Eat," Cliff said. The man sat to his left, and he softly elbowed Marcus to get his attention.

"I know this is hard. But you have to eat," Cliff continued quietly.

"Right. Because we need to be ready first thing in the morning," Max added, overhearing their quiet conversation.

"I'm ready," Marcus said.

"Tell us more about this family you met and have partnered us with," Rafe said.

Marcus took a deep breath. He started by telling them he saw a little boy running between houses. He then talked about Vera and how she welcomed him with her mother Claudia. With a grimace he talked about the healing wound on Vera's face. Margaret shook her head sadly when Marcus went into more details about how she received the injury and how she escaped from her kidnappers, but without her sister. He finished by describing the men of the family and their determination to get Sylvia home.

"Why do they think she's alive?" Rafe asked when Marcus finished.

"I'm not sure. They seem to believe that the Noble Lord keeps the women alive as long as they are of use to him. Some are kept to do the cleaning of the compound. Some are there to work in other ways..." he trailed off as his stomach felt sick again. He couldn't picture Alex being used and violated.

"I guess they need to know for sure either way," Max said.

"The unknown is the hardest," Marcus agreed.

They talked longer about logistics and plans. While they sat, Marcus made sure to take bites of his food, filling his body with the fuel he needed. When they broke from the table, Marcus went to the kitchen to help with the dishes. He and Cliff worked in silence as they washed and dried all the items used to make and serve dinner. The chore was methodical, keeping his mind away from the turmoil and chaos that was trying to force its way to the forefront. In a way, it also reminded him he was part of a group, a family, that sat to eat dinner together and cleaned dishes. He knew not many were so lucky.

Once the dishes were put away, Henry convinced Marcus to read to him before bed. Sitting in Alex's room, where Billie and Henry shared their mother's bed, Marcus felt a lump form in his throat. He choked his way through a chapter of *Harry Potter and the Sorcerer's Stone*, with Henry and Billie cuddled up on either side. Marcus felt like he was in a haze as he tucked them in, kissing them on their heads. He felt like a fake and a failure for losing their mother. His own stupidity had allowed her to be with men they didn't know from Adam. And now he was tucking in children that should be tucked in by their mother. They trusted Marcus and the story the adults had told them so much that they never asked again where Alex was.

He all but stumbled into the bunkhouse, startling Cliff who was loading his weapon on his bunk. Marcus didn't want to talk. He didn't want to tell anyone else that he was ok, or that he was sorry. His emotions couldn't handle going over and over how he had messed up. Without a word he stripped and climbed into his bed. Cliff had his own demons, Marcus knew. The man could easily tell that Marcus was in no place to talk and to his credit, he never spoke. Marcus listened as the quiet man finished loading his gun and extra magazines. He then went about packing a bag, moving quietly to the small dressers they had at the end of the bunk beds. None of them had a lot, but they had started to gather necessary wardrobe items that they didn't come to the compound with.

Cliff climbed into his bunk across from Marcus without a word. As if to give Marcus his privacy, he turned toward the wall, not making eye contact before trying to fall asleep. Marcus laid there in the dark for a long time. His body and mind were beyond exhausted. The night before at the Vega house, he couldn't find sleep. Not with the horrible ideas of what was happening to Alex in his mind. He admitted there was also fear there. Fear of what was happening to her, but also fear of what her siblings would do to him when he came home. With that part out of the way, exhaustion pounded at his mind and his eyelids closed slowly.

The opening of the bunkhouse door was his alarm clock just before dawn. A small lantern shined light until the switch was thrown and the few lights in the room came on. Rafe stood at the door and whistled quietly. Marcus sat up immediately and began to throw his legs over the edge of his bed. Rafe didn't say anything as he turned and left the building. The plan was to get out of the gates before the sun rose. They would get to the Vega home just as dawn broke. Mateo and Albert would be ready to join their party then. From there, luck willing, they would drive straight to the brothel ran by the Noble Lord. In his gut, Marcus was sure nothing would go as smoothly as they wanted. However, a plan to try was better than going off half-cocked.

"Did you sleep?" Cliff asked.

"I guess so," Marcus replied.

He couldn't remember falling asleep and was sure he didn't dream. But suddenly it was pre-dawn, and they were getting ready to go. He guessed his body took over and did what it needed to.

"Good. Can't be tired today," Cliff said.

"Lack of sleep couldn't stop me today," Marcus said with determination.

Cliff just nodded and laced up his boots. With guns and bags, the two exited the bunkhouse and went straight to the truck Marcus was driving. He loaded up the remaining supplies and double-checked again what they had. He was carrying the majority of the food, though everyone carried enough for three days on their own. The Duncans knew how to make a meal ready to eat, or MRE, last more than one day when they needed to. Marcus also made sure the large first aid kit that he had put together was where he had stored it. Charlie had given him some of her clinic supplies to add to the kit, in case anyone was severely hurt. Having Charlie with them would be a benefit if a shootout occurred and emergency triage was needed.

While Marcus and Cliff drove the new truck, Rafe, Charlie, Max, and Griffin drove in Rafe's pickup. Storm, who accompanied Rafe everywhere, sat on the backseat between Max and Griffin. Marcus led the way to the gate. The first step of the plan was for Marcus to lead the way to stop one, the Vega home. He pulled into the trees and as practiced he waited for Rafe to pull through and close the gate. All eyes were in the surrounding trees, making sure none of the dead snuck into the compound. Or worse, living intruders. Once the compound was secured, the procession began to move again. Marcus knew the road in the dark and only had his fog lights on to barely illuminate the main road. The trucks turned onto the main highway easily, not another vehicle in sight. They both switched on headlights at the same time as they picked up speed toward town.

The road hadn't changed much in two months. The same accidents were to either side of the highway. Many the Duncan clan had moved to clear the way to and from the compound. Marcus didn't notice much as they arrived into town. The sun was just turning the sky pink in the East as they pulled up in front of the Vega house. The Bronco Marcus had left was sitting in their driveway now. Marcus turned off the engine and Rafe followed suit. Sitting in the truck, Marcus and Cliff exchanged glances. Marcus knew their plan wouldn't be easy. The smell of decaying flesh permeated the cab of the truck, as infected began to descend, drawn by their vehicles.

"Nothing is ever simple," Marcus said.

CHAPTER ELEVEN

"Gone? In what capacity?" 'The Suit' asked.

"All of the Duncans, except the children from what I can tell, have left the compound," Callahan replied.

'The Suit' had been surprised by the call from Callahan. Typically, the Major didn't call, as he rarely had good news to report. 'The Suit' almost snorted thinking about how Callahan didn't want to have his throat ripped out on every phone call. Now, his information had 'The Suit's' mind racing. Where could they be going?

"This isn't normal behavior, sir," Callahan continued.

"What makes it abnormal?"

"The few other times my men have been on recon missions, they have only seen two or three leaving the compound at once. Something must be going on. Also, unless the men didn't have a clear view, it sounds like one Duncan was missing. The oldest sister," Callahan explained.

"So, go in and get the kids," 'The Suit' said.

"I don't think we want to waste our resources there, sir."

"Explain."

"It's doubtful anyone left at the compound has the information we're looking for. If we go in and get their children, the Duncans will be a more volatile group to deal with. I think it would be better to find out where they went."

"And do you have any ideas?" 'The Suit' asked.

"No leads yet, sir. But my men are still in the area. They should be able to determine where the caravan of vehicles went," Callahan replied.

"Are there any indications that they could be moving from their Montana compound?"

"Unlikely. Frankly, the place is a fortress. They won't find the same security or food resources in other places," Callahan said.

"Keep me posted," 'The Suit' said, hanging up without allowing Callahan to continue.

Turning to his bank of monitors, 'The Suit' began to cycle through the satellite feeds he still had. Movement that caught his eye was the infected wandering the streets. He found one large horde that seemed to wander the area around the Wal-Mart. He watched them for a moment, trying to determine a direction. But after they circled in on themselves, 'The Suit' realized nothing had their attention. After a few more minutes of scrolling through video, he was sure he didn't see anyone actually living out in the open.

It had only been a few days since he saw the oldest Duncan woman take the supplies from the FEMA camp at the school. And now she seemed to be missing. He wondered if they could be lucky and the infected finished the job Callahan couldn't seem to complete. If they had to kill one at a time, that's the way it would go. Eventually all of the Duncans would be dead, and 'The Suit' could rest easy with their secret staying secret. Even the doctors working in his underground lab, didn't know where the plague originated. Taking control of the narrative was 'The Suit's' goal. He fed them a story of an attack from a world power and let them fill in the blanks on their own.

He sat back in his luxurious chair, comfortable in his hidden bunker. He could see the light at the end of the tunnel where the Duncans disappeared one at a time. He had taken down the entire US government. No way one small family was going to be the wrench in his plan.

CHAPTER TWELVE

"What in the hell is a dead brothel?" Alex growled.

Standing outside the old civic center building, Alex began to struggle with her captors. She knew it was futile, but she wouldn't walk willingly into something called a brothel, let alone one that had the word dead in its title. Instead of answering her question, a second man grabbed one of her arms and together the two practically lifted her from her feet as they walked toward the door. The front windows were all broken out and boarded. Alex imagined at one time the building was beautifully cared for. Now there were boards replacing glass, with squares cut out for the barrels of rifles to fit through. Some openings held eyes, that followed them as they walked across the street. A catcall came from one window and Alex began to fight even more.

"You have a wildcat there!" Another voice came, yelling from a window above.

"The Noble Lord is going to love her," a reply came from another lookout.

The men dragging Alex laughed along with the other men, but as she fought, they strained to keep a handle on her. With her hands bound behind her again with handcuffs, Alex had little leverage to do any damage that would give her a chance at running. She was also sure if she did start running, the lookouts wouldn't hesitate to shoot her down in the street. She imagined that was where many of the bodies came from that lay decaying at their feet. In her mind she knew that many of the recently dead on the ground weren't infected before dying. She averted her eyes from the bodies as she realized there were also bodies of children laying haphazardly across the road.

Panic rose in her mind and she tried to push it to a dark corner of her brain. She needed all of her focus on what was happening around her. To keep herself distracted, she counted windows, guns that she could see, and men that watched her. When she got to fifteen men, she found it harder to push the fear away. She didn't know what she expected of the Noble Lord's operation, but she found herself shell shocked at the size. Her mind flashed to Marcus. She wanted to believe he was coming for her. That he had gotten her siblings and would come hurtling in to save the day.

However, her fear was screaming at her. She was on her own. How would they find her now? She wasn't able to leave any sort of sign for them. No breadcrumbs or clues to where the gang of men had carted her off to. She thought back to when they had tracked down Rafe after he had been taken by the military. They had clues from the town people that saw him abducted. Alex wanted to scream thinking how they had taken her in an empty alley. No one could have seen them.

Desperation fueled her need to fight against her captors. Her hands were useless behind her, but that wasn't going to stop her. Stepping close to one captor, Alex lifted her leg quickly and snapped out a sidekick at the legs of another man trying to hold her. His leg collapsed under him and as he went down, Alex was ready, bringing her foot up to kick the man in the face. His head flew back, causing his body to follow. Blood flew from his mouth, spraying across Alex's face. When his head bounced off the ground, Alex pulled away from the second man holding her. She only quickly registered the look of surprise on his face when she pivoted and kicked him in the stomach, her leg snapping back to the ground from the rear kick.

"Goddamnit, grab her!" Lewis yelled from the doorway he was about to walk through.

His face was beet red and Alex wanted to make a comment about blood pressure. She didn't have a chance though, as arms wrapped around her from behind. The man lifted her off the ground and her legs flailed. Throwing all of her weight forward the man grunted as he had to follow her momentum. Alex continued her throw as the man came dislodged from her middle. She turned slightly, allowing the man to fall over her. The bitter woman in Alex felt fulfilled as she kicked the man in the groin, with a running start as if she were a star soccer player.

The telltale sound of a gun being cocked near her ear caused Alex to stutter to a halt in her fight. The cold metal touched her cheek and pressure was used to turn her head. The determination in Alex froze like ice in her veins as her eyes met the fury in Lewis' stare. He pressed the gun's sharp front sight into her throat. Alex had the sick feeling that he had sharpened the small piece of metal into a point for this exact reason. She could feel a trickle of blood drip down her neck as she stared at him. Alex wouldn't flinch. She wouldn't give him any leverage over her. He wouldn't know how scared she truly was.

"The Noble Lord only cares about your face. The rest of you can be as ugly as I want to make it. You can still please the men with a few less fingers," Lewis said, his voice laced with menace.

"Anyone that tries to touch me will end up losing more than fingers," Alex said through gritted teeth.

"You don't know when to give up, do you?"

"Never," she replied. Her voice was stronger than she felt at that moment.

The two of them stood, staring at one another. Lewis' red skin tone didn't decrease as Alex continued to refuse to bend to his will. She stared directly in his eyes as he slid the razor-sharp sight down her neck to her collarbone. The sting of the cut was continuous as her skin was broken. She refused to even blink in a way that would show her pain. Lewis wanted her to hurt and Alex wasn't in the business of helping kidnappers.

The standoff was interrupted by a man coming out of the building. He was surprisingly well dressed in dark khaki slacks and a polo shirt. His shoes were brown shiny leather. He walked toward Lewis and Alex carefully, picking his way around the dead bodies that lay in his path.

"Lewis, what is going on here?" The man asked in a clipped, no-nonsense tone. Lewis spared a glance at the man before removing the sharp point from Alex's body. He turned to face the well-dressed addition.

"Clive, please tell the Noble Lord I've brought him a new toy."

"Where is Bambi?" The man called Clive asked, without looking in Alex's direction.

"She jumped from our moving vehicle. We couldn't get her back," Lewis said.

"The Noble Lord won't be pleased to hear this," Clive replied.

"I'll explain it. We chased her down just like he asked. But she ran and got away once. Then she jumped from the van when it was moving. The dead have her now."

Clive sniffed in a dismissing manner, as if to say Lewis and his explanation would never be good enough. Lewis was clearly used to the attitude toward him because he didn't even attempt to straighten his perpetually slouched stance. Alex was trying to determine the hierarchy between the men. It was clear Clive felt superior to the dirty gang member. But Lewis didn't seem very concerned with his judgement.

"I'm no one's toy," Alex said breaking the silence.

Neither man spared her a glance. The clear dismissal infuriated her, and she began to pull against Lewis' grip on her arm. Still ignoring her, he shoved her into the waiting arms of a man. Alex could feel the blood flowing into her face, her temper rising.

"The Noble Lord has been alerted to your arrival. Clean this up before you come to his office," Clive said as he motioned to the two men struggling to get to their feet. Alex hadn't permanently damaged either of them. However, she found herself hoping they felt like they had been hit by a semi-truck.

"Yes, sir. We got this," Lewis responded with a hint of sarcasm.

Clive narrowed his eyes momentarily. Alex held her breath, hoping for a confrontation between the men. When Clive just smiled ruefully at Lewis and walked away, Alex felt deflated. Lewis waited until Clive disappeared inside before turning to address the men.

"You morons need to get it together. The Noble Lord isn't going to pay us anything if you are sniveling all over the street," he barked out.

The men tried to brush themselves off and look capable. Alex stifled a laugh, knowing how easy it was to take down most of the men when they weren't armed. But, knowing they were going to see this Noble Lord they all worked on looking tough and a semblance of worthy soldiers. As Alex was pushed forward, she intentionally dragged her feet, tripping over the dead bodies. She forced the man holding her to slow down and support more of her body weight. She looked around, her mind trying to come up with a plan. Her eyes landed on Lewis and she found him staring at her, his gun in his hand again.

"I see the wheels turning, bitch. Don't even think about trying to run again."

"I'll be thinking of nothing else until I kill you," Alex said. Her voice was light and casual. Completely contrary to the thundering of her heart.

Lewis just continued to stare as she was forced to the open

door of the Dead Brothel. The entrance was dark and musty. The smell of decay and unclean bodies hung heavy on the air. The blanket of stench smacked Alex in the face and she had to breathe through her mouth to stop herself from gagging. As her eyes became accustomed to the dim light, she looked around the long lobby. Men watched her from their posts at the windows. Some sneered, others catcalled. Alex just ignored them, working to memorize the set-up in the room. If she had the chance to escape, she would take it. And she couldn't risk being lost in the cavernous building.

The inside of the building boasted tall ceilings and ornate decorations on the walls. Alex could see where construction had been in process in the old world. Now the tools were in disarray, holes in the walls were uncovered and the scaffolding was now used to post shooters at high windows. Graffiti marred the beautiful old walls. Words of adoration for the Noble Lord and graphic depictions of sexual acts were the greeting to any visitor. Alex hated the Noble Lord even more now that she saw the destruction of what was once a beautiful building.

"What do we have here?"

Alex's attention was brought around by a female voice. Behind the bars of a ticket booth a woman studied Alex with hard eyes. One of her eyes was swollen and bruised, a gift from any number of men around them at the moment. However, the woman didn't seem to be in the booth against her will. A cigarette hung from thin lips, smoke curling around her face. Her hair hung in oily strands, clearly, she was a brunette but had bleached her hair. Now roots showed prominently. She raised her eyebrow at Alex as she realized Alex was just staring at her without saying a word.

"A new piece for the Noble Lord," Lewis said proudly.

He moved forward and the woman flipped open a large book that sat on the counter behind the bars. She flipped pages, scanning the names and dates from what Alex could see. Lewis was clearly feeling impatient as he shifted from foot to foot.

"Also, we brought the Noble Lord's property that this woman tried to steal. That should get us extra rations."

"We shall see, Lewis."

Lewis leaned against the counter, trying to look alluring. Alex thought he just looked like a dirty clown.

"Come on, Bets. Do me a solid. My boys and I worked hard for this one. And we stopped thieves from getting his stuff," Lewis said.

The woman called Bets grunted noncommittally and continued her search. When she finally found the page she was looking for, Lewis stepped back uncomfortably. Alex felt intrigued about what the book held and what would put the look of apprehension on the gang leader's face.

"Lewis, you are still in the hole for the last advance you were given. And Clive said you lost the pet, so that's not going to help you," Bets said.

"I'll discuss it with him," Lewis said. He then grabbed a handful of Alex's hair, pulling her head back painfully.

"This one is full of fire. She's worth more than that pet plus one."

"That woman has a name. It was Leona. She was no one's pet. Neither am I," Alex said.

Another grunt from Bets who was noting something in her book. No one paid any mind to Alex's sudden statement. She realized that these people were probably used to outbursts, screaming, and fighting. Nothing Alex did would surprise them. Suddenly, Clive appeared again, and he motioned to Lewis to follow him. Shifting his grip to Alex's handcuffed wrists, Lewis pushed her forward. Alex tripped at the sudden thrust and Lewis tightened his hand painfully on her arm. She tried to pull away once, but his fingers cut into her skin and she decided to save her energy.

As they walked away from the lobby, they passed by a large staircase. Three men stood at the bottom, looking bored. Alex could see light streaming from open windows and a curve that led the stairs toward the back of the building. She tried to slow her steps, hoping to see someone coming or going from the stairs, but there was no movement. When she began to pull away from Lewis again, he yanked her roughly to push her through the open door at the end of the lobby. The next room was at least triple the size of the lobby, with huge ceilings. Exposed beams went across the roof. Hanging from the beams were makeshift walls, created from thick canvas that hung to the floor. Crude openings were cut into sections of the canvas to create doors to the rooms.

The sounds were the first thing that struck Alex. Soft crying echoed from somewhere far off. The angry words of a man bounced off the walls, reaching Alex and turning her stomach. The sound of slapping flesh, whether in anger or forced passion, she couldn't distinguish. Self-preservation demanded that she try to flee as she began to backpedal. A man came through one of the nearby canvas openings, buttoning his pants and carrying his shirt in his hands. He glanced over at Alex as Lewis struggled to continue forward motion with her.

"She new here?" The man asked.

"Maybe. The Noble Lord will meet her and decide if she's up to standards," Clive replied, in a tone that sounded like a car salesman instead of a man harboring the rape and torture of women.

"I like fresh meat," the man replied as he continued to get dressed.

"If you like your meat attached to your bones, you'll stay away from me," Alex hissed.

The men, minus Clive, laughed as if Alex was the stand-up comic of the apocalypse. Then with brutal force, the man whipped out a palm and slapped Alex across the face. Against her will, her head flew to the side. She stayed like that for a beat, before turning back and looking at the man. Blood welled from a split in her lip and she stared directly at the man as she slowly licked it. The man's eyes followed the movement of her tongue and Alex was sickened by the way his eyes grew hot. He reached down and adjusted himself without taking his eyes from her. Disgusted, Alex spit blood at the man's feet and waited for the next blow. Just as the man started to get angry, Clive stepped in front of him.

"If you want to hurt the property, you'll have to pay for the marks. You know the rules. And until the Noble Lord accepts her, she's not for sale. Come back later," Clive said, as he dismissed the man with a wave.

With one more look over her body, the man walked away without a word. It was the second interaction that clearly stated that Clive was in a place of power in the hierarchy. Alex put him on the list in her mind. The list she was keeping of the people she needed to deal with. Cutting down the organization from the top was her first goal. She realized it was a lofty goal, as she was still handcuffed, her hands behind her back, her shoulders beginning to ache. Until she was freed, she wasn't going to get much more done, so she went back to making her mental notes of the building.

At the end of the rows of makeshift rooms, an ornate set of double doors sat propped open. The lighting inside of the large room beyond was made up of lanterns and small candle flames. Warm firelight reflected on white walls. At the entrance, Lewis pulled Alex to a halt and handed her off to one of his gang members. Lewis followed Clive into the room and the two disappeared around the corner. Low voices could be heard, but words couldn't be distinguished over the noise from the large brothel. Alex stared at the flames leaping and dancing in the fireplace that took up a significant portion of the far wall. The heat it emanated could be felt across the room at the open doors where she was being kept.

Her gaze was blocked by a large man. Jerking herself back to the situation, Alex looked up at the imposing figure. The first thought that struck her was, he didn't look like a drug dealing, self-appointed ruler. His thick blond hair had a wave that was obvious with its length ending at his shoulders. Alex also noticed his eyes were blue. They weren't a beautiful blue like her sister's. There was a coldness in the man's eyes. His smile reminded Alex of the men on infomercials late at night, smiling and selling you all the things you really didn't need. That smile widened as Alex locked eyes with him.

"Hello. I'm the Noble Lord of Montana. You are?"

"Leaving. As soon as you let me out of these cuffs," she replied.

A deep rumble of laughter came from the Noble Lord's chest, joined by other hoots of amusement from the surrounding men. They clearly took their cues from him, not reacting until they saw how their leader would.

"Well, I'm not sure I can call a beautiful woman like yourself a name like Leaving, but if that's what you prefer."

"I couldn't care less. I won't be here long."

Without a warning that Alex could detect, the Noble Lord struck out with a backhanded blow that threw Alex off her feet. Without her hands to catch her, she again hit her head when she went down. The earlier laughter died down and Alex tried to concentrate on the flames across from her as stars danced in her vision. The large man folded at the knee to get closer to Alex's vantage point.

"Something you will learn quickly; I don't allow mouthing off. However, you're new here. You'll learn the ropes first and then I'll expect you to fall in line," he said. His voice was even, without a hint of malice. His intended meaning was all he needed to enforce his will. Straightening, the Noble Lord turned to Clive.

"Take her to Coral. Tell her to get her cleaned up and presentable. Under all that dirt and blood, I can't tell what we have. Her body will fetch a decent price," he said.

The Noble Lord reached down and grabbed one of Alex's

arms, pulling her to her feet. He shoo'd off the men that attempted to help him, clearly having no problem getting his hands dirty once in a while. He pulled Alex close to him, crushing her breasts to his chest. He stared down into her face and Alex was again struck by how handsome the man was, but it didn't disguise the cold and ruthlessness underneath. She imagined he used those facts to feed his power over the people that fell at his feet. Without looking away the Noble Lord spoke.

"As my pet has been lost by Lewis, this may work as a replacement. We shall test her out after she's been cleaned up. No one else is to touch her, are we clear?"

No one argued with him. For the first time, Clive acknowledged her presence by taking her arm and moving her toward the door. The look on his face was one of disdain, as if handling her was far below him. His fingers were tight on her arm and Alex wondered how far she would get if she was able to break away from him. She couldn't run while her hands were cuffed. That would be a death sentence outside where the dead roamed. Alex wondered if that death would be better than what she could be facing.

Her mind conjured all the terrible things happening in the brothel. Clive walked her through the rooms again, winding away from the lobby where they entered. The screams from abused women and grunts of men taking their pleasure surrounded Alex. She longed to cover her ears and block out the horror she was walking through. In only two months this place had been created and women had been found to fill the rooms. Where had they all come from?

A blood-curdling scream stopped Alex in her tracks, causing Clive to run into her. They both turned to look back toward the sound. A woman, naked from the waist up, covered in blood, ran from a room. Her hand was held to her neck where blood continued to flow. Behind her the flaps of her room seemed to tangle and then a man stumbled through. It was clear how the injury had happened, his face was covered in blood. Alex could see from her vantage point that the man's eyes were black as night.

"He's turned. Let me go. Someone needs to kill him!" Alex screamed.

Her voice was lost in the commotion. Clive did nothing but turn them back to the hallway out of the brothel. He didn't acknowledge Alex's warning and she struggled to get away from him. Her thoughts whirled. The man was one of the infected. That meant the woman would turn next. The entire brothel could be a mass of death before they knew it. That was fine with Alex, though her heart hurt for the women. If she could get away from Clive, maybe she could help some of them before escaping herself. She was a sitting duck with her hands behind her back.

Before Clive began to climb the stairs, two gunshots rang out. Alex jumped and ducked slightly.

"Stupid woman. They don't shoot the merchandise. Climb," Clive said evenly.

"I'm not merchandise," Alex said.

Clive sniffed dismissively as was his habit and Alex fantasized about breaking his nose so he could never do it again. She decided that part of her escape plan should include that, and she felt a sliver of determination growing again. They would have to release her eventually if she was merchandise. And by then she would have a plan in place. A plan that would destroy the brothel, the Noble Lord, and get her back home.

The upstairs seemed to have escaped much of the destruction of the survivors. Where the downstairs walls were covered in graffiti, holes, and unknown stains, the upstairs was an off white. The color reminded Alex of walls that were painted long ago, a white that had darkened over the years as the building was used. But she was sure in the time before, the building was used for happy things. Happier than women being violated and sold, while armed men gunned down anyone that opposed. She tried to put herself in that happy place. It was a picture in her mind, she could almost feel it. Then a scream would reach her ears and she knew she was fooling herself.

A door opened after Clive rapped on it with his knuckles. A small grandmotherly woman held the knob and blocked them from entering. She looked at Alex, dismissing Clive as if she was used to the process. Alex looked between the woman and Clive, finding the man to look bored with the whole situation.

"Another new girl already? I just finished with the last. I need a break," the woman said.

"By demand of the Noble Lord, Coral," Clive replied.

"I figured that much out since you wouldn't bring anyone up here unless he demanded you do it. You tell him I need a break. I'll keep her here until I'm ready to get to work."

"He won't be thrilled."

"He'll deal," Coral said.

Without another word, Coral took ahold of Alex's arm and yanked her into the room. She shut the door in Clive's face, just as he looked ready to argue some more. For some reason, Coral didn't care about the Noble Lord and his demands. Alex wondered what power the woman had that she didn't fear retribution from the man. Clive didn't knock on the door again, leaving Alex in her care. Alex stood in the middle of Coral's room. She turned in a circle, taking in the vast expanse. The room looked like a dressing room, with mirrors, dressers, and makeshift closets full of clothes. A vanity sat against one wall, with a circle of lights surrounding a mirror. The table was covered with makeup, makeup brushes, perfumes, and many things Alex couldn't identify.

Alex had no idea what to say as she turned again to find Coral moving around the room as if Alex wasn't there. She used a small stove in the corner to boil water and pour a cup of tea. As the tea bag sat to steep, Coral dug a set of keys from her pocket. She went to the back of Alex and unlocked the handcuffs holding her wrists. Alex let her arms fall to her sides. She didn't have the strength in her shoulders to move them on her own. A screaming ache burned in her upper back, shoulders, and arms. She tried to rub at the areas, but she could barely lift an arm yet. She eyed Coral, as the woman finished making her tea. The question of friend or a foe came to Alex's mind. The old woman turned to look at Alex, a steaming cup in her hand.

"Tea?"

CHAPTER THIRTEEN

"Do you take sugar?"

Alex just stared at the woman in surprise. After what she had
been through the last two days, the woman was offering her tea.
The woman was older than Margaret if Alex was to guess her age.
Her long gray hair was braided to the side and hung over her
shoulder. She exuded a grandmotherly vibe, very different from
Margaret. When Alex first met Margaret, she was pointing a
shotgun at Alex's face. Thinking of the woman she had brought
back to the compound with her shot an ache into Alex's heart.

"It's not drugged, if that's what you're thinking," Coral
continued.

Alex hadn't been thinking that, but now that Coral suggested
it, Alex didn't think it was out of the realm of possibilities. Drugs
were flowing like currency in the brothel. Why wouldn't the
Noble Lord use it to create more compliant women? Alex just
continued to look at the woman warily. Coral wasn't fazed by it.
She turned with the cup and added two sugar cubes to it. After
stirring for a moment, she brought the cup to Alex and waited as
Alex found the strength to raise her hand and take the cup. The

warmth in the cup spread through Alex's fingers, causing her to sigh quietly.

"Why don't you sit down, girl?" Coral said, pointing toward a couch at the far end of the room. "You'll be here awhile."

"I'd like to leave," Alex said.

"I'm sure you would. But if you value your life, you should just obey orders."

"Is that what you do?" Alex asked.

"We all do what we need to, to survive."

"That's not really an answer. You know what is happening here. And you help," Alex accused.

"Sit down. Before you get yourself riled and do something you regret," Coral replied. Her voice was still soft and non-threatening. But Alex detected something under it, a warning of what she was facing.

Weakness knocked at the door of Alex's mind, as she realized she couldn't fight her way out when there were so many men guarding the building. She sat on the couch, cradling the tea between her hands. She took one tentative sip, allowing the warmth to infuse her body. She couldn't remember the last thing she had to drink, and she wanted to gulp the tea down. Coral seemed to know the drill, because the next thing Alex knew there was a large bottle of water and a bowl of soup sitting on the coffee table next to her. The smell made Alex's stomach growl loudly and Coral snorted slightly at the sound.

"They never bring them here fed and ready to work," the older woman said.

"They shouldn't bring anyone here in the first place."

"Maybe not. But the world isn't what it was," Coral said.

"So, this is the solution?" Alex asked.

"I'm sure you don't think so right now. But behind these walls, you'll be provided for and kept safe."

"Didn't seem like the woman that just got bit was kept safe.

You can't have a brothel with people coming and going like they do and not end up with the infection inside the walls," Alex said.

"Well of course the infection comes in. That's the idea. Why did you think this place was named the Death Brothel?"

Alex sat, in shock at what the woman was implying. The idea hadn't come to her, even after she saw the name outside. Her mind hadn't gone to that and she realized that was part of her problem. She couldn't think like the enemy.

"So, this is a place for men that have been bitten to get their last lay?" Alex asked, her voice incredulous.

"And women, I guess. There are a few men down there," Coral replied. She shrugged her shoulders. "It's what people find important. Drugs and sex."

"And the Noble Lord has made sure he can provide that in spades," Alex said.

"What do you believe you can do with this information? Asking questions isn't a safe practice here."

"Are you going to report me?" Alex asked. She looked at the woman, again wondering if she could think of her as a friend. Or if she was just an agent for the Noble Lord and did his bidding willingly.

"Nope."

Coral's response came without hesitation, giving Alex the sense that she could believe her. Setting the tea aside, Alex picked up the bowl of soup. She was surprised to find large chunks of meat in the broth. Remembering that she was accused of stealing from the Noble Lord, she realized they probably ate quite well in the brothel. Coral puttered around the room, but didn't bother Alex as she ate every bite of soup and drank half of the bottle of water. Once she was done, her body felt pleasantly sleepy. She wanted to curl up on the couch and sleep, knowing if she was going to escape at any point, she would need the energy for it.

"You're going to fall asleep sitting up," Coral commented.

The woman moved to a small curtained area that Alex hadn't

noticed before. Behind the curtain sat a bed with a wrought iron frame. It was ornate and pretty, completely out of place in the brothel. The room's one small window showed the light outside was waning and it was like a button was pushed in Alex. She was tired. As Coral motioned for her to follow, Alex stood and met her at the pretty bed.

"This is usually my room. But when I have a girl here, this is where she sleeps. The frame is good for, well, for keeping guests," she finished.

Alex's eye was caught by additional metal at the foot of the bed. When she looked closer, she realized it was a length of chain and a metal cuff. She swung her gaze back to Coral. Alex knew her eyes were widened in shock; however, she couldn't decide why she was surprised. Of course, the prisoners wouldn't be left on their own, where they could wander out at any time.

"Do you often have guests?" Alex asked.

"All the girls are brought to me before they are given a room downstairs."

"To do what?"

"Prepare them. Clean them. Find them clothes to wear," Coral said. As she spoke, she pointed to different stations in the room. Alex could see it now. She was the stylist for the brothel members. Alex felt ill.

"How could you?" Alex demanded.

"How could I not? You've been outside for a while. I can't survive that on my own. The Noble Lord found me hiding in an attic. I'm too old to work downstairs, so he gave me this job."

"It's not a job. It makes you an accomplice to him."

"Maybe. But it's not the way I see it. Now lay down before you fall down. I'm too old to pick you up off the ground."

Alex looked back at the door. Could she get away from Coral? Did the woman have any weapons? Alex doubted the Noble Lord would trust her enough for that. With the cover of night coming soon, Alex knew it would be dangerous to be out in the open without a weapon or sense of direction. Was it more dangerous than being in the brothel?

"Don't make plans, girl. There are armed guards everywhere. They won't hesitate to come after you. I heard they didn't get that poor Leona back. She's probably dead now too."

"I hope not. I helped her escape," Alex said.

"Well then, you already have one strike against you. They don't take kindly to women that don't obey. You are better off just making your peace with things," Coral said.

Without another word, the woman prodded Alex to lay down on the bed. She immediately placed the metal cuff around Alex's ankle. The process was fluid, Coral having many women to practice on over the time she had worked for the Noble Lord. She ran her finger along the inside of the cuff, ensuring it wasn't too tight against Alex's skin. Alex laid stiff and nervous, waiting to see what the woman would do next. Coral pulled the thin blanket over Alex and placed another bottle of water on the table near the bed.

"I know this is rough, but try to get some sleep. Things will look better in the morning light," Coral said.

Doubtful, Alex thought to herself. She didn't answer Coral, just turned her back to the curtain and waited for the woman to leave. The sound of swishing fabric and footsteps retreating let Alex know she had a small amount of privacy for the moment. She sat up in the bed immediately and tugged on the chain, testing its connection to the bed and to the metal cuff. The chain was welded to the bed and without tools there was no way Alex could separate the two. The chain was connected to the cuff by a thick metal hoop. She tried to pull her foot from the cuff, straining and scraping her skin.

She stopped, breathing hard. Looking around the small sleeping area, Alex couldn't find one thing that could be used as a tool or weapon. The set-up was prepared for the exact reason of keeping someone confined. Someone that didn't want to be there. It wasn't there for saving people that needed help, like Coral. It was for the women that were kidnapped and kept against their will. With that in mind, nothing was in the room except the bed, one blanket, and a small stool being used as a table. Even as Alex thought about using the stool as a weapon, she realized it was plastic.

Slowly she lowered herself back down to the bed. The sheets were strangely clean and soft. Alex pictured other women locked in a room doing the brothel laundry. There had to be a large amount of it. Her mind circled the meaningless subject as she laid quietly. With her thoughts away from her predicament, Alex felt her eyelids droop. She was tired. Her mind didn't want to close down, in fear of someone coming for her. Her body had other ideas. She sank deeply into sleep, with dreams colored of torture and the Noble Lord laughing at her as she screamed.

"Wake up, girl."

A voice accompanied a light shaking at Alex's shoulder. Feeling groggy, Alex opened her eyes and looked up at Coral. A pale light seemed to filter into the room, and Alex couldn't believe she had slept through the night. She felt suddenly alert, remembering why she was chained to the bed. Sitting up immediately, Alex rubbed her eyes as the other woman unhooked the metal cuff from her ankle. She moved the curtain for Alex to exit first.

On the small coffee table, a plate of biscuits and eggs sat, steam still rising from the eggs. A mug of black coffee sat next to it. Alex stood looking at it and Coral added a bottle of water as well.

"Eat up," Coral said.

"I'm not hungry," Alex lied.

Coral didn't say anything else, just picked up her own plate and began to eat. She watched Alex, waiting. Alex wanted to be stubborn. She wanted to throw the food at the woman and escape the room. But she still had no way of getting out. Her plan had stalled until she could get away from Coral and find her way downstairs without guards finding her. She finally sat down and took a bite of a biscuit. There was butter in the middle, making the biscuit soft and delicious. Drinking water to wash down the bread, Alex finished the biscuit in a few bites.

"So, you're going to be here with me a few more days. The Noble Lord had to leave late last night to handle business. I received a message that you will be kept here until he's ready for you."

"Why does he trust you?" Alex asked.

"Trust me to do what? Not help you escape?" Coral asked. At Alex's nod, she continued. "He knows I depend on him for safety. And he always has a backup plan."

"What's the backup plan?"

"Armed guards on this floor and at the foot of the stairs. They won't hesitate to kill you if you should escape. Then they would come for me, assuming I helped you. Which I wouldn't."

"What if you could be safe elsewhere?" Alex asked.

"No such place," Coral said.

An idea formed in Alex's mind. She knew it was a long shot. The Noble Lord didn't know about her home. If he did, they would have attacked them for their supplies by now, Alex had no doubt. Not to mention the women on the compound. Candace flashed in Alex's mind and she couldn't fight the shudder that ran down her spine. What would these men do to an innocent young teenager? She didn't want to know the answer to that. The idea of giving Coral sanctuary wasn't pleasant, but it could give Alex a bargaining chip. In the end, Alex decided to hold that chip close to the vest and not give away more information about herself than she needed to. Coral could turn around and tell the Noble Lord the plan and the location of the compound. Alex would die before putting her family at risk.

Her family. Alex looked into her eggs as tears threatened. Her babies, Billie and Henry, had no idea where their mother had gone. Alex was so thankful to know that her brother and sister would take care of them and keep them safe always along with Easton and Candace, the teenagers she adored. They had only been together for a short time. She wanted more of that. More time to teach them, become a family unit, know them. They were such good kids and she knew they would stay at Billie and Henry's side. Nothing could break her family unit. Not even her death.

"What's wrong, girl?" Coral asked, breaking into Alex's thoughts.

"My name is Alex. Not girl."

Shrugging her shoulders Coral said, "Doesn't matter. The Noble Lord will name you as he sees fit."

"My name is Alex. And it'll stay Alex."

"Say what you will. Everyone breaks," Coral said.

"With your help, I suppose," Alex replied.

"I have nothing to do with that."

"No? Seems you get the merchandise ready for sale. I'm sure girls come in here and see you, this grandmother looking figure. They get a shot of hope, thinking there's no way you could hurt them. But really, you're just plumping up the meat," Alex said.

As she spoke, Coral narrowed her eyes. She didn't like Alex calling her out. Alex just smiled. There was no joy behind the smile, only hatred. She wouldn't fall into complacency, no matter how well Coral fed her. She knew the place the woman held in the organization. The Noble Lord held her, but without chains or locks on her door. She stayed willingly. And helped the devil himself.

"Where are you from?" Coral asked.

"None of your business."

"Do you live safely? Have you had to do things you regret to survive?

"Nothing I can't live with. Can you say that?" Alex asked.

"I'm still alive. I can't change what I've had to do," Coral said.

A knock at the door put a stop to their conversation. Alex again wondered what position Coral held with the Noble Lord that afforded her such respect like not barging into her space. Coral turned and opened the door enough to look at the visitor. A hushed conversation followed, and Alex strained to hear what was being discussed. Coral shook her head making a tsking sound, clearly not agreeing with what was being requested.

"You can deal with his anger later," Coral replied as she slammed the door in the person's face.

She then turned to Alex, inspecting her again. Rifling through her drawers and hanging garments, Coral pulled out an assortment of items. She laid them on the couch next to Alex. She then went to the stove and placed a pot over the burner. While she messed with the bottles of perfumes, soaps, and makeup, Alex looked at the clothing sitting next to her. She could feel heat in her cheeks as anger flowed. The garments were barely enough to call clothing. Pieces missing, lace, ties, and leather seemed to be the general theme. Alex wasn't overly modest about her body, she stayed in shape. But how she chose to present it was one hundred percent her choice.

Alex couldn't touch the food in front of her any longer, feeling sick about what process was starting. Coral pulled a large metal tub near the stove and motioned to Alex. Alex didn't obey, just looked at the woman.

"Let's go. Time to get cleaned up," Coral said.

"I'd rather not."

"It's not really a choice."

"What happened to waiting for the Noble Lord to come back?" Alex asked, hoping to stall until she could escape the nightmare.

"Plans change around here all the time. You need to be cleaned up and ready for tonight," Coral said.

"What's tonight?"

"You might call it orientation," Coral replied.

"I'll pass," Alex said. She sat back into the couch with her arms crossed in front of her.

Coral sighed, annoyed with Alex's stubborn tactics. Without another word, she went to the door and opened it. She motioned to someone outside and a guard entered. His gun immediately trained on Alex.

"She needs some motivation to comply," Coral said.

The man didn't say anything. It was a well-rehearsed action. He was used to dealing with the women that fought the process. He moved to Alex's side and pointed his handgun, which Alex identified as a Glock G19 with a modified grip. She wondered absently who he stole the gun from. The gun rested against Alex's temple as she glared at Coral.

"Now, will you get over here before he has to shoot you," Coral said.

"I don't think he will. The Noble Lord likes his pets," Alex replied.

Alex didn't have much warning as the butt of the gun struck her across the jaw. She was knocked into the couch. It only took her a moment to recover, despite the stars she was seeing. As she shot to her feet, Alex had to rein in her pain and anger. She wanted to strike back. But when she turned to the man, his Glock was trained on her face. His eyes willed her to step out of line. He wanted to shoot her, would enjoy it, relish it. Alex wouldn't give him that satisfaction. She took deep breaths, working to bring her heart under control.

"He likes his pets, but he doesn't care about marks," Coral said. The gunman grinned at Alex then. She gritted her teeth and stared back, her eyes promising the man pain when she had the chance to get free.

"Just come here and get cleaned up. Then we'll see about putting something on your face, so you aren't too bruised for the Noble Lord," Coral said.

Alex knew she didn't have a choice. She walked woodenly to the space next to the stove. Coral bent and removed Alex's boots and socks. She turned to the gunman that was watching and shoo'd him back out the door, as if she knew Alex had reached a point of not resisting any longer. Once the man was gone, Coral motioned for Alex to remove her pants. She stood for a moment, staring at Coral. The woman just raised her eyebrow in challenge and Alex unbuckled her belt and unbuttoned her jeans. She slid the material down her body as Alex stood still as a statue. Coral grabbed her arm and made her step into the bucket.

Once there, Coral pulled Alex's practical underwear down and tossed them to the side. Alex's flushed as the woman inspected her body as if she were just a product to be sold. Next, she began to unbutton the flannel shirt that Alex was wearing. Underneath was her sports bra and Coral instructed her to raise her arms so she could remove it. Alex stood nude, in the metal bucket, shaking from head to toe. As Coral began to roughly scrub at her skin, Alex stared at the empty space above her head. A tear trickled down her cheek as embarrassment and anger pumped through her body. She crossed her arms across her breasts and Coral pulled them down as she thoroughly cleaned her chest.

Coral climbed up a small step stool and poured water over Alex's short choppy hair. As she washed, the woman talked about getting Alex a proper haircut. Alex didn't respond. In a moment of anger, Alex had chopped her long tresses off at the start of the plague. The long hair had been used against her and she couldn't risk having it happen ever again. Alex gulped down the emotion that rose to her throat and an image of her husband came to her mind. He had loved her long hair. When they made love, it would fall across his body. He would fist his hands in it to bring her face to his for his kisses. More tears fell from Alex's eyes, meeting with the soapy rinse water and were washed away before Coral could see.

The water was warm, but Alex was frozen to the core. She couldn't allow her mind to dwell on what was happening to her. If she began to think about being treated like livestock, panic would blind her to any chance of survival. Panic was the beginning of a breakdown that Alex had no time for. She tried to detach herself from Coral's attentions. In truth, the process was probably only five minutes. To Alex, it felt like a lifetime. When Coral wrapped a fluffy robe around her, Alex almost collapsed. She gripped the front of the robe to her body, wanting to stitch it to her skin, to never have to be naked again. Coral let Alex move back to the couch while she cleaned up the showering supplies.

On the couch, Alex tried to pull all of her body inside the robe. She felt violated, even if all Coral did was clean her. The old woman didn't seem phased by the process or by Alex's reaction. Alex's wet hair started to get cold and her shivering intensified. With all the supplies stored, Coral turned back to Alex. She brought a towel and rubbed it through Alex's hair. In a normal circumstance, having her hair washed and dried may have been relaxing. Against her will was as far from relaxing as it could get. Alex pulled her knees up and hid her face in the robe. She had showered normally the last few months, as the compound ran well on the solar-powered battery storage they had. Water came from the well and didn't rely on the city at all. However, being out, fighting the infected, and scavenging could make anyone filthy again.

"Almost done, girl. Then we'll get you some clothes to wear," Coral said. Alex lifted her head and glanced at the clothing again that sat on the couch.

"Those aren't clothes. They're scraps."

"They are what the Noble Lord and the guests prefer."

"I don't really care," Alex said.

"You'll need to adjust your attitude before you see the Noble Lord. He doesn't take kindly to his pets giving him lip."

"He'll have to adjust or kill me. I'm not going to just shut up. I'm being held against my will. I won't stop fighting to find a way out," Alex said and she pushed Coral away from her hair.

Alex was done with the woman touching her. She rifled through the items Coral had picked for her. She found the ones that seemed to cover the most skin and took them with her to the small bed alcove. Coral didn't try to stop her, just watched her as she went. Behind the curtain, Alex sat on the bed for a moment. *How do I do this?* She thought to herself. She weighed her immediate options. If she didn't get dressed and go where Coral told her, she could be harmed or killed by the gunman outside. If she tried to run from the room, the gunman was waiting for her. She went to the small window that was in the alcove. Looking out she couldn't see a fire escape or anything to use to get to the ground from the second floor. She could see guards wandering around the area, smoking cigarettes and laughing as they kicked the dead bodies that were in the street.

She was trapped. Her heart sunk with the realization she was without options. A horde of the dead would have been a welcomed situation. Something she could control. She knew what to expect with the dead. She knew how to fight them, knew how to end their lives. On the second floor of the old building, Alex knew she was up against a wall. She sank back down on the bed, wondering about her family. Hope was dangerous. She wasn't sure if she should allow herself the blossom of belief that someone would break her out of the brothel.

Resolution was the last thing she clung to. She would play the game for now. The Noble Lord would blink. And when he did, Alex would be ready to make her break. She was on her own. And going down without a fight wasn't in her DNA.

CHAPTER FOURTEEN

"Nothing is ever simple."

Marcus hit the steering wheel. Cliff just prepared his weapons. The walkie next to Marcus came to life.

"Well this looks fun," Max's sarcastic voice came across the air.

"Let's just start clearing them out. Albert and Mateo will come out to help. I'm sure of it," Marcus responded.

"We can handle this. Just get the people we need so we can go." It was Rafe's voice this time and Marcus guessed that he took the walkie from his smartass sister. They didn't have time to mess around.

Marcus pulled his knife, thinking a closer fight was going to be impossible to avoid. He jumped from the truck and immediately stabbed a small infected man in the head. The sound of slamming doors echoed and the Duncans were in full force. Griffin and Max fought well as a unit, watching each other's backs as they dispatched the dead. Rafe with his dog Storm took down infected on their own. Charlie sat behind the wheel of the truck now, ready for a fast getaway if necessary. Marcus noted all of this in the split seconds it took between kills. The infected seemed to just keep coming.

The sound of gunfire took Marcus by surprise and he looked up to see Mateo hanging out of the attic window again, his rifle at his shoulder. His shots weren't perfect, but he was trying to slow down the horde that was coming. Marcus was thankful he didn't try to shoot near the group of living on the ground, knowing one wide shot and they could be faced with a second emergency. Albert appeared from the side of the house, coming through the gated yard. He joined the hand to hand fight with the Duncans. His movements weren't as practiced and smooth as the Duncans. He wasn't someone who had trained all his life for the fall of society. But his blows to the infected were affective in bringing them down and ending them permanently.

Marcus didn't have a moment to be disgusted by the black gore that covered his hands. He grabbed the next infected by the throat as it snapped at him, wanting to rip Marcus apart. The skin of the throat was rough and decomposed, causing Marcus' hand to slide as he tried to push the infected away. He brought up the hunting knife and slammed it home in the infected's forehead. As the body fell a piece of skin stuck to Marcus' hand. He wanted to gag, he wanted to throw up. No matter how many infected he killed, the dead still grossed him out. Living in a horror movie, faced with every disgusting thing you watched and grimaced at, made for a very rough world.

A lull finally came, and Albert rushed them into the house. Max and Griffin stayed outside to deal with the straggling infected, while Charlie fussed over Storm and put him back in the truck to prevent him from following to the house. Rafe, Marcus, and Cliff followed Albert into the living room of the house. Here all of the men stood, breaths heaving as they fought to regain air into their lungs. Albert stood watching Rafe with surprise on his face. After cleaning their hands as best they could, Albert offered Marcus his hand and they shook.

"Hello again, Marcus," Claudia said as she entered from the kitchen. Vera was following close behind.

"Hello, Claudia. This is Rafe and Cliff. Two of the members of our compound with the Duncans."

"You promised to come back. And you did. I knew you would, despite what my doubtful brother said," Claudia said, shooting a look at Albert.

"You are as good as Marcus boasted. I didn't think that was possible," Albert said.

"I appreciate that Marcus had good words to say about our family. But I really don't think we have time for pleasantries. I don't wish to be rude, but we should get going before the infected gather again," Rafe said.

Albert nodded and headed up the stairs. Two backpacks already sat next to the door as well as rifles. Marcus looked to Vera and Claudia, suddenly nervous to leave the women alone in the house.

"Are you sure both Albert and Mateo should come? What if you need help?" Marcus said.

"I can shoot. And we have plenty of supplies. There should be no reason to leave the house until you all return," Vera replied.

"I understand that your daughters were also taken. That's where you got that?" Rafe asked, motioning to the long wound on Vera's face.

Vera nodded. "They are ruthless. I didn't want to leave Sylvia. But she made me. If one of us didn't get back here, no one would tell our family what happened and where she was. I fought a guard who tried to get me for free. He marked me up with his knife for resisting. I got lucky. The Noble Lord doesn't give anything away for free. The guard was killed immediately. I was damaged goods. So, I wasn't watched closely as I sat in my room bleeding. It was then I escaped."

"You walked all the way home? How did you make it?" Rafe asked.

"I hid in a nearby house first. Found it empty and the owners had left food behind. I drank the water from the toilet tank. I packed up what I could carry and set out. While at the brothel, I had found an old concert flyer. It had the address on it. I remember it. Once I knew where I was, it was easier to find my direction. It took me twelve days to walk home. I walked all day, sometimes into the night if I didn't find somewhere to sleep."

"So about five hundred miles. That means they are with Alex there now unless they went somewhere else," Rafe said.

"The men that work for The Noble Lord, they are desperate. Some are druggies. Some are criminals. But they are all loyal to the power the Noble Lord has. The guard he killed for trying to take me, he was tortured, not just killed outright. Everyone could hear his screams. They do those things publicly, so everyone knows what happens to those that cross him," Vera said then shivered, as if hearing the screams again.

"That's how he controls people from 500 miles away," Marcus commented.

"Yes. His strength has been spread by the men that follow him. They follow him because he has the drugs. He has illegal drugs but also a large store of pharmaceuticals. People go to him for all sorts of reasons," Vera said.

"How do we hit him? What's the weakness?" Rafe asked.

Marcus knew where his mind was, because Marcus was thinking it too. With a man that had a reach as far as their piece of Montana, how would their small group make any difference? Marcus couldn't help the fears of failure from squirming into his mind. It was like having worms in his brain. The fears burrowed into his thoughts, leaving their trail even after he pushed them away. Failure wasn't an option. He knew the Duncans would never give up when one of their own was missing. They would do the same for any on the compound. But Alex was different. She was the head of the family. She was the oldest sister. Rafe and Max would never leave their sister behind.

"I'm sorry, Rafe. I don't know. There are so many men. Some that come and go, with no schedule to predict. If somehow..." Vera trailed off, lost in her thoughts.

"If what, Vera?" Marcus asked.

"There are so many women inside. They are kept separated by makeshift rooms. But if you could get them to fight, stand up for themselves, they would add to your numbers."

"Do you think they would fight?" Rafe asked.

"I just don't know. I didn't meet many of them. The ones I did meet seemed broken and resigned to their fate."

"My Sylvia will fight," Claudia said, cutting into the conversation. She had watched the men listen to her daughter and the pride on her face was apparent. Her daughter had fought and escaped to come home. Now the information she had would save her sister and maybe countless other women.

"You don't know that, Momma," Vera said quietly.

"Yes, I do. I know my babies. And my girls are fighters. She just needs the chance."

Marcus chose to not mention the possibility that Sylvia was already dead. It sounded like while the Noble Lord needed the women for his business, he didn't allow anyone to cross him. Marcus could easily assume that he would kill a woman for the same offenses as a man. He found himself praying to whatever cosmic source out there that Alex didn't cause waves. He knew she was thick-headed and wouldn't do well with a man trying to abuse her. He could only hope they made it to the brothel before anyone laid hands on her.

The idea of Alex being violated made bile rise in Marcus' throat and he had to cough to stop himself from throwing up. After a few deep breaths he had himself under control and found Rafe looking at him. Marcus just shook his head, trying to clear the thoughts and to let Rafe know he was fine. He knew Alex. She would fight until she was broken and bleeding before allowing the Noble Lord to sell her off like livestock. Marcus had strong faith in all of the Duncans, but especially Alex. She was strong, caring, and sensible at all times. He knew before she was taken she was struggling with her responsibilities, but he had no doubt that she would rise to the pressure.

When Marcus tuned back into the conversation happening around him, he found that Vera was drawing a rough sketch of the building. Admittedly she didn't know much, only what she had seen while she was transported from room to room. She never saw where the Noble Lord stayed. She only saw him the once, when he took the guard for execution. She described a snake smile that tried to be charming, but it was from a killer. She didn't know who he surrounded himself with, but she was sure it was a number of men. The number of men in the building seemed to fluctuate with who was there to take advantage of the women or who was there to get supplies.

"What door did you escape out of?" Rafe asked.

Vera showed them a backdoor area she had drawn. "The guards tend to leave this door unlocked. I heard them talking about it. It's the fastest way for them to get to their post at the back of the building. The door is unlocked, but no one guards it. They assume the guards outside would catch anyone coming or going. They are lazy."

Rafe nodded and Marcus wished he could be a fly on the wall of his brain. He knew the one thing the Duncans had in common was planning. They always had a plan. They were always prepared for each scenario. With the limited information they had, the plan was going to be hard to create. But Rafe and Max would still insist on having the plan. Even if they needed Plan A, B and C. They all needed to know what they were supposed to do, to execute their plans. Marcus knew he was one that had the hardest time obeying the plan. He made a mental note to really try harder this time. Alex's life hung in the balance. And that was his fault in the first place.

Mateo and Albert joined them then, both armed with rifles

and hunting knives on their hips. Claudia disappeared into the kitchen for a moment. When she came back out, she had two packages in her hands. She handed them to Mateo and Albert. Mateo tried to scoff, but she silenced him with a look. They spoke quietly in Spanish. They could have been yelling and Marcus would still not have understood the words. His bout of High School Spanish had failed him long ago. It was clear that Claudia was giving them stern instructions. They both listened respectfully. Out of the corner of his eye, Marcus saw Vera swipe a tear from her face. He realized they were preparing their goodbyes. He hoped it wasn't necessary.

Rafe went to the door and had a hushed conversation with Max who was still standing guard. Once it was confirmed the coast was clear, Marcus, Cliff, and Rafe exited to give the Vega family time to say goodbye. It was a short moment later that Albert and Mateo joined the group, looking stoic. The men decided to join Marcus and Cliff in the truck they were driving. Rafe's truck was already fairly full with the two couples plus Rafe's dog, Storm. Communication was confirmed through the walkie talkies again. With everyone ready to go, Marcus was instructed to take lead as the Vega men would give directions.

On the road the four men stayed silent except for little comments on direction. Each had their own reason to be on the ominous mission. Cliff watched out his side of the truck, keeping an eye out for anything out of the ordinary. The thought made Marcus snort, which caused all three passengers to look at him. He shook his head at them and didn't comment on his inner monologue about how nothing was ordinary about fighting the dead who walked the planet. There was nothing ordinary with having to rescue women from a drug lord, who was now a self-proclaimed ruler. Somehow this was his life now and he accepted that. But it was far from what anyone would call ordinary.

"What was in the package," Marcus asked Mateo.

"Momma made tamales for us to have on the ride. She is afraid we won't eat," Mateo replied quietly.

"Tamales? That sounds delicious. When this is all over, maybe she'd make some for us."

"I doubt it," Albert said.

"The Duncans want to open the avenues of trade with the other living in the area. Maybe we could trade something you want," Marcus said.

"Milk. We have lots of milk," Cliff said sarcastically.

Marcus laughed a little at that. The adults had all gotten tired of drinking milk with each meal. But Alex insisted they use it while they had it and that it was a source of calcium that everyone needed. No one really argued because she made a good point. Margaret had also been working on fresh cheese and Marcus looked forward to trying that when she perfected the process. In the larger picture, Marcus realized how lucky they were. He agreed with Alex, Rafe, and Max about trading. Others didn't have the fresh foods that the compound had. Trading could bring supplies they didn't have and they could help people in the process.

"Mama would like the milk. I guess we'll see if we all survive this," Mateo said.

"We will. Have faith," Marcus replied.

"If we thought it was possible to get Sylvia back before, we would have done this already. This feels like a suicide mission. But since you were determined to go, we couldn't not come as well," Albert said.

"With the Duncans the odds will be more in our favor than you realize."

"Six additional people against thirty or more? You have your faith. I will keep my realism," Albert said.

Marcus didn't try to explain. They saw how Rafe fought. That wasn't even near the extent of his abilities in combat. There was no way to explain to the men how the Duncans were raised, how they had continued to live their lives and how they were prepared for anything. Even if Marcus told them the stories of the tight situations they had found their way out of, the men would probably assume Marcus was lying. Marcus knew that if he hadn't witnessed things since meeting up with Alex, he wouldn't believe it either. The family was the strongest force he knew. There was no way he would believe that a ragged band of drug addicts would be able to defeat them.

The sun was just reaching the middle of the sky when Marcus had to slowly bring the truck to a stop. The road was littered with dead bodies, but also walking infected that stumbled across the road. In a quick guess Marcus figured there were thirty infected at least. Cliff picked up the walkie talkie to reach out to the truck that was idling behind them.

"Infected blocking the road. How do you want to do this?" Cliff asked.

"Can we get around without having to handle them?" Max's voice came back across the speaker.

"Don't think so. Too many dead bodies. Someone fought here already or ran a lot of them down. We might get stuck," Cliff responded.

"Charlie will stay in this vehicle in case of an emergency. Pick one of you to stay behind the wheel to drive while the rest of us clean this mess out," Max said.

With the plan decided on, Marcus and Cliff readied their weapons. After some debate it was agreed that Mateo was the youngest of them, so he would stay with the truck. He grumbled about being faster than the old men. His complaints fell on deaf ears, as the men weren't going to change their minds. Marcus nodded to Cliff and Albert. They all jumped from the truck at the same time. As soon as they slammed their doors shut, the sounds of doors behind them let them know the rest of the hunting party had joined them. Moving to the first bodies in the road, Marcus grabbed the ankle of one and pulled it to the side of the road. The skin was papery and felt detached from the muscles below. The feeling made him think too much of what was happening with the bodies, so he tried to blank his mind.

The noise they made drew the attention of the infected that continued to walk. The collective growl and groans from the group gave Marcus goosebumps. The noise was a dinner bell ringing, calling all hungry infected in the area. Just behind him, Max chopped down two infected with her tomahawk. She sighed deeply, irritation coloring her voice when she looked over to Marcus.

"Let's get the road clear before they bring the whole family to the feast."

"Roger that," Marcus replied as he dragged another body off the road.

On the opposite side of the road, Cliff was mirroring Marcus' actions. Between the two of them they had the road fairly clear of bodies that blocked the trucks. Max, Rafe, and Albert watched their backs, killing those that tried to come up behind them. Marcus looked over to Cliff and saw an infected coming through the trees. Without a word, Rafe threw a blade that imbedded in the infected's head. It fell less than ten feet from Cliff's feet. Rafe stalked over to retrieve his blade and turned to work closer to Cliff.

It was this camaraderie that made the Duncans different from others that were surviving the plague. They never turned their back on each other. And that included everyone living on their compound. They didn't treat Cliff or Marcus any different than a Duncan sibling. Rafe stood watch over Cliff, cutting down the infected that came near them as Cliff continued to clear the road. Marcus could hear Max behind him and knew she was doing the same thing. It was this trait that earned Marcus' unwavering respect and loyalty. Nothing would pull him from the Duncans. They were good people. Doing the right thing, even as the world fell into despair. Even faced with the hardest situations, the siblings stayed within their moral compass as often as possible.

The vehicles inched forward every time Marcus and Cliff cleared a spot. By the time they reached the end of the blockage, the walking infected were also dead. Everyone was filthy and sweating, so they decided to park down the road a few feet and clean up. At the back of the pickup, Marcus dropped down the tailgate and fished a clean shirt from his pack. Sitting in the truck for hours while covered in black muck wasn't his idea of a great trip. Using as little water and sanitizer as possible, they all cleaned up their hands and arms. Max and Rafe worked on their blades, cleaning off the bodily fluids before storing them back in their belts.

A tap at his arm had Marcus turning to find Charlie with a sandwich in her hand. She smiled at him as she handed the sandwich and a soda can to him. Hopping up into the bed of the truck, he and Cliff ate their sandwiches in silence. Cliff tended to always be quiet unless the situation called for his voice. That was rare and Marcus knew his grief was all consuming. Marcus for one was glad the man hadn't given up completely. He knew from conversations with Alex that she worried about him greatly. That was her heart. Thinking of her kindness caused a lump in his throat and he had to stop eating. As a distraction he looked over at Mateo and Albert who were each eating one of their tamales. They looked delicious and Marcus said so.

"My sister makes some wonderful foods, she loves cooking. Her tamales are the best," Albert replied.

A picture began to form in Marcus' head. He decided that when, not if, they rescued Alex he would talk to her about trading with the Vega family. The Duncan compound had a plentiful bounty of food. They were creating a higher production as Rafe worked with Margaret and Issac to expand the garden. Soon they would have so much space growing food that they would need additional hands to harvest. Marcus could imagine that Vera and

Sylvia would enjoy helping in the garden in exchange for some of the produce that they picked. They could trade pork, milk, cheese, or butter that was made at the compound as well. Even with the fall of society, eventually things had to improve again. Eventually, humans had to come together again. Marcus knew Alex would support the idea.

Lunch finished, everyone climbed back into the vehicles to continue their drive. When the sun began to dip, Rafe called a stop to the procession. Marcus tried to fight. He couldn't think of sleeping another night while Alex was being subjected to horrors at the hands of the Noble Lord. Rafe wouldn't be moved. The Duncan siblings agreed that going into the brothel when they were exhausted and not ready was a suicide mission. A mission that could get not only the group killed, but possibly Alex. That was a risk no one wanted to take.

They pulled the vehicles off the road and positioned them behind a row of trees. It wasn't perfect camouflage, but any vehicle driving quickly by wouldn't notice them. The cabs of the vehicles weren't large enough for everyone to sleep. Rafe and Charlie pitched a small tent together with their dog, Storm. Rafe insisted they were safer than everyone else with their early warning system. The dog had proven to be helpful in a number of close calls, so Marcus couldn't disagree. Max and Griffin set up their bed in the back of Rafe's truck, spreading out their sleeping bags and using their bug out bags as pillows. That left the four men in the truck Marcus drove.

"I'll sleep outside," Marcus said, offering before anyone else had to. While he felt somewhat safe in the bed of the truck, sleeping outside felt ominous.

"I can sleep sitting up," Cliff said.

"We'll take the truck bed, Marcus. You and your friend sleep inside the cab," Albert said.

Marcus was going to argue and say it wasn't about being the one with the most courage. However, the stern look on Albert's face stopped him from saying anything. He held up his hands in surrender and got out to help the men make beds in the truck. It wasn't going to be the most comfortable sleeping with the hard metal of the truck bed, but Albert didn't change his mind or complain. The Vega men kept to themselves as dinner was eaten before everyone turned in for the evening.

Sitting in the cab of the truck, Marcus couldn't even begin to think of sleeping. In his mind all he saw was the infected woman tied up in the bus he and Alex found. His stomach was in knots. He didn't want to be negative, but he felt like something bad was coming, something worse than losing Alex. He couldn't be sure if it was Alex suffering that had him so anxious or something else.

"You going to stop fidgeting tonight?" Cliff asked. The bigger man was trying to lay on the back seat, his knees pulled up to make space for his torso.

"I just can't stop thinking about the bus, the woman with the bites and burns. What if...," Marcus trailed off.

"That's not going to be Alex. You know her. She's too strong. And valuable. This Noble Lord will figure out how smart she is and realize she's better off alive than dead," Cliff said.

"Valuable is what I'm worried about," Marcus said.

Cliff went silent and Marcus was sure his mind was now in the same place. The Noble Lord wasn't going to care about her abilities with a gun or knife. He wasn't going to ask her about her knowledge with animals or plants. The fact that she could navigate by the stars would matter not at all. The assets the Noble Lord would be interested in would be those of the bare necessity. That thought had Marcus staring out the windshield until the sun began to peek over the horizon.

CHAPTER FIFTEEN

The guard had to drag her forcibly from the room. Alex wouldn't put one foot in front of the other. She never felt more naked than she did right then. Clad in a black lace babydoll, that was thankfully solid enough to cover her breasts, and black boy short panties, Alex was pushed from Coral's room. The older woman lit a cigarette as Alex fought. She never looked at Alex, just stared out her small window. Alex wanted to scream at her, hit her, make her hurt. But she knew it wasn't going to work without the guard intervening.

At the hall the catcalls started. Whistling and names were called her way. One guard gyrated his hips at her and Alex took a threatening step toward him until he raised the gun he was holding. When she immediately stopped, his laugh was loud and obnoxious.

"Real tough behind a weapon," Alex said with a sneer.

"I'll be sure to put my name on your dance card. You're quite the feisty one," the guard said between laughs.

The guard leading Alex grabbed her arm and pulled her toward the stairs. Not wanting to fall down the stairs, Alex stepped carefully down each step. She wasn't given shoes, something she was sure was on purpose. It kept her off balance and feeling vulnerable. A plan put into place by the Noble Lord she had no doubt. The man was all about controlling his merchandise. At the bottom of the staircase she was led back to the large ballroom. The sounds of women being abused and taken against their will reached Alex's ears again and she wished she could cover her head. Her stomach roiled thinking about how these women were people's mothers, sisters, friends, daughters and now they were here. Prisoners of the Noble Lord.

"I thought the Noble Lord wasn't here. Where are you taking me?" Alex asked.

"Shut up, bitch. You go where we tell you to."

"The Noble Lord ordered no one to touch me. He's going to be angry," Alex said. She tried to push whatever buttons she could, hoping to delay what was coming. And give herself time to escape. The look of apprehension that crossed the guard's face told Alex she had hit the right button.

"If you just take me back to Coral, no one needs to know about this," Alex continued.

"I said to shut up," the guard said. He yanked Alex to him so he could hiss in her ear. "You pissed too many people off already. People willing to pay well for their chance at you."

Alex turned to look the guard in the face. He didn't shrink away, and Alex saw him glance down at her mouth. Alex let her lips dip up in a small smile. His eyebrows rose as he tried to gauge the change. Taking a chance, Alex stepped closer and went up on her tiptoes, as if she was going to give him exactly what was on his mind. Without warning, she sank her teeth into the guard's lower lip and bit down as hard as she could. When she tasted blood and the guard began to holler in pain, she let go and stepped back.

"Do you think anyone is going to get a chance at me?" Alex yelled.

The guard swiped at his lip. Finding blood, a red bloom began on his face as anger began to rage. Raising a hand his swiftly brought it down against Alex's face, causing her steps to falter backward. She didn't let any reaction show on her face, except a smile. *Let them believe I enjoy the pain*, Alex thought to herself. She realized that in her mind she was sounding slightly hysterical. There was a lot she could handle, a lot that wouldn't break her. However, the path they were throwing her down was one she didn't know she could come back from.

Bleeding from his lip, the guard roughly took Alex by the arm again and began to half drag her down the aisle of canvas rooms. Eyes were everywhere, watching what was happening. Alex tried to search out friendly faces, but most of the women that she found turned away before making eye contact. None of them were fighting. They seemed broken and unresisting to their fate. She wondered how many of the dead women in the road outside were ones that had the courage to run.

Alex was led beyond the canvas rooms to a door leading off of the ballroom. The door swung in and Alex was shoved through. She turned to run back at the guard, but the door slammed shut before she had the chance. Immediately she tried the knob, unsurprised to find it locked. Movement behind her made her spin and put her back to the door. She wanted to see her attacker. The room was lit by candles along a bookshelf and on a small corner table. In the limited light she strained to see what was in the room with her.

"The trouble you caused me, I want to know if it was worth it," a voice came from the dark. And Alex knew immediately who it was.

"Didn't get enough beatings, Lewis?" Alex asked.

The gang leader came from the shadows, circling around a small couch that dominated the center of the small room. His eyes blazed in the candlelight and Alex knew she had touched a sensitive subject. Standing against the door in the sheer babydoll, she felt exposed and weak. She held her head up and leveled her glare at Lewis. His grin was slow and malicious.

"I'm taking my payment from you. Whether you like it or not. And I'll make sure you don't."

Alex didn't move as he came toward her slowly. Just as he thought he was going to grab her, Alex pivoted away from his advance and punched him in the jaw. Lewis grunted in pain, but he didn't slow as he turned to follow Alex into the room. As he perused her, Alex's eyes flew around the room, searching for any weapon to use to defend herself. The room was strategically sparse, preventing anything from being used by the women to save themselves when locked inside.

The sound of a belt being unbuckled caught Alex's attention. She watched as Lewis slid his belt from its loops. In her mind the movement was the most threatening thing she had ever seen. Lewis stared at Alex, his gaze lewd and hungry on the parts of her body that the lace didn't cover. He laid his belt over the back of the loveseat. Alex eyed it for only a moment, as a plan quickly played out in her mind. She realized Lewis had close to thirty pounds on her, so her strike would have to be fast and successful.

Before Alex could react, Lewis' hand snuck out and he grabbed her arm. He hauled Alex to him, grabbing both of her wrists and holding them behind her back. Alex coughed, trying to not smell his putrid breath as he leaned close to her face.

"You aren't as tough as you try to act. You'll submit if you want to live," he whispered in her ear.

His lips grazed her ear and then her neck. Alex couldn't stop the convulsion that shook her body. Lewis chuckled quietly as he continued his exploration of her exposed skin. His free hand slid over her shoulder and down her chest. When he reached to cup her breast, Alex flung her body backward, taking them both to the ground. She knew the move was going to hurt. Lewis released her wrists as he flailed trying to keep his balance and Alex only had a split second to brace herself for the impact.

When she hit the ground, she rolled to the side immediately and sprung to her feet. She cursed to herself when she saw that Lewis hadn't actually gone down. The man spun to glare at Alex before launching himself at her. Alex took her chance then, grabbing a candle from the nearest table. Lewis didn't realize what was happening until the candle was extinguished on his eye. The scream Lewis released didn't sound like it came from a man. It was high pitched, ringing with fury and pain. He dropped to his knees, pawing at his injured eye. It was the exact move Alex was waiting for.

It wasn't more than a few seconds. Alex grabbed the belt from the back of the loveseat and ran to stand behind Lewis on the ground. Quickly she looped the belt around his neck and tightened it until gasping sounds came from his mouth. He tried to fight his way to his feet, however when he got one leg straight Alex side kicked him in the knee causing him to fall again. With him on the ground, Alex planted a knee between his shoulder blades and pushed down, while pulling up with the belt. Lewis scratched at his neck, trying to pull the belt away. His hands flung in Alex's direction, trying to stop her.

Fueled by panic, he lifted himself and Alex off the ground. Alex struggled with her balance, but she didn't let go of the belt. Using the knee that wasn't pressed against Lewis's back, she quickly kneed him twice in the ribcage. With no air in his lungs already, Lewis fell to the side, gasping. Faraway in Alex's mind she thought he looked like a fish out of water. She then corrected herself. He was a shark, with deadly teeth. But even a shark had weaknesses. That part of her brain laughed internally as she noticed Lewis turning blue then purple.

Alex's hands burned with pain where the belt cut into her skin. She wrapped the belt around her hands again, to pull tighter on Lewis' throat. She feared the belt would break or slip from her sweat-slicked hands. But as the seconds turned into minutes, Lewis stopped fighting. Even though he didn't move, Alex didn't let go of the belt. She knew in extraordinary circumstances it could take ten minutes for someone to die from asphyxiation. There was no way she was willing to take the chance if she let Lewis go, he would still be alive.

Her body was soaked with sweat from the exertion she was using to hold Lewis to the ground and the belt tight around his throat. She had no idea how much time had passed. A banging on the door startled her. Looking at a nearby candle she was sure it had burned down an inch since she had been in the position of holding the belt. Her body ached, her joints begging to be moved. Slowly, Alex unwound the belt from her hands. Her fingers were purple from the blood flow being cut off. She shook them and then almost cried out as they began to tingle painfully.

"Lewis! Man, the Noble Lord is back. We gotta get that woman out of there. Zip it up!" A guard's voice came from the closed door.

Alex began to panic again. Her eyes flew wildly around the room, looking for any escape. The one window in the room was boarded and she ran to it. Knowing she was on the first floor, she knew if she could get the boards off the window, she could escape. The guards outside weren't anything she couldn't handle on her own. She just needed to be out in the open. Outside she could easily find something to use as a weapon. She could run away as far as possible from the brothel. The Noble Lord would never find her. And if he did, she would be with her family. He wouldn't get his hands on her.

At the window she inspected the wood planks. They were nailed in multiple places along the windowsill. She slid her tingling fingers between two of the boards and tried to grip one of the barriers. With all of her strength she yanked back on the board. It didn't budge. Her will to escape wouldn't allow her to give up. She gritted her teeth and threw her whole body backward. Two more yanks and the board made a groaning noise. Alex froze, wondering how loud the sound really was. In her head it sounded like a gunshot, however, in reality the sound didn't bring any guards running.

When the first board broke free from the windowsill, the cracking of the wood was louder, and Alex coughed trying to cover up the sound.

"Lewis, don't be playing any sick games with her. If you leave any marks on her neck, the Noble Lord will know something happened," The guard yelled again.

Alex snickered to herself, thinking that guard was going to be surprised to find that she wasn't the one being choked. Turning back to the window Alex felt tears well in her eyes. What she hadn't seen originally was the boards on the outside of the window as well. Breathing deeply, Alex wrestled her emotions back in check. Grabbing a second board on the inside she began to yank at it. She was sure this board took longer to come off, but when it did it was remarkably quieter. With two boards off on the inside, a space opened that Alex could fit through if she could get the outside boards off.

"Who's using this room?"

The voice made Alex's blood freeze. She felt the tears coming to her eyes again. With renewed vigor she began to push on the outside boards. They bent and groaned, but she wasn't making fast enough progress. The sound of the guard sputtering outside, trying to come up with a good excuse as to why he was guarding the room came through the closed door. Alex knew her time was coming to an end and she wasn't close to enough to escape.

"Move aside, now," the voice demanded.

Just as one of the boards on the outside of the window came free and bright sunlight burst into the room, the door opened and the Noble Lord stormed in. His eyes were furious, and Alex tried to shove herself through the space she knew was too small. *Please*, she begged in her mind. The Noble Lord only had to take three long strides across the room to grab Alex around the waist and haul her back from the window. The ragged wood scraped along the exposed skin of her back and arms as he yanked her. She tried to hold on to the wood, even when she knew it was futile. The Noble Lord ripped her free and flung her across the floor.

Alex had never been thrown like a doll, but that was exactly how it felt. She flopped and hit the ground with a thud. The guard that had brought her to the room was roughly shoved into the room by another henchman. Alex didn't take time to notice any of them as she was trying to breathe through the pain of bouncing off the hardwood floor. Everyone was silent in the room and Alex realized they were taking in the scene of a dead Lewis and a partially opened window.

"Get someone in here to fix this god damn window, before we have any walkers getting in. And have someone throw this piece of trash out front," the Noble Lord said, motioning to Lewis' body.

The guards that were standing around, shook themselves from their shock and rushed to do as they were ordered. The Noble Lord then turned to the guard that had brought Alex to Lewis. His lip was slightly swollen from where Alex had bitten him. His face was white as a sheet as his leader walked up to him.

"I was pretty clear with my orders in regard to her, wasn't I?"

"Sir, it was Lewis' idea," the guard stammered.

"Is, or should I say was, Lewis the leader of this state?" The Noble Lord said. His voice was cold as ice.

"No, sir."

"You know the punishment for disobeying. Take him to the balcony. Call an assembly," the Noble Lord said to the henchman holding the guard.

"Sir, please, no. I'm sorry. I made a mistake. I can be loyal. It was stupid," the guard said, blubbering through tears that started to show on his face.

"Get him out of my sight. And make sure she's there," the Noble Lord said, pointing to Alex.

She laid still on the ground, watching the whole interaction.

When another guard stepped toward her, she began to scramble back, toward the window again. She knew it was futile, but she couldn't just lay down and obey. The guard grabbed her and yanked her to her feet. The movement caused her to cry out in pain, her hip feeling badly bruised, The Noble Lord turned and looked at her then, stalking back into the room. He grabbed her chin and forced her face up to look at him.

"You saved me the trouble with Lewis, but I don't allow the women to kill my men. We'll think about an appropriate punishment later," he said, before he smashed his mouth against Alex's.

He tasted of cigarettes and Alex fought to pull away. When he tried to force his tongue into her mouth, she made a move to bite him. He pulled back with a chuckle and looked at her without releasing her face.

"You'll learn to submit; you might even enjoy being my pet. I'll treat you well if you behave."

The Noble Lord turned and left and Alex was dragged along behind. Alex spit at the ground and she wished she could spit on the Noble Lord as he laughed at her. When they exited the room, the large ballroom was full of people. They didn't salute, yet stood at attention. The women stared at the ground, some completely nude from being with the men that paid for them. Alex wanted to scream at them, to fight, to have the strength in them to get away. But there was no escape for them all. In her mind, Alex vowed to change that. She would save as many of the women as she could.

She was led back up the staircase that led to Coral's room. Instead of going to the room she was familiar with, the guard pushed her through a set of double doors. She had to shield her eyes from the sudden glare of sunlight. They were facing the street, above the front entrance of the building. Her eyes adjusted to the light and Alex began to study the balcony and what was nearby. Everything was a potential escape plan and she couldn't waste the chance to find a weak point. Her eyes fell on an old fire escape that seemed to be pulled up to the side of the balcony. She looked away from it before anyone caught her staring. She wondered to herself if the fire escape still worked and unfolded to the ground.

Below them, the inhabitants and customers of the Dead Brothel filed out. Women were barefoot and had to gingerly step around the carcasses of the dead that littered the streets. Alex could see where Lewis' body had been thrown near his black van. She could see some of the men she remembered from his gang making their way to the van. Before the Noble Lord began to speak the van started and they drove off. Nearby the Noble Lord turned to whisper to a guard. The guard nodded and left the balcony. The Noble Lord made sure Alex couldn't hear, but she could assume the men were guilty by association. They knew it and took off before revenge could be exacted on them. The Noble Lord didn't take pity on anyone and Alex knew he sent men after the gang to bring them back for punishment.

The murmur of voices halted immediately when the Noble Lord raised his hands. Alex was dumbstruck with how the man had so much power and yet he was nothing but a drug dealer. Everyone below lifted their eyes, waiting for his words. The Noble Lord waited, prolonging the attention he was receiving. Finally, he brought his hands down and spoke.

"We don't have many rules here in The Noble Lord State," he began.

Though Alex hated him she found herself riveted to hear him speak. It was a window into a psychotic head. And that window may give her insight into beating him.

"I believe I lead using a fair rule, but also a strong hand," he continued.

Alex looked down as a murmured reply rose to meet him. It was an agreement, a thank you, a worship of a man that rose himself into status.

"With that strong hand, I find there are times I must discipline even the most beloved of my children. Please, always remember, I do not take joy in this discipline."

His children? Alex thought. She realized the man thought of himself more as a god than just a leader of men. While he tried to claim he didn't enjoy hurting the people, Alex could see glee in his eyes as he turned with a blade in his hand. The guilty guard struggled against those that held him. He sobbed roughly, begging the Noble Lord to spare him. He was pushed to the balcony edge, on display for all.

"When those I trust the most do not follow my word, they can no longer wander my land," the Noble Lord said.

Everything seemed to happen quicker than Alex would have guessed. The next steps were clearly planned and rehearsed. One guard stood behind the guilty man, grabbing his forehead and yanking his head back while another forced his mouth open for the Noble Lord. Once in position, the Noble Lord reached into the man's mouth and grasped his tongue. Using his hunting knife, he sawed through the man's tongue. The screams that came from the man's throat were inhuman. Alex bent at the waist, covering her ears against the painful sounds. The Noble Lord took the tongue and turned to the crowd.

"The tongue is taken, to prevent further lies, here or in the afterlife," he said.

To Alex's horror, the crowd cheered as the tongue was flung into the outstretched hands. She shook her head in disbelief. Were these people faking their adoration of the Noble Lord, or were they all just as twisted as he was? The Noble Lord then turned back to the guilty man, who now had blood dripping down his face. His noises no longer made sense and he was no longer fighting the hands that held him. The Noble Lord reached up with his knife and cleanly removed one ear and then the other.

Alex couldn't take any more. She turned to run, run anywhere she could get. A guard blocked her path and forced her to turn back. Bile rose in Alex's throat and there was no stopping it. She turned away and cowered in a corner as her stomach contents emptied onto the balcony ground. The guard left her there, not wanting to deal with the vomit or smell. Alex would have bathed in it if that would have stopped anyone from touching her. She squeezed her eyes shut and covered her ears, trying to block out the evil that was happening feet away from her.

"The ears are taken, as their purpose was never fulfilled," the Noble Lord bellowed. The rising cheer after his voice told Alex he probably threw the ears to the crowd.

Moments passed and Alex was suddenly grasped and pulled to her feet. She pivoted, ready to fight the guard that had grabbed her. Instead, she was face to face with the Noble Lord. His eyes were bright and wild, his face flush with pure sadistic joy. He pushed her to the edge of the balcony to stand next to the now disfigured man. Her feet felt sticky and when she looked down, she realized she was standing in the man's blood. The Noble Lord held her by the back of her head and forced her to look up over the crowd.

"I demand respect. I am the Noble Lord of this land. You live and die by my grace and obey as ordered. This is my pet. Henceforth she is not to be touched by hands that are not my own. Let this be the lesson to those that dare defy my orders," the Noble Lord said.

With that he released Alex and turned to the guard he had maimed. He looked at the man for a moment before plunging his knife into his gut and sawing the blade up his torso. As blood and internal parts of the man began to spill, the Noble Lord moved away and the guards holding the man threw him over the balcony edge. The cheer from below erupted and Alex couldn't stop herself from looking down. The women seemed frozen, watching the scene unfold. Men that stood near the body began to stomp on it. They began to kick the body, rolling it away from the brothel. They all seemed used to the display. They knew their roles, what was expected of them, what to do to please the Noble Lord.

The barbaric execution over, the Noble Lord turned, and Coral came out onto the balcony with a bowl and towel. The Noble Lord smiled at her and thanked her. At that moment Alex found the whole interaction insane. He acted like he wasn't cleaning blood and guts off his hands in a white porcelain bowl of water. But he stood there, working the soap into a lather a few times until the suds stopped turning pink. When he was done a guard handed him his towel and the Noble Lord inspected himself to ensure he was clean. Once happy with the outcome, the Noble Lord dismissed Coral who actually bowed to him before walking back inside.

Alex stood rooted to her spot. Her feet stuck to the concrete balcony, the blood pooling beneath her. She was completely lost in the moment, not sure what her next step was. How could she escape? Was it a better fate to just throw herself from the building now? She looked back over the edge of the balcony. As she contemplated the idea, she placed her hands on the edge, careful to not touch where dried and fresh blood caked the wall. She lifted to her toes to get a better vantage point. Would the fall kill her? She guessed it was unlikely as it was only one story up. Unless she could make sure she fell on her head. But then she could end up in a coma and who knew what they would do to her then.

Boots behind her was the only warning she had before she was lifted into someone's arms. When Alex turned to fight, she was shocked to see the Noble Lord. She crossed her arms over her breasts, which bulged at the top of the babydoll she wore. He was too close for her comfort and she squirmed hoping he would put her down. Instead he instructed one of the guards to clean her feet.

Once all the blood was removed, the Noble Lord still didn't put her on the ground. Alex assumed this was more of his show of control, to show that he was claiming her. Her skin crawled where his hands rested on her back and thigh. She turned to look away from him, trying to be as far from him as she could while he held her against his chest. She heard him breathe deeply and felt air move through her hair. She shuddered, realizing he was smelling her. Pushing, Alex tried to break free from his hold.

"If I drop you now, you're headed down the stairs. If you survive that, I will punish you. You won't like my punishments. They aren't nearly as enjoyable as other things," the Noble Lord said to her.

As the Noble Lord leaned his head toward her to whisper, his long hair tickled her neck and goosebumps rose on her arms and legs. The Noble Lord made a noise that sounded like a chuckle when he rubbed his thumb along her leg where the goosebumps stood. They stood at the top of the stairs and Alex looked at the old wooden steps. Again, she found herself thinking how dying could be preferable to what plans the Noble Lord had for her. She could barely stomach the intimate way the Noble Lord tried to hold her now. If he tried to touch her later, she would rather find a way to leave this world than be subjected to that.

The Noble Lord walked down the stairs, carrying Alex as if she weighed nothing. He didn't breathe hard or take a break. Alex decided he didn't seem to use his own product because he was in better shape than any drug addict could be. That thought discouraged her. She had hoped he would be weak and eventually show a hole in his facade. Just a small window that would allow her to escape before she was harmed. He held his head high, unafraid of anyone in his employ. All of the surrounding guards carried guns, while all Alex saw on him was the knife he used to filet the disobedient man. In Alex's mind that meant he didn't believe any of the men would shoot him in the back.

In the main ballroom again, people were finding their way back to their rooms. When the Noble Lord passed, women directed their eyes down, not daring to look directly at the leader.

Alex stared at each person they passed, looking for anyone that would hold her gaze. Even the men now avoided looking directly at her. After the Noble Lord's declaration she was completely off-limits, even to look at. Alex thought that was at least one saving grace. She now only had to worry about one set of hands coming near her. How long could she prevent him from taking what he wanted and what she would rather die before giving?

CHAPTER SIXTEEN

Light danced along the ornate ceiling, creating shadow creatures that Alex imagined could come to life. Her right hand was numb, but she wasn't going to complain. Being tied to the bed was terrifying, but the Noble Lord had left her alone. Once entering his main office, the Noble Lord carried her into a large bedroom. In the middle of the room a large four-poster bed sat. Alex almost scoffed at the ridiculousness of the furniture. She wondered where they had scavenged it from and how it seemed to be important enough to worry about during the apocalypse.

The Noble Lord set her on her feet and Alex immediately moved out of reach, putting the wall at her back. The Noble Lord didn't pay attention to her movements. He went to a large wooden chest that sat against a wall and pulled a length of rope from it. Without a word he grabbed her arm and dragged her to the bed. Alex tried to plant her bare feet, tried yanking away from him, but his grip was a vice on her skin. Alex became more panicked when he grabbed her by her arms and tossed her onto the bed. She tried to roll away from him, but he was fast. Grabbing her right wrist, he wrapped the rope around her and the bedpost.

Alex laid there, trying to get as far from him as she could. He looked at her dismissively and turned to walk away. He first went to a small closet. Alex could see him remove his shirt and pants before she turned her head. His body was toned, strong and as Alex guessed, capable of snapping her like a twig. She wouldn't have him catching her studying him, He would think she was admiring him, while really she was only counting the number of ways she'd like to kill him. She didn't turn back toward him as she heard his boots move across the floor. At the door he hesitated, and Alex held her breath.

"Don't worry, pet. I'll be back later. Business to handle."

With that, he left the bedroom and left Alex tied in place. That had been hours ago. Twice men had come in to stoke the fire and add logs. With the lace lingerie Alex was wearing, the warmth from the fire was helpful. In the room, Alex felt as if she was insulated from the rest of the brothel. At times she heard raised voices, but she could never truly tell what the arguments were about. She wondered what type of business the Noble Lord did all day. She imagined his false power was difficult to maintain and he had to have time to flex his grip over the people.

She knew the torture and execution earlier in the day was directly connected with his need to be respected. She thought about the way he talked, almost as if he had been studying how royalty should speak. It was laughable to Alex, but the rest of the people seemed to bow down to him. The power he held was over their safety and their supplies. Those that lived and frequented the brothel were protected by numerous armed guards. They would prevent any sort of infected getting in. In addition, none of them were missing meals while under the roof of the Noble Lord.

He was working to control all of Montana, Alex understood that. What she didn't know was how he was doing it? Her family had been into town a number of times and had never encountered the gangs loyal to the Noble Lord. They had taken supplies that they wanted, shared supplies with those that needed it, and had moved freely in and out of buildings. No one ever challenged them or said there was a power they were reporting to. Alex wondered how that was. The Duncans didn't go into town daily. They chose to stay safe behind their walls unless completely necessary. She imagined it could have been just a coincidence that they never happened upon the thugs.

Cramping began in her shoulder and Alex pulled herself up on her knees again. She rotated her position to keep blood flowing through her limbs. She flexed her right hand and again tried to untie the rope. Even if she got free, the bedroom area was windowless. She knew one door led to the Noble Lord's office. There was one other door, but she had no idea where it led. If she had a weapon, she would be willing to take the chance.

Crouched in the bed, massaging her hand was how the Noble Lord found her. He yawned loudly when he walked in. He eyed her for a moment and then went to his closet area. He undressed, leaving his clothing on the ground. He stalked toward Alex in nothing but boxer briefs that hugged lean thighs. He ran his hand through his blond hair and Alex knew he was trying to appeal to her. He didn't. Her stomach was roiling with trying to decide how to get out of the situation she was in. He stopped before he reached her and studied her.

"You've hurt your wrist," he said.

"I didn't tie myself up," Alex replied.

"Well, we couldn't very well have you wandering free, could we? You have proven to be...difficult."

"I'm not sure what you mean," Alex replied, feigning innocence.

"The women here, some have fought. Some have died trying. But never have I seen a woman kill a man with a belt," the Noble Lord said.

"First time for everything. I could do the trick again if you untie me," Alex shot back.

The Noble Lord grinned at her. The smile was one full of

malice and challenge. Alex vowed in her mind to kill the drug dealer the first chance she got.

"I think I like you right where you are," the Noble Lord said, his grin fading.

Alex had never been with any men before her husband, Blake. And since his death at the start of the plague she had done nothing but mourn his loss. However, looking at the Noble Lord, she knew what desire looked like. His eyes raked her body, lingering over her black lace covered breasts and her long bare legs. She cursed Coral again in her mind remembering how the woman had shaved her legs, making everything perfect for the Noble Lord. Alex tucked her legs under her, trying to get into a position that would give her some leverage.

Fear had her staying completely still, waiting for the Noble Lord's attack. Instead of coming near her, the Noble Lord yawned again and went to the other side of the bed. Pulling back the covers he slid onto the soft mattress. He let out a sigh of a man that had struggled through the day. Alex watched him get comfortable, but she didn't move her position. Suddenly and without warning, the Noble Lord snapped out a hand and grabbed her ankle. He yanked her down onto the bed until she was lying on her side, facing away from him. Her arm was painfully pulled taunt against the bedpost. Alex tried to pull away, but his arm was barred around her waist.

To Alex's horror, the Noble Lord adjusted his position, until he was spooned against her. She could feel his skin against hers, the hair of his legs scratching along the smooth skin of hers. He slid his hand under the babydoll, placing it on the bare skin of her stomach. She could feel other things as he pulled her tighter into the curve of his body. Alex couldn't stop the gag that was threatening. The Noble Lord didn't move, only laughed at her.

"You should get used to this, I enjoy companionship in bed when I sleep," the Noble Lord said against her ear. The shiver that passed through Alex was completely involuntary.

She felt dirty. Every inch of her skin that he touched felt tainted with evil. Her mind went blank, except for the sole purpose of getting away from the Noble Lord. Alex gripped the portion of the rope that connected her to the bed. Yanking as hard as she could, she pulled herself away from the Noble Lord until she could slide to the floor. He didn't fight her, only watched her with a raised eyebrow. She began to fight against the rope with an intensity that even shocked Alex. The situation felt like an out-of-body experience. She knew what she was doing, but couldn't remember making the decision to do it.

As her skin became raw and blood began to show, the Noble Lord finally tired of her behavior. With a huff, he got out of the bed and walked to her. Alex backed to the wall and waited for his next move. He walked straight to her and Alex knew he was going to strike her. When his hand flew toward her, Alex ducked and came up with a left-handed jab to his solar plexus. The punch was quick and he bent slightly in surprise. Alex didn't stop as she came up with an uppercut to his jaw. That sent the Noble Lord stepping back a few paces. He rubbed his face for a moment, his eyes burning into Alex's.

"You are feisty. You like to fight, I can give you a fight."

He went to his closet and came back with a knife. Alex drew back, preparing for him to try to cut her. Instead, he went to the rope and cut it easily. He threw the knife toward his closet, out of Alex's reach. Then he turned to her and before she could register what was happening, he slapped her hard across the face. Her head cracked against the wall and she almost fell. She quickly shook the spinning from her mind, realizing this could be the shot to escape. If she could kill the Noble Lord, she could escape and end the torture for the women in the brothel.

"Let's see if we can bring you down a few notches, shall we?" The Noble Lord said, motioning for Alex to come to him.

Alex waited, looking for the trick. Any weapons the Noble Lord had in the room were in his closet. She knew he'd stop her before she got there. Alex had fought men larger than her, but that was in a gym, during training sessions. Now she questioned if she could defend herself against the size of the Noble Lord. Standing opposite her in his boxer briefs, Alex sized him up. He was wiry, but not in a thin or weak way. She imagined that if he wasn't a monstrous drug dealer, women would find him very attractive. He carried himself with pride and confidence, a man that was used to winning the fights he was in.

"You killed Lewis with his own belt. Bring on your best, pet."

"My name is not pet," Alex growled quietly.

"Your name doesn't matter to me. You are here to be my pet and I'll call you whatever I choose."

Quickly, the Noble Lord became bored with Alex's stalling and he stepped forward with an attack. It was exactly what Alex was waiting for. She preferred to defend and then attack. That way she could see how he would move before she committed to a strike. The Noble Lord feigned right, but then came up with his left and slapped Alex before she could move. She was expecting the blow, allowing it to land. It gave her the chance to step in closer and strike him in the throat with a knife-hand.

The Noble Lord's eyes widened in shock at the sudden blow to his windpipe. He stumbled back a step before advancing again. This time Alex wouldn't just allow him to come at her. She leapt onto the bed and after two large steps, landed on the other side. The Noble Lord was rounding to reach her, but she managed to bypass him to get into the more open space of the room. He whipped around faster than Alex was planning and he threw out a leg, kicking her feet out from under her. She went down hard but was able to catch herself with a hand before she fell face first. The Noble Lord was on her before she could recover.

A thick forearm wrapped under her neck as he lifted her and her feet dangled as he held her with an arm banded around her waist and one at her throat. Alex coughed and kicked. Her heels beat against his shins, but he didn't react.

"You might be a wildcat, but you aren't as strong as you think," he hissed into her ear.

Alex scratched at his forearm as she angled her chin down. When her mouth was close enough, she clamped her teeth around a thick piece of flesh. She bit down hard, trying to break the skin. The stinging pain caught the Noble Lord off guard. He dropped her and Alex fell to her knees.

"Bitch. Biting is a weak move."

Alex scrambled away and jumped to her feet. She pushed away the blackness that tried to intrude into her vision and gulped deep breaths of cool air.

"There is nothing off the board when you're surviving," Alex said with a nonchalant shrug of a bare shoulder.

"You can survive here. Be happy. If you just stop fighting. Give me what I want, and you'll be treated like a queen," the Noble Lord said.

"A queen or a pet? You seem confused," Alex replied.

"You have more strength and courage than any other woman that's been brought through those doors. You aren't equal to me, but you are the closest I've found."

"Don't go falling in love, I'm not interested," Alex said snidely.

She could feel herself channel her inner Max. Thinking of her sister opened a deep longing in her heart that was almost a physical pain. She shoved the picture of Max away and locked it back into a box. A box where she was keeping everything she loved. The people she wanted to get back to so badly. Her children, her friends, their home. They were all far off thoughts that she tried to not pull to the forefront of her mind. It was too painful to even think that she may never see them again.

"Love? The apocalypse isn't about love, pet. It's about power. And together we could control so much," the Noble Lord said, breaking into Alex's inner thoughts.

"I don't want power!" Alex yelled.

With that Alex launched herself at the Noble Lord. He tried to catch her, but she slid to one side and punched him in the ribs. He turned to follow, but she snapped out a kick that hit the back of his knee, causing him to fall sideways. Alex wanted him to fall further, but he quickly found his balance and bounced back to his feet. He pivoted quickly and blocked the next punch that Alex tried to throw at his face. Without hesitation, he punched her square in the eye, throwing her backward off her feet.

The sound of Alex crashing into a small side table brought guards running into the room. The table collapsed under the impact, wood splintering across the floor. Air whooshed from Alex's mouth as she landed flat on her back. A sharp pain cut through the haze and she grabbed at her thigh. She grabbed the small shard of wood that had impaled her skin and yanked it free. Blood dripped to the floor as she rolled back to her feet. She carefully stood in the middle of the pieces of the broken table, gasping for breath. She could feel the swelling of her eye already and the pounding pain of every beat of her heart.

The guards leveled guns at her, their faces covered in masks of surprise and confusion. The Noble Lord stood ready, but motioned them all back with a slash of his hand.

"Everything is fine here. Leave," he demanded.

The guards didn't question the order as they filed back out into the main office, closing the bedroom door behind them. The Noble Lord looked down at Alex's leg before meeting her eyes again.

"You're bleeding all over my bedroom. That's just unnecessary."

"Sure, let me just turn it off for you," Alex replied.

The Noble Lord shook his head at her obstinance. He began to circle to one side, so Alex limped the other direction. He closed the distance between them slowly as he made his circle smaller as he moved. Alex waited, knowing she wasn't going to beat him in hand to hand combat. She had to be smarter. She couldn't be faster with the lame leg. Her eye was going to swell shut soon, she could feel that. Doubt clouded her thoughts. Could she beat him on her own?

"Just let me go. I'm more trouble than I'm worth," Alex said.

"No woman is worthless here. If you don't stay with me, you'll be useful in other ways," the Noble Lord replied.

"Like the women you're selling out there? I'll kill any man that comes near me," Alex said.

"You'll have to try harder to convince me of that," the Noble Lord said.

With that the Noble Lord stepped forward abruptly and grabbed Alex by the upper arms. He pulled her to him until their chests touched. They were both breathing hard and Alex felt some success knowing she had made him work for what he thought was his easy conquest. His bare skin pressed against Alex and she started trying to yank her body away. When she realized she could feel his excitement from the fighting with her, she physically gagged. Every cell of her body screamed in protest and disgust. When he leaned down and ran his nose along her neck and jawline, Alex couldn't take anymore.

When her knee came up to hit him in the groin, he easily sidestepped, anticipating her move. Instead Alex brought her heel down to stomp on his toes. His eyes flew up and pain flared for a moment, but it was the only reaction he had. He released one of her arms and raised a hand to strike her. It was exactly what Alex had hoped for. Locking his remaining arm in place, she hyper-extended his elbow and clamped down on the pressure point in his arm. A small look of surprise crossed his face as he stopped his motion of hitting her and went to grab her again. Before he could, she used a flat palm strike and slammed the heel of her hand into his nose. Then she released his arm and stepped back far enough to front kick him in the stomach.

The fast attack caused him to bend down slightly and grab his nose. She didn't think she was able to break it, but it was enough to bring tears to his eyes. She didn't want to waste the chance to attack. She ran at him, grabbing his head in both hands and taking it down as she brought her knee up to meet his face. When he pulled back and fell to his knee, Alex saw blood on his cheek where her knee had connected. Setting up her next attack, Alex took a step back before she ran toward him, with the intent of kicking him in the face.

He was fast. When Alex looked back on the fight, she would marvel at how fast he was. Again, he anticipated her move and was ready when she got close. He bear-hugged her and stood as he moved. Next thing Alex knew, she was slammed into the ground, her body reverberating with the impact. The Noble Lord looked down at her, his eyes on fire, blood seeping from his cheek. Alex felt ice-cold fear as she stared up at the malicious evil. He quickly straddled her lower body, controlling her legs before he locked his hands around her throat.

"You will need to learn where you belong here, pet."

Alex struggled, raking her nails against his skin, trying to kick her lower body free. Her lungs began to burn as they demanded air that she couldn't get. Alex reached up and tried to grab the long hair that fell in the Noble Lord's face He just laughed and lifted his head out of her reach. She slapped at his arms, his legs, his ribs. Nothing stopped him from slowly squeezing the life from her body. *Better this than to be anyone's pet*, Alex thought to herself. She could feel her body slowly stop responding to the commands her mind was giving it. Alex fell into the black, knowing it was her end.

In the darkness, Alex saw a figure. The body was moving, and the sound of rhythmic wood chopping met her ears. She felt confusion, not sure of where she was or how she had got there. Her memory was fuzzy, but she knew she was safe with the figure and she walked forward. As she got closer her surroundings began to brighten and she was standing in the middle of a field. When she looked around, she realized she was on her compound, behind the walls. The sun was bright, but she couldn't feel the warmth. Before she could wonder why that was a voice spoke.

"What are you doing, Alex?"

Alex spun back toward the figure who now had an axe resting on his shoulder. Mitch Duncan looked at his daughter, a disapproving look on his face.

"Dad?" Alex asked, surprised to see him there.

"Last time I checked."

Max got his sarcasm; Alex had almost forgotten. He was always the one with the great one-liner to pick on his kids. He wasn't mean spirited; it was just the way he knew how to show affection.

"What are you doing here? I'm not even sure...how I got here?" Alex said.

"You're here because you gave up," Mitch replied.

Then he turned and swung the axe in a large arc, impaling it into a block of wood. Alex stared at him as images assailed her. The Dead Brothel and the Noble Lord came to focus. She quickly realized she was probably dead. The Noble Lord had choked the life out of her. The realization made her heart ache. Though she knew that Rafe and Max would take care of her kids, they had already lost their father. Now Alex would be gone. How would they survive that?

"How was I supposed to keep fighting, Dad? I tried. The Noble Lord won."

"That's crap, girl, and you know it," Mitch said.

"I couldn't stay there. Let him do what he wanted to do to me," Alex said quietly. Even knowing she was talking to her dead father, she felt the embarrassment of talking about that subject with him.

"Let him? Alex, you've never let anyone do anything to you in your life. Why is this different?"

"He was stronger than me. I can't beat everyone that comes at me."

"Is that how I raised you?" Mitch asked.

"What does that matter? You're gone. The world has fallen apart. We have been doing the best we can," Alex said. She was defensive, even knowing she was probably imagining everything.

"I know. And I'm glad you all listened to me. But this is different, Alex. You need to fight, harder than you ever have. Remember who you are. You are a Duncan. My grandbabies need you. Easton and Candace need you. The compound needs you."

How does he know Easton and Candace, Alex thought to herself? *Because it's your imagination, Alex.*

"I'm not enough to help everyone. I can't lead the way you think I should," Alex replied.

"I didn't raise a failure in my family. I always knew who you were, Alex. And that hasn't changed."

"You were wrong. Even you can be wrong," Alex replied.

"Was I wrong about this?"

Mitch turned to sweep his hand around the compound. Alex looked away from him and could see people moving around the house. Everything was too bright, too white. Her imagination was letting her see her family again and she was thankful. Maybe she was dead and with her father while they were both looking down on the Duncan household. Mitch led the way toward the house. Closer, she could see Margaret and Candace on their knees in the garden. She saw Easton digging a hole fifty yards away from the bunkhouse. Alex cocked her head, wondering what it was he was doing. But her attention was pulled back to the house where a blonde head bounded out with a smaller dark head following. Her heart swelled as she watched Billie and Henry run, followed by her niece, Jack. Margaret lifted her head from the gardening and looked over to the children with a smile on her face. But even at that distance, Alex could tell the woman was worried about something.

What would happen to her children with her gone? Margaret would be a caring grandmother figure; Alex had no doubt. But that didn't replace parents. Alex looked over at Candace as she pulled weeds with determination. She and her brother had already lost one mother. Losing a second one would be a nail to their hearts. Alex wished she could save them any pain. But as she thought about that, the sadness faded as she watched the younger kids run and play tag. Billie ran to the garden and yelled you're it as she poked Candace in the shoulder. Brushing the dirt off of her knees, Candace stood and chased after the kids. She grabbed Henry and swung him around before singing he was it and putting him down. The kids' laughter flowed over Alex; a balm to her battered soul.

"They're getting big," Mitch remarked, pulling Alex's attention back.

"Yes. They are."

"I would have liked to meet Candace and Easton. They seem like good kids. You are doing right by them. But that isn't a surprise."

"They are wonderful. You would have liked them. They are determined and are learning fast," Alex replied, as she fondly watched Candace running with the younger children.

"Because you're a good teacher, Alex," Mitch replied, looking back at her.

"Where are Rafe and Max? If this is my imagination, shouldn't they be here?" Alex said. She was talking more to herself than her father.

"They need you. And no matter what you think, I know you are a leader. You can protect them. Just like Rafe and Max are coming to protect you now."

"What? What do you mean? Protect me how? No one can protect me if I'm already dead."

"Did I say you were dead?" Mitch asked.

"I'm talking to you and you're dead," Alex said.

"I thought this was all your imagination?"

Without warning, her father took up a fighting stance facing her. Alex didn't think so much as just react. It felt so normal to fall right into the lessons he always had with her as a child. At any time, Mitch would challenge his children in hand to hand combat. His belief that you never knew where the next attack was coming from. Alex fell into an easy defensive stance. She feigned and blocked as Mitch threw a few punches at her. Then as Alex expected, Mitch tried to sweep her legs. She jumped back and then took a leap at him with a fist up. She stopped before connecting and turned away. She didn't feel out of breath. However, she knew she had beat him this round.

Alex turned to her father. She was surprised to see one of his rare smiles splitting across his face. He seemed to study Alex before reaching out a hand and touching her short hair.

"I like your hair like this. It was a smart decision. But that's because you're a smart woman."

Alex tried to grasp his hand, to hold it in her own, to ground herself in the moment. But when she reached, he was suddenly further away. He smiled again and waved at her. It was then Alex realized she was moving away, not Mitch moving from her. She struggled, calling out to him. She could feel tears on her cheeks. What she wouldn't do to have her father back, to help them, to protect her children. All the while he smiled and waved, as the darkness took her again.

CHAPTER SEVENTEEN

"Were you trying to kill her?" A female voice said.

"Don't question me, Auntie. Just finish sewing her up," a harsh male voice replied.

"If you want to keep this one, you're in for a fight. She's different from the other women you've kept in this room," the female voice said.

Alex tried to focus on the voices around her and try to pull herself back to the world. Her confusion was fueled by her hazy dream of her father and her family at the compound. Was she dead? Who was beating the drum in her head? Why did her leg hurt so bad? If she were dead, would there still be pain? Where was her father? Why had he let her go? So many questions were on her mind. And the surrounding voices were answering none of them.

"I know she's different. That's why I'm keeping her," the male voice said.

"Some women can't be kept. That's this one. You will kill her eventually," the female replied quietly.

Alex pulled at the threads of her memory and she started to realize who was talking around her. She could recognize the pity in Coral's voice as she spoke with the Noble Lord. A slight tug at her leg told her that Coral was stitching up her wound. As she tried to focus on the conversation, the darkness in her mind began to bleed into her conscience again. She struggled, trying to keep it at bay, hoping to learn something from the conversation happening.

"Then I will enjoy her until I kill her, Auntie," the Noble Lord said.

Auntie, Alex thought. That did explain some questions she had about Coral and what place the woman held in the brothel. The doting nephew had saved his aunt from death, only to put her to work in his brothel. But not to work like most other women and that put her into a place of respect. It also explained why Coral didn't have a problem talking back to the Noble Lord or denying his orders. She believed he wouldn't harm her. Alex had a feeling that Coral gave her nephew too much credit. The man was a monster that enjoyed harming and enslaving women. Killing family was likely not something he would struggle with.

"Your mother would turn over in her grave if she could see you now," Coral said.

"My mother was a druggie streetwalker, who got sick from dirty needles. I don't care what her ghost thinks of me," the Noble Lord replied, dismissively.

"She wouldn't want this for you. Or for these women. She was sick, but she wanted to provide for you."

"Well then this job—that was good enough for her—is good enough for the women here," the Noble Lord said.

Coral didn't reply to that. Alex had the feeling this was an argument she had tried before. But the Noble Lord wasn't to be swayed from how he wanted to control people. And in the end, Coral needed the protection she had become accustomed to. She felt the woman's fingers at her leg as she put something cold on the wound and then taped a bandage over it. Despite the violence from the Noble Lord, he was clearly concerned about infection and illness. He didn't want Alex to die. And now that she wasn't dead, Alex wanted to fight for her freedom even more.

She laid with her eyes closed and kept her breathing even. Her mind replayed the conversation with her father. He had more faith in her than she had in herself. She wasn't sure she could do what he wanted her to. But he reminded her of who she was. Duncans didn't just give up when things were difficult. Hell, her entire childhood consisted of difficult times. Mitch Duncan had made sure they could handle themselves in some of the harshest circumstances. And though Alex didn't fully embrace all of her father's lessons like her sister, she remembered everything Mitch wanted them to know

Coral's examination included the probing of Alex's skull and there were a few tender places where Alex had to fight the wince. Then the older woman touched Alex's throat carefully. As soon as her fingers pressed into the area around her trachea, Alex knew there was something wrong. Her neck hurt a great deal, but Alex had assumed it was just bruised. Now feeling Coral's prodding, Alex wondered if something was strained or broken.

"You did a number on her throat. I'm not sure she'll be able to talk when she wakes up," Coral said.

"Permanently? That might be preferable," the Noble Lord replied.

"I doubt it's permanent. The bruising and damage would be much worse, I think, if it were that extreme."

Alex heard the Noble Lord scoff and she wanted to sneer at him. She didn't need her voice to defy him. She would use her wits, her body, and her actions. It seemed her imaginary father's pep talk had stoked a fire deep inside Alex. She began to test her body, checking for additional injuries. She flexed her fingers in both hands, happy to not have any broken fingers. She tried to rotate her ankles. The left with the stitches didn't like the movement, but Alex had no doubt that she would heal quickly. Pain she could handle. She didn't want to be immobile.

"She's waking," Coral said as she quickly took notice of Alex's shifting.

"Ah, good. I was wondering if she was permanently damaged."

Alex took her time as she continued the internal examination. When she was ready, she slowly blinked her eyes open. The room was lit brightly by a lantern. Alex assumed that commodities such as lanterns were only used in emergencies, as the rest of the brothel was lit by candlelight. She turned her head slightly and pain cut into her thoughts. Her throat was definitely injured. She looked at Coral who was trying to see into her eyes.

"How many fingers am I holding up?" Coral asked as she held up her hand.

"Three," Alex said, her voice barely coming out as a raspy whisper.

"Is that the loudest you can speak?" Coral asked.

"I'm not sure," Alex responded. She tried to force her voice louder, but it was too painful against her vocal cords.

"Ok. Don't try. It would be good for you to rest your voice, I think. Your vocal cords are bruised."

Alex didn't bother trying to respond. Her body had already told her what Coral was saying. *Talking was painful, don't force it.* The Noble Lord stood behind his aunt watching the exchange and he stood with a bored look on his face. Alex looked back at him, staring. She was pleased to see the butterfly bandages across his cheek and the bridge of his nose. She had wounded him and that only reminded her that he was just a man.

When his eyes met hers, he smiled ruefully. Without words he told Alex he had won, and she needed to submit. But instead of looking away, Alex grinned wildly back, allowing a little crazy to cross her face. The Noble Lord stopped smiling, but he didn't look away. Alex was pretty sure he got her message. She wasn't done fighting.

Coral stood from the bed and began to pack her supplies. Alex watched as she put away sterile packages and hospital supplies.

The brothel was very well stocked, so it made sense that they would have a full supply of medical needs. Alex wondered how often the women of the brothel were injured. Coral was adept with stitching and some basic medical knowledge. With all the women prisoners, she probably put those talents to work fairly often. The last thing the woman did was break the inside of an ice pack, allowing the interior chemicals to mix and start their reaction. She placed the pack on Alex's throat. This time Alex couldn't hide the wince. Quickly the cold pushed away the pain and all Alex felt was numb.

"Keep this on for a while. Hopefully it helps any swelling inside. But I'm not sure how bad the damage really is. We'll have to wait and see."

"You may go, Coral," the Noble Lord said.

Alex noticed that he didn't call her "Auntie" now that Alex was awake. When he thought she was asleep, he was more vulnerable and gave up more information. Alex didn't give any indication that she knew anything as the two parted ways at the door. The Noble Lord came back to the bed. In his hand were a pair of silver handcuffs. He walked straight to Alex and hooked one side to her wrist and the other to the metal framework of the large headboard. Without a word he went to the other side of the bed and laid down.

He faced her and watched her as she stared at the ceiling. Alex didn't turn to look at him. Not only would her neck not allow the movement, she also wouldn't give him the satisfaction of interacting. Alex was exhausted. Her body demanded time to recharge and begin its healing process. But a part of her was too scared to sleep next to the vile man. Though she was injured, she didn't believe that would stop him from taking what he wanted. She was an easy victim at the moment, no matter what Alex wanted. Her will to live was back, she could feel it flow through her mind. It was as if her father was infused in her cells now, after imagining him during her blackout.

Eventually Alex could no longer fight the sleep she needed so badly. She was able to hold out longer than the Noble Lord. She noted the moment his eyes closed, and his breathing became deep and even. She spent a good amount of time wishing she had something to stab him with. It was frustrating to her to have him so close and vulnerable and yet she could do nothing about it. As she began to fall into sleep, she found herself wishing she saw her father again. When she finally closed her eyes, she could feel herself reaching for him. However, he wasn't there this time. She was reaching nothing but darkness.

With no windows to the outside, Alex couldn't be sure how long she had slept. She was woken by the Noble Lord rolling out of bed. The moment he shifted his feet to the ground Alex was wide awake. And the pain hit her like a ton of bricks. With her free hand, Alex removed the now warm ice pack from her neck. She unceremoniously threw it to the floor. She touched her throat carefully, feeling abnormal swelling. The discovery made her seethe with anger. She would find the chance to make the Noble Lord pay for injuring her.

Alex then ran her hand down her leg, finding the bandage Coral had placed. She peeled up a piece of the tape so she could put her fingers on the skin underneath. She waited a beat and was thankful to not feel any hot skin around the wound. A raging infection was the last thing she needed and being stabbed by wood could leave any number of particles in her body. She dodged a real problem with that.

"I wouldn't mess with that," the Noble Lord said.

He came out of his closet area fully dressed, holding his boots. Alex didn't bother trying to respond. She knew it would hurt and she didn't feel like he deserved any responses from her. He sat on her side of the bed and pushed his feet into his boots. Once done, he leaned over her, his hand resting on her uninjured thigh. He brought himself nose to nose with her.

"You won't be doing that again, will you?" He asked.

Whichever way she shook her head, he would assume she was agreeing with him. So instead she looked away from him. He grabbed her chin and brought her back to face him. Alex stared at him with hate.

"Still some fire in there, I see. Well, we have time to break that," the Noble Lord said.

Then he leaned down and softly kissed her. If Alex had more strength in her neck, she would have ripped her face out of his hand. However, at that moment she was too weak to do anything. Instead, she didn't move a muscle, she didn't kiss him back, she laid stiff. Once he was done, he sat back and studied her.

"It's such a shame that we had to damage that beautiful body. But I think you'll heal and we'll start again."

She didn't answer him, just stared at the ceiling. At that moment she made a vow to herself that she wouldn't be there long enough for him to try to break her again. She would figure out a way to escape and if she could, kill him on the way out. She knew it was going to be hard and she wasn't even really sure how she would make it happen. But she thought about her father's words. She had been raised the way she had been for a reason. She was determined to live up to her father's belief in her. The Noble Lord wouldn't break her spirit or her body again.

Without an answer, the Noble Lord just sighed and rose from the bed. He went back to the closet and when he exited again, he was strapping on the hunting knife he kept on his hip. Again, Alex noted that he didn't seem to carry a gun, only the twelve-inch blade. She wondered if it was arrogance that caused him to not carry something more for protection. On the hopeful side, Alex thought maybe he wasn't adept with using a gun. That would give Alex a step up on him and if she could get her hands on a firearm, she could easily take him out.

"Coral will be back to check on you this morning. Try to be nice to the old woman," the Noble Lord said over his shoulder as he walked toward the door.

Without any additional conversation, the Noble Lord opened the door. Alex then snapped to attention, raising her head slightly to see what the guard set-up was. She could see one man by the door and a muzzle from a second gun on the other side. Two men at least at the door. Both of which were armed to the teeth with weapons to protect their dear leader. The Noble Lord relied on and trusted his guards. Alex toyed with the idea of finding one she could turn with lies and promises. If she could get one on her side, it would be easier to get the weapon she needed.

Hours later Alex was awakened by prodding on her throat. Somehow through the day Alex had succumbed to her need for rest and had fallen into a deep sleep. *Stupid*, she thought to herself. She hadn't heard the door open or anyone enter. Luckily for her this time it was only Coral there to check on her. When Alex's eyes popped open the woman sat back slightly to look at her. Alex looked all around the room, afraid that the Noble Lord had come back with her. Finding the room empty she turned her eyes back on the woman that was acting as a nurse.

"Yes, we're alone," Coral said, understanding Alex's inspection of the room.

"Why?" Alex said with a croak.

"You probably should wait another few days before really talking. But I'm not sure what you're asking. Why are we alone?" Coral asked.

Alex nodded her head slightly, but stilled as soon as pain hit her from her neck.

"The Noble Lord doesn't think you're a threat right now. And we were alone before and you didn't hurt me. How would you now?"

Coral shrugged her shoulders as if the answer was so simple. It was then that Alex suddenly realized that her arm was no longer handcuffed to the bed. Both of her hands laid on her stomach, as if Coral was positioning her for something. Alex flexed the hand and tried to rotate her shoulder. The pain in her neck stopped her from doing much, but the blood flowing freely back through the limb felt great.

"I think we should get you up to the bathroom," Coral said.

Alex didn't argue. Her body needed to relieve itself and she wasn't sure where the bathroom was. She shouldn't have been surprised when she was led to a private bathroom that had been blocked off for the Noble Lord. Coral led her through a hallway that had been blocked by wood, not allowing any view from the ballroom. The hallway led to a door which opened to a bathroom with three stalls and a makeshift shower in the corner. Coral helped Alex into a stall before stepping back to wait.

In the stall, Alex sat heavily on the toilet. She didn't move, long after she was done relieving herself. She hadn't been alone in three days and even the idea of privacy in the stall was blissful to Alex. The bathroom was quiet, with none of the outside chaos reaching her. She leaned over and rested her head on the stall wall. She studied the tile on the ground, black and white squares that seemed to be from a different era.

She closed her eyes for a moment and took some deep breaths. In her mind she memorized the bathroom as well. There was one high window, that Alex couldn't climb out of without help. Three toilet stalls and one large metal tub that was made into a shower. There were two sinks, but one was rerouted for the shower water. There was no escape from this room. Knowing that, Alex marked it off her list of possibilities.

"Did you fall in?" Coral's voice came from the other side of the stall door.

Alex didn't bother trying to respond, as she knew it would hurt. She stood and flushed the toilet. When she came out of the stall, Coral stood leaning against the wall waiting. She came to Alex and put an arm around her waist to help. At the sink, Coral splashed water on Alex's face and patted it dry. She used a wash-cloth to clean away the dried blood that had caked into Alex's hair and skin. *Can't have me looking bad for the Noble Lord,* Alex thought to herself. She guessed he expected his pets to be in perfect condition. *A hard request since he's the one that broke them.*

Looking into the mirror, Alex inspected her face and throat. She experimented turning her head from side to side. Her muscles were stiff and tight. The pain was still there, but it was getting more manageable. She continued to stretch for a moment, working the kinks out of her body. Laying in a bed for twelve hours or more straight wasn't normal for Alex. With her injuries and laying stationary, muscles she had forgotten about were angry with her. The cut on her thigh hurt, but it was a speck in the larger scheme of sensations in her body.

When she was done, Coral led her back to the bed. She helped Alex climb into the tall bed and then she propped her up on pillows. While they were in the bathroom, a tray had been brought in. On it was a steaming liquid-filled bowl and a bottle of water. After Alex was settled, Coral held a spoon to Alex's mouth. Alex eyed the spoon and the woman with distrust.

"I'm not here to poison you. If he wanted you dead, he wouldn't have stopped when you passed out," Coral said, nodding toward her throat.

Alex conceded that Coral's reasoning made sense. She opened her lips slightly and Coral slid the warm liquid over her tongue. It was a broth of some type. Though Alex couldn't have felt hunger if she tried, the warmth spread down her injured throat into her belly, making her shiver. Coral set the bowl down and pulled the thick comforter over Alex. The blanket did little to make Alex feel better, but she knew the warmth would soon set in and her body would appreciate that.

"Do I call you Auntie?" Alex said in a whisper.

She watched Coral for her reaction, her widening eyes were the only indication Alex received that she had hit a nerve.

"My name is Coral, you know that."

"I know that you are the Noble Lord's aunt. And he respects you in the only way he knows how," Alex said.

"You are delusional. The Noble Lord doesn't respect anyone but himself."

"In general terms, sure. But I have wondered about you. He doesn't treat you the same. He listens to you. And I now have my answer. My new question is, why do you let him do what he does?"

Coral didn't answer Alex, but instead held the spoon to her lips again. Alex didn't hesitate to allow the spoon-feeding to continue. When she was handed the water bottle, Alex wanted to guzzle the water. Yet, she knew it would only make her sick if she did it too fast. She took sips before placing the cap back and giving it to Coral. When the woman tried to give Alex another bite, Alex shook her head slightly and stared at Coral. She wanted an answer to her question.

"No one lets him do anything," Coral finally said.

Alex opened her mouth for the bite. The broth was filling her with pleasant heat, and she wanted to drink straight from the bowl. But she thought if she could delay Coral leaving, she may be able to gather more information about the Noble Lord and his organization.

"Maybe not. But I think he listens more to you than you are willing to admit to me. Look at me, I'm not in the position to use any information. Be honest."

Her hand swept her body, highlighting the bruises and injuries. Alex hedged her bets that Coral was lonely. That she had no one to talk to in this apocalyptic world. She now lived to serve the Noble Lord. And Alex knew that wasn't a fulfilling life. If she could position herself as a confidant for Coral, Alex thought she may be able to obtain information that was useful to her escape. While her body was in the state it was, she didn't have much else to do.

"I don't know things about the Noble Lord and his operation," Coral said.

"Ok. If that's how you want to be. How long has this place been like this?" Alex asked.

"The drugs were his business before the dead. The women started a few weeks after. He took this place over when he realized he had a moneymaker."

"So, not long," Alex said. Her voice was getting quieter as the pain intensified with each word she spoke.

"No. It looks like something he's worked on for a long time. But this building was a good find. It was being used by FEMA. The Noble Lord and his men, shall we say evicted the workers? They already had separate rooms set up for survivors. The Noble Lord had the manpower and he pushed them all out."

"Pushed or killed?" Alex asked.

"Doesn't really matter now," Coral replied, shrugging her small shoulders.

Alex could guess for herself, the menace of the Noble Lord was apparent. He wouldn't have left anyone alive that could oppose him. She thought about the bodies in the front of the building, some decomposed and smelling. Originally she had assumed they were the infected that were just left to rot. Now she wondered if some of those weren't the innocent people that had originally called the old building salvation. The hate she had for the evil man intensified.

"I know you aren't really ok with what goes on here," Alex said.

"You'll learn to do what you have to, to stay alive," Coral said.

As she spoke, she straightened the nightie that Alex still wore. On one side the lace was ripped away from the bodice, exposing more of Alex's skin than she would have liked. Beneath the black material, bruises bloomed across Alex's skin. They were darkening by the hour and Alex felt her anger grow at the same rate. She would not be learning to do anything, except fight for her freedom and protect her body.

Coral stood and started to clean up the supplies she had

brought. She then turned and quickly handcuffed Alex again, preventing Alex from even attempting an escape after she left.

"I'll be back in a few hours with a dinner for you. Rest. You'll feel better about everything once you're feeling back to normal."

"Unlikely," Alex replied.

Coral just sighed and left the room. It was clear the woman thought anything the Noble Lord did was worth his protection. The difference between Coral and Alex, Alex didn't need protection. She could take care of herself and the surrounding people. She had killed hundreds of the infected. Bending the knee to the Noble Lord wasn't something she was going to even consider doing. On the other hand, her mind was ready to take Coral's advice for rest. Her eyes slowly fell shut and she was immediately in darkness.

Angry voices entered the bedroom and Alex pushed herself up into a sitting position. She had been awake watching the firelight dance on the ceiling. Her nap had re-energized her and she'd spent some time messing with the handcuffs. When she couldn't open those, she tried to find a way to break the bed to get away. Nothing proved successful so she just laid and stared at the ceiling. The Noble Lord coming in having an angry conversation was enough to make Alex jump.

The Noble Lord strode across the room to the fireplace that had the warm fire burning. A guard had come in numerous times to make sure there was a light in the room and that the fire didn't go out. She guessed it was his job to make sure the room was always ready for the Noble Lord. Behind a very pissed off Noble Lord, two men in military uniforms followed. Alex sucked in a breath and then cursed to herself when her movements set off pain in her neck. One of the men looked over at Alex and then pointedly back to the Noble Lord.

"She's not a problem. She can't speak right now, anyhow," the Noble Lord said, waving Alex off like a fly around his dinner plate.

"We come with a message," the blond soldier said.

"I have told you people, you don't come here. I will meet you when we have our arranged times. You coming in here like this makes my people question who's running this place," the Noble Lord said.

Alex listened intently. She decided that the Noble Lord brought the soldiers into his room to have the ultimate level of privacy. None of the guards would dare enter his chambers without permission. He didn't see Alex as a threat. She would prove him mistaken on that point. Now she found herself wondering if there was a secret behind the brothel that she hadn't discovered. The Noble Lord wasn't in power.

"Our Major is the driving force behind this place you call home. Your guards would not be as efficient without the weapons we have supplied. Don't fool yourself, you do not run this place," the brown-haired soldier said.

Even with only the candle and firelight Alex could tell the Noble Lord's face was flushing with anger. His eyes narrowed as she stared at the soldiers. His hands were on his hip and Alex realized he had them there for easy access to his knife.

"And without me Callahan wouldn't have the drugs he needs," the Noble Lord said.

The name was a shot to Alex's gut. It had been almost two months since the last attack from the Major and his men. Alex hadn't allowed her hopes to get up though. Callahan had captured her sister and tortured her, attacked her home to kidnap Charlie and kill her brother, and again attacked when she was on the compound and she killed his men. She knew all of these failures wouldn't allow Callahan to give up his pursuit of the Duncans. And that was without the connection between Callahan and 'The Suit'.

"The Major wants to continue the partnership you have. But the terms need to change," the brown-haired soldier said.

"Change? Why?"

"The Major needs access to the stores of supplies you have,

not just the drugs. Without the government fully functioning, supplies haven't flowed the way we need. We know you have control of a lot in this area. We need access to it. We have a truck to fill," blond solider said.

"A truck? You just want to fill a truck? Callahan has lost his mind. I don't have that much on hand," the Noble Lord said.

"We know you do."

"And what do I get in return?" The Noble Lord asked, not bothering to deny his supply situation.

"Continued protection from any element that would choose to end your little kingdom status here," brown-headed soldier said.

Alex couldn't believe the conversation. The Noble Lord didn't have the power on his own. He was supported by Major Callahan. The last few days seemed so laughable now. The Noble Lord tried to portray himself as the all-powerful king of Montana and lands surrounding. In the end, he was just a pawn of Callahan's. She could admit he seemed to have no problem getting his hands dirty to demand the respect he had from the people in the brothel. But he didn't win that on his own.

"So, Callahan wants more, and I get less. This partnership isn't going the way I'd like to see it," the Noble Lord said.

"Do you want us to take that back to the Major?" Blond soldier threatened.

The Noble Lord turned and kicked at the wood stack next to the fireplace. He reminded Alex of a little boy that had been reprimanded by his parents. He was pouting, because he couldn't change what was happening. He turned back to the men with a smile plastered on his face.

"Boys, no. Listen, I'm here to support Callahan as needed. Why don't we work out all these details in the morning? You two take your choice of whatever women you'd like tonight, on the house," the Noble Lord said. Both soldiers smiled at the prospect of not sleeping alone.

The Noble Lord put a hand on each of their shoulders as they walked back toward the bedroom door. Once the soldiers left, the door shut solidly after them. The Noble Lord turned to look at Alex, sitting up in the bed, tense and waiting. A menacing smile slid across his face as he began to advance on Alex. She yanked at the handcuffs again, knowing it was futile.

That was when the brothel exploded with the deafening sounds of gunfire and screams of terror.

CHAPTER EIGHTEEN

Midday the vehicles that held those bound to rescue Alex pulled to a stop for lunch. Max argued that they could drive and eat. But, Rafe insisted they look at the maps one more time and try to make a plan of attack before venturing into the city that the Noble Lord resided in. Marcus was too tense to voice his agreement with either sibling. Delaying made him sick. However, the alternative was rushing in, unprepared and possibly all dying before being able to rescue Alex. The Vegas didn't have opinions as they ate their lunch in silence and unfolded the city map in the back of the truck. When they were planning on rescuing Sylvia on their own, they had started preparing with information on the city.

A circled block on the map was their target. In the middle of the circle the words "Civic Center" were printed. Albert explained that they had never actually seen the city. They knew the building because Vera remembered seeing signs and an old plaque that had the establishment date. They had the description of the areas Vera had been allowed to see, including the back door that wasn't closely guarded. They knew there was an upstairs and possibly a working fire escape that Vera had seen during an assembly the Noble Lord called.

"We're not far. Maybe fifteen miles," Mateo said.

"We don't want to go in during the daylight hours. We need darkness to assist us in being hidden until we are attacking," Rafe commented as he rubbed his jaw.

That statement brought a quiet to the group, as they realized they had to kill half the day on the side of the road. Marcus checked his weapons for the thirtieth time. Charlie went through her medical bag, unpacking it all and then repacking it again. The sound of a vehicle engine stopped them all in their tracks. Everyone with a gun took up positions behind their trucks, waiting for the vehicle to approach. Marcus felt his heart hammer in his chest. His thoughts went to the bus he and Alex had found. Did the Noble Lord have more pleasure vehicles like that?

In the distance, Marcus could make out the front of the vehicle approaching. An itch started on his brain and he watched as the car got closer. Just as the black van passed their vehicles it began to slow, as if the driver caught sight off the trucks. At the same time, the itch in Marcus' brain became a thought and before he could explain to anyone he stepped out from behind the truck. He began by shooting out the back windows of the van and then started aiming at the tires. He wasn't the crack shot that Alex was but with the rifle he wasn't half bad.

When one back tire blew, the van began to shudder to one side. Marcus ran forward hoping to stop it before they tried to continue to limp down the road. Footsteps pounded behind him and in a distant place in his mind, he knew someone was yelling his name. The van screeched to a halt after Marcus paused long enough to aim and shoot out the second back tire. As the side door slid open, Albert was suddenly at Marcus' side. He realized that Albert knew what Marcus knew. It was the same black van that took Sylvia and Alex. Both men planted themselves and pointed their weapons at the vehicle.

"Don't kill them, we need to know where they took Alex," Marcus said quietly as the rest of the group joined him.

The first gunshots from the van scattered the Duncan group. Marcus didn't feel fear for his own life. Instead of running and taking cover, he ran directly up to the back of the van, using it as a shield from the gunfire. He watched as Rafe, Max, and Griffin dove behind trees on the side of the road. Albert moved toward Marcus, when his right leg suddenly buckled, and he cried out.

"Tio!" Mateo cried from behind the truck Marcus drove.

Bullets pinged off of the asphalt around Albert as he struggled to get out of harm's way. He yelled at Mateo in Spanish. Marcus assumed he was giving him instructions to stay put with a number of curse words that Marcus did recognize. Marcus watched the man and knew if he didn't move soon, he would be dead. The men from the van didn't have great aim. Hitting Albert in the leg must have been a lucky shot, because now that they all fired at him, nothing was striking the man.

"Marcus!" Rafe's voice came a split second before gunfire erupted from the tree line.

Without question, Marcus knew this was a distraction to get Albert to safety. He ran straight for the wounded man. He grabbed him under the arms and decided the van was closer than the trucks. He grunted under pulling the weight of Albert, dragging him across the road. To his credit, Albert didn't cry out. He continued to hold his gun in both hands, waiting for any target to make itself known. Reaching the van before the gang members opened fire again, Marcus leaned Albert against the back bumper. Albert held his hand over the wound that had blood freely flowing.

"Wait here," Marcus said.

"Where am I going?" Albert replied sarcastically.

Marcus circled the far side of the van, taking the chance that the gang members were all focused on the side where shots were flying. He crouched low when he came to the driver's side window and glanced cautiously in the mirror. He could see someone sitting in the passenger seat, bent down to escape the flurry of bullets that hit the side of the van. Marcus tested the driver's side door and found it to be unlocked. Opening it quickly, he pointed his gun at the man in the passenger seat. Marcus couldn't determine much about the man as he was covered in filth. His face didn't have much skin visible. The smell from the van was one of unwashed bodies that had been sweating and many other activities mixed together. It was all Marcus could do to not cover his mouth with his free hand.

The passenger took a look at Marcus and his gun and seemed to weigh his options. Surprising Marcus, the man dropped the gun and showed his hands in a surrender motion. Marcus motioned for him to climb over the driver's seat and to exit the vehicle. The shots from the Duncans continued sporadically, but return fire was slow coming. Once the man was out of the vehicle, Marcus grabbed him and pushed him against the van. He quickly checked to make sure there weren't additional guns hidden on the man. Satisfied that he didn't have anything to attack Marcus with, Marcus spun the man around.

"How many more of you are there?" Marcus asked.

"Two. There were three, but you killed one," the man replied.

"Tell them to surrender, or they follow in your friend's footsteps."

"Jackson! They're gonna kill us all. Just give up!" The man yelled when there was a lull in gunfire.

"Marcus?" Max's voice came from the other side of the van.

"Far side of the van. I have one of our new friends here. He's surrendered nice and quietly. The rest of his friends should too if they want to see one more morning!" Marcus called back.

He heard the footsteps as Rafe and Max approached from the back of the van. Together as a team the two snuck around the van to the sliding door on the passenger side. Marcus led his captive the same way, with a gun pressed against his head. As they approached the door it slid open violently. Everyone froze and waited.

"Fine. We give up!" A voice said from inside.

"Throw out the weapons," Rafe called back.

Moments later, one handgun came flying through the door. Rafe looked and Max, who just rolled her eyes.

"We know you have more in there. Toss it out, or we light the van up again," Rafe called, his voice sounding bored. Marcus didn't know how he kept himself so calm in order to intimidate the kidnappers in the van. Marcus' own heart was thundering in his throat.

A mumbled argument could be heard and then three additional guns hit the pavement.

"Now step out, one by one, with your hands in the air. Any sort of movements will be a bullet to the face," Rafe said. Rafe kept his voice flat, but the threat was clear to those inside the van.

Two grim faces showed from the opening of the van's sliding door. Both had their hands out front, following Rafe's directions. Their eyes bounced around from Rafe, to Max, then to Marcus who still held a gun to their companion's head. A growl split the air and both men froze noticing Storm at Rafe's feet. Rafe noticed the men's reactions and he grinned coldly. He gave them a moment longer to worry before he snapped his fingers and pointed. His command brought Storm to attention, but his growling stopped.

As the gang members' shoulders slumped, Marcus could see the moment they realized they had to give up. With Rafe watching her back, Max went to the guns and threw them all toward the back of the van. Marcus noticed then that Charlie was crouched at the back of the van, her medical bag open next to Albert. When the guns came her way, she shifted to pull them closer to them without hesitation. Cliff stood guard, gun at the ready over Charlie. The team moved fluidly, knowing what was needed from each of them.

"Just don't take us back to him," one of the men said.

"What's your name?" Marcus asked.

"Jackson. That's Bo you have the gun on, and this is Trevor," Jackson said, pointing to the other man that had his hands up.

"Jackson and Trevor, hands on the van. We're going to search you. One wrong move and again, the answer is a bullet," Rafe said.

The men complied easily, and Marcus pushed Bo to the van as well. All three men were searched thoroughly, and Max produced zip ties for their wrists. Once they were bound to the Duncans' satisfaction, the three men were sat next to the van on the asphalt. A check with Charlie let Rafe know it was a grim situation with Albert. The bullet in his leg hadn't exited. She was going to have to dig it out. And then he wouldn't be able to walk on it. The man argued but Mateo was at his side speaking angrily in Spanish. Whatever the younger man said hit a nerve because Albert squeezed his lips shut.

"We're too exposed here," Max said. Rafe and Marcus had joined her in a small huddle to decide on their next steps.

"Agreed. We need to move off the road so Charlie can work on Albert. These men know something about the Noble Lord, so we need to question them," Rafe said.

Rafe volunteered to drive the van with the three captives tied up inside. Marcus worked with Mateo to carefully load Albert into the bed of the pickup truck. Charlie rode with him, keeping pressure on his wound. Cliff sat shotgun with Marcus again, his gun still at the ready, as if he was expecting an ambush at anytime. Marcus guessed anything could happen at this point. He felt better just having his friend watching their back while he drove, following Rafe off the main road. Rafe turned the van on a small dirt road that seemed to lead to a hiking trailhead. There were no other vehicles nearby. Rafe, Marcus, and Max pulled their vehicles in a large circle, parking them all facing the exit.

Once they were set up, Rafe climbed out of the van. He went to the side of the vehicle and ripped the sliding door open. He pulled each man out and dropped them on the dirt next to the van. None of them argued, just avoided looking at any of the Duncan group. Marcus decided he was done waiting to ask his questions. He pulled his 9mm and held it at his side as he walked toward the gang members. Rafe turned and stopped him just as he approached.

"We aren't shooting them," Rafe said quietly.

"I didn't say I was going to shoot them. Well, I won't kill them at least," Marcus replied. He couldn't hide the fury he felt toward the men that had kidnapped Alex. They deserved anything coming their way.

"That little gunfight is going to attract attention, living or dead. If you let off a shot here, you're revealing our position," Rafe said.

"Ok. Well, if they answer my questions, I won't use the gun."

Lightning quick, Rafe held up one of his many knives. He held the handle out to Marcus, and his other hand was out waiting for the gun. Marcus considered his options for a moment. He knew that Rafe was right, but he wanted to make the men hurt. He wasn't as good with knives as Rafe was. Shooting was more his thing. However, he wasn't going to win with Rafe. Setting his 9mm in Rafe's open hand, Marcus wrapped his free hand around the knife handle. Rafe nodded to him once and stepped aside.

Marcus stopped just in front of the men. None of them looked up to acknowledge his presence. They all seemed folded in on themselves, resigned to whatever was going to happen to them next.

"Who were you talking about before? Who don't you want us to take you to? Marcus asked.

"You aren't working for him? The Noble Lord?" Jackson asked, only his eyes coming up to meet Marcus' glare.

"You wouldn't know me. But I was in town that day. The day

you made a woman believe you were in danger of being eaten by a horde. I was there, helping to distract the dead, so she could pick you up," Marcus said, his voice quiet and menacing. He was getting their attention, as all of their eyes were now on his face.

"I was there. Close enough to hear her screams as you abducted her into this piece of shit van of yours. You drove away before I could follow. But I would never give up on her. We don't leave our family behind," Marcus said.

"The dark-haired woman? You're talking about that Alex woman," Bo said, his voice shaken.

Max came flying past Marcus, her fist striking out in a quick jab that struck Bo square in the nose. Blood began to flow freely from his nostrils, and he cried out as his head hit the van when Max grabbed him by the hair. She crouched down, putting herself nose to nose with Bo.

"That Alex woman, she's my sister. I will kill you if you harmed her," Max said in a growl.

"We didn't...I didn't...I didn't hurt her," Bo stammered. Marcus was impressed with Max's skills of intimidation.

"Then where is she?" Marcus asked.

"He has her," Jackson spoke up. When Max's murderous gaze flew to him, he physically flinched. Marcus was sure he had every reason to be scared.

"He? You took her to the Noble Lord?" Marcus asked. When no one answered immediately, Max bounced Bo's head off the van again.

"Answer him," she said.

"Lewis took her. We were sent to find the Noble Lord's pet that ran away. We had her and Alex was just icing on the cake. She should have gotten us paid real well. But she let the other pet go. We never got paid. We had to run." The words vomited out of Bo's mouth. His face screwed up in pain as Max's knuckles turned white in his hair.

"You had to run? And you left my sister there? Where's this Lewis?" Max asked.

"Lewis is dead," Jackson said evenly.

"Your sister killed him," Bo added.

"Why did Alex kill him? What did he do to her?" Marcus asked, anger beginning to raise his voice.

"We're trying to survive out here, just like you," Jackson said, avoiding the question. He lifted his chin in defiance and Marcus knew it was the wrong move.

Max didn't give any warning as she released her hold on Bo and stood to punch Jackson in the jaw. The man's head snapped back and again she succeeded in bouncing a head off the vehicle. Marcus wondered if she kept count. He had her at three so far. Jackson turned to look at her and the sneer on his face was all it took for Max to punch him again. At the thunk sound, Marcus counted four in his head. Jackson didn't get the chance to aggravate Max any further, as his head slumped to one side and his eyes rolled back into his head.

"Well now he's super useful," Rafe said as he approached.

"He deserved it," Max replied, shrugging her shoulders at her brother. Rafe just shook his head.

"So you aren't the Noble Lord's men. But you do disgusting things to be in his favor. Why is Lewis dead?" Marcus asked, picking up the questioning again. If someone didn't stay on track, they would never gather the information they needed.

"He broke the Noble Lord's rules. He got a guard to take your sister to him in a private room. The Noble Lord said no one was to touch her. Lewis paid for it. Your sister strangled him with his own belt, at least that's what I heard," Bo said. The smaller man was very willing to answer questions now that he saw the damage Max could inflict.

Max looked at Rafe and Marcus, her eyes wide. Marcus knew where her mind was. His own was running to the worst possible scenario. For Alex to do something so drastic, she had to have been in serious danger. It wasn't like Alex to take someone's life in her hands unless she felt threatened. Marcus tried to not think about what Lewis had done to her before she got the chance to kill him.

"Do you know the building?" Rafe asked. Bo didn't answer, just nodded his head slowly.

"Good. That information is going to save your life," Max said.

"I can't help you. He'll butcher me if I do," Bo stammered.

"What do you think we'll do if you don't help?" She replied.

"I don't think you could do the things he does. We ran because he executed the guard that helped Lewis break the rules. He cut...pieces....off of him," Bo said. He choked on his words as if he were picturing the event again.

"You don't know us. You have no idea what we would do to get our sister back," Rafe said.

Bo sat, looking between them, weighing his options. He looked over at Trevor, who's eyes were also full of doubt and panic. But the other man just shrugged, putting the decision solely on Bo's shoulders. The man even looked over to Jackson, but he was still out with his head hanging limply. Bo looked back to Rafe once he realized there was no help for him.

"Ok. What do you want to know?"

They sat in the spot grilling Bo for an hour. At that time a plan began to form, and the gang members were locked inside the van, tied to the rings that were installed into the body of the vehicle. Marcus got angry again thinking about the women they must have strapped to the rings, but he controlled himself as they moved away from the van to discuss their options. It was getting late in the day and none of them wanted to wait any longer. Rafe checked on Charlie and her work on Albert. The little blonde gave him promising information as she hung an IV bag for her patient. Mateo insisted on being part of the planning and he followed Rafe back to meeting with Marcus and Max.

Between the two of them they had two maps spread. They

evaluated the fastest way to enter the town without being detected. Then the plan of how they would get into the building began to take form. Bo had confirmed that the back door was the least guarded as the Noble Lord's men tended to use it for smoke and bathroom breaks. Rafe took the lead on the planning and as he laid out what he wanted to do, the group stared at him in a mixture of surprise and shock.

"It only works if we go in at night," Rafe said.

"If it works," Max replied.

"And doesn't get us all killed at the same time," Marcus said.

"Then it's settled. We go in tonight," Rafe said. Before anyone could argue further, he walked away.

Cliff and Marcus had tasks for the plan and the two got busy with little talking. Max decided they were going to take the van with them to the town. Depending on how many women they got out alive, they could need the extra vehicle for transportation. Where the women would go was a question they hadn't answered yet. Mateo waited for his uncle to wake up from the sedative Charlie had given him. She was able to remove the bullet from the man's leg. However, he wouldn't be walking on it anytime soon.

When darkness began to approach, everyone loaded into their vehicles. Max pushed the three gang members from the van. Using her gun she motioned for them to move into the trees. They stumbled and whispered to each other, as they assumed they were walking to their executions. When they were fifty feet from the vehicles Max threw an old hunting knife at their feet.

"Do not try to follow us. Do not try to warn anyone at the brothel. If I see you again, I will not hesitate to kill you. Am I making myself clear?"

"You're leaving us out here?" Bo asked.

"You're alive out here, right? You're lucky I'm not strapping you to a tree for the wild animals or the dead to feast on you. But my brother tends to be nicer than me and he said that plan was too harsh. If I see you again, he won't be able to stop me," Max said.

The men didn't speak again and Max backed away with her gun aimed at them the entire time. She climbed into the van, with Griffin riding shotgun. All the vehicles started up and began their short trip into town. Rafe took the lead and when they arrived about four blocks from the brothel, they turned the vehicles into an alley. The next step in their plan needed to be done when there was still some light.

"I'm not sure about this," Marcus said.

"We won't let you get eaten," Max replied.

Marcus and Cliff stood in the middle of the street with bags they had gotten from the van. They were hoods the gang members used to kidnap women. They were now going to be used to capture their distraction. Each man held two hoods. Each was trying to catch two infected. Max and Rafe were walking on either side of the street, guns at the ready. Marcus could feel the sweat drip down his face. He understood Rafe wanted a serious distraction, but Marcus didn't like the idea of getting that close to the teeth of an infected.

The first groan made Marcus jump a foot. He turned toward the noise to see Max backing away from a broken out storefront. She motioned to Marcus to come forward and she readied herself with her tomahawk in her hand. Marcus whistled loudly to get the infected's attention. A shambling corpse showed itself and it immediately focused on Marcus in the middle of the street. The flesh from the infected's jaw was missing, but the remaining muscle allowed it to snap in the direction of his fresh meat. Marcus looked at Max who acted like she was looking at her nails.

"Seriously?" He blurted out.

That made Max grin widely as she snuck up behind the infected. Swiftly she grabbed both arms and yanked them back behind the infected's body. With no understanding, the infected

continued to snap at the meal it could see. Without trouble, Max
had the infected's wrists zip-tied together. Once Max stepped
back, Marcus stepped forward with the hood. The smell coming
from the infected made Marcus think of raw sewage mixed with
death. He held his breath, but he couldn't stop the one large whiff
he did get up his nose. He moved quickly to avoid the teeth that
wanted to find purchase in his skin.

Once the hood was over the head, Max led the infected
toward the van. She struggled as its body couldn't react to her
pushing. It was a long process to capture and corral the four
infected they needed for Rafe's crazy plan. There were a million
reasons the plan could fail. Marcus tried to keep his mind from
wandering down the avenue of negative conclusions. He pictured
Alex, thinking about how she needed them. If this got her and
Mateo's sister out of the brothel, it was worth the risk.

"Can we go over this again?" Marcus asked.

"It's not hard, Marcus. We free these four in the brothel. We
wait for the distraction to begin and we go in to find Alex and
Sylvia," Rafe replied.

"And the guards at the back of the building?"

"I'll handle them quietly," Rafe said as he flipped one of his
throwing knives in the air a few times.

Marcus had no doubts about Rafe's accuracy with the blades.
The man was deadly and if Marcus was honest with himself it
scared him a little. Rafe had created a practice area near the
bunkhouse where Marcus slept. The constant and rhythmic
thunk sounds often echoed across the compound. Marcus had
noticed that the targets had very little damage outside of the
bullseye. Rafe had offered to teach Marcus once, but after he cut
his hand, Rafe decided he wasn't ready for throwing.

They lead the hooded infected by a paracord wrapped around
their necks. Rafe and Max watched their backs as Cliff, Marcus,
and Mateo struggled to get the bodies to go where they wanted
them to. As they got closer to the brothel, the loud noises of

people could be heard. Marcus couldn't understand why there weren't more infected nearby. When they got within view of the building and they could see the bodies piling up in the streets, he understood. The infected came close and were easily cut down by the waiting guards.

The back of the brothel loomed in the darkness. The windows were all boarded at the first floor. The second floor showed the soft glow of candlelight in places. The street was pitch black, helping to hide the Duncan group as they hid behind a car wreck. Rafe hissed at them and Max nodded as he crept away quietly. He easily disappeared into the night and Marcus struggled to follow his movements. The infected they held groaned and hissed. The noise seemed loud in the empty street. The sound caught the attention of the guards that stood near the brothel backdoor.

"Did you hear that?" A voice came from the darkness. Marcus could just make out the glow of a cigarette bouncing.

"Walkers coming, I think," another voice answered.

The quiet sound of gurgling met Marcus's ears and he knew that Rafe had struck. The second guard let out a short holler, but it was cut short by Rafe. Marcus stood frozen, holding the ropes connected to the infected.

"The coast is clear," Rafe's voice came from behind the group and Marcus almost let out an unmanly like squeak. The man had silently circled the area to ensure there were no additional guards. Until he had spoken, Marcus thought he was still in the darkness in front of them.

"Let's get these smelly bastards in there," Max said.

The process of getting the infected into the brothel wasn't simple. As a team they forced the dead forward, fighting their bodies that had no coordination. When they reached the brothel door, Rafe tested the knob and everyone let out a sigh when the door opened silently. Rafe peered inside first, then he stepped into the dim interior. His hand poked out shortly after, motioning them in. Stepping inside, Marcus drug his infected through the open door. They had to move quickly if the distraction was going to help them find Alex.

Rafe pointed to another closed door.

"That leads to a larger room. I could hear people in there. We need to let them loose in there," Rafe whispered.

"What about my sister?" Mateo asked. His concern was valid. Sylvia had no fighting experience against the living or the dead.

"It's a risk, but we have to take it. We won't be far behind the infected. Hopefully she stays hidden until we can get her out," Rafe said. He placed a hand on Mateo's shoulder. Marcus knew that Mateo had a hard time moving on with the plan without his uncle by his side. However, the injured man was in no shape to fight and Charlie was tending to his wound.

After cutting the wrist bindings, each infected was shoved through the interior door. Max slammed it shut after the fourth and leaned against it as the infected tried to get back through. It didn't take them long to realize they were in a room with more living.

The screaming started next.

CHAPTER NINETEEN

"What the hell?" The Noble Lord roared.

Alex wondered if his anger was fueled by the frustration that he wouldn't get his hands on her again. Or was he mad that his little utopia was being upset by something else? He stormed across the room again to the bedroom door. Just as he opened it a guard burst through, almost knocking the Noble Lord to the ground.

"Sir, sorry, sir. Infected are in the building!" The guard said.

"So, take care of them," the Noble Lord said.

"There's already a handful injured. I think we're going to need more hands-on deck," the guard said.

"So, go get Clive. He can get men to help," the Noble Lord said, waving his hand dismissively.

"Uh, well, Clive is..." The guard trailed off.

"Clive is what?" The Noble Lord demanded.

"Clive's dead, sir. The infected got him quick," the guard said quickly.

The Noble Lord stood silently for a moment, a hand on his chin as he thought. Alex found herself wondering if the Noble

Lord had actually been in any fights with the infected. He had no problem sending his own men in to die, but wasn't too quick to jump in when he was needed. He turned and paced the room a few times as he thought.

"Sir! I need to get back out there. The women don't have any way to defend themselves," the guard said. His words were punctuated by the high-pitched scream of a woman echoing into the room.

"Go!" The Noble Lord yelled.

The guard turned and ran back through the door. The Noble Lord paced the room. Rubbing his face with his hand, as he seemed deep in thought. The sounds of fighting, fear, and killing were loud in Alex's ears. She yanked at the handcuffs again, panicking at the thought of being trapped. If the infected were to get into the room, she wouldn't be able to protect herself. She rattled the metal until the Noble Lord finally looked over to her.

"Let me go," Alex rasped. The Noble Lord didn't answer, he just stared at her.

"Afraid it's not me you need to worry about now," she continued.

"I'm not worried about you. You won't be my problem soon," the Noble Lord said.

He turned away from her then, and she knew his plan. He disappeared in the room that served as his closet. When he came out, he had a backpack on. Alex couldn't say she was surprised to see him running from trouble. He went to the door of the room and looked over his shoulder before opening it.

"I am sorry we never got to have a good time. You are full of fight. I would have enjoyed breaking you," he said.

"You never would have. You're too weak," Alex said as loudly as she could.

The Noble Lord's face darkened, Alex could see him debate coming back to her to teach her a lesson. Part of her wanted to get him closer so she had the chance of getting free. She didn't want to be left alone. And she would even take the company of this vile man over being left to be eaten by the infected. Her goading the Noble Lord didn't work, though. He took a deep breath and turned back to the door. Alex began to struggle with renewed vigor.

"Don't just leave me tied up! Give me the keys!" Alex called out in a wracking whisper.

For a moment she thought she had gotten to him, broken through the horrible shell of the man. The Noble Lord turned and looked at her, his hand fishing in his pocket. He walked back toward her, his eyes never leaving hers. When he was six feet from her, he stopped and stared. She looked down at the hand he was holding open toward her. In his palm, a pair of handcuff keys sat. He stared at her as he turned his hand over and dropped the keys on the floor.

"See ya," he said and turned for the door again.

"You're a monster," Alex tried to yell. It came out low and broken, her throat burned in pain as she tried to force the sound.

"No. The monsters will be in soon, I'm sure," the Noble Lord said, as he disappeared through the bedroom door.

Alex stared at the open doorway for a long moment. With the door open, the terror of what was happening in the brothel was even more real. She could hear people running, screaming, and the thuds of bodies against the walls and floor. A nearby scream startled Alex and she realized she was a sitting duck. She could see the handcuff keys, so close, but just out of reach. That didn't stop her from trying.

Sliding the handcuffs as low as she could on the bedpost, Alex tried to stretch her body toward the keys. She grabbed the metal chain of the cuff and stretched her arms out straight. Balancing on one foot, she tried to use her other to reach the keys. She was at least a foot away still and she cursed as loudly as her bruised vocal cords allowed.

As she was straightening a woman came running into the room. Alex jumped up and backed up against the wall, judging quickly that the woman was alive. The woman's eyes flew around wildly and came to rest on Alex. She studied Alex for a moment before stepping forward. Alex prepared to jump onto the bed if she needed to retreat any further.

"Are you Alex?" The woman asked. Alex just nodded. The woman turned and ran out of the room again.

What the hell? Alex thought to herself. She didn't even get the chance to ask the woman for the keys before she ran back out. Alex started to stretch to reach the keys again, wondering to herself how the woman knew who she was. She couldn't see the door and was startled when a voice came from behind her.

"What in the hell are you wearing?"

"Max?" Alex said, standing up quickly and turning to see her sister entering the room.

"Lace isn't exactly good for the apocalypse, Alex," Max replied.

"Keys, right there," Alex said, pointing.

Max spotted the keys quickly and was scooping them up when Rafe and Griffin entered the room with a Hispanic man Alex didn't know. Rafe came straight to her and studied her battered face and neck.

"Where is he?" Rafe asked.

"Gone," Alex rasped.

"How long?"

"Five minutes max," Alex replied.

"Stop making her talk, Rafe. It's obvious it's hurting her. Charlie will need to check out that neck," Max said.

When Alex was freed from the bed, she rubbed her wrists. Max threw her bug out bag on the bed and rifled through it until she produced a pair of pants and a long-sleeved thermal. Alex grabbed them, thankful her sister was always so prepared. Alex was slightly taller than Max, but she would wear short pants instead of a lace nightie anytime. When Alex put her injured leg into the pants she hissed.

"He do that too?" Max asked.

"During a fight," Alex replied.

"I knew you wouldn't go down without a fight," Max said.

"A lot of good it did me," Alex said as she pulled the thermal over her head. She let the nightie bunch underneath, not wanting to take the time to remove it. In her mind, she would cut it and burn it later.

"Where's Marcus," Max asked suddenly. The Hispanic boy, who Alex now noticed was standing with the woman that knew her name, turned to her.

"I lost him inside the brothel. He was there and then he went off to help a woman that was fighting off an infected," the man said.

"Marcus? He's here? Who are you?" Alex asked questions in quick succession.

"This is Mateo and his sister Sylvia, long story. Marcus is here. We need to find him so we can split," Max said.

"Which way did he go?" Rafe asked.

"Follow me," Mateo said.

The young man put his rifle to his shoulder and headed back out the door. His sister stayed close behind him, her hand on his shoulder. She was wearing a bra and panties under a jacket that she was given by her brother. Her shoes were clunky working boots. The woman didn't seem to care as she moved quickly into the brothel. Alex watched the new additions and raised an eyebrow at Max. Max just shrugged and pushed her toward the door. Alex held out her hand and it was all the signal Max needed to place a 9mm in her palm.

They exited the bedroom into the general office of the Noble Lord. Blood pooled in places and Alex carefully stepped around in her bare feet. She held the 9mm up in a two-handed grip. Rafe was in front of her and Max was to the rear. Griffin stayed close to Max, watching her back as she watched everyone else's. They fell into an easy team, falling back on years of learning how to work together. When the group exited the office, Rafe looked right, Alex went left, and Max and Griffin took up the center.

Chaos was all around them as people fled from the infected. Women ran by, crying and screaming. Alex wanted to grab them, shake them, and then save them. But she knew there were too many for just her and her siblings to save. They could only do so much. Alex knew what she needed to do. Kill the Noble Lord, so the brothel fell, and the women would be free. As she watched the left side, Alex scanned and didn't see the familiar flowing hair of the Noble Lord anywhere. He had run quickly. Alex cursed, realizing he could have escaped everything.

"This way," Mateo said, as he walked into the center of the brothel rooms.

As they began to move as a team again, an infected came from behind a hanging canvas door. Alex shot it in the eye and continued to move forward.

"Not one of ours," Max called from behind her.

"They're turning fast," Rafe yelled over his shoulder.

"What do you mean one of yours?" Alex asked.

"We needed a diversion," Rafe replied.

"So, you brought in the infected? Kinda risky, brother," Alex said.

"It was a chance we were willing to take. And I figured you could handle yourself for a few minutes."

"Good thing I wasn't handcuffed anywhere else," Alex muttered.

They moved in a tight line, everyone keeping their heads and weapons rotating to watch for danger. Rafe had a knife in one hand and his own 9mm in the other, while Max had her tomahawk and a rifle on her back. An infected woman, in a pink fuzzy robe came stumbling toward them. If it hadn't been for the chunk of meat missing from her thigh and the black flat eyes, she would have looked like she had just rolled out of bed. Max stepped to the side to meet the infected and with a quick swipe of her toma-hawk she cut her down.

"There he is!" Mateo called from the front of the line.

Alex turned to see Marcus between some of the canvas walls. He was facing two men and Alex's blood went cold when she real-ized they were the soldiers the Noble Lord had been talking to earlier. Her mind quickly put information together, realizing if the soldiers knew who they all were, Marcus had a target on his back. Alex turned to see Max staring at the scene as well.

"They work for Callahan. Another long story. But if they know who Marcus is," Alex said.

"Then he's in trouble," Max finished.

The Duncan group followed Mateo as they circled the row of rooms and came to have a clear view of Marcus. As they rounded the corner, one of the soldier's eyes met Alex's and she knew immediately that these soldiers knew the Duncans. He quickly took in the faces of Rafe and Max, who had routinely been on wanted posters since their run-ins with Callahan and his men. Recognition lit his expression immediately and he jumped to make a grab at Marcus. Marcus feigned to one side and brought his fist up to punch the soldier in the face. The second soldier caught on quickly and just as Marcus was about to make contact with the first soldier, he pulled a baton from his belt.

Alex didn't have the chance to ask Max what was wrong, as her sister bolted past her and their brother. Griffin was hot on her heels, taking her lead before Alex could react. But she knew if Max was moving like that, something was not good. In her bare feet Alex fought to gain purchase on the filthy floor that now held more than trash, blood, entrails, and bodies joined the mess. Rafe was hot on Max's heels. As they ran, the soldier pushed the baton into Marcus's neck and his whole body convulsed before falling to the ground. Then the first soldier held out a gun, pointing it at Marcus's head.

"You should stop where you are, or I will kill your friend," the soldier yelled as the Duncans halted before reaching them.

"You don't want him. You want one of us," Rafe said in a calm tone. Alex was glad he was taking lead because her voice would never make it over the noise in the brothel. And Rafe was much more level headed than her sister.

"That's true. But you've killed a number of our people. That makes you and everyone with you fair game," the soldier replied.

Max was itching for a fight, as she bounced on her toes next to Alex. Her eyes were slits as she glared at the soldiers. They were in a stalemate. None of the Duncans were going to just go willingly, but they also couldn't let Callahan's men kill Marcus. Alex turned to look at Rafe and found his hand dangerously close to his throwing knives. Rafe was fast, but she wasn't sure he could kill two men before a bullet hit Marcus. When Rafe met her eyes, she shook her head slightly.

Suddenly there was a female scream, closer than the rest. Alex looked to Max, who would never scream in that manner, but her safety was first on Alex's mind.

"Sylvia!" Mateo cried out, just as he lifted his rifle to his shoulder again. Alex's head whipped to the other side of their group and she realized she had forgotten about the small woman that hid behind her brother.

Two men had come up behind them, while they had their standoff with Callahan's men. One man had grabbed Sylvia around the neck and the other pointed a gun in Mateo's face as they backed toward the soldiers. It didn't take Alex long to realize the additional men were with the soldiers, possibly soldiers themselves. While the two Alex had seen with the Noble Lord wore their fatigues, these two men were in civilian clothes. But they quickly joined the soldiers with Sylvia as their second hostage.

"Here's how this is going to go. You're going to stay where you are. And we're going to leave. We're taking your friend with us. Callahan will want to talk to him. If you do as we say, we'll give the bitch back," the lead soldier said.

"That's my sister, pendejo!" Mateo yelled.

"Well then you should want her back unharmed," lead soldier said. As he spoke, the man holding Sylvia leaned down, pressing his nose to her throat. He took a deep inhale and then an evil smile spread his lips.

"You can take me," Alex croaked.

"You? You aren't even the woman the Major wants. It's her," the soldier said, inclining his head toward Max.

"I've killed more of your men than anyone standing here. Take me," Alex said.

The soldier seemed to consider her words for a moment. He then took in her beaten state and bare feet and he leaned back on his heels. He scoffed, clearly not believing Alex's story. Just as she was about to give him more proof, Marcus stirred on the ground. He turned his eyes to Alex and she could see the relief flood his features for a moment.

"Alex," he said.

"Don't move, Marcus," Rafe warned.

Marcus looked confused for a moment, but then he looked up and saw the gun that was pointed at him His features changed then, from the momentary relief, to fear before settling on well-hidden anger.

"Leave him. He's no one. He can't answer the Major's questions. I'm sure I can," Alex continued.

"Alex, I don't think..." Max started to protest.

"Quiet, Max," Alex said, striking the air with her hand. Griffin reached out to hold on to Max's arm, clearly not sure what she would do if Alex traded herself to the soldiers.

Her sister swallowed her next words, only because of her deeply engrained training of following her leader. Alex was her leader. She may have been struggling before she left the compound. She had questioned her decisions and her ability of leading. However, the powerful leader was back. And she was returning with a vengeance. Alex remembered the dream of her father and his words to her. She also thought about her children, all four of them. She pictured each of their faces in her mind and she knew that standing up for her people was her responsibility.

The soldiers studied her for a moment, weighing their options. Alex stepped forward, hoping to tempt them into taking her deal. She found herself surprisingly at peace with the decision. She would protect Marcus and distract them long enough for her family to escape. That was what leaders did in her mind. The soldier holding the gun on Marcus looked between her and the man he had on the ground. Marcus looked up at him as he climbed to his feet. The gun followed, continuing to point at his face. But he stared the soldier down, daring him to do something.

"So, you'd have a woman sacrifice herself for you? I knew you all were weak," the soldier sneered.

"You have no idea who we are," Max said.

"And you have no idea what you are messing with here," Marcus said.

"Oh, we know enough. And she looks like too much trouble right now, so you're coming with us. We'll just shock you again if you don't come along willingly," the soldier, who Alex had now pegged to be the leader, said.

"I'm no trouble. Look at me. I'm weak. Beaten down. I'll come willingly," Alex argued.

"Stop it, Alex," Marcus said

"Shut up," Alex tried to yell at him, but her voice only came out as a harsh growl.

"You are more important to the family than I am. Go home," Marcus replied, ignoring Alex's outburst.

Before Alex could answer, a growl came from behind her. The

eyes of the other soldiers were enough to warn her that something was coming. Alex spun, just as Rafe released a blade toward an infected that was sneaking up on them. Alex lifted her 9mm, taking aim at a group of infected that followed the first. As she fired, her eyes widened in shock as the group split off quickly and attacked from different angles. They were quicker and Alex was caught off guard. Max also noticed because she let out a string of curses as she stepped up with her gun and shot one infected in the forehead.

In the back of her mind, she heard yelling and a woman screaming. But their first challenge was the infected and being a main menu item on their dinner plate. The inhabitants of the brothel that had been killed by the infected were starting to wake up. Infected stumbled from the open doors of the canvas rooms. Canvas walls fell as the infected walked through them, ripping the bindings as they fought to get to the last living people in the room. Alex was careful with her shots, making sure her ammo was conserved. Every shot hit its mark as she cleared the infected in front of her.

After a few moments of firing, the slide on her 9mm locked open. She looked over at her siblings and found them to be handling the battle on their own. Pivoting around, Alex caught the last soldier as he ran out into the lobby. She didn't wait, she knew Rafe and Max would follow when they could. Mateo was already following but had his hands up as he approached the soldiers. When Alex got to the lobby, she stopped next to Mateo just as Sylvia was shoved back inside by the last soldier. Mateo ran to his sister and embraced her as she cried into his shirt.

"Where's Marcus?" Alex asked.

"They took him," Mateo answered.

"Give me your gun," Alex said.

Mateo didn't hesitate to give Alex his rifle. She quickly checked that it was loaded and without another thought, she ran from the lobby. When she burst onto the street, she stopped, looking up and down the street for the soldiers. A sedan peeled away from the curb two blocks down. As it sped away, Alex stared at it, knowing that Marcus was inside the vehicle. A sinking feeling settled into the base of her skull and she feared worse was still to come to her friend. Her breathing was ragged, and she fought the urge to just run after the car.

As she stood there, her worry and panic caused her to miss the sound of approaching boots. The first blow to the back of her head knocked her to her knees. But when the knee came flying toward her face, she was rolling away and jumping back to her bare toes. Looking up she found the Noble Lord standing in front her, his face red and screwed up in rage.

"You ruined everything. Everything I built is gone!" He roared as he came toward her with a knife in his hand.

Alex was no longer afraid of the man. All of her fear was with Marcus now. Her body was full of hate for the Noble Lord. All of which she reined in and pushed through her veins in the form of adrenaline as the first attempted blow came. Alex easily feigned away from the knife twice, before she grabbed his knife wrist with both her hands. Pulling him to her, he stumbled at first, surprised by her move. When he was close enough, she twisted her entire body, twisting his arm with her. She dug her fingers painfully into his pressure point at the elbow before lifting high at the joint until she heard a loud pop. The knife clattered to the ground and the Noble Lord let out a shrill squeal.

Max and Rafe burst out into the night, just as the Noble Lord tried to swing on Alex with his other fist. There was no power behind it though and Alex easily deflected. The Duncan siblings stood watch as their sister danced around her opponent. Alex raised a fist and punched the Noble Lord in the throat. His uninjured hand flew up to hold his throat as he tried to cough and get air.

"You brutalized women. You imprisoned them or made them believe they had to be your whores to live," Alex said quietly.

As she followed the Noble Lord in his retreat, she noticed the infected coming out from between two homes. The noise of all the fighting in the brothel had brought it from wherever it was wandering. And now it was looking for a fresh meal. The Noble Lord continued his backward motion, having no idea that he was walking to his death.

"You dealt drugs and kept people addicted so they would gather your supplies and women for you. Because you're weak. Do you hear me? You did this to women because your own mommy didn't want you. You even had to keep your own aunt on a leash. You didn't build this. Callahan did. He controlled you. You are nothing," Alex said, revealing all she knew.

Though it wasn't much, it was enough to bring the anger back into the Noble Lord. He came at Alex again, wildly trying to hit her. He feigned a punch, but instead when Alex tried to dodge, he brought an open palm across her face. Alex heard her brother curse behind her. But before he could do anything, Alex stepped back and put all of her weight into a front kick that landed against the Noble Lord's sternum. The blow knocked the wind out of the man's lungs in a rush. And right into the arms of the waiting infected.

Alex watched with no emotion as the infected sunk its teeth into his shoulder. The Noble Lord screamed and turned to see the infected, giving the dead the perfect access to the skin of his face. The infected released his shoulder and lunged forward for his ear and face. As the infected pulled pieces from the Noble Lord, Alex turned and walked back to where she had dropped Mateo's gun. She picked it up and checked it again, though she knew it was loaded.

Distantly, Alex saw her brother and sister watching her warily. She knew they were wondering if she had completely cracked. She moved with confidence, as if she had no worry in the world. Her mind felt detached as she listened to the squeals coming from the Noble Lord and the sounds of ripping muscle and tendons. Max coughed slightly and turned away, the sight too gruesome for her to continue to stare at. Rafe stood completely still, waiting for his oldest sister to make her choice.

When the screams finally stopped, Alex walked back across the street. The infected had its face buried in the Noble Lord's throat, pulling out pieces as it ate. Alex felt the bile in the back of her throat. Bringing the rifle to her shoulder, she cleanly shot the infected through the skull. The body fell across the Noble Lord's chest. Looking at the now dead drug dealing, brothel owner Alex felt nothing as she sighted her shot on his eye and pulled the trigger.

She stood above the body for a long moment. Part of her wanted to ensure that the evil of the man was permanently wiped from the planet. She continued to wait and see if he would move, if his body twitched in any way. Alex wasn't sure how long she stood there, but the hand on her arm made her jump and start to swing the rifle around. When she saw Rafe's face she immediately dropped the muzzle and just looked at her brother.

A moment later Cliff came running around the side of the building. When he saw Alex he ran straight to her. He looked at her injuries and his face that was always stone, became red with anger. It was uncharacteristic for him to show emotions. But that didn't stop him from throwing his arms around Alex and pulling her in for a tight hug. The man had suffered losing his family and he and Alex found a bond that helped him in his survival. Now his hug was a soothing balm for her. She gripped him back tightly for a moment. When she pulled away, she had to swipe at tears that were starting to fall down her cheeks.

"We need to follow them. Where are your vehicles?" Alex asked.

"They're five blocks away. We already know where they're taking him," Griffin said quietly. Max didn't say anything. Her eyes were focused in the direction the sedan had gone, the direction of Callahan's camp.

"We need to go," Alex said again.

"You don't know Callahan, Alex. He won't just release Marcus," Max said.

"He doesn't know me. Taking one of ours again will be the last thing he does."

CHAPTER TWENTY

The group followed Alex as she led the way back into the front of the brothel. She moved quickly and quietly to the staircase near the lobby. They were able to avoid any infected as they climbed the stairs. At the top Alex didn't stop as she went to Coral's door. She wanted her boots back. She wanted to find out what the woman planned to do. She also wanted to slap the old woman.

At the door, Alex didn't hesitate. She had already reloaded her 9mm and held it out in front of her as she entered Coral's room. Alex was pretty confident that Coral didn't have a firearm. The Noble Lord didn't trust her that much. And when things started to go into a frenzy, it was likely the woman didn't leave her room. When Alex stepped into the room her siblings fanned out, clearing areas as they went. Cliff stayed outside keeping watch for them and Griffin stood just inside the door.

"It's good to see you up and around," Coral's voice came from the small bedroom area.

Alex swung her gun in the woman's direction. Coral held up her hands, standing still with four guns staring her down.

"Not with any help from you," Alex said quietly, her throat raw and on fire.

"I stitched you up. I did what I could."

"Alex, we need to get out of here," Rafe said quietly.

"Where are my boots?" Alex asked.

Coral pointed toward a box in the corner of her garment section. Alex went to the box and sorted through. She realized it was full of the belongings of the women that had been brought to the brothel and she felt herself go lightheaded at the number of items. Jeans, shorts, T-shirts, purses, bras, and sensible underwear were piled. Alex couldn't even attempt to count the items that would indicate the number of women that had passed through Coral's door. In her mind Alex mourned for the women that had to be stripped to nothing when they were brought to the old woman.

She found her steel toed work boots. Looking around she easily found a pair of socks and she pulled the items on. Her bare feet were rough at the bottom, but luckily weren't ripped open in any place. She went back to join Max and Rafe. Standing there looking at Coral one last time, Alex turned away without saying another word.

"You aren't going to leave me here, are you?" Coral called out.

Alex spun on her heel. She almost was able to leave, without attacking the woman. Maybe Coral was a prisoner in her own way. However, Alex couldn't understand or forget that Coral helped the Noble Lord break the women that came in the door. The women that were kidnapped and forced into services with men that were infected. Alex thought about the full box of belongings stripped from the women brought to Coral for preparation. She could still feel Coral scrubbing at her body with the rough washcloth as she stood nude in a bucket of water.

"You're lucky I'm not throwing you off that balcony. You know, the one soaked with blood from your nephew torturing people?" Alex said.

"I couldn't have stopped him. Please. Help me," Coral begged.

"How many women said that to you, Coral? How many

women pleaded with you to help them escape?" Alex demanded, her weak voice sounding more forceful than she thought it could be. Coral had the decency to look away at that question.

"I thought so. You are on your own. Hopefully, the next person you meet doesn't know what you've done here. Our paths should never cross again, because I won't be so kind," Alex said.

This time when she went to the door, Coral stayed silent. Max hesitated as Alex passed her. She kept her gun trained on Coral. Alex stopped at the door when she realized Max wasn't following her. Rafe and Griffin left, watching the landing and stairs to ensure no attack came from where they weren't expecting. Alex turned back to her sister.

"Max, let's go."

"What did she do to you?" Max asked quietly.

Alex looked over toward Coral and saw the woman trembling. She could read Max's intentions as well as Alex could.

"Nothing I'm not going to recover from, as long as we get Marcus and get home," Alex answered.

"She should pay for it, Alex."

"She will. She won't survive on her own," Alex said. She then went to Max and pushed her gun down. She locked eyes with her sister. They shared a moment of understanding before turning and leaving Coral's room. Once they were on the landing, the door slammed shut behind them and the click of a lock could be heard.

"You're right. She has no idea what's coming for her," Max said.

Alex felt better equipped to handle rescuing Marcus. They descended the stairs again and Alex ran forward with a hunting knife to end a solitary infected that wandered the lobby area. Once outside, they retrieved a few additional weapons before running to the vehicles the Duncans came in. Alex's leg screamed in protest as she tried to push herself to keep up with the group. But she knew if she wasn't careful she would rip out her stitches.

When she slowed a bit, so did the rest of the group, following her lead and not leaving anyone behind.

They led Alex to a small junkyard where the gate had been closed. Rafe yanked it open and entered. Alex could tell her brother was ready to get back to his Charlie. When they came to three vehicles lined up at the back of the yard, Charlie appeared, a shotgun in her hands. Rafe went to her immediately, touching her face and kissing her on the forehead. A squeal sounded from the back of the white pickup as Sylvia found her injured uncle. Mateo lifted her into the bed, and she bent to hug the older man. They all spoke quietly in Spanish. Alex heard Marcus' name a few times and she wondered if they were debating about helping them get him back.

"So, Callahan's headquarters. You know how to get back there?" Alex asked.

"It's almost a day away, I think. We didn't really drive straight to the compound from there, afraid of leading anyone to our home. But yes, we know where it is," Max answered.

"We go now," Alex said.

"We're coming to help," Mateo said, approaching the meeting between the Duncans.

"You can take a vehicle and go home, Mateo. You rescued your sister. Take her home," Rafe said.

"Marcus brought you to us. He made sure we could rescue Sylvia. We can't just leave him now," Mateo replied.

Rafe nodded, accepting that reasoning, "It's still late, we can drive through the night. But it's not safe."

"The longer we wait, the further they get with him," Alex argued.

"Right now, you clearly are running on fumes, Alex. Let Charlie look over your injuries, make sure you're able to fight. We need to be ready for whatever comes at us," Rafe said.

She knew he was right. But leaving Marcus in the hands of the Major for any longer than necessary chilled her to the core. The picture of Max, broken and bruised when she arrived at the compound, entered Alex's mind. If Callahan could do that to a woman, what would he do to a fit man? As she was working out another argument, Charlie was at her arm, leading her to the black van. Alex put on the brakes and shook her head.

"I'm not getting in that. What happened to the guys that were in it?" Alex said.

"Max and Rafe left them to the infected. One was killed in the shoot out. That's how Albert was injured."

"When we leave, we aren't taking that van," Alex said.

"Of course. I'm sorry. Let's go over to the truck," Charlie replied softly.

Charlie had a large medical bag and she pulled instruments out as she looked over Alex's visible injuries.

"What happened to you?" Charlie asked and then added, "You don't have to tell me, if you don't want to."

"It's ok. Nothing worse than losing a fight," Alex replied.

For the next hour Alex explained her injuries to Charlie, gave her pain estimates and let the doctor poke and prod at all of her sore areas. Charlie cleaned the wound on her leg, deciding the stitches were sufficient unless Alex ripped them by being too active. As she wrapped gauze around her leg to protect the injury, Charlie got quiet. She had instructed Alex to strip down to her undergarments. When she saw what Alex was wearing under the clothing, she had gone slightly pale. Alex knew uncomfortable questions were coming.

"Alex, do I need to do any other exams? Were you sexually assaulted?"

Alex stayed quiet for a moment. Silently she was feeling thankful that she was able to avoid any sort of sexual attack. But another part of her felt extreme guilt. While she had escaped that horror, so many other women hadn't. Sylvia hadn't.

"No. I wasn't. I was lucky," she finally answered.

Charlie stood up then. Though she was a little woman, she

had a demanding presence when she got into doctor mode. She made Alex hold her gaze.

"I won't tell anyone, Alex. Your privacy is very important to me. But we need to take precautions, if..." Charlie trailed off.

Alex smiled at her friend, laying her hand on her shoulder.

"Don't worry, Doctor. I would tell you the truth, even if I thought you would tell my brother. I think you should probably check over Sylvia though. I doubt she was able to fight the way I was," Alex said.

"And from the look of you, you fought hard."

"You must know us by now, Charlie," Alex said with a small smile.

"Oh, I know you Duncans. You don't go down quietly, that's a fact. Listen, Alex, I know I'm not a therapist. But with what you've been through, you should talk about it. It doesn't have to be me, just someone," Charlie said.

"Don't worry. I'll talk to someone if I need to. Right now, I need to focus on Marcus. Am I cleared for duty?"

"I'm concerned about your leg. If you rip that open and end up in a fight with an infected, I can't predict what could happen. I also think you haven't gotten real sleep in a few days. So eventually you are going to crash from the adrenaline you're surviving on right now."

"As long as it lasts me another few hours, long enough to get Marcus back, I'll rest later," Alex agreed.

She pulled on the sports bra Max had given her, throwing the lacy nightie in the dirt. She wanted to burn it, but she didn't want to waste any more time. She finished getting dressed and Charlie went to retrieve Sylvia. It was the first moment that Alex was able to be left alone since she was taken by the gang. She sat heavily on the tailgate of the truck. Her body knew that Charlie was right, a crash was coming. She laid back into the bed of the truck, using the backpack Max brought her as a pillow. She hadn't meant to allow the darkness of sleep to invade, but it crept quickly and quietly until she was dead to the world.

"Alex," a voice came and Alex felt her shoulder being shaken. Panic flared and she tried to jump to her feet. Instead, her brother held her shoulders down carefully until she blinked in the early rays of dawn to see his face.

"Oh my god, I fell asleep. Why didn't you wake me?" Alex demanded.

"We tried. But you didn't stir. Charlie insisted your body was doing what it needed to do."

"Next time Charlie shouldn't make decisions for me," Alex snapped. The look on Rafe's face then made her feel bad about being harsh toward his girlfriend. She looked around as she noticed everyone readying the vehicles.

"We're almost ready to go. You can ride with Cliff and the Vegas. Or with me, but you'll be crowded between Max and Griffin. Not sure you want to endure that," Rafe said, rolling his eyes.

"I'll ride with Cliff," Alex decided.

She climbed off the truck bed and sorted through her backpack quickly. Max gave her extra ammo for her 9 mm. They also brought her rifle with its long-range scope. Alex double checked everything on that, thinking it would be useful if they could get a shot at Callahan from a distance. She put all of her things in the truck Cliff was driving and went to meet with Max and Rafe.

"What's the plan?" Alex asked.

"Why do you think we have the plan?" Max asked.

"I know you, that's why. So what do you want to do?"

"In the daylight, sneaking into the camp is going to be near impossible. Also, if they ever figured out how Max escaped, they would have fortified. We are thinking long range is going to be the best bet during the day. If we can get some sort of visual on Marcus and maybe where they're holding him, we can plan for a night breakout," Rafe explained.

Alex agreed that the plan was sound and had little to add.

Max, Griffin, and Cliff were the only ones to know what the camp looked like. That was months prior, so there was no telling what Callahan had changed to ensure security. They hadn't unpacked anything during the night, so they were on the road less than ten minutes later. Alex laid her head against the glass of her passenger window and watched as they drove out of the small town the Dead Brothel had been located. With the Noble Lord dead and gone, she wondered if someone would find a way to pick up where he left off.

Cliff drove them along quietly. Alex appreciated his ability to read the situation and know that Alex really had nothing to say. Soft murmurs came from the backseat as the Vega family spoke between themselves. Sylvia sat between Mateo and Albert. Though Albert was still in quite a bit of pain, he refused to be separated from his niece and nephew now that they were back together. Alex didn't blame him. They had risked a lot coming with the Duncans and trusting them to get into the brothel. Though she had questions, she would wait on the full story about how her siblings had met the Vega family.

The two vehicles were rounding a blind curve when Rafe slammed on his brakes. Cliff had to follow suit or risk smashing into the other vehicle. Cliff pulled the wheel and they coasted to the side of Rafe's truck. As they rounded the corner, Alex could clearly see why Rafe had stopped. The road was blocked by a car wreck. It looked like three or four cars had somehow crashed and were left in the middle of the small two-lane highway. That was something they could easily fix. It was the thirty or so infected wandering between the cars that created more of a problem. The car wreck was fairly new, judging by the steam that rose from one engine. Some infected were leaning into open windows and Alex cursed when she realized they were still eating the living that had been in the vehicles.

She reached under her feet and grabbed the machete she had taken to carrying. That along with the 9mm on one hip and her hunting knife on the other, Alex was ready for a fight. She looked beyond Cliff and found Max watching her from the other vehicle. The sisters nodded to each other and wordlessly agreed to what was going to have to happen. Cliff stayed in the truck, ready to move at a moments notice. Rafe had Charlie slide into the driver's seat in their truck for the same reason. Everyone was on edge and ready to move when it was time.

Alex slid from her side of the truck. With the meat in the cars, not many of the infected took notice of the new additions. Those that did, were slow and rambled toward the Duncans. Alex took up a stance at the front of the trucks. Rafe and Max flanked their sister and together they moved into the fray. Alex swung her machete with a great downward arch, slicing the top of the infected's head clean off. Alex herself felt slightly surprised and she hesitated.

"Took the liberty of sharpening it a bit more," Rafe bit out as he fought on Alex's left with another infected.

That made Alex grin a bit. Of course her brother would be sharpening their blades. Knives and anything that cut were his specialty. She rotated her shoulders as another infected came her way. Her leg was still tender, and she favored it as she moved forward for the death blow. Black gore stained her machete blade and Alex wondered if she should be worried about how good she felt. Fighting the infected was something she had grown to understand and know how to do. This was easier than dealing with a drug dealer or a brothel. The infected were easy to predict and their end was well known.

One of the infected that had been leaning into a car suddenly noticed the fighting happening nearby. The dead eyes seemed to focus on the Duncan siblings, just as Alex noticed its movements. This infected began moving faster than anticipated and Alex knew immediately they were dealing with one of the fast dead. She signaled to Max and Rafe that she was moving away. The two understood and moved so they were fighting back to back. The fast infected moved around the car, almost like a living human. The telltale dead black eyes confirmed what Alex already knew. No matter how normal it moved, it was still a dead, flesh-eating zombie.

Though it was faster, the decisions it made were still based on the same basic instinct. Attack, eat, move on. When it looked at Alex, it saw a meal and its number one goal was to sink its claws into her. Alex used this knowledge to her advantage, knowing the fast infected would lunge at her. Only a few moments later and the infected had its fingers up in claws and was diving at Alex. She easily sidestepped and brought the machete in a downward blow, embedding into its skull. She stepped on the top of its head to pull her machete free. She wanted to roll it over and study the body for any other differences, but more infected were realizing new fresh meals were close and they were coming for them.

Alex turned back to her siblings, finding them fighting easily. Black blood flew and the ground was becoming slick with bodies and dead innards. Storm danced around nearby infected, distracting them or knocking them to the ground at Rafe's feet. She knew she didn't need to worry about Rafe and Max, but the older sister in her made her work her way back to them so they were all watching out for each other. If she did nothing else right in the apocalypse, she would always be there for her family. That thought brought Billie, Henry, Easton, and Candace to her mind. The love she had for them fueled her as she swung and stabbed the infected as they stumbled within her range.

The infected continued to come, some faster than others. The clatter of metal made Alex jump and she whirled around to see Max grabbing the arms of a large infected man. Her tomahawk had fallen to the ground and she grunted now as she pushed back at the infected. The man tried to lean his face in, his chomping teeth dangerously close to Max's face. Alex sprung into action, without a second thought. She pulled her Bowie knife and jumped to add more power as she impaled it into the temple of the infected. Just as the body crumpled to the ground, Griffin came running around the side of their trucks. His face was pale and he was holding his rifle at his shoulder. Clearly, he almost saw Max lose a piece of her face to the infected.

Though Griffin had been instructed to watch the back of the trucks for any additional infected, he couldn't be told to go back to his post. Max was frustrated, but Alex could understand where he was coming from. Their life together was important. They had a lot to work through still and time to enjoy the renewal of their love. Griffin was terrified of losing Max in this apocalypse. Alex knew the pain of that and she didn't wish it on anyone she considered family.

Before she knew it, the fight was over and the highway was covered in infected bodies. With the all-clear signal given, the trucks were turned off and Charlie came bounding out of her driver's door. She had a small case with her and she went straight to the first fast infected Alex had fought. There she flipped the body over and looked at it. Alex joined her, realizing she was doing the same thing Alex had wanted to do.

"What do you think?" Alex asked.

"I haven't been able to figure it out yet. But I'm taking samples so when we get home I can test against the other infected information I've gathered," Charlie replied.

Alex watched as Charlie cut a piece of flesh from the infected. It seemed the piece was from the original bite sight, but Alex couldn't tell that easily. The infected had started to decompose and it had many rips and tears in its graying skin. Then Charlie took a needle and collected a number of small vials of black blood. She held each up to the light and shook them to ensure they were full and what she needed. Once she was done, she packed all of her samples back into her case.

The little blonde woman then turned to her dog and put her hand to her hip. She shook her head at the gore covering his coat. Alex smiled as Charlie lectured Storm on the ability of fighting without needing a bath after. Rafe approached, but didn't inter-rupt as Charlie found some clean areas on the dog and scratched him lovingly, thanking him for always having Rafe's back.

Rafe then insisted she climb back into the truck. She tried to argue, but he whispered something to her and she just shook her head comically before following his directions.

It took them another twenty minutes to move the infected bodies out of the road. Then they had to maneuver the crashed cars as best as they could. One of them had a man that was just waking up as an infected. Alex quickly used her bowie and ended the infected before it could hurt any of the living. Two of the cars were too badly mangled to be pushed by hand, so Cliff carefully pulled one truck up and used the front bumper to push the other car off the road. The sound of squealing tires and bending metal was loud. Alex stood off to the side, her head on a swivel, looking for any unknown attack. Rafe came to join her as he oversaw the operation.

"This couldn't have happened long ago," Rafe said.

"No, the people in the cars were just turning. So maybe twenty minutes," Alex replied.

"How do you think they crashed?" Rafe hedged. The tone of his voice told Alex he had an idea. She didn't answer him, just turned to gaze to his and waited.

"There were bullet holes in two of the windshields. The two that didn't have people still in them," Rafe said.

"You think the soldiers did this? On purpose? They killed the people in those two cars and left the cars for others to crash into?" Alex said, catching his train of thought easily.

"It's a completely blind curve. I almost didn't see the wreck until we were on top of it. If there were other people driving fast and those two cars were left in the middle of the highway, it would have easily caused an accident."

Alex had to admit, it was a sound plan. Especially because she could see the cars after a blind turn as an idea she would use. It was a good barricade location if you didn't want someone to see it until they hit it. With less and less traffic on the road, people weren't careful with their speeds or even staying on the right side of the road.

"They couldn't be sure someone would hit them. But it was either someone else did and we were blocked, or we hit them and it slowed us down even more. Seems the first is what happened," Alex said.

"That's the most likely scenario," Rafe agreed.

Alex wasn't sure she liked the picture of the soldiers being so cunning. She didn't want to underestimate them either. Callahan's men followed orders blindly and didn't worry about who they would put into danger when they did. The thought infuriated Alex. People thought turning to the government or the military would save them. Instead, people found themselves being shot at and used as pawns in a boobie-trap that could have possibly not worked.

Once the road was cleared enough for the two trucks to move through, they were back on the road. Breakfast had gone by long before and Alex couldn't help but hear and feel when her stomach decided to suddenly growl. Cliff heard it too because he looked sharply at Alex.

"Have you eaten?" He asked.

"No. It's been a while I think," Alex replied lamely.

Cliff picked up the walkie talkie and radioed Rafe's truck. The decision was made to stop until they could get food made and then they would drive and eat. Rafe pulled to the side of the road and Cliff followed. Alex wasn't happy about the additional delay. She jumped from the truck, ready to insist they keep moving.

"We have wasted too much time as it is," Alex told Rafe as he came to the back of his truck. He lowered the tailgate and climbed into the bed.

"I know you feel that way. But we all need to eat to keep up our strength. Let me just get the stuff out and then we can drive," Rafe replied.

A hand on her shoulder made Alex physically jump. She whirled around to see Max behind her.

"Alex, calm down. We will be driving again in five. Go sit in your truck. I'll bring you food," she said quietly.

"When did you decide to take care of people?" Alex asked.

"Since my sister went off, got kidnapped, got beat up, and now looks like she could fall flat on her face at any moment," Max replied.

"I'm fine," Alex said. Max's eyes told her she knew it was a lame lie.

"Remember when I got to the compound? You knew something had gone very wrong the moment you laid eyes on me. You gave me my space. You let me come to you when I was ready to tell you what had happened. I'm going to do the same for you, Alex. But I know when you're lying about how you feel. You can either just keep the false front up, or you can let your family take care of you for a while."

Alex couldn't help but stare at Max. She was aware her mouth was hanging open and Max got a sarcastic smile on her face.

"This Max is only going to last so long, so eat it up while you can," Max said.

"I guess I'll take what I can get," Alex replied.

Max embraced her sister and Alex appreciated the warmth. She hadn't realized how cold she was until she felt the love coming from Max. Her heart hurt from what she had endured and what she had seen at the brothel. The good in Alex screamed to be the savior of all the women. In the end, they saved one and Alex felt guilt inside for that. They weren't an army and had to survive as best they could. Her family coming for her was nothing less than what she had expected them to do.

When Alex climbed back into her truck, she sat still with her eyes closed. She let the feeling of love and caring wash over her.

Even if she was surprised it was coming from Max, it was what she needed and she so appreciated it. Alex felt someone touch her hand and she turned her face toward Cliff. He squeezed her fingers for a moment and she squeezed back. The big quiet man lent his support just the same as her siblings. He didn't look at her, just looked out the windshield, keeping his eyes moving. His hand released hers then and Alex settled into her seat.

CHAPTER TWENTY-ONE

In the distance, behind a pair of binoculars, the Duncan group was watched as they served their lunch and got back on the road. Their every move was noted. The soldier had watched them from the Dead Brothel. Taking one from their group was the sure way to get the entire Duncan family back to Callahan. Private Fletcher wanted to earn the respect of Callahan after they had all lost the Duncan prisoner. The Major had punished all the soldiers that were on guard the night Max Duncan escaped. Some of Fletcher's friends disappeared after that night. He knew they had been dealt with by Callahan.

Picking up the long-range walkie talkie, Fletcher radioed the car that carried the member of the Duncan group. He let them know how far behind them the Duncans were. They had a large head start. Though they had stopped after the man named Marcus somehow got a knife and cut himself free from his bindings. He fought hard, but in the end someone knocked him out with a gun and they had to stop to tend to his wounds. They couldn't allow him to die before Callahan questioned him.

Private Fletcher felt very proud of himself for delaying the Duncans as long as he did. Finding the two cars crashed was pure luck in the middle of the night. It was divine intervention when the two additional cars pulled up at a fast pace while he was looking at the wreck. It wasn't hard for him to kill the drivers in the vehicles. After that, the momentum of the vehicles carried them both into the previous wreck. He couldn't have staged the whole thing himself if he had tried. The sound of the shots is what had attracted the infected from the nearby trees. The injured people still alive in the cars was all they needed to stay near the cars and create the diversion Fletcher needed.

The man posted in a tree nearby, after making sure no infected were following his trail. He waited the night out in his perch. It didn't take long for the screams of the living to end as the infected tore at their bodies. A part of Fletcher felt sorry that those people had to be sacrificed for the good of the country. They had all made their own contributions to the cause. This was just their purpose.

He had actually fallen asleep in the tree at some point and was awakened by the sun piercing the tree canopy he was under. He shook himself out of his stupor and began to panic, believing he had missed the Duncans pass. He tried to calculate the time in his mind and was on the verge of climbing out of his tree when he heard engines. He froze and put his rifle to his shoulder. Watching through the scope he saw the two trucks pull up to the accidents. Fletcher was glad they hadn't crashed into the cars, as it had been a risk to have the blockade so close to a blind turn. Killing them wasn't his plan, delaying them was.

He watched as the Duncans exited their vehicles and attacked the infected with a vigor he hadn't seen from anyone not in the military. The three siblings worked closely together, their skills honed over many years. It was clear to Fletcher now why these three seemed like such a liability to the Major. Fletcher saw Max Duncan have a close call and part of him was cheering on the infected. Her escape was the reason a number of his friends were gone now. And he wanted her to pay for that transgression.

When the family began to move the vehicles, Fletcher humped it half a mile away from where he had hidden his small vehicle. He knew the basic course the Duncans would take. They were doing exactly as predicted, not leaving one of their own behind. While it was an admirable trait, Fletcher couldn't lose focus of the plan. In his car he sped down the little highway, finding a second point to hide. He timed the Duncans and when they didn't show like he expected; he backtracked carefully.

Now he hid in the woods again and watched them as they made food and distributed the meal among the adults. He watched the oldest sister be consoled by her family members and he wondered what had happened to her in the brothel. It wasn't his concern on how the Noble Lord ran his business. Callahan gave the man the power to do that as he pleased, as long as he continued to provide the supplies as agreed. Fletcher had enjoyed a few women over the last month there and he didn't feel regret about that either.

Fletcher now took the time to unpack the larger radio system he carried. This military airborne radio system was the way Callahan controlled the communications between all of his men that weren't at the base. There was a communication hub at base that everyone was required to report back to. As Fletcher was the one with eyes on the targets, he was the one to radio back his progress. After a number of beeps and then passcodes, Fletcher was put through to speak directly with the Major.

"Private, what do you have? Over," Callahan said.

"Sir, eyes on target group. They are on schedule, approximately seven hours behind prisoner vehicle, over."

"All three of the Duncans are there? Over."

"That's affirmative sir, over," Fletcher replied.

"That's good, Private. Keep them in your sights. When you get close to base, I need to know all details of where they are and what they're doing, over," Callahan said.

"Copy, sir, over," Fletcher said.

"This is the most important mission you've had, son. I expect you to succeed. Over and out," Callahan said, and the transmission ended.

Fletcher packed the radio back. As he was finishing his transmission, he saw the Duncans preparing to leave again. The prisoner would be arriving at base in less than three hours. That meant at least eight hours for the Duncans until they got to the outskirts of the city. Fletcher climbed out of his post and ran back to his vehicle. He would get out ahead of the Duncans and wait for them to pass him into the city. Then he could let Callahan know what was happening. The Major trusted him and he wasn't going to fail.

CHAPTER TWENTY-TWO

His head felt heavier than a twenty-pound dumbbell. Marcus couldn't figure out why his mouth felt like he'd shoved a handful of cotton balls into it. Or why he couldn't focus on anything happening around him. He tried to put things together in his mind, but he felt like everyone was foggy and far away. Black seemed to seep from the corners of his eyes, but he shook his head to try to clear it.

And that was about the wrong thing to do at the moment. Pain shot from his head down into his eyes and temples. For a moment he debated throwing up the cotton balls and for some reason that image made him want to laugh. But when any sound tried to come out, everything was muffled. *Ahhh, now I get it*, he thought to himself. He was gagged, which was causing the drying sensation in his mouth. Once he realized that, he was then stuck trying to decide how he had gotten gagged in the first place.

Alex's face flared to life in his mind. And she was scared. That was all he needed to have the story become clear. He had been taken by the military. The same military that had tortured Max, had gone after Rafe, had tried to kidnap Charlie. They took Marcus because he was with them. *Stupid*, he thought. He didn't know anything to even give up. They definitely took the wrong Duncan member. He was useless to them. At least he thought he was.

The surrounding soldiers talked into a walkie talkie and between each other. The fog in his mind made it hard to concentrate on the words being spoken. It was all he needed though, to realize the Duncans were coming after him. The military plan all became crystal clear to Marcus and he wanted to scream. He banged his already injured head against the back of the seat, angry at himself for getting taken, angry at the Duncans for not seeing the trap that was being made for them. He began to struggle with the bindings that cut into his wrists. All he could think was if he escaped, the Duncans wouldn't keep coming. If they killed him and left his body for them to find, then the Duncans would be safe. He needed them to be safe.

His connection to the family had grown over the few months they had survived together. It was impossible to avoid. Everyone treated each other as family, blood or not. The children were smart, quirky, kind, and a challenge for anyone trying to guard their heart. Now they were left behind by their parents who succeeded in their first rescue mission, only to fall into a second one. And Marcus felt his life was forfeit when it came to the parents that needed to get home to their kids on the Duncan compound.

He leaned back and lifted his feet. They were taped together at the ankle, so all he could do was slam his feet into the driver's seat. He got two kicks in before the soldier next to him was able to control him. The car swerved some but stayed on the road. Marcus felt helpless. He thought of the times that Alex tried to get him to follow her common sense plans. He always wanted to go his own way, control what he was doing, and make the plans. Often his plans went awry, but never to the harm of anyone else. Would they even be where they were right now if he had just listened to her days ago in that parking lot of infected?

Using his chin and shoulder, Marcus tried to pull his gag from his mouth. It wasn't working so he turned to the soldier next to him and motioned with his face. The soldier ignored him and he was half tempted to try to wet himself. He didn't need to pee, but he wanted to lie to them to make them stop the vehicle. He couldn't be sure how far behind them the Duncans were. But he wanted them to have the chance to challenge these soldiers before they got back to the base camp.

The soldier next to him dismissed him and continued his watch out of the windows. Marcus struggled against his bindings. They had him in metal handcuffs now. After he cut the first duct tape binding, they seemed to think he was more of a worry than anticipated. He thought of all the stupid action movies he used to watch before the apocalypse. Did he know how to dislocate his thumb and put it back? No. So until he could convince them to take off his handcuffs, he was stuck where he was. The struggling started to annoy the soldier in the backseat and Marcus guessed that was better than nothing.

"I don't care what it is you need, sit still or I will knock you out again," the man said to Marcus before throwing out an elbow that hit Marcus in the stomach.

Air tried to whoosh from his mouth, but the sound was eaten by the gag. He bent over slightly, trying to catch his breath through his nose. The lack of oxygen was again bringing spots into his vision but he slowed his breathing and worked on deep steady intakes of air. The soldier next to him seemed to think this was hilarious as he began to laugh. Marcus glared at him, knowing if he were free he could deal with the man easily. He was barely a man, not unlike many of the other soldiers they had faced since the apocalypse had started. Marcus should have felt bad for imagining the death of a barely adult soldier, but he didn't.

The radio in the front seat flared to life again. This time Marcus could pick up more of the conversation now that he was awake. He deflated when he realized that someone was reporting on the location of the Duncans. Someone was watching them. The Duncans had better situational awareness than anyone he had ever met, so the soldier watching them must have been very well hidden. The Duncans were also doing the predictable thing, following Marcus. He wished they could read his mind and let him go. They would be walking into a trap.

What seemed like an eternity later, houses began to appear in the distance. The soldier sped up, navigating roads that he knew very well. Marcus knew that they were coming to the military camp that Callahan held. He had no plans, knowing he couldn't escape now. The only thing he knew was he wasn't giving Callahan any information. Not that there was information to provide. The pieces they had put together between Max, Rafe, and Charlie, they could only assume Callahan thought there was a secret cure. But after months of Charlie trying to figure it out, she still didn't have a way to solve the apocalyptic illness.

The sedan pulled to a stop at a checkpoint. There was a fence erected across the highway, with a sign that said "Welcome to Rapid City." Marcus didn't have any idea where Rapid City was. He only knew it was East of the compound in Montana because Max had come to the city on her way home. The sun had started to approach the middle of the sky, meaning they had been driving close to twelve hours from the night before. Wyoming? One of the Dakotas? Not that it really mattered, Marcus was only trying to distract his mind from what was happening.

The checkpoint cleared the car through. Marcus didn't miss the sneers and laughter coming from the soldiers. He could imagine the Duncans weren't well-liked among the men and women working for Callahan. The sedan pulled up in a small parking lot. Marcus was yanked from the car, even as he tried to fight. Men grabbed his legs as he thrashed and tried to kick. He was carried horizontally into a cement-like building.

Inside, Marcus remembered suddenly the pieces of Max's story he had heard. She described the building as something used for animals or butchering of animals. When he was thrown into a room, he landed hard on his back, his head bouncing off of the ground. He was left like that and he had to keep his eyes closed to stop the room from spinning. He wanted to vomit, and he figured after the blows to his head, he had a decent concussion.

He was still on the ground when a pair of shined shoes entered his blurred vision. He was lifted then roughly placed in a metal chair. His head hung down, a monster of all headaches splintering his skull. The shined shoes lead to an impeccably pressed uniform. Marcus wondered what servants there were around that took care of the dry cleaning. It took a moment for Marcus to focus on the face. The cold eyes and perfectly combed hair were dead giveaways that this was Major Callahan. Max had described him perfectly and Marcus didn't have to guess twice.

"They're on their way, you know," Callahan said.

Marcus just stared at him. He was well aware of what the man was saying, but he didn't feel the need to dignify anything Callahan did or said with an answer.

"You aren't important to me, Jonathan Marcus Kline. From what I've gathered, you aren't useful to my cause."

He knows who I am, Marcus thought to himself. The Major clearly had done his homework on the people at the compound. What Marcus had to wonder was how he knew who was behind the walls. Callahan had a folder on his lap and he slowly opened the cover. Marcus immediately recognized his own passport photo on the front cover.

"Jonathan Marcus Kline. You haven't really decided who you are yet in life, have you? Construction, barista, bartender and even a stint as a dog walker. How does someone like you fall in with the likes of the Duncans?" Callahan asked.

Marcus just stared at the man. When the chilling smile broke across his face, it never reached his eyes. He nodded to the soldier standing off to the side. Marcus expected torture or worse. He knew what had happened to Max inside the very walls he was sitting inside. So, though the punch to the jaw was expected, that didn't mean it hurt any less. Marcus felt a tooth slice into the inside of his mouth and blood flavored his tongue. He spit at the ground, red tinging his saliva.

"I see your attitude isn't much better than Maxine Duncan. You do stay more quiet, though," Callahan said with a sigh.

The soldier punched Marcus again in the face and followed it up with a punch to the gut. Marcus couldn't stop the sound as the air flew from his lungs. Then he was left like a gaping fish trying to force air back into his lungs.

"You may think you can outsmart me. You may believe that keeping your silence means I will get frustrated. Maybe kill you. But you would be assuming wrong, Mr. Kline."

With that, Callahan rose and left the room. The soldier followed him quickly, leaving Marcus alone on the metal chair, bent over trying to breathe. The door shut with a clang and a deadbolt locking Marcus in. His arms were still secured behind him and his shoulders felt the strain. After he gathered enough breath to stand, he walked the cell, rotating his shoulders as best he could. He couldn't help but picture Max in the same cell. He thought about her injuries and the torture she went through. Mentally he prepped himself for the same routine.

He didn't have to wait long. The door opened again and three soldiers entered the room. None of them made eye contact, only entering to handle their orders. Marcus was held by two of the soldiers while the other pulled out a large pair of scissors. He first cut the shirt from Marcus, slicing up the front and the arms. Next to go were his boots, which were tossed out of the cell. Then his jeans and socks were yanked from his body and thrown into the hallway as well. The soldiers left as quickly has they had come, leaving a shivering Marcus.

Marcus guessed there was some sort of intimidating practice in leaving someone almost naked and handcuffed. And the cell was fairly chilly, causing goosebumps to rise on his chest and arms. If they planned to freeze him to death, it would take colder conditions than mid-spring weather. He continued to pace to keep his blood pumping and his body somewhat warm. After he became bored with that, he did squats and armless jumping jacks.

He was breathing quickly when the door opened again. The sudden intrusion startled him and he backed up to the wall, preparing for a fight. Instead, the polished Callahan entered again. His entourage followed with a chair. The man sat down again, motioning for Marcus to join him. Instead of being pushed and prodded by the soldiers, Marcus walked over and plopped down unceremoniously. The Major looked at him for a moment before speaking. Marcus could feel the weight of his steely gaze as if he had his hands around his throat.

"Feeling comfortable, Mr. Kline?"

Marcus just stared at him.

"You are important enough that the Duncans are coming here for you. If you give me what I want to know, I won't kill them all," Callahan said.

He dropped the bomb with a smirk on his face and Marcus realized he was wrong about the level of evil he thought was in this man. He was all evil. Marcus thought about the offer, but he was sure no matter what he did or did not give him, he would still try to kill the Duncans. And if he was able to kill the adults, the kids were practically defenseless at the compound. The military could easily take the home. Easton would fight back and Marcus tried not to think about the teenager being killed. The younger kids would have no defense, other to run into the woods. If they made it that far. But could he believe that Callahan wouldn't kill them all if he answered his questions?

"I can't trust you. You'll do whatever you want, no matter what," Marcus said, speaking for the first time.

"I work for the United States Government. I'm here to help protect its citizens. Why would I lie about this, to you, to someone I should be helping support at this time of need?"

Marcus couldn't stop his mouth from dropping open. While Callahan said the words, that maybe a more noble man would have meant, his eyes stayed cold. There was no compassion in his voice. He was cold and calculating.

"The US Government is who caused this. And there's no one in power left that matters. Least of all you. See, I know things too," Marcus said.

"You only know what the Duncans have been feeding you. If I'm right, you've been with them since basically the start. You haven't seen what is going on in the rest of the country," Callahan replied.

"My guess is, pretty much the same as here. This plague moves too fast to just stop at state borders. I know that."

"We need to rebuild, Mr. Kline. And the only way to do that is to handle the renegade factions, like the Duncans."

"Renegade factions? The Duncans keep to themselves. They scavenge supplies just the same as everyone else. If you were so concerned about factions, you wouldn't have had soldiers enjoying time at the Noble Lord's little crazy house in Montana."

Marcus knew the moment he hit a sore spot when Callahan's lips tightened ever so slightly, and his eyes narrowed. *Guess he doesn't want people knowing about that*, Marcus thought to himself.

"That was a regrettable incident. The Noble Lord could have been a decent partner. But yet another thing the Duncans couldn't keep their noses out of."

"A regrettable incident? Man, you really are out there. The guy was kidnapping women, enslaving them as prostitutes, allowing infected men to use them. How is that not a complete horror show?" Marcus demanded.

"Men have needs, Mr. Kline. You know that. We were trying to provide those needs as best as possible in the world we are in now," Callahan replied. He was nonchalant, picking an unseen piece of lint from his pants.

"Provide those needs," Marcus repeated. He felt a little dumbfounded. The man referred to kidnapping and rape as if it were a trip to the local supermarket.

"If you are so intent on rebuilding the country, then those kinds of places and those types of people would be the factions you need to deal with. Not a family like the Duncans. They have done nothing to you," Marcus said.

"They have killed my men."

"Ones you sent to their home, to kill them or to take members of the family."

"Charlotte Brewer is not a member of the Duncan family," Callahan bit out. He seemed annoyed now and Marcus knew he didn't like all the information Marcus actually did have.

"She is now. That's the thing about the Duncans, something you'll never understand. As soon as you're with them, you're family. There's no question. That's why they're coming here. I wish they weren't. I wish they would turn around and go home. But no matter what I say, even though I have nothing they truly need, but they will never just leave me behind," Marcus said.

As Marcus spoke, he could feel a lump rise in his throat. He had come to care deeply about the family he was with. Even beyond his initial attraction to Alex, which easily melted away when they became close friends, he cared about each person he had lived with over the last few months. He didn't want to be responsible for anything happening to them.

"And that, Mr. Kline, is why you're still alive," Callahan said.

Marcus shivered, but not from the chill in the room this time. A cold sweat broke out on his brow and he thought about wiping it away. His numb fingers reminded him that he was still restrained. He was being used as bait. While Callahan sat and pretended to study the file on his lap, Marcus glanced around the room. Part of him looked for an escape, though he knew there wasn't one. The other part looked for a way to end himself. If he wasn't alive, he couldn't be used as a pawn. He could only hope the Duncans would turn back and not try to exact revenge on the military camp. They were well outnumbered and the Duncans would know that. They also didn't make losing choices.

Callahan stood carefully, folding his papers under his arm. He looked at the nearby soldier and nodded, confirming orders given before they entered the room. Marcus just waited, not able to determine what was coming next.

"Make it look good, but don't kill him," Callahan said before leaving the room.

Marcus didn't have a chance to figure out what Callahan was referring to before the soldiers stalked toward him. The soldier behind him grabbed the chair he was sitting in, as Marcus thought about standing up, the man yanked the chair from under him. Marcus collapsed to the floor, falling to his back without his arms to catch him. He was just able to save his head from striking the solid ground, but the next blow from the soldier slammed his head backward, cracking it against the concrete. A kick to his ribs sent him sliding to one side, forcing all the air out of his lungs. Marcus couldn't remember the number of times he had been breathless since the soldiers had taken him.

He knew he needed to protect his vital organs. Turning to his side, Marcus tried to curl in on himself, but he had no way to protect his head. The next kick landed on one of his kidneys and the pain caused his back to spasm. His fingers were suddenly grabbed and twisted at an abnormal angle, as the soldier pulled him to his feet. The man wasn't any taller than Marcus, but Marcus couldn't stand up straight. With his hands behind Marcus' head, he yanked him down to meet an upward knee. Marcus' flew backward from the blow, hitting the nearby wall. He started to slide down, but he fought the urge. Staying on his feet would be his goal.

The two soldiers circled him as if he were a penned animal ready to attack at any time. The thought was laughable since Marcus was completely restrained and couldn't even protect himself. One of the men grabbed the metal chair and took a full swing at Marcus' shoulder. Marcus danced away quickly, moving toward the door. Using his hands behind him, he was able to confirm the door was locked so it wasn't an option to end the abuse. The soldiers looked at each other and laughed as they realized Marcus was thinking of trying to escape.

"There's no way out of this room. We won't kill you, though. You heard the Major," one soldier said.

"He didn't say how close to get and he wants it to look good," the second soldier said.

They came at him again and Marcus moved to get away again. But one of the soldiers was faster as his foot snaked out and tangled with Marcus' bare feet. When Marcus went down, it was hard. His chin bounced off of the ground and he again tasted blood in his mouth. Suddenly one of the men stomped on his ankle and Marcus screamed in pain as the joint was pushed to its limit. By the third stomp he knew it was dislocated or completely broken. He tried to stop the screaming, but the pain was more than Marcus had known and he couldn't move his leg to get away from the onslaught.

"Great, now we'll have to carry him," one man said in a low voice.

"Yeah, well, that'll stop him from trying to get away."

Marcus could feel hot tears spilling down his cheeks before splashing to the floor. He tried to turn to his shoulder and roll away, but his ankle was limp, and every movement blinded him with pain. The men seemed to realize he couldn't get away and they took their turns trying to break unnecessary parts of his body. As they worked on breaking his fingers, Marcus welcomed the blackness that finally seeped in and swept him away from the torture. His last conscious thought was he hoped he died and Alex would go back and be safe on the compound.

CHAPTER TWENTY-THREE

Alex hunkered down behind a pedicure chair. The smell of chemicals were long gone from the nail salon. But apparently no one seemed to think it was a place to look for supplies. The front windows were intact and the door had been locked when Rafe had picked it. Once they were all gathered inside, they locked the door again and took stations around the large salon. The sun was still up in the sky when they arrived in Rapid City and they knew there wasn't much to be done during the day.

She shifted slightly, trying to get more comfortable, her injured leg making that difficult. Max pushed over some towels they had found, and Alex created a small place to elevate her leg. Charlie had scolded her when she saw her cut was beginning to swell, so Alex figured she was doing what the doctor ordered. Max had found a case of soda, champagne, and snacks in the back storeroom. With a glance at the salon menu, Alex found it was one of the nail salons that served mimosas and food to their customers. They all snacked quietly as they waited for dusk to fall.

Alex had continued to watch Max since they arrived in the city. There was no doubt this was the right place for the military compound. Max had become tense and nervous. Her eyes darted all over the place, as if she was waiting for someone to jump out and get her. Griffin stayed close and rubbed her back as he tried to calm her. Max had leaned against him, sharing a whispered conversation. Griffin had kissed her on the forehead before they both tried to lean back and relax. Alex was so thankful that her sister had her high school sweetheart. Not only was it perfect that Jack now had her father with her, but Griffin also had a calming effect on Max.

"You all right?" Cliff's voice came from the other side of the pedicure chair. Alex turned so she could see him around the footrest.

"I guess. I just want to get Marcus and get out of here."

"Do you think it will be that easy?" Cliff asked.

"No. But we can't just leave him," Alex replied.

And that was really what she thought. She knew if they were to get Marcus back, they would need to be able to sneak in, grab him, and sneak out. Without seeing the camp, they already knew they were well outnumbered by soldiers and anyone else Callahan had recruited. When they all got into the salon, Alex had told everyone the story of the conversation she had overheard between the Noble Lord and the soldiers sent by Major Callahan. Max wasn't surprised in the least, commenting on the fact that Callahan was a control freak. And she had no doubt the maniac would endorse someone like the drug dealing, brothel owner. As long as he was an easy pawn to control.

"Have you thought about not going in yourself?" Cliff asked, pulling Alex from her thoughts.

"No. Why wouldn't I help?" Alex asked, baffled by his question.

"Because you have the kids. They need you. I don't have any kids. Mateo doesn't have any kids. We could sneak in and do the work. And if it didn't go right...well, no one is losing a parent," Cliff explained.

Alex turned to rest her full stare on Cliff before speaking.

"You are still a parent, Cliff, even though your child is gone. And you are needed in this group, just like everyone else. Just because your baby is gone, that doesn't make you expendable. I would never think like that or take actions because of that."

Cliff looked down at his hands and Alex guessed he was staring at his wedding ring. She knew his wife and son were never far from his thoughts. And Alex could understand that after she had to kill her own infected husband. The pain of that loss was an ache that didn't seem to leave her. If it had been one of her children, Alex couldn't imagine she would keep going. Somehow though, Max was able to get Cliff to the compound. Since then he had been a faithful member of their family. Alex couldn't imagine putting him in danger that she wasn't walking into herself.

"It's not the same, Alex," Cliff finally replied.

"Your importance to this group is the same. And I won't hear of you going in on your own again," Alex said. To end the line of discussion, she turned her back again and leaned against the footrest.

An hour later, the sun began to get lower in the sky and they decided they could get moving in the shadows. Everyone took the time to check their weapons and strap additional ammo in all the places they could. Rafe helped Charlie make Albert comfortable on a bed in a back room. The man made cracks about Charlie trying to wax him with the supplies in the room, but when he tried to laugh, he winced and stopped. The Vega family had a quiet conversation and Sylvia was left with Albert. Alex didn't question the decision, knowing the girl had been put through enough already.

They decided to leave out of the back door of the salon. When Rafe cracked the door and peered out, he held up a hand, indicating there were four infected in the alley. Rafe, Max, and Alex rushed out of the door together, taking down the slow infected before they realized they were close by. The bodies fell to the ground in the alleyway and Griffin, Cliff, and Mateo came out to join them. Together they moved near the wall and made their way to the end of the strip of stores.

When they reached the end of the alley, Rafe stopped short and everyone froze. Instead of looking ahead, he turned his head and looked into the windows of a church across a small road from them. By the way he cocked his head, Alex knew without asking that he had seen something that caught his attention. Alex waited, trusting her brother's instincts to know when to move. He stood extremely still and stared at the same spot for what felt like an eternity. When nothing seemed to move, he finally motioned that it was time to move forward.

They rounded another set of shops and found themselves entering a small housing development. There weren't as many places to hide and move, so they took shelter behind a shed for a moment, before looking at a map again. Alex moved to stand next to Rafe.

"What was that back there?" She asked.

"Pretty sure I saw someone move in that church. But when I turned to look, they made sure to stay unseen," Rafe replied.

"Friend or foe?" Alex wondered.

"My guess, in this town? Foe. We may not be a surprise after all. But there's no way of knowing if there are still residents hiding away from the military," Rafe said.

Alex nodded and they both went back to the map. They determined what housing development they were in and they realized they were closer to the camp than intended. They knew they couldn't approach the gates until dark and decided to wait it out in the yard of the house they were next to. Alex was full of nervous energy and couldn't find a way to relax as they waited for the sun to fall behind the horizon. Max just watched her warily as she paced the wall one way and then the other.

"Sit down, you're making me nervous just by watching you," Max finally said.

"You're already nervous and worried," Alex replied. When

Max didn't reply Alex looked down at her. Max looked away from her sister and Alex immediately felt bad for being short. She sat cross-legged next to her.

"And with good reason. I'm sorry. I'm just thinking about what is happening to Marcus," Alex said, reaching out to put her hand on Max's arm.

"I know. I am too. I of all people know what happens behind those walls."

"Unless they didn't keep him alive," Alex replied quietly.

They sat in silence for a while as the shadows stretched across the pavement. Alex was feeling antsy and uncomfortable, so she stood and began to pace the small area. She needed to be in action. Sitting without forward motion was driving her crazy.

"I'm going to do a quick scouting mission. Make sure there are no hordes or anything nearby," she suddenly announced.

"I'll come with you," Rafe replied immediately.

"Me too," Max said, standing up from her spot.

"Three of us as lookouts is a little much," Alex said.

"We know how to move quietly. We aren't letting you out there alone," Max said, shrugging her shoulders at Alex's argument.

Alex knew she wouldn't win so she conceded and the three of them set off behind the house they were sitting near. Alex led the three of them as they moved quietly across the open backyard area that sat between the houses. When they came to a large green space, Alex darted to the nearest tree. Rafe and Max mimicked her, putting themselves in the shadows of nearby trees. Nothing seemed to stir as they waited. Alex wondered if the military swept the town on a regular basis to clear it of the infected.

Alex stood still, looking out into the park area. The empty swings hung still; no children busy trying to have fun in the last minutes of the sunlight. The slide didn't cause any squeals from children as they'd rush down the spinning plastic tube. If she closed her eyes, she could almost remember laying in the sun at a

Las Vegas park while Billie and Henry ran themselves ragged. She wondered if the world would ever be safe again for that uninhibited type of play.

A low whistle sounded from behind her and Alex turned to see Rafe motioning across the park. Alex squinted, trying to see what he was seeing. She didn't see any infected or anything moving in that direction. She slowly moved back to Rafe's hiding spot to ask him what his signal meant.

"We're being watched," Rafe said quietly. He didn't whisper as much as spoke in a quiet voice to prevent sound from carrying.

"Where?"

"I saw movement in the trees, right off the street," Rafe replied.

"Living?"

"If it was an infected, it wouldn't be still."

"We've seen weird things before," Alex replied.

"Not this. Too normal. I think it's the same person I saw in the church," Rafe said.

Alex realized that meant they had been followed for awhile. She knew that wouldn't just be a survivor watching them. They would have given their position away sooner or would have approached the Duncans. No, she knew this was someone from Callahan's military. And that meant he was a threat.

"What do you want to do?" Rafe asked. Max snuck over to join them in the shadows. The darkness of dusk was starting to fall and sneaking would no longer be necessary.

Alex studied the area. If the stalker didn't know they were spotted, the Duncans could have the element of surprise. The inside of the park was exposed, but trees lined the outside, giving a private illusion. As the sun disappeared the trees became darker and a plan began to form in Alex's mind.

"We need bait," Alex said.

"Draw his attention away from the attack?" Max asked in a quiet voice.

Alex nodded. In quiet voices, the Duncan siblings worked out the plan. Max was the most well known to the soldiers in the area and likely the biggest point of anger by the Major. The men following Callahan's orders would be hard-pressed to pass a chance to catch their escaped prisoner again. Max wasn't completely comfortable being bait. As Alex stared into her sister's eyes, she reassured her over and over that she would never allow Callahan to get his hands on her again. Max's outer bravado was dented slightly when she wilted under the idea of being tortured again. Alex squeezed her shoulder and tried to convey with her eyes that everything would be fine.

Rafe and Alex took positions behind the trees on their side of the park. Max, with a tomahawk in hand, crept into the park center. She didn't let her eyes fall on the area they knew their prey was. While she moved slowly in the open, Rafe and Alex carefully moved from tree to tree. With the darkness almost complete, they couldn't be completely sure the man was still where they last saw him. Not for the first time Alex found herself praying that having Max alive was more important that shooting her on sight. As they hadn't been attacked yet, she was fairly confident this was the case. But seeing her little sister in the wide open, with an unknown enemy in waiting, made her nerves short circuit.

Max stopped at their previously agreed spot, halfway around the park circle from where the intruder was last seen. She was then to turn back the way she came to act as if she were communicating with someone behind the trees. Alex and Rafe were betting on the chance that the intruder would be busy watching Max. With his eyes elsewhere, they could easily sneak up and disable whoever it was. Rafe took lead, his knives the more quiet weapon of choice right then.

When they snuck to the trees closest to the intruder, Alex almost missed the man completely. However, when she allowed her eyes to roam and focus, she realized there was a man up in the tree, not on the ground. He watched through a rifle scope, as Max

used random hand signals to talk to pretend Rafe and Alex. Rafe
motioned to Alex as he noticed the man in the tree as well. They
each froze in their spot. Without needing to communicate, both
Duncans knew what it meant for the man to have the high position on them. If Rafe were to throw a knife and the man didn't
tumble from the tree, he would have easy shots to make against
them. He also had his rifle trained directly on their sister. There
was no knowing if he was just using the scope to watch her, or if
he was taking aim.

They knew how to take necessary risks, yet Alex held up a
hand to let Rafe know she wanted him to wait. He didn't question
her decision, just nodded and stepped deeper into his chosen
shadow. From Alex's tree, she could see the man clearly. She
recognized that he was a soldier, wearing his fatigue uniform.
That confirmed her suspicion that Callahan had sent the man.
She had to wonder how long the man had been watching them.
Alex herself had not been at her top level of performance after
what she had been through in the brothel. If the man had been on
their tail longer than their arrival into the city, Alex blamed
herself for not knowing he was there.

Alex turned to see Max looking around the park again and
Alex knew she was running out of ways to distract the soldier. She
would also be wondering why she hadn't heard the fighting of her
siblings or if they hadn't found anyone, why hadn't they come to
get her. Alex thought quickly and without much thought to what
was coming next, she signaled to Rafe to stay and watch the man.
She then quietly jogged back to the general area where Max was
pretending they were hiding. Alex then followed Max's original
path, her head on a swivel, but her eyes never falling on the
soldier's perch. Alex could see Max's eyebrows raised in question.

"What is it?" Max said near Alex's ear when they were
standing near each other.

"Soldier to my 3 o'clock. He's in a tree. We couldn't get to him
without putting you at risk. Follow my lead," Alex replied.

Max nodded and as Alex walked back toward the trees, she followed carefully. Alex turned her head and focused on the trees she had just come from. She used her hand to signal that they were moving on, pretending to communicate with Rafe. She hoped that their ruse was convincing enough. Once in the trees, Alex ran to the edge before crouching behind some of the last trees outside of the park. Max slid to her side and turned to look back the way they had come.

"What are you thinking?" Max asked.

"If the man is truly supposed to follow us, he'll think we've left the park. He doesn't know that Rafe has eyes on him. I'm hoping our show will bring him out of the tree and Rafe can attack," Alex said.

Just then a high-pitched cry came from the other side of the park. Alex stood up quickly and pulled her knife and 9mm before running back through the park. She could hear Max's feet pounding behind her, the thought of stealth out of their minds now. The sisters burst through the trees on the far side of the park and found Rafe pulling a knife from the thigh of a soldier. The man's hands were pushing on the wound, trying to stop the bleeding. Alex cocked her head and guessed Rafe struck an artery. A move she knew wasn't accidental.

"You're going to bleed out," Alex said. The man didn't look at her, just stared at the blood bubbling up between his fingers. Rafe looked over to Alex and she nodded. Her brother removed the man's belt and created a tourniquet high on his leg.

"We'll try to slow down the process if you answer our questions," Alex said.

Rafe grabbed the man's leg and pushed down on the wound until the soldier's eyes bulged and a painful scream erupted from his lips.

"With all the noise you're making, we can also leave you to be eaten. It's up to you," Alex continued.

The soldier gritted his teeth and met Alex's gaze with a

hatred that she could truly feel. She found it so odd to have a man she never met, regard her with such malice. She could only imagine what the Major told his men when he sent them after the Duncans. Alex couldn't decide which direction she wanted to go with the man. She didn't want to keep him with them. Most likely he already raised the alarm and Callahan knew they were coming. Though that was probably a given already and Callahan didn't need anyone to tell him.

"Is our friend still alive?" Alex asked. The man still didn't answer. Alex crouched down and pulled the man's fatigues closer to her. She found his name stitched into the chest.

"Fletcher is it? Listen, Fletcher. We are reasonable people. We have a friend that is a doctor that could possibly help you with this leg. Or we can get you to the military encampment where they could clean you up. Either way, those are only options if you answer my questions," Alex explained.

"I already know you have Charlotte Brewer with you. She has the cure. We are all looking for her and the cure to save the world," Fletcher said quietly. It sounded rehearsed, something repeated to him over and over again.

"She does not have the cure, so you can drop that stupidity," Rafe said, kicking the man in the uninjured leg.

"Liar," Fletcher hissed.

"Listen here, you little piss ant," Rafe started, but Alex cut him off and motioned for him to step back before he stomped on the soldier.

"My brother has a temper when it comes to the doctor, as you all keep trying to kidnap her or kill him. You might want to be more careful with your words," Max explained casually. She stood easily, tossing her tomahawk back and forth between her hands.

"I'm a member of the United States military. You have committed a crime by attacking me," Fletcher said.

"Your laws or at least your perception of them, mean very little to us," Alex said.

"That's because you're on the wrong side of history," Fletcher replied.

"Are you going to answer our questions, Fletcher? Or are you bleeding out here?" Alex said, bringing them back to the subject.

A small whistle called Alex's attention and she turned to look at Max. In the distance the telltale groaning could be heard, Fletcher's screams calling the infected right to them. The darkness was covering their path, but Alex could hear them on the other side of the copse of trees. She looked back down at Fletcher and wondered how far she would go to get the information from him. Alex knew that her sister would go as far as it took. Rafe could easily be pushed to the edge of humanity if the environment was right. Alex, on the other hand, wasn't sure how much she was capable of. She tried to not see Fletcher as the young man he was. She tried to only picture him radioing their position to Callahan. She could see them taking Marcus from the brothel at gunpoint. Was it enough?

"Seems we have some company coming," Alex finally said.

Fletcher's eyes widened and he began swinging his gaze wildly around them. Using his hands, he began to try to stand on his good leg. Rafe stepped forward and pushed him over again. He hit the ground with a grunt, but that didn't stop him from trying to pull himself away with his hands.

"Do you think that will get you away from the infected? And what if they are the fast ones? We might not be able to stop them before they have dug their claws into your body cavity," Alex said. She then crouched down, bringing herself eye level with the man.

"Answer our questions and we won't leave you here," she said quietly.

Fletcher clearly didn't believe her and Alex was at her limit of patience for the day. Hell, probably for the entire apocalypse. She stood up and walked toward the sound of the infected. She motioned for Rafe to wait and Max joined her. Carefully, Alex picked her way through the trees until she could see the teetering infected. She could tell by their aimless movements that after they heard Fletcher, they had lost the trail. She looked at Max, ensuring she was ready. The two of them could easily handle the three infected that seemed to be in the group. However, the point wasn't to kill them right away.

Alex coughed once and Max called out. Immediately, all the dead faces swung in their direction. Alex waited a beat and noted that none of the infected seemed to move faster than usual. That was what she was hoping for. The slow dead would be easier to manage for what she had in mind. Max turned to her with a look that said, "Now what?"

"Let's lead them back toward Fletcher. Maybe seeing the infected will loosen his tongue some."

"Seriously, Alex?" Max asked.

"Yes, why?" Alex asked, perplexed by her sister's hesitancy.

"This seems a little harsh for you. Even I would think twice before leading infected right to a man that can't run away," Max replied.

As they discussed the plan, the infected got closer and the sisters had to take a few steps back before becoming easy targets themselves.

"I'm not going to let them eat him, well not on purpose at least. I just want him scared. He needs to tell us about Marcus."

"What if he doesn't know anything?"

"We'll find that out and then we'll just drop him close to his people. Let them fix him up," Alex said.

Max didn't question the plan any further. The two of them kept their eyes on the infected as they ran into trees and stumbled to catch their desired cuisine. The sound of their hissing and growling was loud enough to carry to Rafe and Fletcher. The sounds of Fletcher arguing with Rafe was an indication that he knew what was coming. The infected stared at Alex and Max with black bottomless holes in their faces. Their hands were up, fingers bent into claws as they swiped at the empty space in front of them.

When they walked beyond the trees that hid Fletcher, Rafe moved and faced the infected that came their way. He eyed the three and then looked at his sisters.

"Really?" He asked.

"What happens next is completely up to Fletcher here," Alex said.

In show, she slid her knife back into its sheath and crossed her arms in front of her chest. Though she was pretending to be calm and composed, she knew that her siblings wouldn't let the infected get to her. Alex stood over Fletcher and watched his face. He had gone ghostly pale, either from blood loss or fear, she couldn't be sure. He trembled and had a hard time pulling himself along with just his arms. When the infected were fifteen feet from him he swung his gaze to Alex's.

"You can't do this!" He screeched.

"Get louder, they love that," Max said over her shoulder. Alex watched as an infected tried to reach her. Max danced away on light feet, bringing the infected back into the trees, before leading him back toward the group.

"Kill them!" Fletcher cried.

"We will, once you answer my questions," Alex said.

Fletcher stared as Rafe stepped forward to sweep the feet from under one of the infected. The dead body bounced to the ground, with no coordination keeping it from falling in an unnatural pile of limbs. The third infected with the group seemed focused on Fletcher and continued to come forward toward him.

"So? What's your decision?"

"Make it quick, will ya? This is boring," Max called out.

"I...I..." Fletcher began.

"You, what? Is our friend alive?" Alex asked again.

"Yes," Fletcher squeaked.

Without hesitation, Alex pulled her 9mm from its holster. She had already turned her body so she could watch the infected from the corner of her eye. Her arm came up and a split second later she pulled the trigger. The force of the impact threw the infected back off of its feet. The walking dead was now truly dead with a perfect black hole in its forehead. The shot was all Rafe and Max needed to both end the infected they were watching. Almost simultaneously the two thrust their knife blades into the temples of the infected.

After, Rafe bent and cleaned his knife on the infected's blood-soaked nightgown. Max in true fashion came to Fletcher with her knife, black ooze coating the shiny blade. She crouched down next to the man and watched him.

"Alex, what happens if I put this black stuff in his wound?" Max asked.

"Not sure, maybe he'd get sick and turn. We could always try it," Alex said, shrugging her shoulders.

"Charlie needs more experiments," Rafe called from his post, watching their backs to ensure no other infected snuck up. Alex knew taking the shot was a risk, but she knew it was more intimidating to Fletcher.

"Stop, I answered your question, didn't I?" Fletcher said.

"I don't have just one," Alex said.

Fletcher didn't take his eyes from Max, or her filthy knife.

"What else do you want to know?"

CHAPTER TWENTY-FOUR

He couldn't open his eyes. Everything was black and part of him felt a sense of peace believing he was dead. Then the pain lanced through his body and Marcus knew he wasn't that lucky. Using the fingers that hadn't been fractured by the soldiers, he swiped at his face. Something seemed to crust across his eyes. He rubbed for a moment and blinked his eyes. Looking at his fingers he realized it was blood caked on his face.

Internally, Marcus had a conversation with his body. He felt badly that it was so abused, but he needed it to help him out. As he tried to push himself into a sitting position, he moved the leg with the shattered ankle. His cry of pain reverberated around the small concrete room. He laid his face back down on the floor, trying to breathe through the nausea sweeping through him.

Worry clouded his inner monologue. He knew they brought him to the brink of death, but didn't finish the job because the Duncans were on the way. He wanted nothing more than for the Duncans to leave him. He wanted the children to have their parents. He wanted them to survive the plague but also survive long enough to take down Callahan and 'The Suit'. Marcus knew if anyone was to end the insanity of this government faction it was going to be the Duncan Family.

Laying on the concrete ground, Marcus found himself thinking about when he first met Alex. She intimidated him with her strength and the solid head on her shoulders. Immediately he had known she was a force to reckon with and he knew he wanted to be on her side. After a number of mishaps and misunderstandings between the two of them, Marcus had finally found his rhythm. Everyone had a part to play in their group and Marcus was glad he found a place in the life of the compound.

Marcus was aware that this was a form of his life flashing before his eyes. He found himself going back through the last few months. With cracked lips, he tried to smile when he thought about teaching Henry to hammer a nail properly. He remembered Billie demanding that he kiss her hand after he took out a splinter, so the owie would go away. Marcus wondered if he'd had more time, would Easton eventually trust him? The teenage boy saw through Marcus' initial attraction to Alex immediately. Marcus knew if the boy had been capable, he would have killed Marcus to keep him away from his adoptive mother.

His inner thoughts were interrupted by the door opening a lone figure stepping in. Marcus tried to focus but he could only see clearly out of one eye. The man that entered was a soldier. However, the way he looked around before closing the door, told Marcus he wasn't supposed to be in the cell with him. The soldier came to Marcus and rolled him carefully to his back. Marcus groaned through gritted teeth as he worked to make sure he didn't scream again. The soldier was older, his brown hair salt and peppered and lines branching out from the corners of his eyes. Marcus found his age interesting because it seemed most of the men following Callahan were young and impressionable.

"Jonathan Kline?"

"Who's asking?" Marcus asked.

"Do you know Easton and Candace Reynolds?" The solider asked.

Marcus leaned back, trying to get a better look at the man. He stalled, trying to think of a reason the man would be asking about the teenagers.

"I saw their names in your file. I don't know how the Major knows about them. Or how he hasn't figured it out yet, but their names are there. Do you know them? Why is my wife's name not in the file?" The solider demanded.

"Callahan hasn't figured out what yet?" Marcus asked.

"I'm Liam Reynolds. I'm their father."

Marcus gasped and suddenly realized what he was looking at. An older version of Easton. He could see it clearly now. The hair that was turning gray had once been the brown of Easton's and his eyes were critical just like his son's.

"I can see it now. Easton looks like you," Marcus said.

"Where are my kids? Are they safe? What about my wife?" Liam demanded.

"The children are safe. I'm sorry, but your wife didn't make it," Marcus said quietly.

"Didn't make it? What do you mean?" Liam's face was lined with pain.

"I wasn't with them when it happened, I met them later. But your wife was bitten and she begged Alex Duncan to take them with her. She did and has been keeping them safe ever since. She protects them like her own," Marcus explained.

Liam stood up and paced the room for a moment. Marcus could see he was breathing deeply, trying to control his emotions. Though tears glistened in his eyes, he pushed them back and didn't allow them to touch his face. After a few more deep breaths he turned back to Marcus.

"Do you work for Callahan?" Marcus asked.

"I'm in the military. So, it's true that my kids are with those Duncan people?"

The way Liam said Duncan people told Marcus he had to be wary of what he said next.

"Do you believe in what Callahan has done?"

"The Major is doing what is needed to save the human race. The Duncans have the cure and are keeping it for those they want to have it. Have my children been given the cure?"

Marcus had to just stare at the man in disbelief. Callahan had really spun the lies to convince the military that the Duncans were the enemy. Marcus wondered if Liam would believe anything he said.

"I thought you were overseas. That's what the kids said," Marcus replied, changing the subject.

"I was. I was on the way home to surprise them, hero home-coming and all that. But when I landed on the East Coast, I was immediately brought here. The outbreak had just started and Callahan was centralizing forces to combat it."

"Didn't work out, did it," Marcus said.

"It spread faster than anyone could have predicted. The few bitten that were able to fly out and get on trains, spread it within twelve hours to all corners of the country. That was the last real communication we had. We're doing the best we can," Liam said.

"The self-appointed US Government should be able to do better," Marcus said, his speech slightly slurred around his swelling lips.

"Where are my children?" Liam demanded again.

"Safe," Marcus replied.

"So, you refuse to tell me? I could make your situation much worse," Liam said.

Marcus snorted. "Worse than this? I'm already on the chopping block, I'm sure. All I can do is keep my friends safe. And that includes East and Candace."

"They would be safer with me. I'm their father. I'm with the military," Liam said, his voice rising with each word. He grabbed

Marcus by his short hair, forcing his head back so he had to look him in the eyes.

"If you're with Callahan, you're a threat to them. You clearly don't have all the information the Major does, or you would know exactly where the kids were. And for some reason, you're afraid to tell him about your connection. I wonder why that is."

"I'm not afraid," Liam said.

"So, you told them you were coming in here to question me? You have told them that the kids are yours?" Marcus replied, challenging him. He realized his questions hit their mark as Liam's eyes lit up with anger.

"I need to get to them," Liam said.

"Look, man, I get it. You want to be with your kids. You want to protect them. But I'm telling you, what is happening outside of these walls is not safe. What Callahan is targeting the Duncans for is not true. I realize you aren't going to believe what I'm telling you. But I care about your kids. And I want them to be safe. Not locked up here. Or worse," Marcus said.

"What's not true?"

"There is no cure, Liam. Yes, the doctor that is familiar with the plague is there. But she can't cure it. She's been trying. Callahan doesn't want the cure. He wants to destroy the proof of how the plague started," Marcus explained.

"That's absurd," Liam replied, shoving Marcus back to the ground as he stood up again.

"Is it? How did the plague start?"

"Terrorist attack," Liam replied without hesitation.

"Wrong. It was a failed experiment ran and directed by members of the government. And instead of trying to prevent the plague, they allowed the outbreak with little concern for the health of the people working for them."

"That's crazy. Our own government wouldn't kill its people. With the way this is going, there won't be anyone left to govern."

"Easier to control a smaller population. But that part is all conjecture. We only know what we've put together from Max being tortured here and the doctor's research," Marcus said. He tried to turn to follow Liam's walking, but his body wouldn't allow much movement.

"So, you're saying the Duncans are innocent of what they are being accused of?" Liam asked.

"Yes. But you don't have to believe my words. Do you know what I'm doing here? Other than being tortured within moments of my death?"

"Being questioned about the cure, I assume," Liam replied.

"I'm bait. I'm only still alive because the Major knows the Duncans won't leave me behind. They are coming here to try to rescue me. Liam, watch what happens in the next day. If this is the US Government, there should be due process, legal processes, lawyers, my rights. None of that is happening and it's going to get worse," Marcus said.

He wasn't pleading for his life. He knew that was forfeit, unless the Duncans had something really crazy up their sleeves. But now all he could think of was Easton and Candace. They had allowed Alex to become an adoptive mother to them. They all loved each other the way a family should. Marcus had admired it since the moment Alex almost kicked Marcus to the curb when he made a stupid move that put Easton in danger, it was clear she took the protection of the children very seriously. When they had been separated and Alex had been forced to leave them, it had broken her in a way Marcus couldn't even think to help with. He could still hear her wailing cries from the bathroom as they drove away from the last place they'd seen the teens.

Alex had taught them well and they survived the world on their own for over a week. When they arrived at the compound, Alex had changed, she relaxed and was as close to happy as a person could be in the apocalypse. They were a family unit that looked out for each other and took the care of their home seriously. Looking at Liam, Marcus could understand why he wanted to get back to his kids. However, he couldn't imagine putting them all at risk if the soldier's loyalties were too strongly connected to the military.

"I don't have much time. I need to get my kids," Liam pleaded.

"I have less time than you. If you hear anything of what I'm saying, hear me on this. There is no cure. Callahan is lying. And your children are safe. If you are determined enough, you'll be able to find where they are. I can only hope that when you do that, you know how to keep them safe."

Liam seemed to realize he wasn't going to get anything else from Marcus. He looked down at him once more, before moving back to the door. He opened it very slowly and peeked through the crack before sticking his head out to check the surrounding hallway. Marcus assumed it was clear, because Liam disappeared a moment later, the door locking behind him. He wouldn't be back, and Marcus knew that in his mind. However, that knowledge didn't stop him from staring at the door, waiting to see it open again.

Time wasn't relevant to Marcus as he laid naked on the floor. The pain that crackled across his senses was fading as he tried to let himself go into a dark fog again. He had never contemplated suicide before, even with the world falling apart. But as he laid broken and disfigured on the ground, he thought the end would be better than what he was facing. Would the Duncans know he was dead? Would they stop their pursuit into the military zone Callahan controlled? Now that he knew that the Major was the backer of the Dead Brothel, Marcus wondered how far his control spread. Was there any place safe?

In his mind, Marcus didn't register when the door opened again. This time it opened with force, banging into a wall as soldiers filed in before Callahan. When he was lifted into a chair, he couldn't stop the keening wail that ripped from his lips. He couldn't keep his broken ankle from getting pressure and it burned with pain. One of his eyes was completely swollen shut now and his lips were unnaturally large. When he tried to lick across them, he could feel the multiple places where they had split and were scabbing over. He couldn't stop his body from slumping to one side. The feeling of broken ribs was a distant pain in the scheme of things.

Callahan sat across from him, stiff and straight in his uniform. He looked at Marcus with disregard, clearly not concerned with any of the injuries he was sporting.

"Are you awake, Mr. Kline?"

"Bright-eyed and bushy-tailed," Marcus slurred.

"Ah, I see your sarcasm is still intact. I am glad that my men didn't damage you too thoroughly," Callahan said. With that he nodded to his soldiers and they filed out of the room and shut the door. Marcus became more aware, realizing that Callahan was now alone with him.

"Do you think I'm ignorant, Mr. Kline?" Callahan asked.

"There's a lot to unpack with that question," Marcus replied.

"Do you believe that I'm not aware of how this plague started or what the situation is with the cure?"

"It seems your men have been told a number of stories. One being that the cure is in the hands of the Duncans," Marcus said.

"Mr. Kline, I have news for you. There is no cure. And I'm well aware of that," Callahan said coldly.

Marcus stared at the man with his one open eye. Marcus already knew the truth. He could put the pieces together and realize that Callahan knew the truth and was lying to get the troops to obey his orders. But to hear the man say it himself, that changed things greatly. Also, that meant Callahan didn't expect him to live to share what was said between the two of them. A rock formed in Marcus' stomach as he realized this was only confirmation that his days were numbered.

"Oh?" Marcus replied, as he had nothing else to add to the conversation. He was too lost in his own mortality.

"Yes, Mr. Kline. And honestly, I couldn't care less about a cure. Let this plague create havoc across the country. Once it's burned through the easy population, we will come back and save those that were able to survive."

"We?" Marcus asked.

"We don't have a name. I report to a man high in the government chain. Yet, our work has never been part of the government plans. We are what you would call, creative, with our solutions to the problems facing our people."

"So you are the people that had Charlie working on diseases. Those were to be weapons?" Marcus asked.

"Weapons or ways to prevent ourselves from being taken off guard. But most likely, if they had found this plague and were able to create a cure, it could have been one of the greatest weapons known to mankind," Callahan said. It was abundantly clear that the man was bragging about what he felt he had been a part of.

"So how is your piece of the government still around? Last I heard, most of the government is dead," Marcus said.

"That's true. Just one aid, that's all it took. In the beginning, no one knew what a bite meant. The aid was bitten at the airport and rushed to the hospital. When things broke down, the aid was on the shortlist of being in a bunker with some of the main heads of state, including the President. Last communication from that bunker was screaming and the video footage cutting out," Callahan explained.

"But that didn't include people from your faction?"

"It did. But most of us were in other safe places. We had our own outbreak protocol. We are more important than the President and the normal succession of power."

"At least you are honest with your ego," Marcus replied.

"I'm honest with the truth. This is the way things are. I realize you aren't capable of understanding the great lengths we have always gone to protect the US people. And we will continue to do so, once this threat can be contained."

"So, the reason you are after the Duncans, is only to silence them?" Marcus asked. The question had been burning in him since the moment Callahan started the share session. If he knew the truth, could he somehow get it back to Alex? Could they use the information to keep themselves safe?

"They are the only ones that know how this happened. When we come out of hiding and work on fixing the country, we can't have that information tipped to any opposition. Clearly, it could be a snag in our larger plan," Callahan said.

The Major sat looking at Marcus, with a smug look on his face. Marcus couldn't be sure if it was fury or blood, but he began to see red. The egotistical maniac saw no problem with wiping an entire family from the world just to hide the truth. All so his plans didn't go awry.

"Why tell me this?" Marcus asked.

"The Duncans are close now, Mr. Kline. There's a few ways this could go. But it's unlikely you will make it beyond tonight, I'm sorry to say," Callahan said as he folded his hands on his bent knee.

"So I won't be able to tell anyone what I know now," Marcus commented.

"That is the idea," Callahan agreed.

Silence fell between the two of them. Marcus searched his mind, trying to think of any way to get a message to the Duncans. They all knew they were facing a tyrant, but he wanted them to know how crazy the larger picture truly was. It was confirmation that 'The Suit' and Callahan were in together in this government faction. Despair for the Duncans entered his mind. He knew he was done for, but he wanted the family to survive.

A knock had Callahan standing and going to the door. He held a murmured conversation before turning back to Marcus.

"I'm sorry to see things go this way, Mr. Kline. You could have been a valuable addition to our outpost. We need to keep all the living we still have," Callahan said.

"If that was the case, killing the Duncans wouldn't be on your agenda."

"That is regrettable as well. They are strong. But, perhaps it's dangerous to be too strong. They could be the largest threat to the new government that exists currently," Callahan said.

With one last glance, Callahan walked out of the room. The door stood open for a moment before soldiers came in with items in their hands. Roughly they pulled what looked like nurses scrubs on Marcus, covering his exposed skin. They yanked him to his feet, but Marcus immediately collapsed with his broken ankle losing any mobility. The soldiers had an angry conversation between themselves, that Marcus had a hard time tracking. Before he knew what was happening, a wheelchair appeared at the door. He was then shoved into it and his wrists were zip-tied to the handles.

Once the soldiers were happy with their work, they waited by the door. Whatever signal they were waiting for must have come, because the next thing Marcus knew, he was rolling down a dark corridor. When the door at the end swung open, he was pushed out into the night. There were too many lights nearby to see the stars, but Marcus strained to look up. He wanted to remember what it looked like on the compound at night. The beauty of the black sky with the reminder that you were only a small speck in a much larger picture.

He then turned to focus on the direction the men were taking him. Marcus knew this was likely the dead man walking scene in his final moments. They pushed him toward the lights he could see behind another building. Once around the corner, he could see the spectacle. In the center of a large open area, a stage had been built. Floodlights glared, causing Marcus to squint his open eye. The brightness also lit up lines of soldiers standing at atten-tion. In the center of the stage was Callahan, waiting for Marcus.

CHAPTER TWENTY-FIVE

"They just don't seem worried about the infected," Rafe murmured. He looked through the viewfinder of his DSLR camera. After coming home from his time in the mountains, Rafe didn't leave the compound often without his camera. He was always trying to gather information on what was happening in the world. Now that they were outside of the Callahan compound, he snapped photos hoping to find a weakness in the layout.

"Fletcher clearly wasn't concerned either, watching us like he did. Maybe they have controls in place?" Alex replied. She held binoculars to her eyes studying the perimeter of the fencing.

The Duncan siblings, along with Griffin, Cliff, and Mateo crouched on the top of a three-floor apartment building. They were less than two hundred yards from the edge of the facility. Their recon hadn't garnered much hope, as they couldn't find an entrance on any side. The area where Max had escaped before had been fenced again, as well as adding barbed wire to the top and middle of the fence. Callahan hadn't wanted to take any risks after that mistake.

Suddenly, flood lights flared to life in the middle of the

outpost. The brightness caused Alex to look away for a moment, her adjusted night vision going slightly haywire. When she finally could look back she pressed the binoculars back to her eyes and she was shocked at what she was seeing.

"Is that really a stage?" Alex asked.

"Looks like it," Rafe replied.

"Let me see," Max demanded, grabbing the binoculars from Alex. After looking, she handed them to Griffin, before they came back to Alex.

"That definitely wasn't there a few months ago," Griffin said.

"So, Callahan needed a place to be put on his pedestal," Max replied.

"Something is going on," Rafe said.

Alex watched as numerous soldiers seemed to scurry around, completing tasks. She had to agree something was up, as it was the middle of the night. It seemed none of the inhabitants of the outpost were actually sleeping. Soldiers that weren't assigned to some sort of duty started to line up in precise lines, facing the stage.

"This doesn't look good," Alex said.

"We'll have to wait, we can't get in with everyone running around like that," Max said.

Alex knew she was right. However, deep down, she felt like this show had something to do with Marcus. And if she was right, this much attention wasn't good. Callahan was doing something he wanted an audience for. A loud squelch suddenly could be heard and Alex had to look around at her companions.

"Do they really have speakers?" She asked, incredulous.

"Like I said, he doesn't seem concerned with the dead," Rafe replied.

They all waited with bated breath, as the soldiers continued to file in. The quiet click of Rafe's camera was the only noise on the apartment roof. The flood lights gave him all the illumination he needed to capture images. He wanted to take as much information with them that he could. They would study the photos later, look for more weaknesses to handle Callahan. After they rescued Marcus, Alex had reminded them. Everyone agreed of course, but she knew they still had doubts that he was alive. Despite Fletcher telling them that he was alive, there was really no way of knowing what had happened to their friend behind the walls of the outpost.

"Who's that?" Rafe suddenly asked, pulling Alex's attention back to the stage.

"Must be Callahan. He looks exactly how Max described," Alex replied.

Without saying anything she held the binoculars toward Max, who slowly took them. She then shook her head and handed them to Griffin. He kissed her head before putting them to his own eyes. Even in the small illumination of the flood lights, Alex could see red rising on Griffin's neck. It was the only indication of his anger, as he handed the binoculars back over to Alex. He looked Alex in the eye and nodded curtly once. The man center stage was Callahan.

Alex watched as Callahan spoke to some of the soldiers still on the stage. Each of them nodded at their instructions and ran off to complete whatever task their leader had given them. And all of a sudden things seemed to still, as Callahan held up a hand to quiet the crowd. The hair on the back of Alex's neck stood up as she realized something big was about to happen.

Movement next to her, had Alex putting the binoculars down. Max moved and brought Alex's Winchester bolt-action rifle to the edge of the roof. She pushed it toward Alex, looking back toward the stage.

"He's right there, Alex. You could kill him right now," Max said quietly.

She wasn't wrong. Alex was the best shot out of the three of them. When it came to long-range shots, Alex was in the ninety percentile of accuracy. Her .308 slug would fly the distance without question. As she readied the weapon, she thought about the repercussions of killing Callahan while he was on stage in front of his soldiers.

"He'll be a martyr," Alex suddenly said.

"So?" Max asked.

"Even if we kill him now, Marcus would easily be dead shortly after. They will all know who did it. They will come down on us with a force we can't fight on our own," Alex said.

"Alex, that man is a monster. He needs to be dead. We can deal with whatever comes after," Max exclaimed, louder than she should have. Griffin's hand found hers in the darkness.

"Max, she's right. We need to time this right. You know I want him dead too. But he's center stage. Whatever he's told these men, will all be proven right by one bullet," Griffin said softly.

Alex could feel her sister deflate next to her, all of her pain and need for revenge collapsing in on her. Alex wanted to avenge her sister. There wasn't a question of that. The vengeance filled part of her wanted to do it close, by hand, where she could see Callahan's eyes as the life left them. She had no way of knowing if that chance would ever present itself. She could see where Max was coming from, this opportunity was one they wouldn't get again. However, she couldn't be sure the repercussions were something they would survive.

Even though she wasn't sure she would take the shot, Alex wrapped the rifle sling around her arm and settled into position to use her scope to watch the stage. She could clearly see Callahan in her range and she could feel her finger itch to pull the trigger. She placed it outside of the trigger guard, to prevent any accidental shots. Rafe continued to zoom in and take photos of Callahan and the surrounding men. His gasp had Alex adjusting her view, trying to see what he was seeing.

"Oh my god," Alex breathed.

Max now had the binoculars which she lifted now. They all easily found the figure strapped to the wheelchair being pushed up a ramp to the stage.

"If I didn't know they had him, I wouldn't even know that was Marcus," Max said. Alex could hear her swallow heavily.

"What have they done to him?" Alex said to no one in particular.

No one could really answer that. They could all see the injuries on their own view finders. Alex could barely make out the features of his face. It looked like he'd had gone twelve rounds in a boxing ring. One of his eyes was completely shut, bruising was blossoming all along his jaw and cheeks. His mouth looked strange and Alex imagined it was busted in a number of places.

"What is wrong with his foot?" Rafe asked from behind his camera.

Alex adjusted and tears sprang to her eyes. His foot was at an abnormal angle, his entire foot puffed up and swollen.

"I'm not sure Charlie could even fix that," Max whispered.

"Let's hope she can. We need to get him out of there," Alex said.

Suddenly Callahan's voice came across the speakers. His words were clear and understandable to the Duncans at their hiding place.

"Johnathan Marcus Kline, you have been found guilty of treason against the US Government. You have been found guilty of the murder of multiple US Government soldiers on sovereign ground. Do you have anything to say for yourself?"

Callahan held the microphone down to Marcus's face. Alex held her breath, praying that he was able to keep his sarcasm to a minimum.

"Uh, not guilty, your honor?" Marcus said.

"Ugh," Alex said out loud.

"He just can't be serious, can he?" Griffin said, his voice as exasperated as Alex felt.

"There is only one saving grace for you right now, Mr. Kline," Callahan said, moving on without acknowledging Marcus's comment.

"You are associated with the fugitives Alex, Rafe, and Max Duncan. If you can produce them and they give themselves over, you will be spared," Callahan finished.

"He has got to be kidding," Max said.

"Remember, he knows we're out here. Fletcher told him we were coming. This large spectacle is to get our attention," Alex said.

"We aren't going to surrender, are we?" Griffin asked.

"Of course not," Max replied without hesitation. She looked over toward Alex, when she didn't say anything.

"Alex, we are not all going to die to save one, right?" Max demanded.

"Right, of course, right," Alex finally replied. Max watched her, clearly not believing her sister's resolve.

Alex continued to keep her focus on Marcus. Callahan was motioning to some soldiers who came toward Marcus with knives. Her heart began to beat wildly until all the men did was cut the zip ties around Marcus's arms. He rubbed his wrists before he was yanked to his feet. He immediately held up the foot that was disfigured and his cry could be heard across the microphone. But Alex could see his face, see how he was trying to grit and hold the pain in.

"We will allow the criminal to stand to give us his answer. Remember, Mr. Kline, these could be your final words. Choose them wisely," Callahan said. He handed the microphone to a soldier that was holding Marcus up on his feet.

Marcus looked out over the soldiers that were standing in front of him. Alex wished she could call out to him, tell him they were there. They were going to rescue him. He didn't have to tell the maniac anything. But all of her thoughts were in her own mind and no matter how hard she tried to push them toward Marcus, she knew he couldn't hear her or feel her presence.

Finally, Marcus cleared his throat.

"In front of this large audience, I would like to say something," he said, before taking a deep breath. Then he began to shout into the microphone.

"Alex, do not come for me! Callahan will kill everyone! He knows there's no cure and no chance for a cure! He's trying to eliminate witnesses! He's trying to take over the country! RUN!"

Alex jerked back from the gun for a moment before pressing her eye back to the scope. Marcus tried to fight away from the soldiers holding him, but his foot was useless, and he was too weak. The soldiers kept him still and the yell from Callahan was all the warning they had before a gunshot sounded and Marcus's head jerked forward. Blood sprayed from the front as he went slack. The men holding him stepped back, dropping Marcus's limp form to the ground. Callahan stood with his handgun still in the same position it was when he shot Marcus in the back of the head.

Alex didn't know she was screaming. She could hear it, but had no idea it was coming from her own mouth. Callahan's head swung in their direction, his eyes searching the darkness. Max was yelling at her while Griffin was packing up their supplies and throwing on his bag. Rafe was trying to shake Alex, but all Alex saw was Callahan through a haze of tears. Her finger was on the trigger and she squeezed once. She felt the kick against her shoulder and saw Callahan's hand fly to his shoulder as he fell.

"Shit, Alex, we have to go!" Rafe yelled.

He grabbed the rifle from her hands, preventing her from shooting anyone else. Her throat was raw from screaming. Tears streamed down her face. She could hear Marcus's voice echoing in her ears. His last words. He knew he was going to die. He used his last words to tell them the truth and to warn them. In his last moments, Marcus proved that he belonged with the Duncans from the beginning. He died protecting those he loved. Alex could never have loved him in any way more than a friend, but his friendship had become so important to her over the months since they had met. She tried to cover her mouth, to stop the screaming, to prevent herself from hyperventilating, to stop the vomit.

"Alex, you have to get up. I'm sorry. I'm so sorry. But we have to run," Cliff's voice broke into Alex's haze. She tried to focus on his face, but she couldn't stop the burning tears. She put her hand out and Cliff grabbed it, pulling her off the ground.

The group ran down the stairs of the apartment building. Everything was a blurred nothingness to Alex, but Cliff held her hand and pulled her in the direction they needed to go. They ran all out until they reached the place they had left their vehicles. Charlie burst out of the van with a gun, but once she recognized them she ran to hug Rafe. He embraced her quickly before explaining that they needed to leave immediately. Charlie's face was full of questions, but no one had the words to explain what had happened yet.

In the truck, with Cliff behind the wheel, Alex cried as they sped away from Rapid City. They didn't want to go straight home, in case they were followed. However, getting away from the outpost was their number one goal. Rafe followed in his truck and Max drove the van that started the whole horrible nightmare for Alex. She would set that van on fire before it went anywhere near their home.

"Alex, it's going to be ok," Cliff tried to console her.

"Nothing is ever going to be ok," Alex said. Her voice was raw and full of pain. She couldn't get the image of Marcus's head jerking forward as the bullet passed through it. His body being dropped to the ground like trash.

"They won't bury him. They'll just throw him out," Alex cried.

"Well at least you got one for us," Cliff replied.

"No, I missed the kill shot," she said quietly. Alex replayed the shot in her mind. She knew exactly where it had hit him. And it wasn't going to be fatal.

"What?" Cliff asked. He was clearly shocked.

"Callahan will be back."

CHAPTER TWENTY-SIX

An hour later Rafe turned sharply off of the main highway, swinging the caravan into a rest stop area. The weeds and grass had grown out of hand for months and the rest stop was completely abandoned. When Rafe pulled into a spot, Cliff and Max followed suit. Alex could see Charlie in the front seat of their truck, her eyes rimmed red from crying. Alex had to look away, to keep her own sorrow from flooding back. She laid her head back against the seat and closed her eyes against the world. Maybe if she didn't see any of them, they wouldn't try to talk to her.

Cliff had clearly gotten her message, as he carefully exited the truck and closed the door quietly behind him. Though the windows were all up, Alex could still hear the conversation between Cliff and her siblings.

"What do you mean she missed?" Max asked.

"She did just see her friend killed, Max. Give her a break," Rafe replied.

"Which is why she should have made the shot," Max shot back.

"I think it doesn't matter at this point. She needs to be home. And we need to figure out what to do now," Cliff said.

"Home? Can we even go home?" Max asked.

Alex grimaced at the question. She knew her sister's concerns were valid. Callahan knew who shot him. His men would know. And now the major would have no trouble getting the soldiers to follow his orders. They would come for them. And the Duncan compound couldn't fight an army.

"We have to go back. We have to get the Vegas home. We need to get our kids," Rafe replied.

Everyone looked around the group, each looking for confirmation on what the plan was. The slam of the truck door announced Alex's arrival into the conversation.

"We go back to town. We deliver Albert, Mateo, and Sylvia to their home. We then go to the compound. Once home we start packing up for an extended trip away. The wound I gave Callahan will need some help, possibly surgery. That should give us a head start to decide where to go to hide until we can take them all down."

"Where did you hit him, Alex?" Max asked.

"Shoulder. Too far from the heart to kill him. It was my mistake. I allowed my emotions to cloud my vision," Alex explained.

Cliff's large hand settled on her shoulder, trying to comfort her, but Alex shrugged him off.

"Missing is on me. But it doesn't matter. Alive or dead, they would still be coming for us. We need to chop this off at the top. Thanks to Marcus, we now know this has nothing to do with the plague and all about covering their tracks. They will stop at nothing to kill us all," Alex said, her voice full of anger.

"Who's the top?" Rafe asked.

"Callahan is taking direction from someone. I would wager that our guesses around 'The Suit' are accurate. Callahan got his information from someone and 'The Suit' is the one that had it.

We go for him first. If Callahan dies along the way, all the better,"
Alex said.

Max whistled quietly at her sister's statement. Alex knew what
she was thinking. It wasn't like her to want vengeance or to disregard human life. Callahan had been on her list after what he had
done to Max. Now, Alex would make sure the man died. Painfully;
if she had any choice in the matter. It was more like Max to feel
the way Alex was. Yet, Alex had lost too much. She had met the
breaking point and she wasn't sure how to come back from it.

After some additional discussion around the best route back
to Kalispell, everyone began to check the vehicles that were abandoned in the rest stop. Alex and Max worked on siphoning gas
from those that still had it. They worked in silence, Alex having
nothing to say and Max without the words to reach her sister.
They were able to fill the two trucks, with the van left on a half a
tank. Alex stood back from the van and stared at it until Rafe
came to her.

"What do you want to do?" Rafe asked.

"Burn it."

"That would be a spotlight on us, Alex," Rafe replied.

Alex looked around, trying to think of another way to destroy
it. She walked away from her brother and went straight to the
edge of the rest stop. When she peered over the embankment,
she was pleased to see that the rest stop sat on the top of a crest,
a rocky cliff on the other side of the safety barrier. She went back
to Rafe and told him to get all the gas and supplies out of the van.
He didn't question her as he instructed Charlie to move Albert
into a truck and everyone worked together to strip the van of
everything useful.

Rafe tried in vain to convince Alex to not go forward with her
plan. But at the moment, all of her pain, anger, and retribution
was inside of that black van. All she could think of doing was
destroying the one thing she saw as the start of all the chaos
reining around her. She thought of Marcus's body, likely thrown

out beyond the fence for the dead or animals to feast on. Marcus deserved to be avenged. Until Alex could truly do it, destroying the symbol of her anger was the next best thing.

The van was an empty shell as they drove it up the embankment. Once the front of the van was angled on the top of the hill, Max jumped from the driver's seat. All it took was four adults to shove the front half of the van over the incline and gravity began to take over. The van plunged down the rocky hillside. Alex scrambled up the hill to watch the destruction. The van hit a tree and the back end began to spin to the left. Then the entire van flipped over a number of times before finally coming to rest against a large tree trunk near the bottom of the hill. Alex stood and stared at the wreckage and realized it was a perfect representation for what her heart looked like.

"Feel better?" Max asked as she joined Alex to look down at the vehicle.

"Not particularly," Alex replied.

"Sis, you of all people know what I've been through. At the hands of Callahan, obviously. You have been there for me. I just want you to know, I'm here for you too."

The heartfelt message made Alex turn to look at her sister. Max watched her with a careful look, waiting to see if she crumbled. But Alex wasn't going to fall apart. At least not in front of anyone.

"Thanks, Max. I'll let you know. I honestly don't know what I'm feeling right now. I feel sort of numb, ya know?" Alex replied.

"That'll pass. I remember that feeling. Then everything came flooding back at once and it was like I had just escaped all over again. Just remember when that happens, you aren't alone," Max said.

She then squeezed Alex's shoulder, before sliding down the embankment back to the trucks and the waiting group. Alex looked once more toward the van, before turning away from the black mass. She made her way back into the parking lot, stomping her feet to get the dirt off her boots. When she looked up, she found everyone looking at her. She knew they wanted her word on the next steps. She wanted to hide. She didn't want to be responsible. But then the dream of her father came back to her and she knew her purpose.

"We go home. Get the Vegas home. Get our friends and family packed up and leave the compound. For now. We can only hope that once we get are able to come back, there is a home to return to," Alex said.

No one spoke, just nodded before everyone loaded into their vehicles. The drive back to town was long and quiet. They stopped once the sun rose so they could eat breakfast. The entire time they continued to keep watch behind them. No vehicles ever showed on the horizon. But that didn't mean they weren't being followed. The threat was there, and they had to get out ahead of it.

They were pulling back into Kalispell by the next morning. They had stopped to sleep, allowing everyone the chance to recharge. Alex couldn't sleep, no matter what she tried. She was physically and mentally exhausted. But that didn't change the fact that when she closed her eyes all she saw was the blood spraying from Marcus's head. They took turns as lookouts, but Alex ended up take three shifts because she knew she wouldn't be able to rest.

Rafe lead the group as they made their way through residential streets to the Vega home. When they pulled up everything around the house was silent. Alex watched from the truck, feeling detached from the situation. Mateo jumped from Rafe's vehicle and Alex could tell he was worried that no one had come out when they pulled up. But when he got to the door, a woman Alex could only guess was Claudia was flying into his arms, hugging her son to her tightly. Alex could see tears on Claudia's face. Vera came running from the house and Alex guessed Mateo had told them that Sylvia was also in the truck.

Sylvia was just climbing from the vehicle when Vera stopped short of her.

The sisters looked at each other for a long moment. Then they both began to cry as they reached out to hug one another. Alex could imagine the feelings they were going through. She could logically figure they were feeling relief, with Vera's tinged with guilt. Alex could think of the emotions, but for some reason she couldn't feel any of them. She felt cold and far away. When Claudia looked up at Mateo in shock, Alex knew that was the moment he told her about Marcus. Next thing Alex knew, Claudia was coming toward her side of the truck Cliff drove. Alex gritted her teeth then rolled the window down.

"Hello, Alex. I'm Claudia, Sylvia's mother. I've heard a lot about you," the older woman said.

"I've heard a lot about you as well. Thank you for being kind to Marcus," Alex replied, her voice stiff and wooden.

"I'm so sorry. He was a good man. He cared about you and your group greatly. I could tell his emotions and feelings were true," Claudia said.

"Yes, we were family," Alex said, her voice hitched for a moment. Tears threatened behind her eyelids as she squeezed them shut. She wanted to shut out the sympathy, shut out the loss, shut out everything that was hurting her.

The door opening had her eyelids lifting. Claudia stepped into the opening and took Alex's hands in her own. She then looked over to where Vera and Sylvia were still embracing. The woman's eyes were soft and wet, watching her children back together in one piece.

"You've brought back a piece of my soul. Marcus made sure that happened. He promised that he wouldn't give up. And he didn't. He deserves your mourning. I know it hurts like a physical wound. But remembering him is the only way to honor him now," Claudia said.

The pain Alex felt was immeasurable. Though Marcus was just

a friend, his loss cut her heart into shreds. She knew her heart wasn't whole after losing Blake, the loss of Marcus only compounded the grief that she couldn't seem to manage. Now the dam was cracking, and she wasn't sure she could stop the flood once it came. She knew that this was the life of the apocalypse. They wouldn't all survive. Hope had made her vulnerable to the pain of losing someone close to her again. But the feeling of hope was the only thing that kept her moving from day to day.

Claudia seemed to read Alex's face as she went from shutdown, to panic, then unbearable grief. The woman had her arms around Alex before the first tears actually fell. As soon as the comfort was there, Alex couldn't stop the flood of pain that cascaded from her. Claudia rubbed her back, murmuring softly as she did so. Her voice was a quiet murmur as she spoke in Spanish to try to provide solace to Alex. Though Alex didn't understand any of the words, she could tell the emotion behind the meanings.

When the older woman pulled back, she placed her hands on Alex's wet cheeks. She looked into her eyes as she spoke.

"Don't fear the grief, Alex. It will eventually come on like an inevitable tide. Better that it's the evening tide and not a tsunami you never escape."

Alex nodded her head before Claudia stepped back out of the truck open doorway. Alex watched as the mother went to embrace her daughter. Sylvia buried her face in her mother's neck and her body shook with what Alex knew were sobs. The young woman had been through a lot at the brothel. Alex knew she was lucky compared to Sylvia, who was kept in one of the canvas rooms where the men could purchase time with her. Alex tried to believe that Sylvia would survive the emotional wounds she experienced while being held captive. She knew that the physical ones would heal eventually, leaving scars that she would grow used to.

They took the time they needed to say their goodbyes to the Vega family. Charlie set up Albert with a few additional pain killers she could spare. She instructed the family on how to change his dressing at least once every other day. She also promised to come back and check on him in a week or so, after she'd convinced Rafe that it was necessary. Claudia insisted on packing food for them all, despite the fact that they weren't far from home. Seeing what Claudia had cooked gave Alex ideas for future partnerships with the Vegas. However, that was something to think about later. Now all she could picture was her compound, her children, and how they needed to make plans.

The drive to the compound was without incident, which Alex was thankful for. She couldn't handle another run in with the infected or Callahan's men before she got home and felt safe for at least a day. When the gate came into view, Alex took a deep breath of relief. That feeling was quickly squashed by something stronger when she saw Billie and Henry walking over the crest of the hill blocking the house. Behind them was Easton with his sister Candace. When they saw Alex in the truck, they all broke into a run, meeting the truck before it could even park in the driveway.

Alex embraced the younger kids first, squeezing them each and kissing their heads. She then walked to Easton and Candace. She could clearly read concern on the teenage boy's face.

"I'm ok," she said just before Easton grabbed her in a bear hug.

"We already lost one mom," he said quietly.

"I know, shhhhh, I'm ok," Alex said, comforting him the way Claudia had just done for her.

Candace was next and she buried her face in Alex's neck and Alex just let her hold on as long as she needed to. Rafe had told Alex that the younger two hadn't known she was in trouble. But the teens had heard what was happening and clearly, they had been scared.

Behind them, Alex could hear the kids chatting with all the adults that were getting out of the trucks. Jack had joined them now and was being hugged by her parents. It was such a happy reunion for everyone. Even Rafe's dog, Storm, had bound toward the house, barking crazily. Alex was pretty sure it was part happiness and part angry dog for being left behind during some of their fights. Rafe crouched down and scratched the dog and talked to him like he was a child. Charlie had broken off from the group and had gone up the hill to meet Margaret who held Aiden. His little arms were out for Charlie before she got to the top. Alex felt tears sting her eyes as she thought about how the little boy had also lost his parents. But as Charlie swung him up and around, his giggle was high and happy. Alex knew he would someday need to know what had happened. But for now, he was safe and happy.

"Where's Marcus?" The question came from Billie and Alex tensed immediately. Candace still had her arm around Alex, and she could feel the change in her body.

"Oh no," Candace breathed quietly. And then her hand flew to her mouth and tears began to form in her eyes.

"What?" Easton asked.

"Mommy?" Billie asked, realizing something was very wrong.

Alex sat down in the grass and beckoned to Billie and Henry to join her. As Henry settled into Alex's lap, Billie sat across from her so she could see her mother. Max sat down as well, taking Billie's hand in her own and gave a comforting smile to Alex. She knew how hard this would be and she wanted to give Alex support as best as she could. Alex looked into the deep dark eyes of Henry as she took a deep breath.

"Marcus isn't coming back," Alex finally said. Henry's lip began to quiver, and Alex hugged him into her body, wishing she could just take all the pain.

"I'm sorry, baby," Alex said.

"What does that mean? He's not coming back? He left us?" Billie asked.

"No, Billie. He cared very much for you both. He wouldn't have left if he had a choice."

"He's dead," Billie said flatly.

"Did the sick people get him?" Henry asked, sniffing back the snot that threatened to flow down his face.

"No. Someone else did. Someone just as bad as the sick people," Alex said.

"Are you going to get the bad person, Mommy?" Billie asked.

Alex looked at her daughter. Her eyes were shining with tears that wanted to fall. Her knuckles were white where she squeezed her aunt's hand. Alex knew she was fighting to be tough and it broke Alex's heart. She wanted her daughter to be able to act her age. Instead, she was in the middle of the apocalypse where she could lose any of her loved ones at any time. Alex met her eyes and she knew the only answer she could give her kids was the truth.

"Yes. I'm going to get the bad man."

Later that night, after the younger children had been put to bed, the adults sat around the living room. Rafe fiddled with wires that lead to the TV from his computer. Finally, finding the right connection, a photo of the military outpost came to the large screen. The group wanted to discuss the location and what they had learned before any of it faded from memory. Alex had to admit out loud that she couldn't remember much, everything was hazy. Of course, everyone understood where she was coming from. Margaret laid a comforting hand on her shoulder from where she stood behind the couch.

"We're going to have to leave the compound," Alex finally said. The small talk hushed in the room.

"He knows who shot him. He'll send everything he has at us now. I did nothing but piss off a hornet's nest. All because I let my emotions control my trigger finger," Alex said.

"You did what any of us would have done," Max said.

"Griffin didn't when he knew what was happening to you," Alex said.

"Well, he left his mark," Max said. Alex knew she was thinking about how Griffin had beaten one of the soldiers before they had left. A solider that now stayed on their compound. Partially as a survivor, partially as a prisoner. Alex made notes about how they would have to take him with them when they left as well.

"I appreciate that. But I was reckless. I put us all at risk. I'm sorry. We will need to make plans," Alex said.

As Alex spoke, Candace suddenly jumped from her place on the couch. She went closer to the TV and stared. Easton watched for a moment, trying to figure out what she was looking at.

"Wait, go back a few photos," Easton said, as he stood and joined Candace in the middle of the room.

"Oh my god," Candace said quietly.

"It can't be," Easton said.

"What? It's can't be what?" Alex said. Concerned for her adopted children, she stood and went to them. She looked at Candace's face, but it was sheet white. Easton was more emotional, his face beet red, as if he was angry.

"Ok you two, explain. What is going on?" Alex demanded.

Candace lifted one finger and stepped closer to the TV. She pointed to a man standing on the stage in the military outpost. The photo was taken prior to Marcus being brought out. Rafe had zoomed in close to the man, apparently trying to identify what they were doing on the stage. Alex could make out sandy brown hair and a grim looking face. But when she stared, something was familiar about the man. She couldn't make out his name, but she felt like she had seen him before.

"It's our Dad," Easton said.

Alex suddenly realized why the man looked familiar. He was an older version of Easton, confirming that there was no question about who the man was. Their father was on the stage where Marcus was killed.

CHAPTER TWENTY-SEVEN

Alex poured over the photos from the execution. She could track, who she knew now was Liam Reynolds, from the crowd to the stage. He then stood on the stage as Marcus was brought out. Alex tried to discover from the photos of what part Liam played in the death of Marcus. But when the gun came out of Callahan's holster, Liam looked shocked and when Marcus' body was on the ground, Alex tried to guess he looked sick. They didn't have photos after that, as that was about the time Alex had shot Callahan.

She pushed away the computer and lifted the glass of tequila to her lips. She was not typically an alcohol sipper, but the tequila was the good stuff according to Margaret. So she sipped it and let it burn down to her stomach. She looked up as the chair across from her scraped across the floor. Easton flopped down and his eyebrows rose when he saw she was drinking.

"It's been a long few days," Alex said in her defense.

"I know. I'm sorry," Easton said.

"You have absolutely nothing to be sorry for. You know that, right? Nothing that happened is your fault."

"My dad...he just stood there," Easton said quietly, his words strained.

His shoulder seemed to fold in on him as sadness and anger weighed him down. Alex couldn't handle the boy beating himself up. She moved to the chair next to him and took his hand in both of hers.

"Look at me, East," Alex said. It took a moment, but he finally met her gaze.

"Whatever is happening with your father, whatever he's done, whoever's side he is on, none of that matters. You are my boy. Your mother gave the responsibility of the safety of you and your sister to me. She wanted me to take you and care for you as I do my own. And I do. You understand? Nothing changes."

"Candace is wondering if we should go find him."

"If that's what you want, I will help you do it. Safely. But I have to tell you, if he's with Callahan, he must know you are here," Alex said softly.

"That's what I told Candy. He had to know we were here. They've sent men to kill us. And his children are here," Easton replied. His anger was rising again.

"Maybe he didn't know you were here then. Maybe he wasn't informed of Callahan's plans. He's your father. And whatever you want to do, I will support," Alex said. She squeezed Easton's hand again before sitting back.

"He's been in the military since just after I was born. He's career. He's been gone more than he's been present in my life. He's never been home for one of Candace's birthdays. But he wasn't a bad father. And he always made sure Mom had everything she needed to take care of us. When he was home, he was loving and funny. I can't imagine he would just go along with Callahan and his crazy plans," Easton said.

"Ok. I think it's best we try to make contact with him. I'm not sure how to do it yet, but we'll figure something out. I can't let you feel torn like this," Alex said with a small smile.

"Because you really are like a mom to us," Easton replied with his own smile.

"I'm not trying to replace your family, I never wanted that. But you do grow on a person," Alex replied, bumping her shoulder into Easton's.

"I guess you do too," Easton laughed.

"If it helps to settle your mind, I've been reviewing the photos. From what I could see your father and his facial expressions, I don't think he knew Callahan was going to kill Marcus."

"That does help, some. You know Marcus wasn't always my favorite person. But I never would have wanted to see him dead. I'm so sorry Alex," Easton said.

"Thank you. And I know, you would never hurt anyone just because you didn't like them. Try to get some sleep, East. Tomorrow we plan for leaving. It's going to be rough until we know we can come back," Alex said.

"Goodnight, Alex."

"Night, Easton."

When she was alone again, Alex unfolded a map across the kitchen table. She studied all the ways she could trace from Kalispell to Callahan's outpost. There were only a few direct routes and some that went many miles out of the way before cutting back to Rapid City. Max and Rafe found their way into the kitchen and they settled in with Alex.

"What are you thinking?" Rafe asked.

"The kids want to contact their father," Alex replied.

"How is that going to work, Alex? 'Hey, Callahan, can we call a timeout while we talk with one of your soldiers? Give us a fifteen minute head start then we're back to trying to kill each other'," Max said.

"I'm still trying to work that out, Max. He's their dad. I can't just send the kids into the outpost on their own. If Callahan knows they are here, he could execute them just like Marcus. If their father is really a Callahan lacky, who knows what he would make them do?"

"Why do they even want to go? Couldn't they just let it go?" Max asked.

"Would you? If it was Dad?" Alex said.

Max didn't respond, because they already knew the answer to that question. The siblings all studied the map for a while longer. They agreed to use the soldier they had for information. Former Private Smith slept in a military vehicle, locked in for the night because no one trusted him. He knew nothing of what had happened to Marcus or Alex. But they would bring him up to speed so they could formulate a plan. Alex thought maybe they could use radios. If they could figure out what channel the soldiers were on, maybe they could trick someone to putting Liam on the radio. Once he was on the radio, they could give him limited information about where to meet the kids.

"That's the best I have right now," Alex said.

"We also need to talk about where we're all going to go," Rafe said.

"Agreed. We can't stay here, for a while at least. If we can convince Callahan we're gone, he might stop checking here. Then we could come home. Or we kill him and 'The Suit' and finally get on with surviving," Alex said.

"I like the killing idea," Max said.

"I do too," Alex agreed.

"I think it depends on what opportunity presents itself. It might not be easy to get near him. We need to think survival and keeping our family safe. Callahan and 'The Suit' are secondary," Rafe said.

"It's not a secondary concern if they keep trying to kill us and our families," Alex replied.

"We take all the vehicles. In the end, if we have to, we can sleep in them," Max said, changing the subject.

"We'll need them all, if only to pack all the supplies we should take. I still have some of the pig left that we last butchered. We have the meat salted so it will be able to transport much better. I also want to take all the produce in the root cellar. It won't stay good forever, but we could eat as much of it as we could until it spoils," Rafe said, throwing ideas out there.

"Those are good ideas. We can get to work on packing the RV with food that can fit in the fridge and freezer in there. They run on a generator and battery, so we just need to make sure we keep the RV full of fuel. I want to make sure everyone packs as much of their clothing as they can as well. We won't be doing laundry out there," Alex added.

"We have those boxes of MREs too. Those will come in handy," Max suggested.

For the next few hours the siblings made lists and added to them until they had a final decision of what they thought was a good set of supplies needed since they were feeling forced to leave the compound for a long period of time. Each of them had specific duties to start the next day, as well as who to enlist into additional tasks. Though they had no specific shelter planned, they knew they could travel and work with what they found. They were resourceful and could fortify whatever they found along the way.

"The only end to this is Callahan dying," Alex said. They were getting ready to head their separate ways to bed when she spoke.

"I'm not sure that's the end. 'The Suit' is still out there," Rafe replied.

"So they both have to die," Max said, shrugging her shoulders as if it was easy as that.

Alex didn't feel as sure. It wasn't that she wasn't prepared to pull the trigger again, she would do that in a heartbeat. She just didn't know how they would accomplish getting close enough to the Major to make sure they succeeded. They would have to lure him out of his safe military outpost. Alex tried different scenarios in her mind, trying to figure out how they could anger Callahan enough, that he came after them himself.

When she entered her room, she found Billie and Henry sleeping in her bed. She changed clothes and squeezed between her children. She tried to force her body to relax. Her leg still hurt, though Charlie had cleaned it and put fresh bandages on. The doctor was happy with the progress the wound had made and that she had luckily not ended up with an infection. The rest of her body was covered in angry black and purple bruises. Every way she tried to lay in bed, she ended up on one of the injuries. She finally decided to lay on her back, with her arms curled around the kids. She tried to clear her mind, but instead tears leaked from her eyes, sliding down her temples and into her hair.

Alex laid there thinking about Marcus and his last words. He confirmed what they were all pretty sure of. Callahan knew there was no cure. He knew it wasn't possible. And even knowing that, they still came after the Duncans. To silence them. To kill the truth about how the apocalypse started. Alex couldn't allow that to happen. They had to spread the word to those that were still alive. She wondered if there were even enough people still alive to fight the corrupt rule of this government faction. Hope bloomed in the darkness of her chest and though she wanted to fight it back, she knew it wasn't in her nature to not try. As she fell asleep, Alex was imagining posters papering the walls of every town they came to.

Her next thought was of pain as an elbow jammed into already bruised ribs. She woke with a start and felt bad when Billie sat up in bed with panic in her eyes. The room was mostly still dark, the sun barely coming to kiss the edge of the mountains. Alex shushed Billie, insisting she sleep more while the sun was still down. Once she was sure her daughter would stay in bed, Alex carefully shimmied down to the foot of the bed to get up. She was tying up her boots when the door cracked open and Max stuck her head in. She nodded to Alex and left again to wait in the hallway.

Max hated mornings, but with as much work as they had, early rising was their only option. When they came downstairs, they could already smell coffee and the sisters knew they were beat to the punch by Rafe. Both Rafe and Charlie were standing in the kitchen. They talked softly and turned when Alex and Max entered. Charlie let the wisp of a smile come across her face when she turned to pour them coffee. None of them spoke as they stood around the kitchen, drinking the dark gold. Alex had to wonder when and how they would have hot coffee like this on the road. Instant mix only went so far for so long.

"We ready for this?" Alex finally asked, breaking the tense silence.

"Are you sure we have to leave?" Charlie asked.

She stood with Storm at her leg, her hand buried in his thick fur. Alex guessed it was for her own comfort more than anything. The dog looked up to them as if he understood every word the humans were saying.

"Pretty sure. Callahan must be furious that we injured him. He'll be out for revenge, even if it makes no sense," Alex replied.

"He's calculated. But I think the only thing that could break the facade is his own mortality," Max said.

Slowly the rest of the adults began to filter into the kitchen. Whether it was the rising sun or the knowledge that big things were coming, everyone woke up without prompting. Everyone had their fill of caffeine and Margaret set to making breakfast for the household. Candace came in shortly after, not a hair out of place for just waking up, to assist in the cooking. Alex kissed her on the forehead when the girl came in for a hug. Easton followed, though he didn't look as put together as his sister. He held his hand out for a mug and Candace put his coffee, very light with lots of sugar, in his grip.

Alex looked around and decided while the young children still slept, it was the best time for a pep talk. She cleared her throat.

"I know today is difficult for us all to fathom. We came here, some of you because you just trusted us to bring you somewhere safe. We thought this would be our salvation through this sickness. Instead, we have to run again, out into the world that feels so unsafe. And I'm sorry for that. But I promise, whether we come back here, or we make a new home, we will stay together. We do everything we can to be safe."

The room was silent, every eye on her. Margaret looked into Alex's face and smiled, encouraging her. She nodded, letting Alex know she was with her. That vote of confidence helped.

"Last night, something else occurred to me. In Marcus' final moments, it was important to him to let us know what was happening in Callahan's mind. We can't allow the truth to die with Marcus, or with any of us. I intend to do whatever I can to spread the truth. I think before we leave, before we have no power or printing capabilities, we should make up flyers. Maybe some sort of booklet too. Something we can give survivors as we see them. Or even posters we could nail up so anyone who passes sees them. Charlie, I was thinking since you have so much information, maybe you could work on that today?"

Charlie nodded enthusiastically.

"I have just the thing in mind. That's a great idea, Alex," Charlie replied.

"Do you think people will believe us?" Max asked.

"I don't know. But at least the truth will be out there. It will be out of our heads and in the hands of others. If we were to fall to Callahan, we know it won't be in vain," Alex replied.

The room went silent again, a somberness falling on them all. Alex hated to bring the real threat to them. But they were a team. She couldn't hide what was really happening from them.

"We have a list of tasks to complete today. We're thinking it will be best to leave in the cover of night tonight. In the chance the compound is being watched, we want to make it as hard as possible to follow us," Rafe said. It was just like him to bring things back around to the necessities.

"Tonight? That's so fast," Candace said from her position at the stove.

"We have to assume they won't delay on striking back. Our first stop will be the Vegas' home in town. Charlie wants to check on Albert and make sure they have everything they need before we leave," Rafe said.

"Where are we going?" Easton asked. Alex knew his question was loaded. He was thinking of his dad and he was asking Alex of how they were going to find him.

"We will be heading toward Rapid City," Alex said.

"Wait, what? Why would we go right into the lion's den?" Cliff asked.

"We need to give Easton and Candace the chance to contact their father. It's possible he could help us. And it's possible he has no idea that Callahan is lying," Alex explained.

"Alex..." Cliff trailed off.

"I know, Cliff. It's going to be dangerous. We're going to use a roundabout route, hoping to keep us from accidentally running into troops. Once we make it, that's when we figure out how to contact Liam Reynolds," Alex explained.

The mudroom door opened and in walked Issac and former Private Smith. All eyes turned to Smith and he halted quickly in the entrance to the kitchen. He looked to Alex, completely ignorant to why everyone was staring at him.

"And in walks our perfect weapon," Max said quietly.

"Weapon?" Smith echoes.

"We'll see if Smith can make himself useful once we get to Rapid City," Alex agreed.

"Rapid City? Why are we going there? Callahan will kill me!" Smith cried.

"Shut it, Smith," Rafe shot back.

And to his credit, Smith knew when it was smart to keep his mouth closed. He immediately stopped his protest and walked into the kitchen to accept the coffee Issac handed him.

Small discussions continued, but once Rafe handed out the morning chores to everyone, the group disbanded. Alex was left in the kitchen with Smith standing across from her. Rafe and Max had decided she would be the best to question him about Liam Reynolds. Max scared Smith and Rafe was afraid he'd strangle the man after he helped take him hostage. Alex was the last one left with a cool head, though that cool head was slowly becoming more of a liability she feared.

"Walk with me, Smith," Alex suggested.

He fell in step behind her, without question. Alex lead the way out to the barn. She picked up two large baskets and handed one to Smith. They made their way to the back of the compound where the fruit trees were planted in a few small lines. Alex was happy to see pears still on the branches and some apples. She pulled an apple down and took a bite. It was cool and sweet, perfect to pack away in the RV for snacks as they drove. She tossed the bitten apple to Smith for him to try and he did. He moaned quietly at the taste of fresh fruit before holding out the apple to her.

"Keep it," Alex said.

"Thanks," Smith replied.

"You've never tried to escape, Smith. Even though we keep you locked up and under constant supervision. You've never tried to escape. You've never tried to turn on us. Why is that?" Alex asked.

"Uh, well, if I'm not here, I'm back with the Major. And he's volatile. After going missing like I did, he would kill me no matter my explanation. Especially because Rafe escaped when I was still alive. It would be blamed on me," Smith explained.

"So, you're afraid of Callahan?" Alex asked.

"Everyone is. You should be too," Smith replied.

"I'm not sure fear is what I feel."

"Well, excuse me for saying this, but you're stupid," Smith said.

Alex looked at him over her shoulder as she pulled another apple to drop in her basket. Smith worked on the tree next to hers and had stopped to look at her as he made the comment. She turned to him.

"I'm anything but stupid. I just know Callahan doesn't have as much power as he thinks," Alex said.

"Power or not, he's ruthless. And will level this place if you stay," Smith replied.

"Which is why we're leaving."

"But, going to Rapid City? That's the worst direction to go. Let's go west. Oregon or Washington. Lots of water. Lots of land to grow things," Smith said.

"There are things we need to handle before we can stop looking over our shoulders," Alex explained.

"I'm not sure that's a good enough reason."

"Do you know Liam Reynolds?" Alex asked.

Smith frowned at her sudden change of subject. He turned to pull another apple from his tree as he thought.

"Should I?" He finally asked.

"He's a soldier in Rapid City. We need to reach him. Do you know him?" Alex asked.

"Maybe. I didn't know everyone's names, but faces I'm better with."

"I thought that might be the case," Alex said.

Reaching into her pocket, she pulled out a photo that Easton had given her. It was worn at the edges and Liam looked a few years younger than he did now. But his face was the same as the photos Rafe took just hours before they arrived home. Smith looked at the photo of the happy family smiling into the camera. Easton and Candace were little kids sitting in their parents' laps.

Easton kept the photo on him at all times, his way of remembering his mother.

"I know him. He's not a normal grunt, like most of the people Callahan has. So many of us were straight from boot camp when the Major recruited us. This man is higher up, I think he's a First Lieutenant. He wasn't in the Major's inner circle. I think people with rank scare Callahan. He's afraid they will challenge his leadership," Smith said.

"Is he a good man? Would he turn us in, if we tried to reach out?"

"There's no way for me to know that. Those are his kids, wouldn't he want to protect them?"

"I would hope so. But if he believes we are the enemy, he might turn us in to Callahan with a deal to spare his children," Alex said. She had put a lot of thought into the what ifs of the situation.

"That's one option I guess," Smith said absently.

They picked fruit in silence for the remaining time. Alex went through each tree, making sure they had all the ripe fruit in their baskets. Margaret had been busy canning a lot of the food from the trees and garden. But having fresh fruit and vegetables would help them manage the initial hunger during travel. Alex wanted to be sure they prevented malnutrition. Powdered and dried foods would only fill so many vitamin needs. Alex added to her mental list to add the multivitamins they had as well.

Using a wheelbarrow, Alex and Smith carted the fruit toward the RV, where they would store a large portion of the food during their travels. When they passed the bunkhouse, Alex noticed a shovel and a pile of dirt. She stopped for a moment, looking at the spot. It felt familiar to her, but she didn't remember it being there before she was taken to the brothel. She tried to wrack her mind until Smith interrupted her.

"What is it?" He asked.

"That hole? Where did it come from?" Alex asked.

"When you were gone, Rafe gave Easton the job of digging a hole that would eventually be an outhouse," Smith explained.

For a moment Alex felt lightheaded and confused. When it came to her, she covered her mouth and almost cried out. She knew how she recognized the hole. Pictures of her near death experience flooded into her consciousness. Alex fell to her knees, trying to catch her breath.

"Oh, crap. Alex? What's wrong?" Smith asked, crouching down next to her.

Alex wasn't listening to him or registering his voice. She could see her father, hear his words in her ears. She had stood in the field with him, watching as Easton dug the hole, the children were running and playing. All while she was close to dying on the floor of the Noble Lord's bedroom. There was no way of her knowing that Rafe had instructed Easton to dig. She didn't know they were putting an outhouse there. The digging hadn't started until she was gone. So then how had she seen it?

With questions buzzing around her mind like angry bees, she forced herself to stand up. She shook her head at Smith when he asked if she needed help. Instead she pulled herself up tall and felt calm fall around her. Her dream hadn't been a dream. If she knew about the hole, then she knew talking to her father must have been real. His words and his plans for her, were all real. At that moment she finally found herself believing she could be the leader that Mitch Duncan had worked so hard to train. Alex would survive. She would protect her family. And she would end the threat that loomed over their heads.

CHAPTER TWENTY-EIGHT

Liam Reynolds wasn't sure anyone would notice he added his own name to the rotation of scouts. Normally he wouldn't be allowed to leave his post of housing management. The post was typically slow and quiet. He didn't think he would be missed for at least a few days. By then he'd be far enough away that they wouldn't be able to stop him.

He packed a light bag, nothing anyone would notice. He made sure to pack an extra pair of clothes, water filtration tablets, a few MRE meals and a map. He had the documents he had stolen about the Duncans packed at the very bottom of the bag. He didn't need anyone seeing them if they searched his bag. When he checked out the Hummer, the sergeant in charge of the vehicle pool checked his records and easily handed Liam the keys.

Liam had never been as nervous as he was when he pulled through the exit gate. He checked the rearview mirror every few minutes, expecting to find someone chasing after him. He was as close to positive as he could get that no one had put connected the kids to him. Their last name wasn't very original. And Liam knew Callahan didn't know the names of all the men under his leadership. There were a few hundred soldiers on the base in

Rapid City. He knew they had just over 200 hundred civilians as well that he was responsible for setting up with housing. Callahan never cared about learning their names.

For the few months since the apocalypse had started, Liam had followed directions without question. He hadn't wondered why they were shipping the children that came into the outpost to California. He believed Callahan when he said it was for their safety. And Liam had stood the same group, with the same speech. It was for their safety. We had to ensure the survival of the human race. The only way to do that was to keep the children safe. The promise of safety was what convinced most parents to let their children go.

Now Liam had to think of his children. His babies, who weren't babies anymore. He wondered again if what Marcus had said was true. Were his children safe with the Duncans? Did his beautiful wife fall to the plague and give the care of their children to strangers? And the most burning question to him, were the Duncans really the enemy? No cure. No cure possible. Those words played over and over in Liam's head. He had held onto the hope that Callahan spouted to the outpost. He didn't understand the lie. If there was no cure, shouldn't they be working together to eradicate the plague and all the infected?

Liam thought of the chaos that had followed the shooting of Callahan. The Major had been rushed to surgery under the best doctors they still had. The word had quickly spread that the shot was not fatal and the Major would recover. Liam had been in shock from the murder of Marcus that he hadn't been able to react when Callahan fell on the stage. He knew that plans were being made to retaliate. That knowledge was what pushed him to leave and go after his children now. He couldn't have them in the middle of a war that didn't concern them.

He led the Hummer down the freeway, avoiding crashes as necessary. After about an hour of driving, he pulled off into a small truck stop. He surveyed the area before turning off the engine and pulling his bag to the front seat. Unfolding the map he had found he used the information he had stolen from the Duncan file to give himself a general direction. He traced the numerous routes he guessed he could take. The most direct route would be the quickest of course. But he was worried about running into other soldiers there. He took some time and finally decided on a route that would take him on a lot of smaller highways. He knew the soldiers determined to make the Duncans pay wouldn't go that way.

He packed up his items again and then decided to check the gas station for any supplies. Taking so little on the road made him nervous. Since the infection started, he had never gone without a meal. He knew some basic survival skills. And one he knew that was most important was to scavenge as often as possible. He checked his weapon and quietly exited the truck.

He kept his head on a swivel as he approached the building. At the broken door, he banged on the metal and waited as the echo died down. Nothing came from the shadows. He didn't smell the unmistakable dead smell. Entering the truck stop store, his feet crunched on broken glass. The store had been ransacked, not surprising Liam. He went down the aisles and filled a bag with the individual items he could find.

On his way out of the store, he stopped short in front of the cash register. There was a turntable of post cards. He thought again of Easton and Candace. Grabbing a few cards with different pictures, he ran back to his vehicle. He thought of their tradition of him sending post cards from wherever he was at. He could only hope they forgave him for not being there for them.

CHAPTER TWENTY-NINE

The RV was decided to be the last in the convoy. It was the tallest vehicle and it would block the view of the others. Alex waited behind the wheel as everyone loaded their last-minute items and found their seats in their assigned cars. Bille, Henry, Candace and Easton were with Alex in the RV. Margaret and Issac drove her Bronco. Cliff had Smith as his co-pilot in one pickup. Rafe, Charlie, Aiden and Storm were in Rafe's truck. Griffin was behind the wheel of the military truck they had stolen, along with Max and Jack. Though Jack begged to be in the RV with the kids, Griffin was having a hard time letting his daughter far from him when they were out of the walls of the compound.

Rafe was the last to get into his truck, as he locked the house, let the cows and pigs out into the pasture and cursed at the rooster he still wanted to kill. Alex watched him stand for a long moment, watching the animals. She knew he was connected to them and she felt bad for him having to leave the home he had worked hard to maintain. Unlike Alex and Max, Rafe had never left Montana. When their father died, he was in the perfect position to take over the care of the compound. They all just knew it had to be done. Alex was thankful for the time Rafe had spent keeping the home in working order.

The safety they all felt behind the walls of the compound was bleeding away as they all prepared to drive away. The interior of the RV was jammed with boxes of foods. All the canning Margaret had worked on, the MRE boxes, the fresh fruits and vegetables. The fridge was all full of what meat, milk and eggs they could hold, though it wasn't much. Alex knew the fresh foods would make the first days easier for the group. But before long they would need to start scavenging and always making sure they had what they needed. The Bronco was full of blankets, sleeping bags, pillows, tents, tarps and tools. Each pickup had a tarp tied down over full beds of supplies they would need to be on the road.

Charlie had gone into town to check on Albert Vega before they loaded up to leave. She had been happy to report that his wound was healing well and they were prepared to take care of him after Charlie was no longer close. Claudia sent an ice chest full of tamales, cooked rice, beans, sodas and candies. Charlie relayed the message that Claudia had been cooking for an entire day to make sure she had something to send with them on their trip. Albert also sent the message that the Duncans had somewhere to hide, should they ever come back to Montana.

Alex was thankful to have made allies in a world that had fallen apart. Though their own group had grown some, Alex realized the world felt very lonely without neighbors and friends outside their own walls. The world had gone so quiet, that Alex found herself wishing for the noise of traffic just once more. She knew she was the only Duncan sibling that felt that way. Both Rafe and Max were happy without society around to interfere with their lives.

Rafe was finally settled in the truck at the lead of their little caravan. The CB Radio sitting on her dash came alive with Rafe's voice.

"Radio check," he said.

Everyone took their turn and answered back. Easton answered for the RV. While Charlie was checking up on Albert the day before, Rafe was scavenging all the military and FEMA vehicles for CB radios to install so they could stay in constant contact. Between Rafe, Issac and Cliff they were able to figure it how to install the radios in each truck and the RV. Alex felt better being able to communicate as they drove and should they get separated somehow, they could reach out if close enough.

The giggle of Henry reached up to the front of the RV and Alex looked over her shoulder. She was happy her son was laughing at his cartoon playing on the small RV tv. She knew losing Marcus was really weighing down on the kids. But they were resilient and would keep surviving as they had been. It was no life for a child, but with no better options, what the Duncans could provide was the best they were going to get. Alex and Easton's eye met as they both turned to look back at the road.

"I can't believe this is really happening. We worked so hard to get here," Easton said.

"I know. But as long as we're together, we can do this," Alex said.

"You're always so sure everything will be ok."

Alex thought about her inner turmoil and doubt she had been experiencing. Hope was something hard won for her. Often she wanted to give up, no longer fight, accept things for the way they were. But when she thought about her kids, all four of them, she couldn't bring herself to fall apart. It was her they looked to for strength and guidance. If she wasn't strong, she wasn't the example they needed. Her hope was really placed in them, even though they weren't aware. Hopes of them learning everything she knew so they could survive once she was long gone. Hopes that they bonded and took care of one another, like Alex, Max and Rafe. Hopes that they found happiness even though the world was falling to the infected.

"I have to be sure. Because I have you, Candace, Billie and Henry. I will never believe that there's not a way to survive so you all have a life to live," Alex finally replied.

"That was deep, Alex," Easton grumbled in his teenage way.

"Sometimes parents have emotions, East," Alex replied, laughing.

Rafe's truck began to drive through the open gate. After he was through the gate shut. The plan was he and Charlie would check the area to ensure there were no infected or soldiers waiting for them to come out of the compound. When the gate opened again, the rest of the convoy would know it was safe to leave. A gunshot sounded and Alex tensed. She leaned forward in her seat, as if that would help her see her brother and what was happening. A few more gunshots echoed into the compound.

"Those are 9mm shots," Alex mumbled.

"So Rafe's gun?" Easton asked.

"Most likely."

Alex was only talking to ease the tension in her stomach. It was the first time she had hoped for the infected. She didn't want to find out there were soldiers in wait for them outside the walls. It was long moments later when the gate opened again. Rafe had backed his truck almost to the fence. The CB radio crackled with his voice.

"Just infected. Not many. We handled it. It's clear. Over," he said.

"You and Charlie ok? Over," Alex replied.

"All intact, no issues. Over," Rafe said.

"Let's get this show on the road, over," Max chimed in.

The vehicles all slowly made their way through the gate and onto the well worn dirt road beyond. The trees stood tall on either side, shadows dancing under the moonlight. The warmth from the day had warmed the RV and Alex figured they would need the AC on at some point. Candace opened some of the windows just a crack to let the cool air blow through. The forest was quiet now that Rafe had cleared it of the infected.

The RV was the last to pull through the open gate. Once they were clear, Easton hit the button for the gate and Alex watched it close in the side mirror. When it stopped, she didn't drive away immediately. She stared at the gate, remembering how relieved she had felt when she finally arrived there a few months ago. She thought about how her heart had nearly stopped when Easton and Candace had made it and were on the other side of the gate. The image of a broken Max coming through and then finding Rafe and bringing him home. That was all through the gate her father built years before.

"Alex?" Easton said.

Her eyes left the mirror and looked at the boy in her co-pilot seat. His eyes were full of question, his eyebrows raised up. She nodded to him and swallowed hard to keep any tears from threatening. She put the RV into drive and guided the large beast down the dirt road.

Glancing back to the gate once more, as it began to disappear around a corner, Alex made a promise in her heart. Someday, they would come home.

ACKNOWLEDGMENTS

Thank you so much for joining the continuation of the Sundown Series! I hope you enjoyed this look back into Alex's side of the the Apocalypse and how the Duncans never leave a loved one behind. To keep up with more of their stories, be sure to follow along on my website courtneykonstantin.com. I also post updates on my Facebook page at https://www.facebook.com/AuthorCKonstantin.

As always my brainstorming bestie was by my side during the writing of TORMENT. Thank you for reading every message I sent, no matter how long and all over the board it may have been. You always know when to rein me in when necessary, and push me further when I need it.

Thank goodness for a fantastic editor that keeps my comma mess to a minimum!. Pam Ebeler from Undivided Editing keeps me on track with those evil little things, making sure I am able to concentrate on the bigger picture. Thanks for all your hard work Pam, I appreciate you!

Thank you to Podium Publishing for the fantastic cover for TORMENT. Seeing Alex ready for battle really helps the story hit home!

15659384R00217